PENGUIN BOOKS

IN THE BEAUTY OF THE LILIES

'John Updike's genius, his place beside Hawthorne and Nabokov have never been more assured, or chilling. One puts down this novel with the intimation that America is, very near its center, the saddest country on earth' – George Steiner in the *New Yorker*

'This is his strongest work for years ... Family sagas are almost always gripping; one filled with such sharp portraits as *In the Beauty of the Lilies*, and underpinned with the sheer intelligence and fascination of Updike's ideas, is pretty well irresistible' – Philip Hensher in the *Mail on Sunday*

'Updike's familiar qualities are on display: his infinitely flexible prose; his unfailing sense of place; his awareness of the complex relationship between public events and people's private lives ... Finally, and most powerfully, there is the breadth of his sympathy, an always impressive combination of sharpness and benevolence' – James Walton in the *Daily Telegraph*

'Almost from its opening moments, John Updike's rigorously considered new novel displays a depth and a narrative confidence that make one sigh with sweet anticipation. This is the Updike of the Rabbit books, who can take you uphill and down with his grace of vision, his gossamer language and his merciful, ironic glance at the misery of the human condition ... *In the Beauty of the Lilies* is stirring and captivating and beautifully written' – Gail Caldwell in the *Boston Globe*

'At the end of it, we feel that we understand more about that peculiar spiritual condition known as America – its crazy credulities, its destructive uncertainties, its brashness, its murderousness ... it is the best description of religious emotion or feeling I have ever read' – A. N. Wilson in the *Evening Standard*

ABOUT THE AUTHOR

John Updike was born in 1932 in Shillington, Pennsylvania. He attended Shillington High School, Harvard College and the Ruskin School of Drawing and Fine Art at Oxford, where he spent a year on a Knox Fellowship. From 1955 to 1957 he was a member of the staff of the *New Yorker*, to which he has contributed numerous poems, short stories, essays and book reviews. Since 1957 he has lived in Massachusetts as a freelance writer.

John Updike's first novel, *The Poorhouse Fair*, was published in 1959. It was followed by *Rabbit, Run,* the first volume of what has become known as the *Rabbit* books, which John Banville described as 'one of the finest literary achievements to have come out of the US since the war'. Two of the volumes, *Rabbit Is Rich* (1981) and *Rabbit at Rest* (1990), were awarded the Pulitzer Prize for Fiction. Other novels by John Updike include *Marry Me*, *The Witches of Eastwick*, which was made into a major feature film, *Memories of the Ford Administration*, *Brazil* and *In the Beauty of the Lilies.* He has written nine volumes of short stories, and a selection taken from *The Same Door*, *Pigeon Feathers*, *The Music School* and *Museums and Women* is published by Penguin as *Forty Stories.* His most recent and highly acclaimed collection is *The Afterlife and Other Stories.* His criticism and his essays, which first appeared in magazines such as the *New Yorker* and the *New York Review of Books*, have been collected in five volumes. John Updike's *Collected Poems 1953–1993* brings together almost all the poems from five previous volumes, including *Hoping for a Hoopoe*, *Telephone Poles* and *Tossing and Turning*, as well as seventy poems previously unpublished in book form.

John Updike

IN THE BEAUTY OF THE LILIES

PENGUIN BOOKS

PENGUIN BOOKS

Published by the Penguin Group
Penguin Books Ltd, 27 Wrights Lane, London W8 5TZ, England
Penguin Books USA Inc., 375 Hudson Street, New York, New York 10014, USA
Penguin Books Australia Ltd, Ringwood, Victoria, Australia
Penguin Books Canada Ltd, 10 Alcorn Avenue, Toronto, Ontario, Canada M4V 3B2
Penguin Books (NZ) Ltd, 182–190 Wairau Road, Auckland 10, New Zealand

Penguin Books Ltd, Registered Offices: Harmondsworth, Middlesex, England

First published in the USA by Alfred A. Knopf 1996
Published in Great Britain by Hamish Hamilton 1996
Published in Penguin Books 1996
5 7 9 10 8 6 4

Printed in England by Clays Ltd, St Ives plc

To Martha

who loves ancestors

and also descendants

In the beauty of the lilies Christ was born across the sea,
With a glory in his bosom that transfigures you and me:
As he died to make men holy, let us die to make men free,
While God is marching on.

—Julia Ward Howe,
"Battle-Hymn of the Republic"

Chapters

IN THE BEAUTY OF THE LILIES

i. *Clarence*

IN THOSE HOT LAST DAYS of the spring of 1910, on the spacious, elevated grounds of Belle Vista Castle in Paterson, New Jersey, a motion picture was being made. The company was Biograph; the director was David W. Griffith; the title was *The Call to Arms.* The plot took place in medieval times, and centered about a lost jewel beyond price. For the setting of a medieval castle, what better than this Belle Vista, popularly called "Lambert's Castle" after its builder, the local silk baron Catholina Lambert? The rolling lawn with its groomed, medieval-appearing oaks and beeches commanded a hazy view of New York City, less than fifteen miles eastward of the crowded rooftops of Paterson lying sullenly snared within the lowland loop of the Passaic River. From this height the human eye could discern the strip of brick mills clustering about the Falls and its three millraces designed by Pierre L'Enfant, the dour but majestic brownstone spire of Father William Dean McNulty's Cathedral of St. John the Baptist, the white wedding-cake tower of City Hall, the fantastical varicolored Flemish façade of the Post Office, and the ribbed dome, not ten years old, of the Passaic County Court House, upon whose columned cupola a giant gesturing woman persistently kept her balance. The distant spires of New York City were a photogenic marvel, their apparently weightless suspension within the mists of summer heat belying the mass of human suffering and striving their enchanted profile rested upon. But the moving-picture camera was aligned to exclude any such modern view. The cameraman waited impatiently in the muggy, coal-gas-poisoned New Jersey sunshine, fearful that a random cloud might suddenly throw his aperture-setting out of adjustment. A faint scent of oil arose from the encased fine gears and sprockets.

It was two in the afternoon, and the heat was at its peak. In spite of it, the actors Mack Sennett and Dell Henderson had donned metal armor, and the star of the film, little Mary Pickford, sweltered in the tights, velvet cape, and heavy brocaded tunic of a page. She was to mount a horse and gallop with a supposedly momentous message across the wide castle lawn, whose every hard green blade reflected back colorless sunlight. The horse's great barrel of a body, as several men in overalls helped Miss Pickford up into the saddle, felt hot, and emitted a stench of sweat and wet horsehair. The sunbaked leather of the saddle scorched her buttocks and thighs, and the tousled hair of her steed's mane seemed to lead her consciousness invitingly down toward the roots of a shady tangle. The petite star was but seventeen. The hotel accommodations in jam-packed, clattering Paterson had not conduced to an easy night of sleep. She felt distinctly less than herself; however, it was not until the close-up—Griffith was mad for this new artistic toy of his, the facial close-up—that she lost consciousness. The page was, for the third take, excitedly delivering the message whose exact words would be spelled out on the screen in white on black, ornately framed: "Sire, the king bids the troops to attack the Saracen infidels!" Two grips in shirtsleeves were holding large foil reflectors to bring further light to play on her fine young features, whose natural pallor was enhanced with powder. In this intensified heat a darkness welled up at the back of her brain and she fainted. The sweet moist scent of June grass and the ammonia of smelling salts seemed to rush simultaneously to her nostrils. When she came to, Mr. Griffith, though ever the correct Kentucky gentleman, was furious, as not only had she wasted a half-hour of daylight—this was Monday, and the schedule committed him to finishing the film by Friday—but she had besmirched with grass stains her expensive tunic of brocaded white silk.

At the moment when Mary Pickford fainted, the Reverend Clarence Arthur Wilmot, down in the parsonage of the Fourth Presbyterian Church at the corner of Straight Street and Broadway, felt the last particles of his faith leave him. The sensation was distinct—a visceral surrender, a set of dark sparkling bubbles escaping upward. He was a tall, narrow-chested man of forty-four, with a drooping sand-colored mustache and a certain afterglow of masculine beauty, despite a vague look of sluggish unhealth. He was standing, at the moment of the ruinous pang, on the first floor of the manse, wondering if in view of the heat he might remove his black serge jacket, since no visitor was scheduled to call until after dinnertime, when the Church Building Requirements Committee would arrive to torment him with its ambitions. The image of the chairman's broad, assertive face—the froglike, nimble, downturned mouth of Harlan Dearholt, a small silk-ribbon millowner, whose short blunt nose supported a pince-nez that gave off oval flashes of blind reflection—slipped in Clarence's mind to the similarly pugnacious and bald-crowned visage of Robert Ingersoll, the famous atheist whose *Some Mistakes of Moses* the minister had been reading in order to refute it for a perturbed parishioner; from this perceived similarity his thoughts had slipped with quicksilver momentum into the recognition, which he had long withstood, that Ingersoll was quite right: the God of the Pentateuch was an absurd bully, barbarically thundering through a cosmos entirely misconceived. There is no such God, nor should there be.

Clarence's mind was like a many-legged, wingless insect that had long and tediously been struggling to climb up the walls of a slick-walled porcelain basin; and now a sudden impatient wash of water swept it down into the drain. *There is no God.* The irregular open space of the parsonage in which he had paused and been assailed by this realization was defined by the closed door to his study, the doorless archway into the dining room, the inner front door with its large decoratively frosted pane framed in leaded rectangles of stained glass the color of milky candies, and the foot of the dark walnut staircase that, in two turnings punctuated by rectangular newel posts whose points had been truncated, ascended to the second floor. Drafts from the front doors, and the linoleum-floored vestibule between them, lifted dust up the stairs, Mrs. Wilmot often complained; and so it seemed that the invisible vestiges of the faith and the vocation he had struggled for decades to maintain against the grain of the Godless times and his own persistent rationalist suspicions now of their pulverized weightlessness lifted and wafted upstairs too.

It was a ghastly moment, a silent sounding of bottomlessness. Outside, on Broadway, a farmer's cart was wearily dragging its way uphill, turning up Straight Street to the bridge and the road to Haledon and the rural north of Passaic County after a dawn descent to the Main Street market. The horse's metal shoes broke their syncopated music slightly as they crossed the double trolley tracks embedded in the cobbles; the hickory axles squealingly protested the moment of uneven stress, of torque. The driver was singing something to himself; Clarence first thought it was a hymn, in German, until a snatch of tune came clear, from the new waltz, "Let me call you sweetheart, I'm in love . . . with . . . you." The driver had a young voice, or else there were two men mounted in the front of the cart, a man and boy. From the kitchen, behind a door that swung either way, came the voices of Mrs. Wilmot and Mavis, the little Irish servant girl, undertaking, in their armory of ponderous, pitted metal utensils, the daily labor of the evening meal; some members of the Church Building Requirements Committee, including the chairman and his ample wife, had been invited to dinner, along with a few of the parish orphans—a newly created Italian widow with her two daughters, and an aging broad-silk weaver newly unemployed, thanks to his political imprudence.

Life's sounds all rang with a curious lightness and flatness, as if a resonating base beneath them had been removed. They told Clarence Wilmot what he had long suspected, that the universe was utterly indifferent to his states of mind and as empty of divine content as a corroded kettle. All its metaphysical content had leaked away, but for cruelty and death, which without the hypothesis of a God became unmetaphysical; they became simply facts, which oblivion would in time obliviously erase. Oblivion became a singular comforter. The clifflike riddle of predestination—how can Man have free will without impinging upon God's perfect freedom? how can God condemn Man when all actions from alpha to omega are His very own?—simply evaporated; an immense strain of justification was at a blow lifted. The former believer's habitual mental contortions decisively relaxed. And yet the depths of vacancy revealed were appalling. In the purifying sweep of atheism human beings lost all special value. The numb misery of the horse was matched by that of the farmer; the once-green ferny lives crushed into coal's fossiliferous strata were no more anonymous and obliterated than Clarence's own life would soon be, in a wink of earth's tremendous time. Without Biblical blessing the physical universe became sheerly horrible and disgusting. All fleshly acts became vile, rather than merely some. The reality of men slaying lambs and cattle, fish and fowl to sustain their own bodies took on an aspect of grisly comedy—the blood-soaked selfishness of a cosmic mayhem.

The thought of eating sickened Clarence; his body felt swollen in its entirety, like an ankle after a sprain, and he scarcely dared take a step, lest he topple from an ungainly height. His palms and armpits had broken out into a sweat. Precariously, seeking to suppress the creaking in both the floorboards and his leather shoes, he slithered across the dining room to the kitchen door, and harked there with his lean head tilted, like that of a doctor listening for a heartbeat in a patient who has sustained a trauma. In his sallow temple a blue vein insistently, fearfully pulsed.

"My goodness, Mavie," he heard, "don't be so stingy with the brown sugar—we Americans like our ham *sweet.*" Stella's buoyant and bossy voice was itself sweetened by its Southern accent, which seven years in New Jersey, and six before that at a pair of cold parishes on the plains of Minnesota, had diluted but not expunged. He had met her in Missouri, at a dismal struggling church in a gaunt wooden town perched on the river bluffs. She had played the piano at services in lieu of an organ, and run the little Sunday school, with its score or so of pupils. She was overweight and swarthy and plain; feminine beauty was confined to her lively black eyes, with their liquid gleam of mischief and need, and her fine head of thick dark hair, loaded with chestnut highlights and with tortoiseshell devices to hold its waving, buckling, spraying mass in place. His gratitude for her lending the church her vitality—for keeping him company in this failing outpost of Presbyterianism in a land of river-fed, whiskey-fuelled license and of shouting, loutish Baptists—had led imperceptibly, with no clear dividing-line where he could have called a halt, to their marriage. They had been swiftly blessed with two children, a boy and a girl, and then, seven years ago, with a second boy, whom they, after some mild dispute, had agreed to name after the young and virile President.

In her full-bosomed sweet voice Stella was saying, "Then we add two level teaspoons of dry mustard—now, pay attention, Mavie, and watch how I scrape it level with the knife—and just a *splash*, half a teacup you could say but I never measure, of the dry breadcrumbs we pounded fine, to give the basting body, and then we add the moistener, you can use most anything but spit, my Aunt Dorothea used to say—she was a character, dear old Aunt Dode, all bent over like a comma. You can use drippings from the ham, or prune juice, or my daddy down home used to favor a shot-glass of elderberry wine"—

pronounced *waaahn*—"but Mr. Wilmot with his tender tummy likes his cider vinegar, so here goes three tablespoons: one, two, three, like *that.*" *That* became two syllables, *tha-yit;* he could mentally see Stella's chins doubling as she looked down lovingly into her task. "Now I'm going to let you stir a minute while I see how you trimmed the fat. I declare, I think you cut too deep, Mavie. You're meant just to slice away the *rind*, all but a collar around the shank bone here, and leave all the good fat you can—it has another hour in the oven to go, and we don't want it all dried out, now do we, little sweetheart?"

Clarence could not hear Mavie's murmured, chastened reply. Her people came from Cork, and she lived in that jostling mob of unpainted wooden houses below the mills called Dublin; she was saved from the silk mills, where girls spent ten-hour days at the ribbon looms, by domestic service here. She came before seven in the morning and left at six-thirty, when the Wilmots' dinner was on the table, unless they were having company, in which case she stayed to serve the table. But on non-laundry days they sometimes allowed her to walk back home and help out her mother with her younger siblings. It was the usual Irish situation: a brood of children, and a father who wasted his wages in the taverns. A profligate race, stubbornly professing an antique creed. Mavis had fascinating fine small hands, red-fingered from being much in soapy water, tentative and fumbling as a child's hands are, and a serious face whose lips were as pale as her fair skin. After a Thursday when she could steal an hour from work and join the idle young people on Garrett Mountain, her face would show a burst of reddish freckles. Then Stella, who had a Southerner's fear of the darkening touch of the sun, and yet whose own face imperceptibly turned dusky in the summer, would chasten Mavis playfully for "overindulging in the out-of-doors."

"Then, while you do that—really *stir*, dear, and don't be afraid to mash with the back of the spoon—I'll take the big knife and cut the fat in nice long diagonals—see?—and when

I'm done you can take the tin of cloves and stick one each into the *exact* middle of each diamond-shape! Oh, *don't* we have fun! Little Teddy just loves pulling the cloves out and sucking each one like a tiny chicken-bone!"

The eavesdropping clergyman, numbed by his sudden atheism, had half-intended to push open the swinging door and enter the fragrant brightness and let his unspeakable wound be soothed by the blameless activity there, but he lost heart and turned away. He stood baffled, looking about the dining room for some exterior sign of the fatal alteration within him. *There is no God.* With a wink of thought, the universe had been bathed in the pitch-smooth black of utter hopelessness. Yet no exterior change of color betrayed the event. The mahogany dining table, with its pedestal legs and much-waxed top of faintly mismatching leaves; the Tiffany-glass chandelier, shaped like an inverted punchbowl with scalloped edges and imitation tassels cleverly fabricated in glass and lead; the bow-front sideboard, with its flaking veneer of curly cherry; the brown wallpaper, unchanged since the manse was built in 1880, its alternating idylls (a couple picnicking in courtship, a child chasing a hoop) framed in scrolling lines whose silver glints were nearly smothered by three decades of exposure and ingrained dust: none of these mute surfaces reflected the sudden absence of God from the universe—His legions of angels, His sacrificed Son, His ever-watchful and notoriously mysterious Providence, His ultimate mercy, the eternal Heaven so hard to picture yet for which our hearts so unmistakably yearn, the eternal Hell which even calm, gentle, reasonable Calvin could not conceive as other than indispensable to God's justice. With the mystery of His freedom vanished the passionately debated distinctions of sublapsarianism, supralapsarianism, and infralapsarianism, in regard to the precise moment when God imposes election. The mahogany tabletop in silence reflected with a tinted blur the colorful bowl suspended above it, a bowl emptying itself world without end. At the rim of this vast purge, this volcanic desolation, the house's furnishings stood unchanged, temporarily enclosing and protecting the clergyman and his family.

Temporarily, for few of these elegant if well-worn downstairs furnishings were his; they came with the parsonage and would pass to the use of the next minister and his brood. Only upstairs, in children's beds and bureaus thriftily acquired as needs arose, and a linen-laden cedar chest—Stella's cumbersome dowry—that had trailed them throughout the upper Midwest, and a scuffed mahogany fourposter they had bought second-hand in Oshkosh when the rope bed the parish had supplied gave them both painful backs, and a somewhat saccharine framed print of the Heinrich Hoffmann painting of Jesus praying in vain in the Garden of Gethsemane for this cup to pass from Him while the disciples slept—a gift of the parish in leaving Granite Falls—and a few crackled family portraits and small items of quality in silver and ivory descended to him from the Wilmots' wealthier days as Manhattan importers and merchants, before the Civil War bred a rougher set of entrepreneurs and sent the declining family into the farmlands of New Jersey—only upstairs was some of the furniture theirs, to carry with them on their next move, to his next call. But where would they go without his faith to carry them? His faith was what paid their way.

Yet would he call it back, his shaky half-faith, with its burden of falsity and equivocation, even if he could? In his present state he was a husk, depleted but at last distinct in shape, as if, after a long, enfeebling captivity, a secret anger and resentment at his captors could be felt moving tinglingly through his veins. The cowardice of men and women in the face of the natural facts had forced upon him the discreditable role of magician. Ingersoll, among his other thunders, had promised the clergy liberation, unchaining them from mouldy books and musty creeds. He must look up the passage. He was shaking, a look at his hands discovered. A slight lumpy soreness, as if after a mismanaged swallow, had intruded itself into his throat. Anxious now not to deflect the women's attention from the ham to himself, he walked with Indian stealth, suppressing the scrape of his leather soles, back through the spot on the dark wood floor where his theocentric universe had collapsed. The milled and carved configurations of the spiky staircase and the inner vestibule door with its big frosted-glass pane rimmed in milky translucent colors were as they had been ten minutes ago. The cap of the walnut newel post nearest him was an elongated four-sided pyramid upon a brief neck of several turnings of half-round molding; the detail presented itself to him as having a glowering Oriental aspect, as if the Gothic and Chinese styles were carved by the same barbaric hand, guided by the benighted, hopeless mentality which seeks ornament as a distraction from the intolerable severity of the universe. Bare, pure, devoid: even the Bible contained the information, in its less exegized verses. *All is vanity and vexation of spirit. How dieth the wise man? as the fool. If Christ be not raised, your faith is vain. If in this life only we have hope in Christ, we are of all men most miserable. My God, my God, why has thou forsaken me?*

Clarence had preached on these texts, sought with his striving, affecting, rather fragile tenor voice to find the way around them, but there was, it now clearly appeared, no way. He went back into his study, his book-lined cave that smelled of himself, scented with the odor of his tobacco and of paper piled on paper, undusted books and yellowing magazines, pamphlets, manuscripts from his own hand, never to be again consulted. Miss Brubeck, the church secretary, kept a superior semblance of order at his office in the adjoining church building, where his sermons and blurred carbons of his letters, struck off on that frenetic modern device the typewriter, filled green metal filing cabinets with the tidy hopefulness of bodies awaiting Resurrection; here in his home study the disarray of death reigned, its musty surrender to chaos. The door was a somewhat ecclesiastical yellow oak construction with a rounded top that in the humid heat of summer tended to stick, unless one pressed with some force down on the knob; the embossed knob had been worn to a crescent of polished brass on its top side by years of such pressure from his and predecessor palms. His hand was unnerved and enfeebled by the physical shock that a motion of his mind had imparted. The latch clicked and he took a consciously deep breath, stepping in and closing the sticky door behind him.

He was safe among books, books which had so much danger in them. He wanted to look up that quotation from Ingersoll. *Some Mistakes of Moses* rested in its rusty-red covers sideways on his much-consulted row of the Kegan Paul *Pulpit* commentaries, next to those of *The Expositor's Bible;* the passage came early, in the first chapter, ministers leading the parade of those—teachers, politicians—that Ingersoll wished to free from the tyranny of the Bible. Here it was:

> The hands of wives and babes now stop their mouths. They must have bread, and so the husbands and fathers are forced to preach a doctrine that they hold in scorn.

Well, not exactly scorn. In pity, more. The doctrine had for these years past felt to Clarence like an invalid, a tenuous ghost scattered invisibly among the faces that from sickbeds and Sunday pews and the oilcloth-covered kitchen tables of disrupted, impoverished households beseeched him for hope and courage, for that thing which Calvin in his Gallic lucidity called *la grâce.* Grace Clarence had pictured when his faith was healthy as an interplay between men and God, achieved within the mystery—imagined as a glass globe, transparent only in decorative spots and bands where the frosting had been buffed away—of Christ and His placation of that otherwise ineradicable sin inherited from Adam, leaving men with, in a phrasing Clarence had once found delightful, "a lively tendency to disobey God." This faith that he offered to represent lay not in them, the aggrieved and wounded and disappointed, and not in Clarence, housed and paid that he might serve them with this elusive commodity, but between them, in their agreeing thus to meet in faint hope of daily miracles. Not an invalid, perhaps, so much as an infant that he must tenderly nurture and indulge and take great care not to harm. Ingersoll went on with his own, lively evangelical vigor:

> It is a part of their business to malign and vilify the Voltaires, Humes, Paines, Humboldts, Tyndalls, Haeckels, Darwins, Spencers, and Drapers, and to bow with uncovered heads before the murderers, adulterers, and persecutors of the world. They are, for the most part, engaged in poisoning the minds of the young, prejudicing children against science, teaching the astronomy and geology of the Bible, and inducing all to desert the sublime standard of reason.

Clarence stopped reading. This sentence, like hundreds of others mocking and scourging the Christian faith, which he had turned aside at the time of initial reading with a hardened skepticism of his own, a thick skin bred of his education in apologetics, must have sunk in—each bit of scoffery a drip carrying away his vocation's modest mountain. He looked at his pallid hands resting on his green desk blotter, hands as fumbling and blind as Mavie's, though twenty years older, coarser with masculinity and weathered with age. A nerve in the flesh connecting his thumb and forefinger jumped. He lifted his eyes to the wall of books opposite his desk, rows of books in subtly ridged cloth the careful dull colors of moss and clay, the dour greens and browns of putrescence, their titles in fading, sinking gold: *Apostolic History and Literature* and *Systematic Theology* and *What Is Darwinism?* by Charles Hodge, *The Atonement* and *Popular Lectures on Theological Themes* by his son Archibald Alexander Hodge, both professors at the Princeton Seminary before Clarence Wilmot arrived there in 1888. He did take a course with Benjamin Warfield—as erect at the lectern as a Prussian general, with snowy burnsides—whose *Introduction to the Textual Criticism of the New Testament*, lost in this wall of accumulated titles, should have fortified him forever against Ingersoll's easy sneers, and with William Henry Green, whose *Higher Criticism of the Pentateuch* and *Grammar of the Hebrew Language* had given the slender young seminarian many a headachy midnight back in Alexander Hall. In those student days, hungry for knowledge and fearless in his youthful sense of God's protection close at hand, he had plunged into the chilly Baltic sea of Higher Criticism—all those Germans, Semler and Eichhorn, Baur and Wellhausen, who dared to pick up the Sacred Book without reverence, as one more human volume, more curious and conglomerate than most, but the work of men—of Jews in dirty sheepskins, rotten-toothed desert tribesmen with eyes rolled heavenward, men like flies on flypaper caught fast in a historic time, among myths and conceptions belonging to the childhood of mankind. They called themselves theologians, these Teutonic ravagers of the text that Luther had unchained from the altar and translated out of Latin, and accepted their bread from the devout sponsors of theological chairs, yet were the opposite of theologians, as in the dank basement of Greek and Aramaic researches they undermined Christianity's ancient supporting walls and beams.

It had given Clarence as a divinity student a soaring sense of being a trapeze artist to look down into these depths of dubiousness and facticity—Mark, the oldest of the Gospels, ends in air in the best manuscripts, at verse 16:8, with the tomb simply empty and the women bearing sweet spices for the corpse confused and *afraid!*—and then to return from the daze of the library to the firm and reassuring ground of Gothic, semi-bucolic Princeton, where his eminent instructors radiated an undisturbed piety and his fellow students, though festively disputatious, appeared uniformly stout in their vocations, vigorously proof against disabling spiritual wounds. Melodious bells would toll six o'clock; dinner would be served. Now, while yet another dinner in his life's long but finite chain of meals was being prepared, the spines of his books formed a comfortless wall, as opaque and inexorable as a tidal wave. The two volumes of Strauss's *Das Leben Jesu* stood out as a square of fusty darkness, a blot almost absorbing their slimmer companion, the crimson-bound *Vie de Jésus,* by Renan. There was a tide behind these books that crested in mad Nietzsche and sickly Darwin and boil-plagued Marx. For all its muscular missions to the heathen and fallen women and lost souls of the city slums, the nineteenth century had been a long erosion, and the books of this century that a conscientious clergyman collected—the sermons of Henry Sloane Coffin and the apologetics of George William Knox, the fervent mission reports of Robert Speer and the ponderous Biblical dictionaries of Hastings, Selbie, and Lambert—Clarence now saw as so much flotsam and rubble, perishing and adrift, pathetic testimony to belief's flailing attempt not to drown. *New Light on the New Testament. Life on God's Plan. From Fact to Faith. Our New Edens. The Principles of Jesus Applied to Some Questions of Today. Calvin, Twisse and Edwards on the Universal Salvation of Those Dying in Infancy.* Clarence had groped his way around his desk, in his study's perpetual twilight, and stood reading the titles, looking for one he might take hold of in his terrible sinking, his descent through the shadows of this stifling afternoon into the bottomless, featureless depths of Godlessness. The stout old books—Bunyan's *Pilgrim's Progress* and *Grace Abounding to the Chief of Sinners,* Thomas à Kempis's *Imitation of Christ,* and the forty-four volumes of Calvin's *Commentaries,* with uniform spines a bright ivory like that of unplayed piano keys—were ignorant but not pathetic in the way of the attempts of the century just now departed to cope with God's inexorable recession: the gallant poems of Tennyson and Longfellow, phrasing doubt in the lingering hymnal music; the blustering historical novels *Quo Vadis?* and *Ben Hur;* the cunning pseudo-affirmations of Emerson and his hyperactive spiritual descendant Theodore Roosevelt, after whom Stella had insisted on naming their youngest child, as if to infuse into their progeny a vitality from above. Clarence's spectral white hand floated past his copy of *The Strenuous Life* and tugged out *The Origin of Species,* its cover stained and warped by his frequent if discontinuous readings—blood-chilling dips into the placid flow of calm, close, inarguable natural evidence, collected from stag beetles and starfishes. As if by Providential guidance but in truth owing to the binding's having absorbed the effect of his recurrent reference to the passage, the pages fell open to a paragraph which had more than once made him smile with its hypocritical benignity. Darwin, a clergyman's son, reaches out to the dismayed reader with reassurance:

> I see no good reason why the views given in this volume should shock the religious feelings of any one. It is satisfactory, as showing how transient such impressions are, to remember that the greatest discovery ever made by man, namely, the law of the attraction of gravity, was also attacked by Leibnitz, as "subversive of natural, and inferentially of revealed, religion." A celebrated author and divine has written to me that "he has gradually learnt to see that it is just as noble a conception of the Deity to believe that He created a few original forms capable of self-development into other and needful forms, as to believe that He required a fresh act of creation to supply the voids caused by the action of His laws.

But how little, Darwin could not have but noticed, he had left "Him" to do. "His" laws as elicited by the great naturalist's patient observation were so invariable, as well as so impersonal and cruel, as to need no executor. Leibnitz had not been wrong; Newton had led to Deism, from which it was but a brief step to Diderot, Robespierre, Saint-Just, and the horrific, but authentic, philosophy of the Marquis de Sade. Was it in here, or in *The Descent of Man,* where Darwin offered the missionary Livingston's numbness while in the mouth of a lion as a possible consolation for all the slaughter tirelessly exerting its sway over the world? Clarence flipped about in hopes of recovering the passage, gave up this hope, slipped the volume back into its place on the shelf, and permitted himself a deep inhalation and exhalation of breath. Life's mechanisms persist in the condemned man even as he mounts the steps of the gallows. *There is no God.*

The fault was in himself. Not Darwin or Nietzsche or Ingersoll or scientific materialism with all its thousandfold modern persuasive corroborations was to blame for this collapse, this invasion of his soul by the void: the failure was his own, an effeminate yielding where virile strength was required. Faith is a force of will whereby a Christian defines himself against the temptations of an age. Each age presents its own competing philosophies, the equivalents of Godless stoicism and hedonism, of Mithraism and astrology, of ecstatic and murderous and obscene cults such as still rampage through Asia and Africa. The body suffers its pain and seeks its pleasure; what more, without revelation, is there to know than this? Skepticism and mockery surrounded the first apostles and wrought their deaths and tortures. Christ risen was no more easily embraced by Paul and his listeners than by modern skeptics. The stumbling blocks have never dissolved. The scandal has never lessened. Even in the age of the cathedrals, Vikings razed the coastal monasteries and Saracens slaughtered armies of the faithful, calling them infidels. Sweeping negations lurked in the reasonings of Abelard and Duns Scotus. Luther's terror and bile flavored the Reformation; Calvin could not reason his way around preordained, eternal damnation, an eternal burning fuelled by a tirelessly vengeful and perfectly remorseless God. The Puritans likened men to spiders suspended above a roaring hearth fire; election cleaves the starry universe with iron walls infinitely high, as pitiless as the iron walls of a sinking battleship to the writhing, screaming damned trapped within. The rational alternative to absolute pre-election, it was painstakingly demonstrated by more than one lecturer, was a God somehow imperfect, maimed, enfeebled, confined to a quarantined corner of things. What all the genteel professors at Princeton Seminary had smilingly concealed, Warfield and Green and the erect, pedantic rest, and the embowering trees and Gothic buildings had in their gracious silence masked, was the possibility that this was all about nothing, all these texts and rites and volumes and exegeses and doctrinal splits (within Scots Presbyterianism alone, the Cameronians, the Burghers and Antiburghers, the Auld Lichts and New, the Relief Church and the United Secession Church, the United Free Church and the Free Church and the further seceding "Wee Frees")—that all these real-enough historical entities might be twigs of an utterly dead tree, ramifications of no more objective validity than the creeds of the Mayan and Pharaonic and Polynesian priesthoods, and Presbyterianism right back to its Biblical roots one more self-promoting, self-protective tangle of wishful fancy and conscious lies. Jesus the Son of God? The Son of Man? What could either mean? The church fathers who had thrashed through their epic distinctions had been centuries ago reduced to rat-gnawed bones and scraps of brown skin in their catacombs: clots of dust circling about a non-existent sun. Two copies of *The Presbyterian* on his desk, folded open to the "Books and Book News" pages, testified in every phrase to the problematic, euphemized absence at the heart of all this cheerful church activity:

> "Christ Invisible Our Gain," by A. H. Drysdale, D.D. . . . Dr. Drysdale's arguments are cumulative, and his last chapters are the best. There is a vital connection between the absent (but present) Christ and our spiritual life.

In another issue, Clarence had marked, for possible purchase, in his tidy blue pen—marks left as if by an extinct creature, the believing clergyman, looking to bridge the unbridgeable—*The Next Step in Evolution:*

> His argument is that the promise of the coming is fulfilled in the spread of Christ's doctrine and the reproduction of his life and spirit in the world, and that, therefore, he is coming, and, in a sense, has done, now. Those who cannot agree with Dr. Funk's understanding of it, will nevertheless admire his spirit and share his love and adoration for the divine Redeemer.

Below this, *Judge West's Opinion, Reported by a Neighbor:*

> Judge West's opinions of the world and all things therein, are those of a cheerful optimist who has a substantial faith in the

goodness of God and the excellence of his creation. The neighbor puts various hard questions to him, concerning life, death and the experience of mankind, and gets more or less satisfactory answers from the optimist's point of view. The collection of the Judge's opinions does not make a great book, but a cheerful one, and will help a questioner to see the bright side of things, where perhaps he thought there was none.

What sad pap, Clarence thought. *Cheerful optimist, substantial faith, goodness of God, excellence of his creation.* Paper shields against the molten iron of natural truth. With its fantastic doctrines and preposterous rationalizations the church ministers to life—credulous, pathetic human life. Hope is our sap, our warm blood. Clarence had lost his sap—not suddenly but over the nearly twenty years since seminary, when he and his cohorts, like soldiers training to brave the terrors and shadows that beset Christendom, had brimmed with the jolly, noisy juices of militant, masculine faith. It had been his vow, his vocation, to keep the faith, and he felt his failure within him as an extensive sore place, which rendered all his actions at his desk stiff and careful.

Mechanically in his pale steady hand he wrote a few letters, one to an enterprising salesman of church supplies who had attended service and now was offering at reasonable rates a whole range of padded kneeling cushions, with rolled or fringed seams, to replace Fourth Presbyterian's tattered, compressed, faded array, and another to a former parishioner, now moved to Paramus, who wished him to perform a memorial service for his father, who had died in Leghorn, Italy, and whom Clarence had never met. In both letters, he politely regretted his inability to oblige. He marvelled that his handwriting still flowed, with a light evenness of pressure and studied care of letter formation, much as it had before his soul had been upended and emptied. The envelopes licked and stamped with George Washington's pigtailed violet profile, Clarence looked over the financial figures preparatory to tonight's meeting of the Building Requirements Committee, and satisfied himself that the church could by no means afford the new addition, to accommodate church socials and an expanded Sunday school, which some of its headstrong and overzealous members were proposing. Pearls before swine, good money after bad. Why add to all the echoing, underused ecclesiastical structures in Christendom when Irish and Polish immigrants slept six to a room a few blocks distant?

Stealthily, not wishing to bring upon himself, in his weakened, shamed condition, the attention of the women, Clarence left his study, passed through the double-doored vestibule, and darted his body for a moment into the oppressively hot outdoor air in order to retrieve the copy of the Paterson *Evening Times* from where it was thrown, cleverly folded, onto the front porch each afternoon at about four o'clock. With this prize he retreated back into his study, to his leather sofa, comfortingly marred with permanent creases and missing buttons, where he read with his head up on two large cross-stitched pillows as compressed by his habitual head as the church's kneeling cushions were by generations of knees. The dominant headline was BOARD OF EDUCATION TO BE ELECTIVE. The long-agitated issue of whether the people or the mayor should control the Board of Education was coming to a head among the aldermen. Another local story told of a number of "Paterson citizens, who hail from the so-called highest respectability of the town," whose uproarious behavior on a trolley car—"It was on the return trip to Paterson from Palisade Park, in the early hours of the morn, and the way they whooped things up was a caution"—reached its climax when

> the men, having exhausted their stock of noise producers, their ribald songs, their stale jokes, proceeded to indulge in a game of crap. Cries of "Oh you babe," "Hand that money over," and a hundred others could be heard above the noise of the wheels and the roar of the car as it sped along the rails. A number of passengers shocked at the conduct of the men appealed to the conductor. "If I interfere," he said to one of them, "I may get a punch in the nose."

Elsewhere and equally unedifyingly on the page were JAMES MENOW IS SHOT AND IS IN A SERIOUS CONDITION and FOUND THE OPIUM IN BLACK MAN'S POCKET, this second item concerning "Fon Fen, a Chinaman, of No. 326 Market Street," two of whose customers, one colored and one white, were detained by the police as "suspicious characters," a jar of opium being found in the colored man's coat pocket. Other items were the marital troubles of one Samuel Barrmore, a résumé of the terrible damage done by last Saturday's whirlwind of a storm, the renovation of the Broadway baths, and the cancellation of a performance of an opera at the Lyceum "on account of the small audience that was present." The weather column promised "decidedly high temperatures." On the global side, Clarence skimmingly read of the devastating record floods that had peaked recently in Germany, Austria, and Serbia. In Mexico, President Díaz had proclaimed martial law and arrested hundreds who had been plotting his downfall, and in New York, Theodore Roosevelt, Jr., was marrying Miss Eleanor B. Alexander at the Fifth Avenue Presbyterian Church. Clarence looked through the list of ushers—Francis Roche, John W. Cutler, Hamilton Fish, Jr., E. Morgan Gilbert, Fulton Cutting, Eliot Cutter, Grafton Chapman, George Roosevelt, Monroe Roosevelt, Kermit Roosevelt—for a familiar name, perhaps the son of a Princeton acquaintance, and found none. The happy event gave the *Evening Times* excuse to recount another, the triumphant return of the former President from his world travels two days ago, on Saturday, June 18:

> From the time the Kaiser Auguste Victoria arrived at quarantine the welcome was a royal one. The revenue cutter Manhattan met the Victoria and took aboard the President's family and the President later made the trip up the Hudson on the Androscoggin. There was one uproarious welcome all the way up the river, and at the Battery he was welcomed by Mayor William Jay Gaynor and a delegation of Roosevelt's former Army Rough Riders. As his escort proceeded up Broadway, a shower

of ticker tape fell from the skyscrapers of the financial district—an unprecedented display of enthusiasm.

Of the present chief executive there was little notice save four lines stating that President Taft had signed the railroad bill but did not sign the statehood bill, mention that all the Taft family was headed for New Haven to be present at the graduation from Yale of young Robert A. Taft, and a fear expressed that Colonel Roosevelt's return might open wider a breach in the Republican Party; as a sub-headline put it, *Former President May Assume a Dictatorial Air in Affairs of Nation to Which President Taft Will Not Tamely Submit.* On the sports page, the New York baseball team continued to sit comfortably atop the American League. The Giants held down second place in the National, and the Lyceums defeated the Totowas, 3 to 2. A sportswriter confidently boasted that in exactly two weeks Mr. Jim Jeffries would rid the white race of the embarrassment and outrage of a negro heavyweight boxing champion, Jack Johnson, whose disturbed condition was indicated by his recent carousing and refusal to train and his firing of his manager, Mr. George Little. Ominously, the Japanese army, according to reports from a number of sources, appeared to be massing for an invasion of Korea. The world rolled onward, in other words, on its usual riotous course of bombast and deviltry, with or without God. Clarence felt not just forsaken but insulted, as when, still at Princeton, he had been spurned by a girl of good family whom he had decided to court. Eliza Cutler had been her name. The insult dwelt in the pit of his belly. To beguile himself from awareness of the sore and shameful void opened within him, Clarence pulled from his shelves not a volume to help him prepare for next Sunday's sermon—the very prospect sickened him—but a squat book, *The Trimmed Lamp,* by the author O. Henry, who had died a few weeks ago, at an age only a few years more advanced than Clarence's was now. Piqued by its Biblical allusion, the clergyman attempted to read the title story, which concerned two young city shop-girls with a man, Dan, between them, but before he could arrive at the twist and moral at the end dozed off in the arms of . . . nothingness.

The heat of the day relented with a forerunner of the evening breeze, which gently scraped the window shade against its frame. In his dreams, he seemed to be trying to fix a lock on his bedroom door, lest one of his children barge in upon his and Stella's privacy. But the lock grew large and clumsy beneath his hands, curved and wooden to the touch, like an old ox yoke shaped by visible chisel-marks or like an axle to adjust or grease which he had perilously crowded himself beneath a heavy wagon's underside. The great iron-tired wheel near his head creaked to turn, and he awoke with a start. There were brittle, chuckling noises from the dining room; the women had started to set the table. His mouth was parched; he wondered if he had been snoring. The now-crusty wound of faithlessness was still there in his consciousness, like a muddy shirt allowed to dry where it had been tossed. *There is no God.* Croakily, Clarence ventured his first utterance aloud for these three hours. "Have mercy," he whispered, smiling at the futile sound of it, his voice scratching at the air like a dog begging to be let in at the screen door.

"Mr. Dearholt, would you like to favor us by saying grace?"

The oval glasses, the confident broad false teeth, flashed. Dearholt had a voice preeningly rich and rounded, rebounding off the cavernous wet walls of his mouth. He often left his mouth half-open after an utterance, as if a delightful addendum might instantly set it in motion again. He responded, "Reverend Wilmot, I would never dare presume to do so at the table of a man of the cloth."

Dare: Did Clarence imagine a glint of danger there? Dearholt was the owner of a small mill—thirty employees, a dozen looms—and an expert in spotting weakness in both machines and operators. Clarence's suggestion bordered on the eccentric, though he hoped it might pass for elaborate courtesy and habitual modesty. He had now a secret—God's non-being—to protect. He bowed his head beneath the leaden silence above them, the rectangle of twelve downcast faces in the sickly yellow light of the scallop-edged Tiffany chandelier, and reached upward with his oddly roughened voice, which sounded fragile and muffled in his own ears. "Heavenly Father," he began, blankly, and found in his practiced lexicon of sacred usage further words: "In these troubled times instruct us in Thine activating covenant and loving mercies so that we may render back unto Thee a worthy portion of the blessings which Thou bestowest, even to this meal and the fellowship of our gathered company. We dare lift our voices in petition not through any merit of our own but by virtue of the gracious intercession of Thine only Son, our Lord and Savior Jesus Christ."

"Amen," Dearholt loudly said, as if driving an extra nail into a shaky construction.

Yet, that awkward duty discharged through a dryness like chalk powder in his mouth, Clarence found he had a fair appetite. The sweet ham with its congenial tang of cider vinegar, the steaming bowls of vegetables glazed with melting butter and sugar in Stella's rich Southern style, the three sorts of potatoes—mashed, boiled, and "Dutch" fried—and the long suspended field of glittering silver and glasses seemed to bid him live at his own wake. Present at the meal, while pale little Mavis hesitantly served, were his wife and three children, Jared, Esther, and Theodore; Mr. and Mrs. Dearholt; Mr. and Mrs. McDermott, he also of the Building Requirements Committee; Mrs. Caravello, with her two dark-eyed, dark-browed teen-aged daughters, Maria and Sophia; and Mr. Kleist, the recently fired broad-silk weaver, a wiry, edgy German of about fifty, bristling with grievances and theoretical remedies.

Mrs. Caravello's husband had been a dyer's helper who had died prematurely of the damp, the cold and the heat, and the vicious chemicals of the job, which could strip a man's skin from his hands and stain his skin beyond the reach of any soap. Caravello had been, like many of the immigrants from northern Italy, resolutely anti-clerical, and his shy, buxom widow had showed up one Sunday in a back pew of the Presbyterian church guiltily, as if betraying her husband's ghost but unable to control her need for God's society. Clarence was embarrassed by her—her halting English, her humid heavy good looks, the dark gauzy hair on her forearms and upper lip—but Stella's impulsive embrace had swept her up and installed her among her many parish pets; the two daughters, themselves nubile, were a few months ago baptized in the creed of Calvin at a private weekday ceremony around the marble font in the empty church. The three Italians, scattered about the dining table, formed pockets of silence, yet with their glowing olive skins, and hair centrally parted and pulled tautly back into shining buns, and curvacious lowered lashes, they were disturbing presences, radiating the life force in their wordless sexual need.

The born Protestants worked around them, snapping at each other. Clarence followed the conversation, when he could, almost with amusement, hearing all the voices, including his own, distantly, as if his ears were plugged with wax. At times his hearing withdrew entirely, while his mind turned away and visited the new emptiness within him, marvelling at its extent, grandeur, and searing persistence. *There is no God.*

"Troubled times," Dearholt quoted back at him with an uptilted chin. "What do you see troubled about them, Reverend? I would call these exceptionally good times, for the U.S. of A. and the city of Paterson both. The silk business is going full tilt and the locomotive works will come out of their slump as sure as I'm sitting here—it *has* to happen, what could possibly replace rail as the cheapest, fastest way to move bodies and freight across this enormous nation? Alexander Hamilton was dead right, the Passaic Falls make this the finest manufacturing site in the Western world; it just took a century or so for the reality to catch up to the vision." This must be from a speech he was accustomed to delivering, for as he gave it his bright, slightly protuberant eyes and flashing spectacles roved merrily around the faces at the table. "Why," he went on, "we're becoming such a showplace they're making movies right in on Garrett Mountain; any number of people I've talked to have seen Mary Pickford, ducking in and out of that little hotel over on Barclay Street, owned by Bill Ruffing and George Marion. The actors use it for changing rooms."

Clarence felt obliged to interject another voice. "I suppose, Harlan," he began, and with several awkward ahems scraped away at the hoarsening obstruction that clung to his vocal cords. "I suppose there are always fortunates to whom no time appears troubled. But for the run of mankind, if we take to heart what I was just reading in the *Evening Times*, misery is more the rule than the exception. Floods, revolutions coming and going, armies poised to invade. The faster the telegraph wires bring the news to us, the worse it seems. Locally, shootings, drunken misbehavior, drugs, conflict between the races."

"You sound discouraged, my friend," Dearholt genially barked back. "Struggle and survival, it's been ever the way of the world. I enjoy it; it tests a good Christian's mettle." He swivelled his head, mouth ajar, as if projecting a beam of light from a lighthouse.

"And what, sir, may I ask now," Kleist broke in, with a Teutonic accent that made him seem more aggressive than perhaps he meant to be, "do struggle and survival have to do with being a Christian? Turn the other cheek and trust in the Lord, that's the message as I understand it was handed out."

"Fight the good fight, Mr. Kleist. Jesus was no namby-pamby. He knew life was a ceaseless battle—read the parable of the seeds. He warned us right out, He came to bring a sword."

"Yes, but did He intend the sword to be always in the hands of the rich?"

"If it's me you're referring to, my good friend, I'm far from rich, as my missus here will attest. We live within our means and set a table more modest than this one here at the good reverend's. I worked my way up from bobbin boy and when I graduated to a loom gave twelve hours a day of hard labor for half the weekly wage the weavers of today are grumbling at. Ask the men and women I employ if I'm not on the floor before they show up and if I'm not doing my figures when they're safe at home, or more likely squandering their pay in the corner saloon."

"As it happens, Mr. Dearholt, I *do* know men fortunate enough, if that's the word, to have been in your employ, and they tell me there's nobody keeps a stricter watch on the off-minutes and there's nobody keener on stretching."

Mr. McDermott, halfway down the table, announced, "I'm not certain, sir, that all at this table know what stretching is." He was a loom-fixer for Empire Silk—a tall man, gentle and precise, who loved the looms, though their clatter had taken away some of his hearing.

"You can't live in Paterson," Clarence heard himself saying, as if on the other side of a wall, his own hearing having difficulty, "and not know about stretching."

Jared, his older son, sixteen at his last birthday, laughed at the far end of the table, as though his father had made more of a jest than intended. Jared was a quick, hazel-eyed, predatory boy, more like his grandfather Jared than like Clarence. He was seated next to the older Caravello daughter and may have felt obliged by that tc call attention to himself. Seated next to his mother, little Teddy, whose eyes were chocolate-brown like hers but without the merry gleam—little lusterless passive pools of watchfulness instead—looked toward his father worriedly, sensing the grown man's distress and disorientation. Tonight even Teddy's lovingness struck Clarence as a bothersome burden.

"Stretching," McDermott was going on with his Scots pedantry, aiming his explanation most directly at the non-comprehending Italian widow, "signifies raising the ratio of operator to machines, which has become possible with all the marvellous improvements in the looms. The first improvement was the changeover from hand-power in the Eighteen-eighties, and then, more recently, the invention of these devices that stop the loom when a shuttle thread breaks, or when a warp end breaks. Before, you see, the operator had to spot the break and stop the loom himself. So a man now can operate two machines instead of one, and receive a higher pay."

"But far from *twice* the pay," Mr. Kleist added in his pushing German voice, "though they do twice the work."

"No, now—not twice; let's not exaggerate. The gain of productivity amounts at most to two-thirds."

"Regardless of the exact figures," Mr. Dearholt impatiently intervened, "the point is that the fools resist progress at every point, just as the Luddites did a century ago. Men never learn: progress is inevitable, and everyone benefits by it in the long run. The anarchist mentality you see in Paterson now would have us all still walking the fields with wooden plows, looking at the rear end of a horse."

Kleist's face, a bit concave, like Punch's or the man in the moon's, went rigid with the effort to keep his temper, and to organize his angry tumble of thoughts. "The men that own the plants benefit, there's no argument there. But those same weavers that accepted the stretch-in for higher pay, within a few years they saw their pay back to where it was, and them having twice the machines to run."

"Competition, Mr. Kleist, competition," Dearholt smilingly responded. "The costs in Paterson must be equal to those in the mills of New England and Pennsylvania, or there will be no jobs for anyone. It's the owners who must cope with the costs and try to keep Paterson industry competitive. The generals look after the soldiers, that's the way it must be, or the battle is lost."

"And now at Doherty's, where I used to work," Kleist went on, "they doubled the looms again, four to a man now, two in front of him and two behind. We wanted to strike but Doherty had bought out the union, the AFL; it ordered us back to work, saying they had worked out an agreement we'd be paid more. Paid more until it suited the bosses to bring wages back down to where they were, with twice the broad silk being produced!"

"Aye, but they're such beautiful machines now," McDermott said, leaning his long head forward and his voice softening with tenderness. He had jutting half-white eyebrows and a chin with a dimple in the center like a scar healed. "They almost run themselves; the men in charge can go to sleep on their feet."

How strange faces are, Clarence thought. If we were turned upside down, would our underparts do as well for identification—to express our identities, our souls? We would still congregate, still converse, with visages once thought obscene.

It was time for someone else to speak, but no one expected it to be Mrs. Caravello. "My husband," she exclaimed. "Work with wet feet all day, all day! Come home so tired fall asleep in chair. Work kill him—kill him as if with gun!" And with an amusing vulgarism she held a plump hand in the air with a finger pointed like the barrel of a revolver.

"*Mamma,*" the older of the two girls reproached her, adding softly, blushing, "*Silenzio è sorte nostra.*"

Nothing cowed Dearholt. His smile broadened, to expose back teeth as perfect and porcelain as those in front. "Work is the way of the country, my good lady. Those afraid of work should have stayed home, in the old country, where the competition is less open, less honest and strenuous, and everyone is taken care of, deserving or not, the village idiot right along with the man of initiative. All dressed up, and nowhere to go, that's present-day Europe for you. Those who don't like it here are welcome to go back. Anybody in my plant I hear expressing anarchist ideas, out they go, Jew or Italian or whatever. No free rides, Mrs."—her name escaped him—"that's the way we do things here. I hear talk about worker ownership of the mills—we have it already! *I* was a worker, a bobbin boy, as I may have said. Catholina Lambert himself, head of Dexter, Lambert, began as a humble worker, back in Yorkshire. Doherty, Bamford, John Ryle himself, who got silk started here—all came from Macclesfield, back in the English mills."

McDermott, at Mrs. Caravello's side, confided the friendly fact, "Catholina Lambert built the Castle. Wonderful masonry and woodwork, up in the Castle."

Dearholt kept at her, with his friendly fierce smile: "The English and Scots who got here faced a wilderness. They had to fight cannibalistic savages! Those of you who have come later are fortunate—Paterson holds no redmen, does it? We have cleared thc way for you! Your children and grandchildren will thank us, my dear lady, even if you cannot find it presently in your heart to do so. Am I overstepping, Reverend? I mean everything I say kindly, to encourage *all* of my fellow Americans. Courage and faith, that's all we need. *Faith.*" He made a fist and vibrated it. "There's where the power to succeed comes from, in a land God has favored with such a wealth of opportunity."

Mrs. Caravello misunderstood the gesture as hostile. She protested, "Rich think nothing but more rich here. Not like Italia—*pittura,* opera."

Jared spoke up again, in his strident adolescent voice, seeking perhaps to save the Italian woman from too much attention. "Jamie Cressy got taken to the opera in New York City and said it was horrible. Everybody fat and screaming and he couldn't understand a word."

Stella now, as if to shelter her son, let her voice with its music from gentler climes sound out: "Oh, but the angelic harmonies the soprano and tenor make! And the bits of history you learn! It's so much healthier, I think, than sitting in a dark smoky building watching the moving pictures, the way all the young people do nowadays! The young people you see on Market Street look pale as ghosts, and I blame the moving pictures—those, and cigarettes."

Esther, now that the young people were beginning to speak,

said, "Mother, it's so em*bar*rassing, with the real people on stage! They're all so *loud,* and I always worry, what if somebody makes a mistake! With the motion pictures, everything is done perfectly, and it's always the same! And you don't have to get all dressed up to go!"

Clarence, though the debate before him seemed a carnivorous phantasmagoria projected on a wall of his inner void, felt obliged to answer his Building Committee chairman, who had asked if he was overstepping. "Not at all, Harlan," he pronounced, belatedly, feeling thick-tongued and with a waxen distance placed between himself and these vigorous eyes, chewing mouths, clumps of hair. "What better place than church premises for a frank expression of our views? Speak the truth in love, St. Paul enjoined."

"When the workers of the world unite," Mr. Kleist advised Mr. Dearholt and Mr. McDermott, "let's see how you and your kind like being stretched. Come the revolution, see how the bosses like being stretched on the rack."

"Welcome to the *industrial* revolution, Mr. Kleist," Dearholt said, beaming at his own humor. "The better the machines become, the fewer workers we're going to need. Those who don't take the work that's offered, at a wage that keeps wholesale prices competitive, are welcome to try the bread line, or to go find gold nuggets in Alaska!"

"Invention's a force altogether for the good," gentle McDermott urged everyone. He had long brown teeth crowded in the front like a beaver's. A paste of masticated food stuck in their irregularities. "Already it's made the world a tenfold better place, and there's more to come, believe you me. What they can do with those Jacquard cards!—they'll soon be running an entire assembly line."

"And where is the benefit for those without capital?" Kleist asked, his aggressiveness somewhat softened as Stella's sweet ham and three kinds of potatoes percolated through his digestive system. "What profits invention makes possible are gobbled up at the top, and squandered on yachts and mansions and marrying off their daughters to dukes and counts overseas!"

"Not at all, Mr. Kleist, not at all," Dearholt said, playing now the Christian placator. "The very clothes you are wearing—a century ago, only a gentleman could have afforded that suit. The profits from ever more sophisticated machines come straight to you, the consumer, in the form of cheaper goods. Even the poorest among us benefits, though he may not know it."

Done unto one of the least of these, Clarence remembered. Ah, but there is no God.

Little Teddy, gazing from the far end of the table into his father's face, burst into tears. Clarence heard the child distinctly whimper, as Stella bowed over the boy, "Dad looks funny."

Stella glanced toward her husband, but unlike her son did not see into him, just registered with satisfaction the fact that an appropriately dressed man was filling the space at the head of her splendidly supplied and dressed table. The younger Caravello daughter, who had been casting her limpid long-lashed eyes sideways toward Jared, now spoke up, claiming her American rights. "I like America," she said, in an English scarcely accented. "It is a hard country but you are free. Back in Italy, Papa used to say, there were three tyrants—the *padre,* the *signore,* and *il tempo,* the weather. Here there is only one tyrant, money. And a man with money can belong to himself." She faltered, alarmed by the circle of silent attention she had commanded and perhaps uncertain if her last sentence had been grammatical. "In the old country others always owned you; there was always fear. They used God to make fear."

"*Silenzio,* Sophia," her sister hissed.

"I think that's very well said," Stella announced, in a voice so syrupy and complacent that Clarence doubted she had been listening. In a sharper voice she called, "Mavie. It's time to clear, dear." To Clarence their young Irish maid loomed, in the muddy rainbow glow of the Tiffany lampshade, as an angel, pallid and meek and neutral, above the garish faces of his guests, her childish fumbling fingers floating the disgusting plates away, stacking them on the oval serving tray on its folding stand. Surely the loaded tray would be too heavy, with its thick plates and ponderous pronged accompaniment of silver, for her to lift. But she did it, with a pained wince of a saintly pale-lipped smile that only he observed; with stiffened back she bore off the tray through the swinging kitchen doors, to its fate of hot suds and, for the silver, Parlor Pride polish. The table talk, having inflicted in its clash so many cuts to heal, had fallen quiet, and Clarence dismally perceived that it was his hostly duty to start it up again, upon an innocuous topic. He cleared his throat and said, "I read in the *Evening Times* where young Teddy Roosevelt and his bride won't be returning, after their honeymoon, to the East. He's going to take up residence in San Francisco, where he's to be the district manager for the Hartford Carpet Company."

"My lands," Stella said, rising to assist Mavis in bringing the dessert but wishing to help her husband revive the conversation. "They might get swallowed up by another earthquake."

"Disasters are everywhere, Mrs. Wilmot," Dearholt assured her, "as your good husband has earlier stated. Even in our own proud city we have suffered, since the turn of the century, a fire gutting the entire downtown, two furious floods, and an actual cyclone! Still, Paterson prospers as never before. Two hundred silk plants, over five hundred manufacturing establishments in all, producing upward of sixty millions in annual product value!"

"And forty thousand men and women paid starvation wages for the privilege of being slowly worked to death," Kleist interjected, his eyes narrowing in amused expectation of protest from the representatives of ownership and management. He had turned his radicalism, it seemed to Clarence, into a social trick. A performing monkey on a string of ready indignation.

With painful seriousness McDermott rose to the bait: "Starvation wages, far from it, for the skilled workmen. A good loom-fixer, or a Jacquard-card puncher, or even a broad-silk weaver, they're up another level or two from your average dyer fresh off the boat from Genoa."

"Bosses' toadies, twice as bad as the bosses," Kleist hissed.

Well, Clarence reflected, of God's existence or non-existence, what did it all amount to but the paper-thin difference between death as the end of it all, no worse than a long untroubled sleep, the end of desire as well as capability, and death as the beginning of fresh adventures, a life beyond imagining, full in God's sight, and grotesque to picture—the scramble of Resurrection, the open-mouthed monotony of eternal choral praise? For most men this was all religion was, this gamble at the back of their minds, with little to lose but an hour or so on Sunday mornings. But for him, alas, it was a livelihood, and his manhood's foundation. There is no God, no foundation. The floor of his stomach chafed, overfull.

Mavis and Stella brought in the dessert, two pies hot from the oven, a mince and an apple, the slices of apple laid one upon another as tidily as a fish's overlapping scales, and heaped up high beneath a blanket of cinnamon and brown sugar and piecrust thumbed at the edges to a kind of baked spiral. He had often seen Stella's plump hands do the trick, running around the rim of the pie in less than a minute. Mavis carried on her tray the pies and between them a crystal bowl of the season's first strawberries and a side-dish of whipped cream twirled to a peak like a heterodox church's white spire. In spite of the panic gnawing at his stomach, Clarence felt in his mouth a welcoming rush of saliva.

The other members of the Church Building Requirements Committee arrived in time to be offered coffee and dessert if they wished. The late arrivals endeavored quickly to take on the conviviality of those elect who had dined together. The mingled, forcefully amiable faces and voices pecked at Clarence's muffled awareness. Kleist merrily escorted the Caravellos out into the warm evening, where light still lingered on the streets; Stella and the two committee wives retired to the parlor while Clarence ushered his committeemen into his study, where chairs were grouped away from his desk. The meeting, after a prayer for guidance offered by the chairman, Mr. Dearholt, debated the wisdom of the new two-story Sunday-school and church-social wing, which could be built on an adjacent lot, extending through to Fair Street, prudently acquired in the wake of the 1902 fire against the possibility of just such an expansion. The cost would come to a mere nineteen thousand dollars, it was estimated by a reliable contractor known to Mr. Dearholt—indeed, his brother-in-law. Such an addition not only would relieve the gloomy cramping of the present basement Sunday-school rooms but would provide a well-lit and up-to-date upstairs space rentable to suitable outside groups for an amount whose pleasant effects on the budget would vary according to the renter's means and worthiness. The space would accommodate fellowship dinners and educational events and musical evenings which would attract, in the competitive bustle of respectable Paterson, new young members. Young members are the lifeblood of any church if it is to serve the needs of coming generations. "Growth, growth," Mr. Dearholt pronounced emphatically. "Any organization that is not growing is dying, though it may take years for it to realize the fact. The Congregational Church over on Auburn Street is an example. One day, to coin a phrase, it woke up dead!"

A chuckle ran through the committee, which seemed inclined to agree. Clarence found the prospect unutterably depressing. The unbuilt annex sat like a stone across his chest: the workmen, the excavations, the noise, the dust, the debt to be financed, the thousand details to be wrangled through, the disappearance from this section of the city of the pleasant little rectangle of green shade, with its stucco birdbath in a bed of impatiens, its signboard announcing the coming services and the week's religious motto, its wrought-iron bench for the contemplative of whatever denomination. His face must have expressed dismay and discouragement, for all turned to him in expectation of having their enthusiasm checked.

"It wearies me," he confessed, "the thought of so much effort and expense directed to a merely material end. Nineteen thousand dollars: such a sum would support a score of families for a year, or would enable a foreign mission to relieve only Heaven knows how much misery in one of the Asian famines. I think of the interest, the running expenses, that will be with us far into the future, a burden upon our children's children. The Psalmist admonishes, 'Except the Lord build the house, they labor in vain that build it.' Is a church effective in direct proportion to its physical size? Please ask yourselves, gentlemen, how much of your sudden passion for building is rooted in motives of competition and envy. Just because Trinity Methodist, our good neighbor further up Broadway, has expanded, and reconstructed its entire chancel the better to display the voices of its paid choir, does not oblige us to match them, dollar for dollar. Surely our Presbyterianism is not so crassly worldly as that." He permitted himself a dry theological jest. "The Methodists are, after all, followers of Arminius, who argued against thrifty Calvin and said men were free to spend. Seriously, a church is a community whose strength lies in purity and zeal, not in its buildings. The present edifice sits harmoniously on its lot, and the leftover green park is a kind of gift we make to the neighborhood in general, to the weary passersby." Weary himself, he sighed.

The eyes of the committee fastened on him with an oppressive brightness and curiosity, detecting in his very cadence something already defeated. Not one voice sprang up to argue against him. Mr. McDermott at last said quietly, kindly, "Ah, but how will purity and zeal be known, unless we make of them an outward and visible sign? Our buildings are the means by which we announce ourselves in Paterson. Visible prosperity is not a virtue, of course not, but Calvin's creed allows that it may be a sign of God's grace." His tone was not accusatory but softly probing, like a doctor's.

And Clarence did feel sick, not just in his stomach but in his chest, always his frailest part, since a boyhood fever and a spell of what they called consumption. He took breath with a little difficulty, and could not shake the touch of hoarseness. "My friends," he said, "the church belongs to you, and not to me. That's the meaning of Presbyterianism. I am a teaching elder, but you are the ruling elders. I am with you only for the length of my call, whereas many of you have been baptized here and will be buried here; this is the church of your lifetimes. I just wonder"—he scraped away an obstruction in his throat—"if going forward in a very practical way is not sometimes"—again, he struggled to clear his voice—"a path of avoidance, avoidance of the deeper issues. . . ." He trailed off.

The committee, their voices coming to the rescue, briskly agreed to establish a subcommittee to look, in view of the minister's lack of enthusiasm, more closely into the likely costs, both immediate and continuing. A friendly conference with the Trinity Methodists, as to the drawbacks and results of their own expansion, might not be out of the question. Of course, you can bet that—and they named several industrial aristocrats who sat prominently among the Methodists—contributed heavily. Some said as much as half of the needed total came from two or three pledges. Mr. Dearholt, his oval glasses flashing, in his clarion voice ventured to hope that no lesser generosity might be met with in their own ranks. Their parish was not impoverished, though the three older Presbyterian churches in the city of course offered stiff competition and contained many of the oldest and most distinguished families. He would take the liberty of informally inquiring, here and there, among sound and discreet men whose acquaintance he happened to enjoy. Might he make an approach—non-binding, of course—to an architect experienced in ecclesiastical additions? Nothing less than full Gothic, in matching rough-faced brownstone, was his own personal vision—an imposing addition that would blend seamlessly with the existent structure, whose beauty and integrity our pastor quite rightly cherished.

Clarence felt that he was mentioned with a touch of orotund gravity, as if he had, in some sense, passed on. With Dearholt on the subcommittee, the thrust of its report was in no doubt, only the details. Still, he was relieved, as the meeting concluded in a jocular mood, to have put off to a future meeting any real decision. Vagueness and procrastination are ever a comfort to the frail in spirit. He marvelled at himself, how the diction of belief had still risen to his lips. Perhaps this afternoon's revelation would sink harmlessly down within him, to join in unspoken, half-forgotten depths the grotesque sexual dreams and nocturnal emissions of his youth.

Stella was waiting for him in their bedroom, awake. Shadows hung in the corners, away from the feeble electric bulb whereby she was darning a black sock; she was sitting upright in the mahogany fourposter, in a white cotton nightie and a frilled cap bulged by the containment of her hair. She explained that Mrs. McDermott and Mrs. Dearholt had taken the streetcar home, after a nice chat over the rest of the strawberries and cream. "How was the meeting?" she asked.

He removed his black coat, hung it tidily over the back of a ladderback chair, and with an upward strain of his jaw and grimace of difficulty undid his detachable celluloid collar. "Dearholt steamrollered for the addition, but I asked them if they weren't wanting this just to keep up with the Methodists. It gave them a little pause, though I expect they'll end up going ahead. I should just get out of their way, I suppose, but the Sabbath school is struggling to fill its classes now, with so many of our better families moving out to Clifton and Totowa." He sat down on the cane-bottomed rocker to remove his black shoes and socks. "Oh, my, Stel dearest, what a weariness I feel! I wonder if I have energy for all this."

"All what, Clarence?" From her voice she was still concentrating on the darning threads.

"All this church—all these good people, wanting something

from me no mortal man can provide. All this simulation of zeal." He could not tell her how even pronouncing words had become a heaviness, now that the true nature of reality was revealed. *There is no God.* Perhaps everybody, back to his professors at Princeton, had known it already.

"You'll feel better after a good night's rest. Little Teddy thought you looked tired."

"I heard him, all the way to my end of the table. Poor child, he's sensitive."

"More so than Jared and Esther?" she asked, still squinting at the sock stretched on its wooden egg, picking her way among the black threads. "They're the ones that get the marks at school."

Even attempting to discriminate between his children was in his brain-weariness almost beyond him. "Maybe not. But they're getting on in life. Both have jobs after school, and Esther has a beau. Teddy's being left behind."

"Not by us."

"Ah, I hope not."

She glanced up, and decided to ignore the enigma of that remark. "Dinner was spirited, I thought," she said.

He had to laugh, even in his stupefaction. The world distracts us from its own ruin. "Spirited is one way to describe it; some might say it was a quarrelsome disaster. You never should have invited Kleist; he's gone fanatic since they laid him off. He even had our demure Italian guests rallying to the red flag."

"It's healthy for people to exchange frank views," she said. "It's good to have the different sorts mix. If you let Paterson's class factions divide the Christian church, there's nowhere left where the sides can hear one another. Our Lord was never afraid of a good discussion." As if fearful of seeming to know his business better than he, she subdued her tone. "That McDermott seems a sweet soul, and Mr. Dearholt means well—he just rubs you the wrong way."

"He wants to take over Fourth Presbyterian as his own little business on the side, and the way I'm feeling tonight he can have it."

"Why, Clarence, you're sounding almost sinful! There's nobody like you around, for learning and compassion."

"Compassion! Isn't that a sickly thing, when as Kleist said the millowners have all the swords? Aren't these so-called Christian virtues just as Ingersoll and the radicals claim, an excuse for doing nothing, a way to keep the poor quiet while the rich get richer?"

Stella put aside her completed sock and told him, "I've never read a word of Ingersoll and don't intend to. He mocked God yet went on living off the fat of a land made prosperous by God-fearing men and women. And you shouldn't be reading him either—something's troubling you, everybody noticed it tonight."

"Really? I tried to hold my tongue and let the others talk."

"You always do, dearest. It wouldn't hurt for them to hear their minister speak his mind now and then."

"Ah, Stella, I don't half know what my mind is any more." He went in his suspenders and black trousers into the bathroom, to spare her the sight of him naked as he changed into his nightshirt. He did not want to come any closer to confessing his secret, the still-raw sore of Godlessness within him. He brushed his teeth with baking soda and took a swig of Mrs. Winslow's Soothing Syrup to ease his throat and help him sleep. When he came out, Stella was already unconscious, in the sudden way of a healthy animal. The brown-shaded light burned directly into her sagging face. She had never been beautiful but there had been a square-jawed compactness that was loosening and bloating with age. She was looking more and more like an overfed man. He thought of slender little Mavis asleep in her corner of an airless room down in Dublin, her hard-working small hands curled against her chin, her fresh crop of freckles fading into the milk-soft skin. He pulled the chain on the lamp so gently his wife would not waken and slithered into a dark space beside her that might as well have been his tomb, except that the heat of this June day followed him in, and the whine of mosquitoes, and the desolate stir of his mind, and the muttering noise of the city putting itself to rest. The clatter of horseshoes and iron-tired wheels on cobblestones was mixed with the receding friction of a Broadway trolley car and the occasional snuffling crescendo, punctuated by sharp coughs of frustrated combustion, of the horseless carriages, or motorrigs—Ford Model Ts and Oldsmobiles in the main—which the more advanced citizens of Paterson were inflicting in ever greater numbers upon the old uneven, dung-strewn streets. The young century was thronged with a parade of inventions that amused Clarence when little else did, and the presumptuous, ragged, hopeful sound of a doughty little motorrig brought a ray of innocent energy, such as messenger angels would ride to earth, into his invalid mood. The hoarse receding note drew his consciousness to a fine point, and while that point hung in his skull starlike he fell asleep upon the adamant bosom of the depleted universe.

His next day's duties, thick-headedly enacted while an underlying fever of confusion sought to repel the virus of atheism, included calls upon the sick of his parish. Clarence walked the two blocks to the mews behind Hamilton Street and took out the parson's buggy. Betsy, a compact old gray Morgan, had a blood spot in her left eye and greeted him by rotating her little white-fringed ears. He flicked the reins listlessly, settling his eyes on her heavy croup and agitated tail as she tugged the lightweight box, with its spinning slender wheels, along the polished cobbles of Parks Boulevard. Mrs. Van Scoyk was at home recuperating from her fifth difficult accouchement. The baby could be heard squalling in the next room, as a nurse vainly cooed and crooned. "As soon as I hold the cunning little angels in my arms," Mrs. Van Scoyk told her visitor, "the agony flies right out of my mind, as if it never happened!" Miss Harriet Bartle, active in his altar league, was for an indeterminate stay abed on a floor in Paterson General, originally "Ladies Hospital," in Wayne, suffering from a siege of nervous indisposition whose exact symptoms and deeper causes could be comfortably left veiled with other female mysteries while he delivered a little gossip and offered up a brief prayer at her compliant, wistful bedside. Barnert Memorial, opened a mere two years ago far out on Broadway, to serve the immigrant masses in all their flourishing ills, was—like St. Joseph's, Paterson's oldest hospital, founded by a priest and five Sisters of Charity—rarely on Clarence's rounds. Mr. Orr, however, lay near death in Barnert. He had been a manual laborer—a hod carrier to brickmasons, a crate-handler for grocers, a paid helping hand to those with heads enough to be tradesmen or entrepreneurs—and never able, somehow, to achieve the ease of a wife, home, and family. Yet he had been a tenaciously faithful attendant at church, always seated on the lefthand side of the nave, midway down the set of side pews underneath the painted-glass memorial windows presenting a sextet of Protestant martyrs and heroes—Wyclif, Huss, Calvin, Knox, Cromwell, Bunyan, all seen, save for the armored Protector, at pulpit or desk with expressions of dire resolve. Beneath their sternly rapt visages Clarence had missed, these last months, Orr's small, dingy, beadily staring face, hanging on the sermon with an intensity that shamed the sermonizer, whose habit of dramatic hesitation frequently tempted his mind to wander even as his tongue proceeded. Today Mr. Orr, who bore as testament to his parents' piety the Christian name of Elias, was poorly; Clarence found him asleep, his head on the starched pillowcase looking little bigger than a withered gray apple. Disease had thinned his russet hair unevenly, so it seemed patchy like a newborn baby's, and chronic pain had cut deep lines along his nose and between his brows. Clarence would have tiptoed away, but within Orr's sunken sockets two wet dark gleams forced apart the crusty melding of his wrinkled lids; the man grunted in lieu of welcome and made a gesture at elbowing himself higher in the bed, before lapsing back into supinity.

"Don't bestir yourself, Mr. Orr. I didn't come but for the briefest moment. How is your cure progressing?"

"To say I'm fair would be saying too much, Reverend. I'm very weary of the pain. It won't be long, I can feel it in my marrow. With all how hot it's been these past days, the cold has not let go its grip on my feet, and trust my words it's climbing higher."

"This unseasonable muggy spell has got us all down. My wager is you'll be up and about within a week or two."

"Ah, don't talk foolishness, sir, in trying to be kind. I'm nearing the end, and I'm ready to face the verdict. Reverend Wilmot, tell me true now. The time for soft talk is by. What do you think my chances are, to find myself among the elect?"

The little face in the pillow emitted an odor of dental rot and stale mucus that afflicted Clarence's nose six feet away, though the ward was perfumed with alcohol and ether. "In all frankness," he said as gravely as he could, into the small monkeyish face, "I should estimate your chances to be excellent. Have you, in the course of your life as best you can remember, ever enjoyed a palpable experience of the living Christ?" Clarence's mouth felt dry, dragging forth this old formula, with its invitation to hallucination and hysteria.

Mr. Orr's eyes had forced wider apart the enclosing folds of skin; the bleached circlets of his irises were aswim in yellowish rheum threaded with blood. "I cannot honestly recollect ever enjoying that. I've searched my heart, but it's hard to say, now, isn't it? Some of these women, they boast of the Lord as if He comes to pay court every night. I've had what you might call promptings, during prayer and on rare occasion in the middle of the day, while about business of another sort. But I wouldn't want to make claims for them as palpable experiences. A palpable experience, I guess you'd have no doubt—isn't that so?"

He had struck a note of sly wheedling that brought home to Clarence the cruelty of a theology that sets us to ransacking our nervous systems for a pass to Heaven, even a shred of a ticket. "You're too modest, Mr. Orr. Anyway, some among us teaching elders hold that there can *be* no palpable experience—

just the impalpable experience of existing in God's grace, won anew by His Son Jesus Christ."

The silence that greeted this was perhaps longer than Clarence imagined it. Then Orr said, "Well, if I'm not to be among the saved, it was laid down that way at the beginning of Creation, and what can a body do? Tell me, sir. What can we poor bodies down here do?"

Clarence was taken aback; dying was making the man conversationally ruthless. "What we can do, Mr. Orr, is to do good to our fellow man and trust in the Lord and enjoy His gifts when they are granted to us. I don't see how any deity can ask more of us than that."

Orr closed one eye, as if to sharpen his vision from the other. "You don't. Is that right? You talk like it's six of one and a half-dozen of the other. We're not dealing here with any deity, we're dealing with the true and only God. He asks the world and then some."

Clarence thought to respond, but his voice was slow to come, and the withered little laborer, opening both eyes, went on challengingly: "Reverend Wilmot, my life's been hard. I never had advantages. I never thought I had enough to spare to take a wife, though there were several that were willing, when I was young and able. Having put up with a hard life for sixty-six years, without much comfort in it but hope of the next, I'm not afraid to face the worst. I'll take damnation in good stride if that's what's to come."

"Oh come now, Mr. Orr!—there can be no question of your damnation."

"No, sir? No question. And why would that be?"

Clarence weakly gestured, unable politely enough to frame his impression that Mr. Orr was not worth the effort, the effort of God's maintaining and stoking and staffing an eternal factory of punishment.

The man's suspicions were aroused; he repeated the scrabbling effort of his elbows to raise himself in bed. "Damnation's what my parents brought me up to believe in. They were regular pious folk, from Sussex County. There's the elect and the others, damned. It's in the Bible, over and over, right out of Jesus' mouth. It makes good sense. You can't have light without the dark. How can you be saved, if you can't be damned? Answer me that. It's part of the equation. You can't have good without the bad, that's why the bad exists. That's what my parents held—pious folk, good people, lost their pig farm to the banks in the Panic of '73, never got their heads above water since. Every night, before supper, we used to sing a hymn. Even nothing on the table, we used to sing a hymn. 'Now the day is over, night is drawing nigh.' That sort of thing. So tell me, Reverend Wilmot, where's the flaw in my reasoning? You're a learned man—that comes across real clear, Sunday mornings."

Clarence had had such conversations before, but usually they were abstract, amiable disputes among professionals of the faith; laymen on their deathbeds he had generally found modest and mannerly, anxious not to embarrass the minister of God come to offer rote comfort, their thoughts absorbed by their bodily upheavals and their final arrangements with loved ones. He sensed that Orr was terrified, and he knew that even as recently as yesterday he would have had stronger answers for him. But he forced out the words. He said, "You've left God's infinite mercy out of the equation, Mr. Orr—there's the flaw. Jesus spoke of Hell and outer darkness but He only condemned devils to it for certain, and who of us can claim to be a devil? Who would be so proud? God showed Man His love twice—when He created him out of clay and when He gave His only begotten Son to redeem him from Adam's sin. In the Old Testament, we read how He loved Israel, His chosen people, even when they strayed. Don't bother yourself about damnation, I beg you, my good friend, but think instead of the glorious Resurrection and life everlasting. Think of the thief on the cross, to whom Jesus said, 'Today shalt thou be with me in paradise.' Not that the state of your health is comparable to the thief on the cross. You've got a peck of years left in you, I can tell by your argumentative spirit. You're on the mend. You'll be back in your pew under the Reformers' windows before we know it."

The dying man turned his ashen, shrivelled face to study his comforter. "Don't you believe in damnation at all?" he asked.

"Me myself? Absolutely I do. Without a doubt, absolutely. But not for you, Mr. Orr. Not for as hard a worker and as faithful a churchgoer as you. Certainly as a matter of abstract doctrine there has to be a state of non-election. And—who knows?—there may well be in the world men wicked enough to be eternally damned."

"Them Oriental potentates with all the jewels and wives," Mr. Orr offered.

"Exactly."

"And all the Jews."

"I can't go along with that, I fear. Our Savior was a Jew. One of the most outstanding men in Paterson, Nathan Barnet, is a Jew."

Mr. Orr closed his repulsive pained eyes, and sang in a voice surprisingly high and true, " 'Shadows of the evening, steal across the sky.' " Clarence imagined, with relief, that his presence had been forgotten, but Orr's eyes opened again and he announced, "I never heard enough damnation from your pulpit. Many mornings I had to strain to take hold of what you *were* saying, Reverend. I couldn't figure it out, and got dizzy listening, the way you were dodging here and there. A lot of talk about compassion for the less fortunate, I remember that. Never a healthy sign, to my way of thinking, too much fuss and feathers about the poor. They're with us always, the Lord Himself said. Wait till the next go-around, if the poor feel so sorry for themselves on this. The first shall be last. Take away damnation, in my opinion, a man might as well be an atheist. A God that can't damn a body to an eternal Hell can't lift a body up out of the grave either."

"Mr. Orr, to relieve your mind—"

"Young man, don't worry about relieving *my* mind. I told you, I can face it. I can face the worst, if it was always ordained. God's as helpless in this as I am."

"Well, now, that's just it, isn't it? How can a God be considered helpless—"

"If He's made His elections at the beginning of time, He is. He can't keep changing His mind. I guess that's something He can't do. Well, in a few days I'm going to know what His mind was and is. I'd promise to tell you from the other side, but I'm no Spiritualist. There's this side, and then there's the other, just like there's saved and not saved. You take counsel with yourself, Reverend Wilmot, and see if you can't think a bit more kindly of damnation. To tell a man he can't be damned has logical consequences you haven't taken into account. There have to be losers, or there can't be winners. That's what the Bible tells us, and Mr. Herbert Spencer too."

"That's an arresting connection," Clarence said, startled for the moment out of his profound discomfort.

"I've given things some thought," Mr. Orr said, not without pride. "I've had no missus and a lot of lonely nights to do some pondering and a little reading. All the modern thinkers have come around to it—a lot of losers, a few winners. Eternal damnation it has to be, if there's any sense to any of it at all. Mark my words."

"I have and will, Mr. Orr. I wish you well. Forgive me"—he gratefully stood, lifting his thin, tilted, handsome head away from this foul deathbed into a level of atmosphere smelling of ether and antisepsis—"if I can't quite believe damnation is for you. Maybe more for the likes of me. I can see the signs of election sparkling right in your eyes."

The little man as if spitefully closed them, leaving his caller gazing down at a shrivelled yellow death mask.

Some weeks later, when that debilitating onset of June heat had settled into a daily drone of July temperatures in the nineties, the cycle of the lectionary had brought round, to the tenth Sunday after Pentecost, the thirteenth chapter of Matthew, the parable of the tares:

As therefore the tares are gathered and burned in the fire; so shall it be in the end of this world.

The Son of man shall send forth his angels, and they shall gather out of his kingdom all things that offend, and them which do iniquity;

And shall cast them into a furnace of fire: there shall be wailing and gnashing of teeth.

Attendance was sparse; the gentry of the congregation would be enjoying with their families the breeze and waves of the Jersey shore or the heights of the Catskills, and those unable to afford summer homes or rentals would have trooped by mid-morning to the shaded picnic groves of Garrett Mountain. Clarence, mounted into the pulpit through the skeleton choir's wavering "Amen," looked toward the left wall and was sorry to see that Mr. Orr's round, implacable, attentive face was gone, forever gone, from beneath the translucent row of unsmiling Reformers. The minister had meditated hard upon this sermon, to please the dead man. Feeling the plain back Geneva gown upon him as a gentle, inhibiting weight of consecration, and aware at his throat of the encasement of the upright wing collar which he wore, with a white bow tie, in modern echo of the traditional clerical bands, he faced the upturned faces scattered through the varnished pews. Paper fans imprinted with oily Biblical scenes methodically beat back and forth in front of these sweating, courteously expectant faces. He commenced in a quiet, factual voice, "The notorious agnostic Robert Ingersoll, whose imprecations did so much to arouse and refortify the church of my father's generation, once began an essay as follows:

" 'One great objection to the Old Testament is the cruelty said to have been commanded by God. All these cruelties ceased with death. The vengeance of Jehovah stopped at the tomb. He never threatened to punish the dead; and there is not one word, from the first mistake in Genesis to the last curse of Malachi, containing the slightest intimation that God will take his revenge in another world. It was reserved for the New Testament to make known the doctrine of eternal pain. The teacher of universal benevolence rent the veil between time and eternity, and fixed the horrified gaze of man upon the lurid gulf of hell. Within the breast of non-resistance coiled the worm that never dies. Compared with this, the doctrine of slavery, the wars of extermination, the curses, the punishments of the Old Testament were all merciful and just.' "

Stella and the three children—hard-mouthed Jared and fair-haired Esther looking superior if not quite sneering, soft-bodied Teddy gazing with that aggravating undercurrent of fright—were seated in the front pew, and Mr. and Mrs. Dearholt, having elected for this weekend to stay and roast in Paterson, were behind them, with four empty pews intervening. Dearholt's oval glasses flashed; his wide wife wore a ghost of a deferential smile behind her dotted veil. Clarence had captured the congregation's attention. He had knotted his strait-jacket; now to get out of it, like the great Houdini.

"What might we say to this fierce indictment? That there is pain and brutality in the Bible, no one denies; it describes Mankind, and pain is a fact of human existence. The God of the Old Testament did not distance Himself from His chosen people; He participated in their struggles and made Israel's enemies His own. Israel's own transgressions grieved Him and incited Him to a terrible wrath. Ours is no aloof Lord—no Buddha beyond it all or Zeus making light of mortal travail. Among the world religions Christianity is unique in presenting a suffering God, a God who took human suffering upon Himself and in His agony gave birth to mankind's salvation. He defeated death, which means He had to lay His hands upon death, as the Old Testament Jehovah laid hands upon Jacob and wrestled with him all the night long. We do not worship a God immensely above us, out of human reach, but One Who does not disdain to touch us, to lay even rough hands upon us, and in that brief Lifetime recounted in the New Testament to descend to our condition, and to speak to men in metaphors drawn from their daily lives.

"For what does a farmer *do* with tares, with weeds? He *burns* them, to keep his fields tidy and to destroy those weed seeds, which otherwise would find fertile soil and bring forth in the next season a crop of weeds greater than ever. The economy of agriculture demands selection, demands winnowing. Earlier in the Gospel of Matthew, John the Baptist announces to Judea's generation of vipers, 'Every tree which bringest not forth good fruit is hewn down, and cast into the fire.' One greater than he, John the Baptist announces, will come and 'baptize you with the Holy Ghost, and with fire: Whose fan is in his hand, and he will thoroughly purge his floor, and gather his wheat into the garner; but he will burn up the chaff with unquenchable fire.'

"Pity the chaff, will say some to whom the mercies and the justice of Christ are obscure. Pity the weeds, and the fruitless fig tree. But"—Clarence paused, gazing about, his pale-blue eyes distended, his mouth ajar beneath the drooping sandy mustache—"I suggest to you that men are not plants, they have minds and souls and free wills, they are responsible for their deeds and for the eternal consequences of these deeds. They have *made* themselves chaff, if they are so judged when the great farmer comes with his winnowing fan. The tree has made itself fruitless, the weeds—" His voice snapped on the word; he lost his place, his thought, and looked down into his scribbled text, written in a desperate rush of inspiration last night after dinner, and still could not find it. He looked up, and felt how his pause had drawn the congregation's attention tighter to him, like a strangling embrace. "The weeds," he stated levelly, "have grown where they were not wanted, and have elected themselves to be uprooted and cast away."

He changed tone, into a matter-of-fact pitch. "Actually, the number of times that Jesus invokes Hell are not many. The most celebrated verses, and the most severe, come in the fifth chapter, and are echoed with variation in the eighteenth chapter and also in Mark. Our Savior is portrayed as preaching:

" 'Ye have heard that it was said by them of old time, Thou shalt not commit adultery:

" 'But I say unto you, That whosoever looketh on a woman to lust after her hath committed adultery with her already in his heart.

" 'And if thy right eye offend thee, pluck it out, and cast it from thee: for it is profitable for thee that one of thy members should perish, and not that thy whole body should be cast into Hell.

" 'And if thy right hand offend thee, cut it off, and cast it from thee: for it is profitable for thee that one of thy members should perish, and not that thy whole body should be cast into Hell.' "

The words seemed to parch Clarence's throat, which had become fearsomely dry; not one but several audible, partial throat clearings were necessary before he could proceed to his consoling mitigations: "The word translated here as 'Hell' was 'Gehenna' in Greek, based upon the Hebrew 'gehinnom,' a name derived from the valley of Hinnom, a rubbish dump near Jerusalem. Hell is therefore a trash heap, and the fires of Hell, to which Christ sometimes refers, should be understood not as eternal torture but as the purifying action whereby trash—whose accumulation would otherwise overwhelm us in our homes and in the streets of a busy city such as Paterson—whereby trash is returned to nature: is broken down into its basic elements, and returns to air as smoke and heat, and to the earth as ashes. Those who are condemned to damnation have already *condemned themselves* to *non-existence*, as understood in the light of the miraculously full existence which Christ's coming and His redemption has made possible. *Possible* for each of us, but not certain. *Promised*, but not, my brothers and sisters in the hope of that promise, necessarily attained."

Clarence felt his voice giving out, closing up. The effort to push words out into the great space of the church, with its clutch of unresponsive listeners, was taxing his chest; his lungs felt to be heaving within him. His family in the first row was staring up at him with visible worry. "*We,*" he announced, as emphatically as he could, "must bring something to the new covenant. The mountain has come to us, but we must climb it. He who stands at the base of a mountain and refuses to climb it stands in an abyss. That abyss of non-attainment is Hell. That is why the infidel Robert Ingersoll's charge that the New Testament brought Hell into human history is correct and true. Those outside the light of Christ's new dispensation exist in outer darkness—a phrase, *to skótos to exóteron,* unique to Matthew, though it is found in rabbinical writings and in intertestamental writings such as Enoch. Matthew, chapter eight, verse twelve: 'But the children of the kingdom shall be cast out into outer darkness: there shall be weeping and gnashing of teeth.' By 'children of the kingdom' the Gospel-writer means those who *should be* participating in the kingdom, now that its news has arrived—those who *have had their chance.* Those who do not know Christ now are infinitely more ignorant than those who lived before He came. By not accepting Christ, we make ourselves trash, fit for nothing but to be burned on the dump of Gehenna. The pain of having lost Christ will be so great we will not feel the flames. That is the meaning of Hell—a giant space of comprehended loss, of self-recrimination, of *self-despising*"—he had to pause here, his voice clinging precariously, with a painful, scraping grip, to a crumbling inner slope; he finished in a hoarse rush—"that has been carved from the universe by Christ's cosmic victory."

There was more, a concluding and uplifting paragraph addressed to the late Mr. Orr's concerns, and meant to brighten, for all who shared the ideas of this departed spirit, the darkest corner of their Calvinist heritage. "Election," Clarence strove to say, "is not a leaden weight laid across our earthly lives, rendering our strivings as ridiculous as the"—he fluttered the fingers of his free hand, and a young person in the congregation tittered—"as the wrigglings of an impaled insect or bug or butterfly. Election is not a few winners and many losers, as we see about us in this fallen, merciless world." He must hurry, he must shorten; he had hardly any voice left; he could hear his listeners rustling in their dryly creaking pews. "Election," he mouthed, "is winners and non-players. Those who do not accept Christ's great gift of Himself waste away. They become nothing. Election"—the word hurt and scratched—"election is *choice.* Our choice. It is God's hand"—he stretched out that same white, long-fingered hand that had been an impaled insect—"reaching down, to those who reach up. If we cannot feel God's hand gripping ours, it is because"—and now his throat felt catastrophically closed, his breath reduced to a trickle, a wheeze—"we have not reached up. Not truly." He could speak no more. He felt strangled, his voice scorched to less than a whisper, a dry web stuck in his throat. The faces of those looking to him for faith pressed upon his chest in a hushed throng. Their paper fans had stopped beating.

For moments that approached eternity he hung there, in the pulpit, his milk-blue eyes protruding, his mouth ajar, until Stella from her front pew leaped up, turned to face the congregation, and with a smile and in her sweet-pouring unabashed Southern accent recited what came by second nature after a lifetime of observant Sunday mornings: "Blessing and glory and wisdom and thanksgiving and honor and power and might be to our God forever and ever! Amen. Mr. Wilmot has been battling just the most terrible catarrh. Now let us all join in singing hymn number three seven seven, 'Soldiers of Christ, Arise'!" The organist, Miss Miriam Showalter, glanced over at Clarence questioningly, and at his nod hit the first chord, and the congregation with a thin and ragged shuffle stood and sang,

"Soldiers of Christ, arise,
And put your armor on,
Strong in the strength which God supplies
Through His Eternal Son."

The hymn had six verses; as they unfolded in these manifold healthy throats, Stella sidled around the altar rail, as expertly as if dodging around her kitchen table, and conferred with Clarence in whispers: "Apostles' Creed or Nicene?"

He nodded, irritably. She should know that the Nicene was said only on Communion Sundays. "Apostle's," he silently replied. His lips were able to move even in the midst of this curious disgrace, this oubliette that had risen up around him with its slippery invisible walls. His cheeks felt hot, but his fingertips felt cold, and a shiver kept passing uncontrollably across his chest.

"Which prayer of thanksgiving?"

"You choose," he mouthed, exasperated. In the midst of this grotesque affliction, he was expected to worry about details. She had the book of worship in her hands; she had been at a thousand services; she could lead these sheep out the door. He wanted only to be alone with his miserable miracle, his glaringly clarified condition. The hymn concluded,

"From strength to strength go on;
Wrestle, and fight, and pray;
Tread all the powers of darkness down,
And win the well-fought day."

The congregation, more rustlingly and coughingly than usual, seated itself, and Stella stepped forward to the rail and called into the varnished depths of the ill-attended church, "With gladness, let us present the offering of our life and labor to the Lord." The two ushers, bumping together at the back, launched themselves with tentative, mismatching footsteps down the aisle. Stella looked at Clarence with a wild dark glance and then dartingly about the chancel, her composure shaken; languidly, in a daze of ironic impotence, he stepped to the side bench where the felt-bottomed collection plates reposed and presented them to the ushers, with a grave nod meant to soothe the disquiet in their faces. Kindly, long-chinned Mr. McDermott was one, and Mr. Cyrus Terhune, the stout proprietor of a Market Street dry-goods emporium, the other. Behind Clarence, as he gave the two men the briefest of ceremonial bows, Stella ringingly declaimed, "Remember the words of the Lord Jesus: It is more blessed to give than to receive." She seemed, to his ear, to be overacting.

In view of the sparse size of the summer choir, the organ was supposed to accompany the collection with a solo, but Miriam Showalter's hands were still, as if they had been stricken along with his throat. The wooden plates floated through the hushed pews eerily, hand to hand, the drop of coins dulled by the felt. The plates came forward with the ushers; Clarence took them—the wood felt warm from their grips—and turned and lifted them up to the stained-glass Jesus, Who was darkly ascending, with gracefully upturned hands and uprolled eyes and unweighted toes pointing downward and the hem of his robes a-flutter, between the two ranks of dusty organ pipes. In reflex Clarence opened his mouth to say the customary words; but Stella's voice rang out instead: "Yours, O Lord, are grandeur and power, majesty, splendor, and glory."

"All in the heavens and on the earth is yours," the congregation dubiously rumbled, "and of your own we give you."

He was wondering now if he might not find it in him to pronounce the prayers, but Stella had firmly found her place in these familiar, inflexible procedures. "We praise you, God," she sang out, with a swelling confidence, "for you are gracious. You have loved us from the beginning of time and remember us when we are in trouble." The sound of a woman's voice pronouncing the syllables of this litany was of course a blasphemous astonishment to most of its hearers, yet they had little choice but to respond, "Your mercy endures forever," and to be led through the Lord's Prayer and the morning's final hymn, "O Daughters Blest of Galilee," and to be sent forth into the world, "rejoicing in the power of the Holy Spirit," and to be blessed. Stella had looked toward her husband, asking with her eyebrows if he was up to pronouncing the benediction, but he shook his head impatiently, and so she melodiously, theatrically bid "The Lord bless you and keep you. The Lord be kind"—*kaaand*—"and gracious to you. The Lord look upon you with favor and give you peace." He joined in the "Amen" but not the "Alleluia!"

Miriam Showalter's burst of postlude Bach sounded angry. Stella, seeing Clarence move to follow the choir in his robes, showed an inclination to process to the entrance ahead of him, as befit her role in the service; but he restrained her with a grip that sank deep into the fat of her upper arm in its sheath of summer batiste.

"Go to the children," he directed, hoarsely yet audibly.

Her eyes flared; her mouth tensed in a little "o," making wrinkles all across the arc of her slightly hirsute upper lip. "You can talk again! What on earth happened?"

He shrugged helplessly, began a sentence with the word "God," then waved it away, saying, "It won't do."

"I would say not," Stella responded, turning on him her broad rounded back. Her wifely ability to sympathize, he saw, had been curtailed by her liturgical triumph, her taste of forbidden fruit. Briskly maneuvering her corseted heft, in her voluminous dress trimmed with ivory Valenciennes lace, upon her small, button-shoed feet, she stepped down from the chancel, replaced her book of worship in the pew-back, and also her chromolithographed paper fan, and collected her parasol and black leather purse. "Well, that was an experience," she sighed to her children. Their three children, all that was left of those who had witnessed Clarence's disgrace, stared in amazement, even Jared, with his clever slant eyes and wised-up mouth, too stunned to mock the event.

At the narthex door, next to the bell-ropes, Clarence found his voice sufficiently restored to function at a conversational level. "Mr. Proctor . . . thank you . . . yes, a catarrh . . . most inopportune, but it should pass . . . Mrs. Wharton . . . yes, another hot day . . . the lawns do need the rain." Most of the several dozen churchgoers declined to mention the uncanny indisposition they had witnessed; but a greater-than-usual constraint hovered above their perfunctory courtesies and murmurous hurry to be off into plain daylight.

The Sunday passed at first as if nothing unfortunate had happened. Clarence had never been physically strong, not even in his youth, and small nervous collapses and sudden disinclinations to do the usual were laid to his excessive learning and delicate earnestness. His father, Joshua Wilmot, had been an overbearing spade-bearded farmer who had developed a gravel pit at the rear of his ninety acres into a profitable sideline of supplying stone and sand to local builders, which he then had expanded into a lumber-and-brick business, locally retailing what he bought wholesale from larger suppliers. His older boy, Peter, had been groomed to inherit the enterprise; Clarence, who had followed Peter into the world after a run of three girls—Rachel, Esther, and unfortunate Phebe, born with a humped back and an extra thumb—was, from the start, of a retiring, obedient nature, and had sidled into the ministry as a path of least resistance. His happiest boyhood times had been spent in silent communication with a piece of printed paper, whether it be the local newspaper or an adventure romance by Mayne Reid or, at Princeton, the New Testament in its original Greek. Today, he and Stella and their three offspring had been invited to Sunday dinner with one of the more prominent of their parishioners, Amos Thibeault, the owner of a little wire manufactory tucked over on McBride Avenue behind the larger mills, and the owner of an impressive Second-Empire mansion, bristling with iron spears at the edges of its many mansard roofs, on Park Avenue beyond Carroll Street. The occasion passed stiffly but without any marked embarrassment. The hostess but not the host had been present in the church when the minister's power of speech had failed, and so Clarence's silence at lunch, and his wordless head-shake of refusal when invited to pronounce the blessing, were not unexpected.

As, with an expression of morose benignity, he sat consuming his share of pork roast and its ample vegetable accompaniment, his wife and children—except for the youngest, little, careful, tongue-tied Teddy—were exceptionally animated and conversational. He was a vacuum they were moving into. On the long walk home to Straight Street and Broadway, the family was silent, sensing itself to be imperilled. A wagon selling ice chips tinted and flavored by a variety of irresistibly sweet syrups was passed without importunities; a crowd of near-naked working-class children uproariously and defiantly splashing in the puddles around a gushing public faucet aroused no comment or combative exchange from the Wilmot children; the vulgarly vivid plantings of petunias and marigolds that the Italians and Polish had established in their front yards around plaster statues of a blue-gowned Madonna drew their eyes but no remark. These were not fashionable neighborhoods. The residents displayed themselves on their sagging wooden porches and stoops in shirtsleeves and loose, uncorseted dresses that permitted glimpses of more than dusty ankles and callused bare feet. Foreign languages—operatic ribbons of Italian, rapid stabs of Yiddish, mushy thrusts of Polish—floated through the air as shadows reached across the brown little lawns between the weedy, battered hedges; dark-eyed glances insolently grazed the straggling family of Protestants. The three Wilmot children walked with eyes down and scattered to their rooms and thence out into their own neighborhood when they arrived at the manse at four o'clock; they knew their parents had to talk, and feared that the family destiny was pregnant with something vague and dismal.

"Well, Mr. Wilmot, I must say," Stella began when their bedroom door was closed and her heavy white dress had been returned to her cedar wardrobe, and her corset loosened above her thin chemise of sweat-stained nainsook, "I've heard no thanks for my part in patching over your strange exhibition this morning. Whatever ailed you, dear?"

He wanly smiled; his mustache—which looked dirty, as fair

mustaches do—drooped a little less, exposing his lower teeth. His voice was hoarse and softer than usual but distinct, and unexpectedly sardonic. "My dear, you appeared to enjoy yourself so much I didn't think you needed thanks. In one bound, you overleaped the whole vexed question of female ordination. You were a veritable Louisa Woosley—splendid, my dear! Would that you had my male prerogatives, or I your dauntless faith."

"Faith?" she repeated absent-mindedly. Her corset, though less cruel to the waist and unnaturally compressing than the hourglass fashion of her young womanhood, was confining; first she undid the attached garters, and then the hook-and-eye fasteners down the front, at last dividing and parting herself from the semi-elastic carapace, much as one splits the nubbled belly of a Maine lobster to get at the meat. Physical relief evident in her large face, she moved back and forth in the room in her thin chemise as one forgetful of her generous physical endowment. Stella had had no great height of beauty from which to fall, and seemed little less comely now at forty-three than she had at twenty-six, her age as a bride. Though Clarence and his fellow seminarians had often talked of women, and not always in the most reverent manner, it had been a revelation to him that Stella not only had submitted to sex but in their early years had sought it, when a week or so of abstention had gone by, though he was tired and dragged down by the business of the dour little Missouri parish. It had been years since she, with certain touches of her hands and inflections of those lively lustrous eyes, dark as a gipsy's, had requested her rights of satisfaction; on winter nights, however, the married partners were still a warmth and comfort to one another on the double-troughed mattress of their old mahogany fourposter, and she accepted him without complaint on those rare evenings when arousal came unbeckoned upon him. Tonight, unrolling her stockings and tucking them back in the corner of her top drawer and unpinning her upswept load of chestnut hair so it fell, only slightly marred by gray, slowly uncoiling down her plump back while she gave herself a stern squint in the oval dresser mirror, she seemed unusually vigorous and able; he decided at last to impart to her the burden he had for a month been carrying alone.

"*My* faith, my dear, seems to have fled. I not only no longer believe with an ideal fervor, I consciously disbelieve. My very voice rebelled, today, against my attempting to put some sort of good face on a doctrine that I intellectually detest. Ingersoll, Hume, Darwin, Renan, Nietzsche—it all rings true, when you've read enough to have it sink in; they have not just reason on their side but simple humanity and decency as well. Jehovah and His pet Israelites, that bloody tit-for-tat of the Atonement, the whole business of condemning poor fallible men and women to eternal Hell for a few mistakes in their little lifetimes, the notion in any case that our spirits can survive without eyes or brains or nerves—Stel, it's been a fearful struggle, I've twisted my mind in loops to hold on to some sense in which these things are true enough to preach, but I've got to let go or go crazy. I love you for feeling otherwise, and would never argue a man or child out of whatever they believe, but to me it's all become relics, things left over from our childish nightmares, when there's daylight now all around us—this is the twentieth century! I can't keep selling myself and others the opposite of what jumps out at me from every newspaper and physical fact I see. The universe is a hundred percent matter, with the energy that comes in waves out of matter, and poor old humankind is on its own and always has been."

She had turned from the mirror to gaze at him. Her mannish, heavy face looked oddly seductive, her lids half-closed. Her low hairline gave it a brutish cast: her head's gleaming bounty, with its chestnut highlights and buckling waves, sprang from a line straight across her brow, without a hint of widow's-peak. "Clarence, have you tried praying?" She told him, "Reason isn't everything. There are things beyond it. Believing isn't supposed to be easy. What did St. Paul say? 'We see through a glass darkly.' "

Her tone of soft pleading, somehow sexual after these many years of their laying their bodies to one side, drew him closer to her. He lowered his voice, which felt raw, as if tear-scoured. "St. Paul," he said, "said many excellent things. 'For the Jews require a sign, and the Greeks seek after wisdom: but we preach Christ crucified, unto the Jews a stumblingblock, and unto the Greeks foolishness.' I love the old words, but now they lie dead in me. I don't quite know what has slain them—the infidel modern times, perhaps, or simply my years, it may be, and the fatigue with which the years tax my system—but dead the words are, as dead as the bones in the valley of Ezekiel."

"But those bones lived," she said quickly. "That is the point of the story. With God all things are possible. Perhaps your fatigue will pass, and these doubts with it."

"They are not doubts, alas—they are certainties. I cannot continue in the Christian pulpit, and be a Benedict Arnold in the camp. I fear if I continue to speak I will take hope and reassurance away from those that can still believe." And, as if proving that bones can live, he felt his eyes water and a convulsion of grief long held within himself overtook his face and shoulders; he sat on the edge of the bed, and she with him, setting a hand on his thigh.

"Poor heart," she said. "For how long have you been thinking these hopeless thoughts?"

"Since before the solstice, and it's been building God knows how many years before that." He laughed, snuffling, through the tears, at his unthinking invocation of the empty name. "I felt the leaving like a physical event," he said. "The afternoon before the Dearholts came to dinner."

"Dearholt weighs on a man of your temperament," she said. "He rouses your spirit of contrarity. Clarence: we all have moments, when life seems empty and not worthwhile. But they pass; we push through them, for the sake of the children we have brought into the world and all those others who depend upon us."

"Would I could push through, Stel. For, if I cannot, the burden of failure will fall not just on me but on you, dear, you and the children, as you say."

Her back stiffened so that the old bed swayed and once or twice creaked. "What are you thinking of? Not—"

"Yes. Resigning the ministry."

"Oh, my dear. How would we live?"

"There must be jobs. It would be a rare job indeed that pays less, in hard cash, than this. Even our horse and buggy are parish property."

"But"—her gesture took in the room, the house, the respectability and distinction that hedged them round. "Many a minister and priest, I'm sure, has doubts."

He thought of objecting again to the word, but this seemed pedantic and petty amid the gaping abyss of social consequence that had opened up with this sharing of his impotence.

Stella went on, "But the Word goes on, out through them."

"So I should go through the motions? Perhaps I could, if people did not sense the truth—the lack. They sensed it this morning. It dried me right up. The words stuck in my throat."

"You don't know what those people sensed—they were thinking of a hundred different things, would be my guess. As to the frog in your throat, you've run yourself down and are getting a summer cold, like I said right out," she told him. "Clarence"—with her extended Southern "a," one long syllable—"couldn't you think of it, keeping on, as walking a bridge, from one solid shore to another? The Lord doesn't leave us hanging, if we truly turn to Him. Remember the time when little Jared had the diphtheria, and you and I stayed up together all night watching and praying, and—"

He gently laid his hand on hers and lifted it from his black-clad thigh. "You believe, I know, and it is lovely in you. I envy you, I suppose. But I no longer *can*—if simply willing it or praying for it would do it, don't you think I would have? And the bitter fact is that my respect for the church is still enough that I don't intend to pollute its pulpit with hypocrisy."

She had pulled back, offended by his dismissal of her helping hand. The bed creaked with her shift of weight. "That's all very grand of you, dear, and of course don't bother about me—my life, my position with all the people who know me around here, how everything will look—but what about the children? How will they eat?"

He sighed, exasperated by the smallness of her concerns, when he had lost the entire contents of his universe. "I can't yet think clearly on that. But this parish includes a number of well-placed men with whom I have worked successfully. . . . Surely . . . Or it may be our future does not lie in Paterson. We could go back out west."

"West?" she said sharply. "We escaped the West, and glad of it. Your spirit was too fine for the West; it ground it down, all those ignorant penny-pinching farmers."

"Yes, well . . ." The effort of confessing to her, the faint disappointment he felt now, as if expecting her, against all reason, to rescue him, suddenly left him very weary. To stretch out upon this bed, to merge his head with the down of the pillow . . . He said, "I needed to talk to you first. Now, Stel, do I have your permission to go to Harlan Dearholt? He is head elder; a consultation with him would be the first step in my resignation."

"Permission?" She was angry; it had not occurred to him, swallowed up in his own spiritual misfortune, that she could become angry. "You don't need my permission. You didn't ask it when you decided to abandon your Lord, why ask it now?"

Struck by her characterization, he turned it over in his mind before saying mildly, "I didn't decide, dear. The decision was beyond my control. My Lord decided, if you would rather, to cast me out."

"We cast ourselves out, or deal ourselves in," she said, surprising him with this Missouri touch of riverboat parlance. "You have cold-bloodedly decided to inflict on your family an entirely needless sacrifice. This parish has suited us. Paterson is thriving, it's letting the children make their way, and now, just because— I don't know why I should be surprised. Your own sister Esther warned me, before we married, 'The Wilmots are a cold clan.' "

"But if the requisite faith—"

"Oh, stop this tedious mooning about faith! Faith is something we *build;* it's a *habit.* I always thought—back in Jackson Bluffs I thought—you were a weak reed, Clarence Wilmot, but, but you know the conceit of women"—it had become her turn to laugh snufflingly through the slippery obstruction of tears—"I thought I could make a man of you. Well, all I've done is make a pretty mess for myself and the three harmless souls I brought into the world."

"Dear, no, don't speak so harshly—so unworthily. You'll find me solid through all this, I vow."

Her eyes contemplating him seemed dark as small plums; liverish patches beneath her eyes in the wan electric light seemed to betray some streak of ancient, pagan blood. "As solid as you can be, I don't doubt." She turned her back, the white flesh broad across her shoulders marred by a few raised moles between the straps of her frilled chemise. "Oh, my," she sighed, not so much to him as to a set of ghostly ancestors and descendants that had clustered sympathetically around her. "The trouble a life sees. No wonder they say there's another, to make this one right."

This was her way of conceding him all he sought.

Mr. Dearholt's house on Pennington Street had round, heavy-stoned arches and a round side tower whose conical roof was covered with progressively sized slates and tipped with a glass-balled lightning rod. It projected the gloomy savor and amplitude of a church, and yet the living room had a certain Oriental sensuality, with its ottomans and fringes and patterned Persian carpets. Having heard his unhappy visitor out, Dearholt lifted his head so his oval eyeglasses flashed and, with a friendly grimace of his flawless teeth, said, "Fight on, my friend. Never give up the good fight. You will win through in the end to renewed certainty—of that *I* am certain—if you stay the course. These are passing shadows, a crisis of direction, common to a man at your time of life. When I was just past forty, I had half a mind to throw everything over and head to Alaska and prospect for gold. From boyhood on, I've been drawn to the open spaces—the cowboys in Montana seemed to me to be the most splendid people in the world, and I would have gladly become an Indian if a tribe had ever been so kind as to kidnap me. But the better half of my mind prevailed, and my better half—my blessed Obelia—in her wisdom rode out the storm, and I've stuck the route here in Paterson, as you can see. The city's been good to me. The silk industry's been good to me, for all its ups and downs. Here's where the future's being made, in industrial cities, not in some Wild West that only exists any more in travelling shows where a few shabby survivors sit to be stared at. Once I took my twin boys up to Madison Square Garden, Reverend, to see Buffalo Bill and his gang, and Geronimo was too drunk to move a muscle!"

Clarence felt he was being tugged rather far from the point of his visit. "Mr. Dearholt," he said, "every Christian has doubts; it is our challenge and privilege to wrestle with them. Since student days at Princeton, I have been exposed to thinkers and poets from outside the Christian fold, and indeed at seminary some of the professors themselves gave alarmingly earnest voice to agnostic reasoning—but always, at the end of the day, I could return home, to the burning candle so to speak and the Sacred Book and the childish trust with which I lay me down. My father—a skinflint, some said, but a steadfast churchman, and a double-tither no matter how high or low that year's income—presented for my emulation a stern rectitude. He was Old School through and through; when the local possibility of merging with the Hopewell Congregationalists came up, as sharing the Calvinist heritage, he said he would as soon merge with the Unitarians and Emersonian pipe-dreamers, as he called them. For many years I assumed I had inherited his inflexible faith. So I know what it is to have faith, and now know what it is to have none. If I attempt any of the old formulations, to make myself the target of my own apologetics, or offer my inner voice up in helpless prayer, some irresistible denying force within me knocks the words away. I fear I have read too many atheist thinkers, in an attempt to understand and refute them. Meaning to undermine them, I was undermined instead! Darwin, Nietzsche, Ingersoll—the sons of clergymen have slain the Father above!"

Mr. Dearholt's smile persisted, along with the hard gleams from his oval spectacles. He was not yet bald but his hair was thin enough to reveal the curious shape a man's skull has, as of a dome that has taken a dent or two. "Gadarene swine, Mr. Wilmot—think of the Gadarene swine. Our Savior cast the devils into them and sent them squealing over the cliff into the sea. That is what you must do, sir. Cast out your devils, pure and simple. I wouldn't touch their filthy freethinking tracts myself; life's too short to get yourself hot and bothered. Think of these Huxleyites and Higher Critics and socialist scoffers not as reasonable men of good will like you and me but as devils in disguise, devils sent to test you, sent to test the church. Of *course,* they are clever; of *course,* they seem plausible. The Devil's campaign is not to be sneezed at. He sends good soldiers—smart, sincere soldiers. But they are *enemy* soldiers, Reverend Wilmot, to the likes of you and me. They serve the Beast and the Great Dragon, Gog and Magog, in the battle at the end of the thousand years, before the Devil is cast into the lake of fire, and all are judged. Are you with the devils or with the Lord in the battle is the question. Yes?"

Clarence looked with wonder at the dented curve of Mr. Dearholt's skull, that it would hold such mad and fiery contents. He tried to see timid, ailing, painstaking Darwin and sweet-voiced, pedantic Renan by the apocalyptic light his ruling elder had provided, or even bluff Ingersoll, and could not. As to the socialist scoffers, former workmen like Debs and Haywood, why not scoff, after the misery they had witnessed, and the jail terms to which they had been condemned? These were men groping after justice, after truth, which was a live presence moving always ahead of them, rather than the strangely shaped and petrified old dogmas defended with such vigorous complacence by the man settled, with his cigar and lemonade, before him. Mr. Dearholt was devoted to the newest devices; an electric fan, its head a flattened cage and its body a single brass stem, stood before the fireplace and battered the air so loudly that both men had to speak at an uncomfortable volume. The current of stirred air, Clarence noticed, was directed mostly at his host, lifting stray strands now and then from his dented, gleaming skull.

"Yes, still . . ."

"Yes, still, you are too gullible. Out of your gullible nature you've let the enemy infect your thinking, my friend. Think of your state of mind as a disease. You need to convalesce, to rest. Take no offense; these are trying times, as I heard you say last month when I had the pleasure of being your guest at dinner. August is imminent; what are your vacation plans? Your missus and children should already be out of the city, safe from pestilence somewhere where the breezes blow. That little fellow of yours especially needs some outdoor pursuits; I thought he looked woefully underexercised."

"I haven't thought much about it. . . . My sister Esther and her husband have a house down in Delaware, not too far from the water, we generally go there for a few days. The two older children have summer employment, and the work of the church . . ."

"Will survive without you, I guarantee it. With your permission I will canvass the board of elders and ask that your vacation begin now, the fees for pulpit supply to come out of general funds rather than your salary. I happen to know a man—a man not of our humble parish but of our denomination, whose contributions to the First Presbyterian are significant, believe me—this man among his holdings owns an excellent seaside cottage at Ocean Grove which he and his family are unable to use this August because of a planned excursion to Europe, as a college-graduation present to his older daughter. He had not planned to rent, risking exposing his property to any sort of person who might offer themselves as a tenant. But for a pastor and his family—"

"This is a bewilderingly generous offer, but—"

"Nothing is definite, understand, my friend. But I think I can make it so. I will whisper a word to this man concerning your, shall we say, nervous condition. This is not charity, believe me—entirely a matter of enlightened self-interest on the part of the parish. A sound investment, to ensure a proper return on the call that brought you among us. We were not mistaken; you have the endowments. How does our Book of Discipline put it?" Dearholt closed his eyes behind his glasses; his lids trembled with the effort of memory. " 'Natural, acquired, and gracious endowments fitting him for the office.' That's what it takes, for the church to extend the call. The call went out, you answered. I haven't agreed with every position you've adopted—you are *much* too cautious, in my view, about our building requirements—but you have what it takes, as they say in the mills. I can size a man up pretty quick; that's part of my business. You know, quite frankly, the Presbyterian church of the U.S. of A. isn't getting the kind of vocations it used to—mostly average or below boys looking for the nearest way off the farm or up from the factory floor but with nothing about them of the gentleman. A man of your qualities—your endowments—is treasure not to be wasted. We don't want to lose you in the Almighty's ongoing battle, Clarence."

Clarence brushed at the tickle as a gust from the noisy fan agitated the hair of his long sideburn. "Maimed as I am?"

"Don't say maimed, say momentarily indisposed. Under the weather, as even young men sometimes are, eh? You'll emerge from this siege of trouble strengthened, I am a hundred percent certain."

"I fear that my will—"

"And consider your own personal welfare. Think selfishly for a moment. What lies outside the church for you? Nothing compared to what is within. You are no longer young, my friend. You have invested your assets in the office you occupy. How does Paul put it to Timothy? 'Neglect not the gift that is in thee, which was given thee by prophecy, with the laying on of the hands of the presbytery.' Neglect not the gift that is in thee," Dearholt repeated, and began, "Faith—" He was becoming reflective, as when he revealed his desire to go to Alaska, and interrupted himself, "Would you like another lemonade? Would you disapprove if I fortified it with a splash of something stronger—say, a dash of good old Jamaican rum?"

"Oh no, no thank you." The denomination was temperance, but not as fanatically as the Methodists and Baptists. "My pipe is vice enough. I wonder too if I have not taken enough of your evening. Mrs. Dearholt—"

"Is happy upstairs," Dearholt concluded for him. "Obelia has her embroidery. Faith," he went on, "is not some merely intellectual choice. It is basic human strength. It is manliness, and womanliness. It gives courage and cheer from the infant's first steps to the aged's last breath. Without it, we're not alive, Reverend Wilmot. Without it, we're the servant who buries his talent in the ground. It may seem strange for me to be telling you this, but you need to hear it, as I once needed to hear it, years ago. I was close to forty and the Panic of 1893 had knocked the stuffing out of a little business I had put my heart and soul into. I felt sorry for myself and walked the streets, right here in Paterson, and in the park by the Falls I heard a self-appointed preacher, a man some could say was simple, who catered to the poor without benefit of a church over his head or a vestment over his shoulders, but he told me what I needed to hear, and I've lived by it; it's given me life, and pleasure in life. The Word is life, just as the Book says. The way, the truth, and the life. Everything outside the Book is just the hollow show of life. Oh, it can be plausible. It can be alluring. But the show belongs to the Devil's realm, and in the end, when they wrap the show up, there's nothing left onstage to see, just the fact of death."

Clarence was moved that the other man had opened up to

him so completely his innermost convictions, but he left Dearholt's fine house still believing that the exact opposite was true: life, with its risks and ultimate defeat, lay with the calm, merciless, impersonal truths that godless men were daily uncovering in the wide world spread beyond the moldering walls of the shrinking castle keep. The Christian castle's precincts had become for Clarence so claustral and musty and dark that they felt like the Devil's tenements.

The minister of the Fourth Presbyterian Church was a member of the Presbytery of Jersey City, in the Synod of New Jersey. Clarence one day in August—having evaded the bribe of the Ocean Grove cottage—boarded a train at the Erie Railroad station on Market Street, and then stared out the sooty windows as Clifton and Passaic slid by. Coalyards, small brick factories, summer-tired trees, backyards dingy in their proximity to the tracks scattered and broke into a gap of Aquakanonck farms before Nutley and Belleville yielded to the outskirts of Newark. Slowing its pace, the train clacked diagonally over the Passaic River and entered upon a glorious stretch of the Meadows—tall tawny cattails and saltwater grasses still as green as spring, flickering with white butterflies and red-winged blackbirds—before crossing the Hackensack into the city of his destination. The presbytery kept its modest offices on the sixth floor of an eight-story building a healthy little walk from the station. A creaking birdcage elevator lifted Clarence to a hall lined with carefully lettered doors half of frosted glass. The presbytery was hardly to be distinguished from Spitz and Quinlan, Legal Attorneys, or I. H. Levine, Expert in Chiropractics. The waiting room was equipped with well-worn, uncushioned oak furniture and an overweight receptionist-secretary. When she sighed and heaved up from her desk and went into a room whose ajar door revealed shelves of archives arrayed in boxes of marbled cardboard, the action was performed with the aid of a cane, her massive hips seesawing with a strenuousness painful to see. Clarence spied in a gap between her long skirt of navy serge and a black shoe that seemed less creased than the other some inches of drab brown stocking covering what he took to be a prosthetic leg. Yet her amber hair, in whose uniform bright tint some artificial rinse was implicated, gleamed a glossy pompadour, and a smile dimpled her plump cheeks with a quicksilver coquettishness. *When thou makest a feast, call the poor, the maimed, the lame, the blind:* thus does the church, built upon the stone which the builders rejected, declare its mercies to a ruthlessly selective world. Clarence meekly returned her smile and for fifteen minutes' wait shared with this other maimed person a companionable silence. He would miss, he thought, all such nooks in the ecclesiastical maze, wherein a blameless quotidian industry concealed and overarched the essential unreality. His journey had taken over an hour and left his summer suit of cream-colored linen wrinkled. Through the room's one window he enjoyed a view whose foreground consisted of tarred flat rooftops burdened with wooden water tanks and chairs and even weather-soaked couches for residents escaping the swampy heat, and whose middle ground was a green waste of marsh grass and cattails brutally bisected by railroad tracks on a built-up embankment, and whose hazed distance held lower Manhattan, its granite-girded skyscrapers bristling like a conglomerate horn on the nose of a rhinoceros whose body could only be guessed at. Faded white letters on a nearby building advertised BEECHAM'S PILLS and elsewhere his eye picked up advertisements for WEINTRAUB BROS. HIGH CLASS TAILORS and SHINOLA and DR. WERNET'S POWDER FOR FALSE TEETH and DREAMLAND, a dance hall or moving-picture theatre, presumably.

His perusal of the cityscape was interrupted by the emergence of the moderator of the presbytery from his office. Thomas Dreaver had been recently elected to the post; like Clarence a clergyman, he was younger than expected, younger than his petitioner. Pale and rounded in feature, with short fair hair brushed away from a central parting, he wore a single-breasted, slate-blue business suit and was businesslike in manner, save for an extra smoothness, a honeyed promissory timbre to his voice that marked him as an executive of Christian business. For some perverse theatrical reason Clarence had, for this fateful encounter, dug into Stella's cedar chest, packed with clothes from their past, and found his one surviving rebato, worn in his Missouri days to distinguish himself in dignity from the shirtsleeved Baptists, and a black rabat vest. Though Calvinist thinking had always shied from these Roman appurtenances, they had never been officially proscribed, and the Princeton approach had tended to be playfully "high," not even abstaining, in chapel celebrations on major holy days, from colored stoles decorated with the Chi Rho in gold thread.

"I was very troubled by your letter," Dreaver said, yet offered a deft, untroubled smile, while flicking a smooth hand toward the chair in his office which Clarence should occupy.

"And I was somewhat perturbed by yours," said the visitor, seating himself. "My mentors at seminary failed to spell out—or else I was inattentive that day—what a complicated and tedious affair resigning from the ministry would be."

" 'Our vines have tender grapes,' Mr. Wilmot," said the young man. "Not every hand can pick them. And what did Calvin himself say—'It would be a very serious accusation against us to have rejected God's call'?" Dreaver picked up a small flexible black-bound book, the edges of its pages gilded. "Here. Let me read you the section, section fifty-one, from the Book of Discipline. 'If a minister, otherwise in good standing, shall make application to be released from the office of the ministry, he may, at the discretion of the presbytery, be put on probation, for one year at least, in such a manner as the presbytery may direct, in order to ascertain his motives and reasons for such a relinquishment.' "

Clarence interrupted. "I could hardly bear another year of going through the motions. Giving communion, preaching, trying to console the sick and dying—it would be, I can't say blasphemy, but a travesty. And the parishioners would know it. Already, they sense how hollow I am."

"With all respect, I wonder if they do. You are not the source of what they seek. You are God's conduit, merely, and hollowness is no fault in a conduit, is it?" Dreaver held up a finger and read smoothly on. " 'And if, at the end of this period, the presbytery be satisfied that he cannot be useful and happy in the exercise of his ministry, they may allow him to demit the office, and return to the condition of a private member in the Church, ordering his name to be stricken from the roll of the presbytery, and giving him a letter to any church with which he may desire to connect himself.' "

Clarence suppressed a smile; the mass of leaden guilt with which he woke in the morning and lay down at night almost seemed manageable, caught up and segmented in such strict language. "The word 'demit' is new to me," he confessed. "And I doubt I would be presenting a letter to another church; I am not apt to join one when I lack sufficient belief to keep on in the only profession for which I am fitted."

"Yes, well fitted. So your ruling elder, Harlan Dearholt, informs me."

"Harlan is a model of faith. Had I but a tenth of his portion, I would continue in harness without complaint."

With a soft slap Dreaver let the supple black book fall to his desktop and asked, "What has made you imagine in yourself a lack of faith?"

Having already rehearsed in several other conversations the desolating progress of his thought and reading, he summed it up economically, and concluded, "To put it in mathematical terms: it has been bearing in upon me for some time that God is a non-factor—all the equations work without Him. Science still confesses to mysteries, of course—the ultimate origins of matter, how life came to arise, and so on. But how the forms of life have shaped themselves, how men came to descend from apes, how the Bible came to be written, along with similar accretions of folklore—the Hindoo Gita, the Koran—which Christendom does not happen to recognize as sacred: all this became terribly clear to me. The universe is a pointless, self-running machine, and we are insignificant by-products, whom death will tuck back into oblivion, with or without holy fanfare."

Dreaver shrugged—the smallest possible stiffening of his shoulders, under his business suit. "It has appeared that way even at moments to our Lord," he said mildly. "Unfaith is a cohort of faith, as Satan is a cohort of God. It is the shadow that shapes the truth into form, the No that must be said, so that Yea can ring out. I believe your seminary was Princeton, was it not?"

"Yes."

"There could be the trouble. You imbibed conservatism there, and it limits your thinking now. The two Hodges, and Benjamin Warfield—fine men in the old muscular tradition, but quite helpless when the winds of history blow. They cannot *bend*, Mr. Wilmot, and those that cannot bend break. If you had gone to Union, as I did, you would not be afraid to let history into your understanding. Into your understanding of the Bible, into the workings of our lives, into the future of the church. Hugh Black and Charles A. Briggs, whom the old guard rode out of the ministry for his embrace of the Higher Criticism, William Brown and Henry Sloane Coffin, Arthur McGiffert and Henry Jackson Van Dyke—the staunch liberal tradition has nothing to fear from the future; no development can upset it. Remember the Epistle to the Hebrews, how Paul begins?—" 'God, who at sundry times and in divers manners spake in time past.' *Divers manners,* and that includes Darwin and Marx, when the evidence bears out what they say. 'For the law made nothing perfect,' Paul told the Hebrews; they were the conservatives of their time, clinging to every shrivelled scrap of the Torah and the law as if their souls depended on it. 'For the law made nothing perfect, but the bringing in of a better hope did; by the which we draw nigh unto God.' Whatever brings in a better hope, that draws us nigh to God—that's what I gleaned at Union, Mr. Wilmot, where we were taught not to be afraid of science, not to fear admitting that the

Holy Book is embedded in history—that it contains the best wisdom of its time, but that time is not our time. Relativity is the word we must live by now. Everything is relative, and what matters is how *we*, we human creatures, relate to one another. Think of how our two seminaries relate to their surroundings—Union in the middle of the nation's biggest city, and far from the most savory part of Manhattan at that, but drawing vitality and the pulse of reality from it; Princeton sitting down there in fox-hunting country, surrounded by estates and lettuce farms, cut off from the real, urban, industrial world. Its theology took shape in the eighteenth century, when the Deists were the wolves at the door, and hasn't changed since. *Change*, Mr. Wilmot—from the nebulae to the microbes change is the way of Creation, and it must be our way, but for God's sake don't destroy your essential self. Don't give up your calling. I promise you, there is nothing in your beliefs or unbeliefs that can't serve as the basis for an effective and deeply satisfying Christian ministry. You have taken the charge upon you too egoistically: depend upon your parishioners, as well as bidding them depend on you. You are the captain and they are the crew, but the wind in your sails is none of your making."

Mr. Dreaver, one of those fair-lashed men whose eyelids always look pink, spoke all this with a virtually hypnotic smoothness, as if memorized, or at least urged upon troubled pastors several times before. For the sake of the children and Stella, Clarence wanted to believe him. "What about personal immortality?" he asked.

The moderator shrugged, and began to speak confidentially, in a kind of shorthand. Clarence felt the pressure of the next appointment already bearing upon them. "Very little of it in classic Judaism. The New Testament references, ambiguous and various. The Roman Catholic emphasis definitely post-patristic. Purgatory, Limbo, the anatomy of Hell and Paradise—*entirely* invented post–first millennium. Consider this approach: Modern physics proves that nothing is newly created or destroyed, not the merest atom or particle of energy;

in exactly what form our own energy persists nobody knows or pretends to know. Prying into the afterlife, with Spiritualism and the like, breeds goblins and absurdities. State the hope firmly, of endless continuance, and anxiety is eased. Life can go on. *This* life is the one to be lived now, that much is crystal-clear. What did Thoreau supposedly say—'One world at a time'?"

His pink lids opened wider, the intelligent blue eyes under their white lashes asking how much more Clarence demanded of him. Dreaver's eyes' blue was not milky but a steelier echo of the northern seas that, from Orkney to Jutland, had narrowed their seafaring ancestors' gazes with briny winds and a low-angled sun. He spoke with a gliding, quick-tongued New York accent that was consistently light, fluid, easy, even nonchalant, dropping some "g"s, passing over some "r"s. Clarence asked, "The Resurrection?" He felt as a circus trainer must, tossing a ball to a seal who effortlessly, shimmeringly balances it on his nose.

The little shrug again, impatient and alert, with a gaze above Clarence's shoulder as if someone might walk into the room from the outer office. "The Gospels give garbled accounts. The risen Christ was seen here, there, sometimes by crowds. He ate of the honeycomb, showed His wound to doubting Thomas, and wandered off out of history again. Mark's and Luke's accounts of the ascension seem pretty tacked-on; the description at the beginning of Acts' account feels rather theatrical, with the cloud that takes Him out of sight and the two men in white who pop up. Paul testifies to an appearance, to 'one born out of time,' but gives no details, and in the next letter to the Corinthians has developed the formula 'Whether in the body, I cannot tell; or whether out of the body, I cannot tell: God knoweth.' Talk about building a house on sand! What can't be disputed, though, is that the Jesus movement resurrected itself in the months and years after the Crucifixion. Think of the devastation, the humiliation the disciples must have felt—and we all still celebrate the living Christ among us.

Do we not? If there was no Resurrection, something happened just as inspiring and transformative. Here's a crux, actually, where history helps the believer, and puts the burden of explanation on the skeptics." Seeing Clarence about to speak, he lifted a shapely small hand whose palm had a lily's waxen pallor. "And if the Resurrection is only a manner of speaking, a metaphor for the Christian community's revival and growth, why should we scorn words?—words which bring us the only reality the mind grasps." He tapped his glossy, lightly furrowed brow. "Bishop Berkeley, et cetera. Try some William James, if you care. Not just *The Will to Believe* and *Varieties* but the recent books, like *The Meaning of Truth.* Pragmatism—it turns the tables. It's the American contribution to the great debate; you might say it's the healthy Calvinist answer to all those pedantic Lutherans who burnt the ship beneath them and then couldn't walk on water. And actually there are some interesting new developments in German—a man called Husserl, picking up on some old hints of Hegel in *Phänomenologie des Geistes,* and using some of Kant's terminology. I mean, 'the real' isn't quite as self-defining as we intuitively think. Human consciousness is part of it—shapes it. The Resurrection can be thought of as something we have *made* happen, if you follow me, instead of something that happened once and for all, and debatably at that. Welcome to the twentieth century, Mr. Wilmot; we all have some catching up to do. Amazing things are coming out of European physics. Time is the fourth dimension, it turns out, and slows down when the observer speeds up. The other three dimensions don't form a rigid grid; space is more like a net that sags when you put something in it, and that sagging is what we call gravity. Also, light isn't an indivisible, static presence; it has a speed, and it comes in packets—irreducible amounts called quanta. Quanta aren't merely the limit of our measurements; they appear to be the fact. Energy is grainy! All these strainings of our common sense are facts. We don't any more merely investigate reality—Lilliputians crawling over some huge dark Gulliver sleeping there. We *make* it, make it with our minds, our minds and wills. We make God, you could say."

"A personal God?" Clarence asked, mesmerized and feeling betrayed, as Lazarus might have when brought back to life. "The Biblical God?"

"Again, 'existence'? In what sense? 'Personal' is tautological, of course. Why bother to have an impersonal God?—you're back then with Spinoza and calling 'God' everything and therefore nothing. The Unitarians tried that and within three generations they're a spent force. The soul needs something *extra,* a place outside matter where it can stand. The Bible—think of it as the primer of a language whereby we can talk to one another about what matters to us most. It is our starting point, not the end point."

Clarence liked this light-tongued, pink-lidded, preoccupied man, and was considerately conscious of the inroads his troubled case was making upon Dreaver's crowded schedule. He felt like a deficient schoolboy having a privileged hour with a busy tutor. Beyond the brick buildings of Jersey City, with their flat roofs and lettered advertisements for pills and tailors and dance halls, the green patch of cattailed marsh rippled and twinkled in the summer breeze like those vistas of freedom seen from a classroom window, rectangles of a world sublimely free of effortful thought and the problems that exist in books. From beneath the accumulated weight of two months of atheistic dreariness and dread he glimpsed this blithe creation bathing naked in the sun, and felt the eclipse in his heart as some kind of sin which the other man, with his rapid, stabbing equivocations, might lift from him. "You're saying," Clarence said hesitantly, "that within the general indeterminacy—"

"There is room for belief," Thomas Dreaver finished, sinking back in his wooden swivel chair so emphatically that the spring hinge beneath the seat squeaked in surprise.

"Enough space to go through the motions."

"Going through the motions, not at all. Walking toward the light. None of us lives *in* the light; we can only walk toward it, with the eyes and legs God has given us."

How easy it is, Clarence thought, to use the word "God" when the reality has been construed out of existence. The God Who confronted Moses was a terrible burning presence, unspeakable. "But my parishioners expect me to be halfway along the path at least."

"Your parishioners know you are human—don't underestimate them. Mr. Dearholt has supplied me with a sheaf of fond testimonials. You are loved, Mr. Wilmot."

"I don't underestimate them. That's why I wish to quit. To demit," he corrected, smiling. This man made him happy, even as he resisted his counsel. The church was not utterly dead, if bright young men like Dreaver continued to staff it.

"The people see," Dreaver offered, gazing up at the ceiling fan that lackadaisically paddled the torpid air, "the difficulties. They know that out of our common unease and terrors the majestic apparitions of faith are born. What drives them to church, those that come? They need very little from you to complete their quest, but that little they do need, and will forgive you much if you provide it. We have spoken of the Bible as the point of departure; think of yourself—your standing there in vestments, the visible pillar of the institution—as the point of arrival. You have pledged yourself to walk with them toward the light."

"But I can't—"

"Never say can't, Mr. Wilmot. The movements of our innermost selves are various, and unpredictable. They need but a tendency to be suddenly fulfilled, when we least expect it. To yourself you seem unworthy. To me you seem an eminently well-qualified pastor—dignified, conscientious, and admirably earnest that the things of faith not be taken lightly."

"Lightly! Mr. Dreaver, you are putting a positive aspect on what in truth is quite negative. The things of faith for me have totally evaporated."

Now the young man did look tired; the reputed graininess of energy had gone to his voice, which had hoarsened. His intent blue eyes seemed to itch, behind a chronic flutter of his pink lids and pale lashes. Clarence inconsiderately had dumped the full load of his own incapacity upon this upholder of that by which they both lived. Yet the moderator offered a smile, and a dismissive flicker of his hands above the papers that awaited his attention. "What evaporates can recondense," Dreaver said. He picked up the black-bound Book of Discipline but did not open it, since both remembered what he had read. "I cannot permit your demission on the evidence you present, of alterations in your understanding of doctrine. Doctrine is the living, changing expression of a living God, and is properly the subject of ongoing, at times radical, reconsideration. You heard it: at least a year's probation. The General Assembly of 1889 made this rule in response to a situation in the Presbytery of Butler. In 1901 the Presbytery of Chicago and in 1906 that of Puget Sound, with similar cases in their venue, placed on record overtures assenting to the wisdom of the probationary period. In that period of a year this Presbytery of Jersey City asks that you carry on your duties as before, with good faith and a genuine will, and that you submit to searching introspection the motives and reasons that would lead you to consider relinquishment of those duties."

Clarence said, touching his black chest with all his spread fingertips in a gesture of disclaimer and, almost, martyrdom: "I did not *wish* to lose my faith; the reasons came upon me, irresistibly, from outside. They came from above."

"Much of what we blame on the above comes from within," Dreaver said, still soft-voiced but growing impatient. "Quench not the spirit, Mr. Wilmot. The elect are not spared passing through the valley of the shadow of death. The possibility of rebirth lies within you, if you but nurture it. Though both science and our own divines have sought to reason it away, I firmly believe in free will. We make our salvations, as well as our earthly fortunes. However, as moderator I truly have no choice in my disposition of your request. Is the necessity of at least one more year in the clergy so repugnant to you?"

"No—it is pleasant. I know the tasks; they are the only tasks I do know. My poor distressed family will be very pleased. I myself am relieved. But it seems to me you are directing me to behave with blatant hypocrisy."

Dreaver became ever more official; his pallid eyes flashed. "I am asking you to carry for twelve more mere months responsibilities you solemnly vowed to undertake for a lifetime. Please, Mr. Wilmot—renounce your intellectual pride and give God's grace a chance to do its work. This is not hypocrisy, but the meekness that every man in his work offers up to the order of things, whether divinely ordained or not." Dreaver lowered his pained pale gaze, cleared his throat, and set the Book of Discipline aside. The stacked papers on his desktop were all smartly typed, as in the most modern offices. He concluded, "The presbytery will be apprised of this conversation, and all its members shall pray that at the end of the year you will no longer wish to seek demission."

Clarence boarded the train back to Newark with a light head beneath his straw boater. He had no choice; he had been commanded to take the easiest course left him. Swinging his arms, grasping lightly in alternating hands the curved brass handles fitted into the corners of the plush seats as he moved down the swaying aisle in search of a seat, he shed upon his fellow passengers the blessing that his reversed collar proclaimed had descended upon the world. Outside the grated, open windows, the Meadows and the two rivers and the trusses of their iron bridges skimmed past; gulls and ducks shared the waters and islands of the marsh, and red-winged blackbirds flickered from reed to bending reed. Miniature suns bobbled in the water beneath their wings. Then city buildings and dirty backyards crowded around the elevated tracks; weathered white letters on a brick wall welcomed the passengers to NEWARK—HOME OF BALLANTINE ALE. In his light-headed, celebratory mood, he impulsively disembarked at the Erie Railroad station and, walking a few blocks, found a saloon where in spite of his collar he enjoyed a cold draft ale and a hot sausage and sauerkraut on a roll. He strolled back to catch the 2:26 for Paterson, already basking in Stella's relief and the children's joy that for at least another year they were assured of the shelter of the parsonage and the respectability his position extended to them all.

Three years later, during the spring and much of the summer of 1913, a strike of the silk-workers paralyzed and galvanized Paterson, pitting twenty-five thousand workers against three hundred silk manufacturers. Local 152 of the Industrial Workers of the World was the organizer. The strike had begun at the end of February and instantly widened when the police chief arrested three out-of-town IWW agitators at Turn Hall, on Ellison Street. Fifteen hundred assembled strikers had gone wild at seeing Elizabeth Gurley Flynn in the clutches of the law; a steady hail of clubbing from mounted police did not disperse the mob that accompanied her to the station.

In March, the police installed cots at their headquarters and hired a cook and barber to accommodate the platoons of new around-the-clock officers, and the strikers, feeling the pinch and anticipating worse, established a General Relief Committee. The Purity Cooperative Company, a bakery founded eight years before by immigrant Jews, distributed thirty thousand loaves of bread free for each week of the strike. The Order of the Sons of Italy voted to levy its members enough to provide a thousand dollars a week. Picket lines were established to harass and shame scabs seeking to enter the shut-down mills. Big Bill Haywood, head of the IWW, came and went; Flynn was almost constantly in Paterson, throwing her voice over crowds of thousands, emboldening the women who emerged as leading spirits of the strike. Hannah Silverman, seventeen years of age, became the captain of the pickets at the Westerhoff mill on Van Houten Street. Twenty-three-year-old Mary Gasperano slapped a woman strikebreaker in the face and was arrested for the fifth time. A fourth of the more than two thousand persons arrested were women, women and girls like those of the Bamford ribbon mill, who ate lunch on the outdoor factory steps rain or shine, were locked out and docked a day's pay if a minute late, were fined for such offenses as laughing and opening a window, and half of whose pay was withheld to the end of the year by Joseph Bamford; if they left within that year, he kept it. Hoping to appeal to the workers' patriotism, the manufacturers declared a Flag Day, flying American flags on their mills to welcome back employees. The employees did not return. The IWW distributed lapel cards reading *We wove the flag. We dyed the flag. We won't scab under the flag.* Elizabeth Gurley Flynn told a crowd at Turn Hall that the IWW had brought all nationalities of this city together and represented the ideal spirit of America. As she tried to explain a red flag, a dyers' helper leaped to his feet and held up his hand, dyed indelibly red by years of work, and cried that here was the red flag. The thousands in the hall cheered.

The local police, who had neighbors and friends among the strikers, were relatively gentle, and broke bones but never took a striker's life. In April, however, one of the hated special detectives hired from the O'Brien Detective Agency of Newark by the Weidmann Silk Dyeing Company, while putting a group of strikebreakers on a trolley car outside the mill in the Riverside section, fired shots to intimidate an angry crowd of dyers' helpers and killed an employed file-worker, Valentino Modestino, as he stood on the stoop of his own house. The detective was never indicted. The manufacturers owned the police, and the courts. Thousands marched to the Laurel Grove Cemetery and dropped red carnations on Modestino's grave. Red ribbons were worn by the workers, red flags were waved.

Five weeks after the abortive Flag Day, the American Federation of Labor, a relatively conservative trade union that had already enlisted the well-paid, anti-strike loom-fixers, twisters, and warpers, sent John Golden to seduce the strikers away from the socialist IWW, but his scheduled meeting at the Fifth Regiment Armory was swamped by heckling Wobblies waving their red handkerchiefs and their little red books of membership. The strikers' days were filled with meetings—every weekday morning the ribbon weavers met at Helvetia Hall and the dyers' helpers and broad-silk weavers at Turn Hall, being addressed by the out-of-town "jawsmiths"—and speaking themselves, at first shyly, then vociferously, in Italian, German, Polish, English, Dutch, Yiddish, even Arabic. Afternoons, there were shop meetings of smaller groups at Probst Hall, the Union Athletic Club, Degalman's Hall, the Workingmen's Institute. Sunday afternoons, there were giant gatherings across the river in the streetcar suburb of Haledon, which had a socialist mayor and one policeman, who weighed ninety pounds. Spring burgeoned as the strike aged. There were brass bands, mass singing, romance. Flynn, who was blue-eyed and dark-haired and twenty-two and separated from her husband, conducted an affair with the Italian-born anarchist Carlo Tresca, with whom she had fallen in love during the 1912 woolworkers' strike in Lawrence, Massachusetts. On one occasion a meeting in Helvetia Hall was interrupted by the complaint, "Mr. Chairman, there is love going on here," and a vote was taken to expel a young couple who had been kissing.

In May, the tide turned against the strikers. Patrick Quinlan, the first of the out-of-town leaders to be tried for advocating violence, was convicted. The police and Mayor McBride closed Turn and Helvetia Halls, on the grounds that the speakers there had abused the right of free speech. In retrospect, this loss of a rallying place was a crippling blow. Each striker faced alone his hunger, his unpaid rent, the mounting bills. The manufacturers held adamant; the bigger of them had begun decades ago to build annex mills in eastern Pennsylvania, where the wives and children of coal miners would work for lower wages than skilled workers had become accustomed to in the proud old industrial town of Paterson. With these Pennsylvania annexes the manufacturers were able to fill some of their orders.

Men like Lambert and Doherty and Bamford were old-fashioned nineteenth-century entrepreneurs driven by cutthroat competition to squeeze and drive their workers ruthlessly. The same pressures bore upon the smaller, newer silk manufacturers, Jewish in the main, some of whom might have settled, if the union could have trusted them to keep their agreements. The strikers' goals were an eight-hour day and a twelve-dollar minimum weekly wage. The respectable classes of Paterson were solidly with the manufacturers against the spectre of revolution. Of the clergy, only the Reverend Joshua Gallaway, pastor of the Third Presbyterian Church on the corner of Prince and Grand Streets, spoke up for the strikers, saying to an audience in Turn Hall that "without strikes the oppression of the workers of the world will never cease." The more common ecclesiastical view was that expressed by the Reverend W. C. Snodgrass, who preached that "the worker's side was generally fairly conducted by the owners of industry." No view was publicly expressed by Clarence Wilmot, who was treading the seething streets of Paterson as a salesman offering door to door a leather-bound set of facts and pictures called *The Popular Encyclopedia,* for three dollars fifteen cents a volume, paid monthly until all twenty-four volumes had been acquired, forming a priceless home library and a ladder of information up which any literate person, regardless of how early circumstances had compelled him to quit formal schooling, could climb toward improvement and higher status. Upon completion of payment, a handsome walnut-stained two-shelf case for housing *The Popular Encyclopedia* was delivered, gratis, to the home.

This job—hardly a job, since it earned no salary, just a thirty-percent commission, paid on receipt of funds, a dollar at a time, rather than upon the signing of a subscription—was being advertised in the *Evening Standard* when, as an early casualty of the diminished downtown business caused by the strike, Clarence had been released from the sales staff of Goldman's Fine Clothiers for Gentlemen and Ladies, on Main Street. Prior to his position there, he had served out his year of probation in the Presbyterian clergy. On more than one occasion, finding himself waking Sunday morning without a voice, he had enlisted Stella as his substitute. Her sermons, drawing as much upon her Missouri girlhood as upon the Bible, were increasingly admired and enjoyed by the initially skeptical congregation. At the year's end, Clarence had felt no renewal of his vocation. On the contrary, his sense of the emptiness and foolishness at the base of the universe floated like a veil before his eyes, numbed his tongue in social discourse, and proved so debilitating that he gasped for breath whenever the weather changed or day shaded into night. Evenings, after dinner, he almost always needed to lie down. He travelled again to Jersey City and, with the wry triumph of the negatively confirmed, described his condition to Thomas Dreaver, whose distress and surprise were disappointingly modest. Very well, then: the procedures of demission would be completed. The moderator had moved on in his mind, he had written Clarence off; like any good businessman, he must pocket his losses and look to the future.

Clarence sought to emulate him. The Wilmots had some small savings, the financial remnant of his fifth of the gravel-pit fortune when his older brother, Peter, decided to liquidate their gritty inheritance, and with these plus a loan secured on favorable terms from a banker friendly to Mr. Dearholt, they had bought a small wooden house out on East Twenty-seventh Street, with only a margin of yard but with Eastside Park eight blocks away, for the children to get their fresh air and exercise in. Teddy was their main concern; he was now ten, a heavy, quiet, apprehensive child with lackluster brown hair and eyes, who had taken on a paper route to help the family finances. Jared at nineteen was nearly through with his freshman year at Rutgers; he had seen that Princeton was beyond his family's present reach, gone down to New Brunswick to apply and see about a scholarship, saved up his summer money from driving one of the Nagle Brothers ice wagons, gone out for the football team, and was down there now waiting on tables and playing second base on the freshman nine. One of his teammates' father was a trader on the Wall Street stock market and had promised Jared a job as a trading-slip runner next summer. Once the days of his infancy were over, Jared had always seemed to Clarence another man in the house, with an uncomfortable resemblance—the same bushy fox-red eyebrows, the same decisive slash of a mouth, though not framed by a trimmed iron beard—to his own father. With his cocky, good-humored realism Jared had early grasped that his father, even before the collapse of his vocation, was not a person to lean on. The boy had caught, by some wireless telegraphy, the rhythm of the America to come, the nation constantly reinventing itself in cheerful ignorance of all the discouraging books in his father's airless study. He was merry and distant and implacable, the ragtime tunes of the future jangling within him. When he deigned to come home, full of collegiate wisdom and new slang, he was treated by Stella and Esther as a source of authority, though the young man contributed nothing to the household and everything to his own advancement.

Esther, who had grown into a tall, slender, and pale echo of her father, with her mother's rich head of chestnut hair transmuted to a less luxurious strawberry blond, was a month from high-school graduation, and not so caught up in the whirl of commencement and its semi-sacred ceremonies—darkened and complicated this spring by the strike and its plurality of deprivations as they reverberated into the lives of the young—as to have failed to seek employment. She had switched, two years ago, to the secretarial course, and hoped to find employment typing for one of the city's law or merchandising firms. Had her father kept to his own employment, resources might have been found to send her to the Normal School on Nineteenth Avenue, for she had the scholastic aptitude and the steady, erect benevolence of a born teacher. But she was a girl, whose best destiny was marriage, and the route whereby she reached it was among the lesser of the many uncertainties that Clarence faced.

He had not fully grasped how far his resignation from the church would drop him in the social scale; he had somehow imagined proceeding by inertia along the same paths of respectability, only without the encumbrance of hypocritical pretense. Robert Ingersoll had written stirringly of freeing the clergy; well, now he was free—free to sink. He had vaguely thought that, with his languages and love of print's silent song, he might find an appropriate niche as an instructor, in a genteel, private boys' school. It was what he should have become in the first place, had not his father's rock-hard faith insisted that his son go seek an otherworldly profit. As Clarence imagined his new future, he would be, liberated from the dead black shroud of the Geneva gown but otherwise ministerial, deferred to by a lively pack of secular choir boys as he evangelized for the Latin classics or the English poets, or individualized the vague parade of the grim-lipped American presidents as they evolved from Washington to Wilson. But his locally notorious apostasy, he soon realized, put a shudder into headmasters and boards of trustees. It was not so much, they or their representatives assured him, his beliefs or lack of them—this was a free country, after all. There would be no difficulty had he never made a public profession or accepted a call to preach and serve; but since he had, and had demitted, a whiff of betrayal clung to him. He had deserted his post. The world can accommodate many sincere opinions but has no lasting use for turncoats. Having made such a point of renunciation, with a pious wife at his side and a disheartened congregation spread before him, why would he, in his fury of faithlessness, not seek to propagandize credulous children? The climate of the times was against him. The immigrant hordes had brought to America German radicalism and Italian anarchism and Semitic materialism; this was no time for native-born Protestants to grow lax and abandon the sublime values and articles of faith that had induced God to shower down upon them the blessings due a chosen people. It was Harlan Dearholt who with genial frankness explained the nuances of feeling behind the sometimes curt rejections that set the limits to Clarence's professional prospects. He alone of Clarence's former parishioners continued to engage him in intercourse; besides helping him arrange the home loan, he headed Clarence, in the more prosperous atmosphere of 1911, to Goldman's Clothiers, where the former parson's natural courtesy and dignity of bearing enhanced the store but did not lift his wages as high as the twelve weekly dollars the strikers would demand. Dollars had once gathered like autumn leaves on the wooden collection plates; dollars were the flourishing sign of God's specifically American favor, made manifest in the uncountable millions of Carnegie and Mellon and Henry Ford and Catholina Lambert. But amid this fabled plenty the whiff of damnation had cleared of dollars and cents the parched ground around Clarence Wilmot.

Setting out in late winter, when the soot-speckled triangles of old snow were easily mistaken for the bedraggled pieces of newspaper and strike propaganda that blew everywhere, he had first essayed the more fashionable blocks on the East Side, and had met there mostly doors quickly shut by frightened-looking maids, on orders he could hear shouted within rooms curtained from view. In some houses where affluent boredom welcomed a visitor, he met a disposition to make of him the morning's entertainment. The encyclopedia company, which was located not in one of the capitals of the East but in forward-looking St. Louis, supplied to its apostles, along with a smart briefcase holding order forms and sample pages, a glossy handbook that listed for memorization the merits of its product—the more than thirty million words, the twenty-five thousand separate alphabetical entries from Aachen to Zwickau, the close to ten thousand illustrative steel engravings, diagrams, and maps, the over a thousand individual contributors, eighty-five percent of them American citizens, in sharp contrast with an unnamed competitor, whose contributors and emphasis were preponderantly British. The enterprise even had a brute industrial dimension, measured in the hundreds of compositors needed to set the text, the tons of metal involved in the type, the miles and miles of thread to sew the sheets together, the tons of ink and glue—twice as many tons, it turned out, of glue as of ink. Heads of learned societies, members of the United States Congress, learned professors eminent the world over—even these were not spared quantification. Some prospective customers listened respectfully to his tumble of information; some cut him short; most didn't let him in the door. He thought he would grow inured to rejection and scorn, as in his former profession he had grown inured to tales of misery and discontent from his parishioners, but something unhealing and unduly proud in him continually winced at the angrily shut door, the sardonic dismissal. More than one smug householder from the eastern parts of Paterson walked him to the study and unkindly showed him the haughty leather spines—so impeccably ordered on their tall shelf as to suggest that the treasury of knowledge was merely worshipped, never consulted—of the eleventh edition of *The Encyclopædia Britannica.* Then it was his to protest, in a gambit foreseen by his salesman's handbook, "Oh, but the *Popular* is edited entirely by Americans, and is much superior on American subjects. It has an American slant throughout, as well as being written in a more accessible language, and over a dollar a volume less expensive. If you have any young persons in the household—"

"The young persons are grown and flown. There's only me and my missus, and when we want accessible language we'll go down to the Question Mark Bar and hear it spoken by the disgruntled workingmen and their anarchist friends." He laughed, this bespectacled, sallow retired accountant or clerk, his life spent in inky cuffs and green eyeshade in some secluded upper cell of a mill whose battalions of machinery throbbed and shrieked below him. "I don't envy you your task," the man genially conceded, showing Clarence the door without the offer of coffee and cake which his initial hospitality had suggested might be coming, "trying to sell books of knowledge in a city where ignorance is up on a high horse, and two in three can't even speak the king's English let alone read it. I don't know what the country's coming to, Mr—?"

"Wilmot."

"Wilmot. Somehow that name rings a bell. Your face was familiar, too, when I came to the door. I don't as a rule entertain drummers, understand. Ada, that's my missus, is terrified of letting a stranger in, the way burglaries are rising these days, with the strikers feeling the pinch—and they'll feel it worse, mind you me, when the industry gives the reds a shaking out!"

"You can never be too careful, sir. I appreciate your allowing me admittance. Permit me to give you my card, in case you think of anyone who might be interested in subscribing to a down-to-earth encyclopedia, written and edited to patriotic native tastes and yet containing all the world's essential knowledge."

"Wilmot," the man repeated.

"My father was a farmer, like his father before him, in the middle of the state, around Hopewell. His people before the Civil War had been New Yorkers, old-fashioned merchants."

"You've come a good way from them," said the little withered accountant, more registering a deficit than seeking to be unpleasant. Clarence was out the door gratefully, into a raw spring day, under chill rolls of cloud spitting shreds of snow that might be flecks of chimney ash.

Contrary to what he had expected, it was in the working-class districts, neighborhoods close to the river and the Erie Railroad tracks, amid the little clapboard houses with sagging stoops and drawn shades, that he achieved now and then a sale. "My English, not good. Never can read. But my children, maybe. Already they speak good."

"Whatever they want to know, they'll find in here," Clarence said, tapping his tinted photograph of the complete set.

"For the twentieth century, these books are what the Bible was for"—he rejected "bygone times" as perhaps too idiomatic—"times long ago."

"I know nothing," said his possible customer, a wiry Polish Jew with expressive gnarled hands, "just knitting. In old country, since boy"—a hand held at belt level—"know to knit. Father told me, Come to silk mill. He knew knitting, I learned knitting. I come here. Now knitting business bad. Too many mills, making same silk. My boy—no. Go to school, learn from books. I tell him. In America, people learn from books. Not like old country, everybody held in place"—a yellow, veiny fist, held rigidly in mid-air, and the other hand laid on top of it, captive and captor—"never change. Here, change." He removed the left hand, the fist floated upward, its fingers relaxing. "Each man make new self."

Clarence was too eager; a tremor shook the promotional papers he fanned before the man. "*Popular,*" he said. "The word comes from *populus,* the word for 'people.' For just three dollars and fifteen cents each month, you receive one volume, and at the end of two years have the complete set, in a handsome box that is *free.* Your children can look up everything they need for their schoolwork. They will get high marks." He restrained himself from shouting; he was straining his throat.

The man's stained, muscular hands, warped to be the guiding parts of a machine, limply waved away the prospectus, the contract. "Not good time now, mister. Strike. No money anywhere, no money for food. Come back when strike won. Then, lots of money. You a good man. I like your ideas. America the best country."

In another modest house, entered through a tiny screened porch not six feet back from the pavement—a patch of front yard at this time of year brightened by a few crocuses and early dandelions—a tiny well-spoken woman in a buttoned housedress asked him, "Isn't it anti-Catholic? We wouldn't want to have that in the house."

"Madame, not at all. The editors have taken pains to make

the articles on religion uniformly respectful and studiously neutral. No child's faith, of whatever denomination, would be disturbed by studying these pages. Facts—*The Popular Encyclopedia* contains nothing but facts, the facts of the world, clearly and straightforwardly presented." Saying this, he seemed to be sunk deep in a well of facts, all of which spelled the walled-in dismal hopelessness of human life. The world's books were boxes of flesh-eating worms, crawling sentences that had eaten the universe hollow.

A few blocks away, and sounding closer, a booing rose to a roaring sound; the police were trying to break up a picket line, or perhaps some poor scab, shaming himself to keep his family in bread, had dared a gesture of defiance at the mob of his former co-workers. It was the mindless bloodthirsty roar of a crowd at a football game, a boxing match, a coliseum where Christians were being tortured and dismembered; it seemed at its distance to rise and keep rising, a wave of terrible mass, with all the weight of the human ocean driving it to tower and topple.

"But does it tell how His Holy Father is infallible? Does it give due reverence to the saints, or pass them off as less than forever blessed? Does it make out Luther and those others to be heretics?"

"It gives balanced accounts, I am certain, of all the religious controversies that have existed since Arius argued with Athanasius. Remember, madame, that the orthodox Christian creeds were hammered out point by point, and on every point both sides of the debate should be presented."

"Ah, only if it comes out right," said this small defender of the faith, with her curiously precise diction, as if each word were consciously held back from contamination. "On the right side. If a book isn't Catholic, it's anti-Catholic. Father McNulty gave us a homily once, on how the encyclopedia attacked the Jesuits. He forbade us to read it, or anything like it. Jesus said, and it's right in Scripture, that he that isn't with the church is against her."

"That was not *The Popular Encyclopedia* the good father preached against," Clarence assured her. "Most likely it was the *Britannica,* which is composed mostly by British scholars, with no understanding of American subjects and attitudes." But he had lost all faith in this sale; this doughty would-be nun was using him merely as a whetstone to sharpen her prejudices on. His mind was blocks distant as he listened to the hullabaloo whose roar rose and then fell, shattered into a multitude of shrieks and shrill whistles, as the frightened police perhaps began to lay about with their black billyclubs, and the fragile pale girls from the ribbon mills melted and writhed beneath the blows, and the twin tides of desperation swept one against the other.

At times, as he solicited wooden tenements packed in rows near the mills, on Van Houten and McBride and River Streets, on Ryle Road and Broadway, the roar of falling water would penetrate his mind as a constant tumult underlying those of riot and catcall, rally and parade. Since the young Alexander Hamilton had thrilled to the sight of the Totowa Falls and saw in this heedless power the center of American industry, the Falls had plunged and thrashed and thrown up mists, and, though the unharnessed flow had been diminished by the three millraces, the Falls remained an essentially wild thing at Paterson's heart, a distillation of all that is furious and accidental and overwhelming in nature, a gem of pure ruinous uncaring around which the aching generations came and went. The Falls had been here when only the Leni-Lenapes had stood rapt before such careless grandeur, and would be here when Paterson had sunk back into a crooked valley of brick rubble and rusted iron.

One gray forenoon early in April, when the blank sky wore a blinding glare without being blue, Clarence knocked at a narrow house in need of paint along Fulton Street. Clarence was startled by a familiar, delicate face at the door.

"Mavis! Is this where you live?"

"Myself and some others, Reverend Wilmot. Come in, please do. What a start you gave me, there's no telling what a knock on the door will bring these days. Is it Mrs. Wilmot that has sent you?"

He was tempted to back down the two wooden steps that had brought him to this door; the girl had left their service while they were still in the manse, that last, provisional year, during which he was courting his disgrace but had not yet been married to it. Mavie's figure had filled in since then, and her green-eyed gaze no longer quite so shyly flitted away from his face. She was wearing an apron around a thickened waist, but her hands still had red-tipped little fingers and a childlike look of not yet being shaped by the things she touched. Her hair was bundled more loosely, with more of a wiry wildness, than he remembered. "No, not Stella, though she is well, and misses you, I have heard her say more than once. I am knocking on doors, Mavis, one after another, on a commercial quest, and won't trouble you with it. It has made my day less dreary, to have seen you for this moment. You look well. You were a girl when we had to let you go, and now you are a woman."

"What sort of commercial quest would it be, Reverend Wilmot?"

"No longer reverend, my dear Mavie, and that explains the quest. Lacking a care of souls, I am going from door to door trying to sell subscriptions to twenty-four volumes of more fact than fancy called *The Popular Encyclopedia.* I dare say you would have no use for it."

"Well, now, we can't be altogether sure without hearing about it. Please—you must come in and let me give you a cup of tea at least. Many the cup I enjoyed in your own kitchen."

"And many the cup you made and served, for rather little recompense."

"You paid what others did, and always treated me kind. Mrs. Wilmot had a warm heart, and you were every inch the gentleman. Not every master is, I found out soon enough. I was sorry to leave your service, though you could say it's turned out for the best."

The parlor of the little house was tidy, and the furniture

commonplace but not shabby, with an upholstered velour sofa the most elegant piece, decorated with antimacassars and two black pillows holding each a large rose in needlepoint. There were yellowed lace curtains at the windows, and a pair of the kind of florally decorated Austrian-porcelain vases one could buy for five dollars at Greene Brothers.

"Is this the home of your parents, Mavis?"

"Ah, no, they never had more than rooms, even when there were six of us. This is Mr. Czajkowski's house, him and his mother and sister and now myself."

"You?"

A blush tinged her thin-skinned Irish pallor, that pallor which extended even to the dulcet feminine forms of her lips. "We love one another, sir."

"Without marriage?"

"I know, it grates on my family something fierce, but he says why let the priests run our lives, hand in hand with the rich as they are? With the world in chains, what's free but love? I've come a long way in these few years, but I remember the talk around your table as getting me to thinking. Did you truly say you were no longer a reverend?"

"Yes, I gave it up, Mavis. Or you could say it gave me up."

"How could that be? The fine big house, and you looking and acting the part like a man born to it."

"Ah, acting the part, exactly. It often happens that men cannot hold on to what they were born to. I no longer measured up to even my own standards of good faith. These are hard days, for the old beliefs. I am glad that you and Mr.—"

"Czajkowski. It's a name that made me stumble as well, at first—you can see why I'm in no hurry to make it mine. But I'm forgetting the tea."

"Never mind the tea, please. Sit and tell me about yourself. Where are the others in the house?"

"Eva is out on the picket line over at the Dale mill; Joe's mother is upstairs. She's not well in the chest and needs tending; people say it's the lint, all those years."

"And . . . Joe? He is out on strike too?" Though conspicuously fuller in the body, Mavis was thinner in the face. This month of April had seen a new look slip into Paterson—the shifty-eyed, dry-mouthed look of people who had been too long on one meal a day, and that one meal provided by the fickle charity of Wobbly sympathizers in New York.

"Oh, no," Mavis said, with a quick lilt of pride. "He's a foundryman for Danforth and Cooke, earning all of eighteen a week, and the shop solid union. Orders are backed up a year; people can do without silk, but they'll never do without locomotives."

"It would seem not. I'm happy for you, Mavis, and I know that Mrs. Wilmot will be too. She always said you were the brightest of our girls." Clarence wondered, once it was out of his mouth, if this compliment wasn't condescending. He was tired, he realized, now that he found a momentary space in which to rest, and he regretted declining the tea.

"A lot of girls, I can tell you, don't show their brightness; it doesn't sit well with the men, or with their betters of either sex. But one good thing about the strike, it's let it out what women can do. This Mrs. Flynn fears neither man nor beast, and outtalks Haywood and Quinlan and Tresca right up there in front of thousands. When the men talk, we listen; but when it's Mrs. Flynn on the platform, oh," Mavis told him, framing a kind of quick window in the air between them with her childlike hands, and leaning toward where he sat heavily in the center of the new velour sofa, "it's like hearing your own heart speaking."

Clarence felt a pang of jealous discomfort, at this enraptured evocation of ideal preaching. When younger, he had been vain of his preaching, and of the judicious flair of exaggeration he would don with his vestments. A stately power of eloquence seemed to enter him from behind, and he became both actor and audience.

Mavis appeared unable to make herself sit down in the presence of her old employer. As if reading his mind, she set about making them tea, which took her but a few steps away, into a kitchen adjacent to the parlor. They did not need to suspend their conversation.

"Indeed, your own heart speaking?" he prompted.

"I know it sounds grand, but when she calls up the world that might be, instead of the one that is, you can hardly keep from crying at the beauty of it. Women equal, and not slaves kept in the kitchen, and children not having to go into the mills at the age of eight or nine, and there being no workers and owners, because the workers are the owners, and everything an equal partnership . . ." She trailed off, her utopian vision eclipsed by the rituals of the teapot—the warming of the pot with simmered water poured from the battered kettle lifted from the new-fangled porcelain-sided gas stove that Mr. Czajkowski had earned with his forging of locomotives, the quick swishing and pouring out, the careful measurement of the tablespoons of the shreds of Pekoe tea, and the repouring of the hot water preparatory to the steeping. Whole nations in Asia and Africa, Clarence recalled missionary reports stating, were economically consecrated to the white man's coffee and tea, to the great detriment of the native agriculture and diet.

"And yet," he said, playing a gentle devil's advocate to keep up the flow of delightful liveliness from his hostess, "Mrs. Flynn herself, as a wife and mother, appears to have deserted both Mr. Flynn and their infant, for the romantic charms of Signor Tresca."

Rosiness did reappear on Mavis's cheeks, and reddened her throat with quickened spirit. "You know what she says, when people charge her with free love? 'Better that than slave love.' If she wins for women a bit more of self-respect, and daily wages closer to what men receive, then she has been mother to a million happy babies."

He wondered if he dared allude to the baby perceptibly lodged behind her apron, and instead sighed in impotent irony. "My dear, it gladdens me to see you so inspired, so resolute. I am too old, and too Presbyterian in my mental habits, to take much hope from any of this world's prophecies. The strike is failing, you know—the big mills are meeting orders out of their annexes in Allentown and Easton, and the little mills are tied to the bigger. There are too many competing plants—none can afford to concede an eight-hour day."

This bleak opinion was echoed from the pages of the Paterson *Evening News,* which until April had been, if not downright pro-strike, the main purveyor of the strikers' announcements. Mavis responded by silently serving the tea, setting the tray on the low oval table before the sofa. She brought a hard chair set against the parlor wall and seated herself on it to pour. Her freckled forearms were nicely rounded; her touch on the teapot was sweetly practiced. Settling back, her face on a level with his, she bestowed upon him a confidential smile, a broad sad stretching of her lips that granted the world's capacity to baffle us. "And how does Mrs. Wilmot feel about your being no longer among the clergy?"

Was this subtle revenge for his predicting the failure of the strike? "She doesn't like it," he confessed. "How could she? Her goals in life were all achieved; she had no doubts about anything. She cannot imagine why I would indulge such an unfortunate change of heart. She is very conscious of how fallen in status the children are, and how desperate our finances have become. And these things of course are a great weariness to me as well. A *great* weariness, of which sometimes I think I must simply curl up and die. You do not have to be a factory worker, Mavis, to learn how utterly the world can cast you out, once your usefulness is over."

"Tell me about your books," she said, sitting a touch more upright, with a lovely and prim elongation of her white neck, and a two-handed gesture of subduing her wiry, cedar-colored hair.

"Books? My books destroyed me. Books are the bane of mankind, I tell myself at least once a day."

"The books you sell, door to door."

"Oh, those. Quite worthless, really. A less expensive American imitation of a British encyclopedia—an arrangement, in alphabetical order, of articles on everything. An encyclopedia, you might say, is a blasphemy—a commercially inspired attempt to play God, by creating in print a replica of Creation."

"I have heard the word 'encyclopedia.' "

"Of course you have, Mavis. It's in the air now, along with radiotelegraphy and flying machines. Encyclopedias began, more or less, with a Frenchman called Diderot, who set out to demonstrate that materialism was a complete system, accounting for everything under the sun. He was wrong in some details, of course, but basically he succeeded. You don't want these books, Mavis."

"And how much do they cost?"

"Three dollars fifteen cents a month until the full set of twenty-four is obtained in two years' time," he told her automatically. "There are twenty-five thousand separate alphabetical entries, nearly ten thousand steel engravings. Everything you or your children want to look up, it's in there, if not as a separate article, listed in the index. You don't want it, I swear to you—it's the last thing you want. All the information there can be, and it breaks your heart at the end, because it leaves you as alone and bewildered as you were not knowing anything."

"Sir, does it have a name?"

Clarence laughed. "*The Popular Encyclopedia,* but it hasn't been very popular in Paterson, not on any street I've walked, and I've walked most of them. It's written for the common man, they say—as if the common man cares for anything but his bucket of suds and his five-cent cigar. I've sold so few we've had to send Teddy some days down to the workers' relief tent, so he'd get a square meal and not stunt his growth. Oh, how the mighty—but I was never mighty, is the odd thing. God doesn't need a big target, He can hit an hour-old infant square on the nose. But, then, excuse me, I shouldn't be blaspheming. I shouldn't still be using that terrible old word 'God.' "

Finding himself close to tears, he wondered, as he often had in the pulpit, how much of a shameless actor he was. The very material was so theatrical—the rending of garments, the ashes on the head, the kiss of betrayal in the garden, the crying out on the Cross.

"We could afford the three dollars. In addition to what Joe brings home, I still hire out, when Eva is here to look after Matka, and can until—" She blushed once more, in confession of her warm blood.

"The baby comes," he finished for her.

"I want those books for him. Or her."

"Mavis, you don't."

"Don't tell me what I don't, Mr. Wilmot. I'm in my house here." Embarrassed at this spark of temper, the girl looked away, at the corner of the sofa where the needlepointed rose bloomed. "Could you leave me some of your materials, to discuss with Joe? Tell me honestly, though—would these books be a fair start? I know we must look ignorant and common to you."

His face felt enormous, vaporous, as his sales pitch was dragged from him. "Yes, a fair start. The people in St. Louis who put it together are honest workmen. There is more in these books than either of us can ever know. As of the year of our Lord 1913, the facts are here."

"Well, then."

"But can you afford— You mustn't subscribe because—"

You pity me. He couldn't say it, but she heard it. Mavis's pale lips compressed as she bowed her head—her loosely bundled hair haloed by filaments of pure light—to the china pot, and asked, "More tea? If you fight off all your customers like you do me, I don't wonder, Mr. Wilmot, there aren't many of them. Be sure to leave any forms that Joe and I should sign."

Within a week, the forms came through, and his dollar-a-month commission, but after this particular sale Clarence's discouragement deepened, and the trouble in his breathing apparatus bit deeper into his vitality. His body as he dragged it up and down the paved slopes of Paterson grew heavier, though in fact he was losing weight. The rarity of sales drove him, by trolley car and hired buggy, to the neighboring towns of Clifton and Totowa and Hawthorne, but with no better luck than on the East Side streets of Paterson; those with money stocked their own libraries and distrusted goods that had to come importuning at the door. The very name *Popular* had been made suspect, to the ears of the middle class, by the socialist rhetoric of the strike. More than once, when the householder or his delegate came to the door Clarence's voice froze in his throat, and, after a few stammered words that courted rejection, he turned away. As the summer lengthened, the defeat of the strike settled over the city like the stultifying heat, muting the excited sounds of booing and shouting, of rally and massed song, of police whistles shrilling and the hooves of mounted police cantering through the tight streets threaded among the mills. Only the roar of the Falls persisted. By August, in a ragged series of surrenders, the mills went back to work, the dyers' helpers caving in as their families' hunger mounted, the broad-silk weavers accepting what promises they could get from plant to plant, and the ribbon weavers following a week or so later, with a militant residue holding out even longer for at least a nine-hour day. Soon they too surrendered. Then began the manufacturers' counteroffensive of stretching and blacklisting, and the eddies of recrimination among the Wobbly leaders as they felt their high tide of national influence ebb, never to return.

During this summer Clarence took his own defeat indoors, deserting the sunny harsh streets of door-to-door rejection for the shadowy interiors of those moving-picture houses that, like museums of tawdry curiosities, opened their doors during the day. The worshippers within these catacombs sat scattered and silent. In 1913 there were increasingly many such houses, along Main and Market Streets: the Lyric Theatre, the Grand, the Bijou, the Apollo, the Royale, and the Washington Show, the largest and newest, at 137 Main. Some of the original nickelodeons had already passed into history: the Paterson Show, on Market, and the Nicolet, at Main and Van Houten, which had displayed the latest pictures from France in the era when Georges Méliès and the Pathé and Lumière brothers had led the fledgling industry. However, the Kinetoscope and the Wonderful Projectoscope had been invented by Thomas Edison right down the road in West Orange, and Edison's assistant, Edwin S. Porter, had filmed *The Great Train Robbery* in New Jersey, transforming the locale with a few guns and cowboy hats into the Wild West: the "movies" were above all American. When Clarence had paid his nickel—one of the brand-new Indian-head nickels, with a buffalo hulking on the reverse side—and settled into his hard chair in the dark, carefully placing his leather salesman's case upright between his ankles, it was as if his eyes drank a flickering liquor. The passionate, comical, swift-moving action on the screen, speckled with bright scratches, entered him like an essential food which he had been hitherto denied.

Ever since his revelation three years ago of God's nonexistence, he had carried around with him a crusty, stunned feeling—a clinging sense of lostness, as if within a series of ill-furnished, run-down classrooms he found himself in the wrong one, with an urgent appointment elsewhere, for which he was growing every minute a minute more tardy, incurring the growing wrath of some faceless, dimensionless disciplinarian. The sight of his poor family—Stella visibly aged and thinned by their fall, Jared and Esther coming and going with the secretive cockiness of children thrust too early upon their own resources, Teddy at ten growing a shell of deep reserve and plodding stoicism amid the debris of his father's infidelity—was as painful to him as the sight of a sunstruck row of houses on whose doors he was condemned to knock in vain. Within the movie theatre, amid the other scarcely seen slumped bodies, he felt released from accusation. The moving pictures' flutter of agitation and gesticulated emotion from women of a luminous and ideal pallor licked at his fevered brain soothingly. Images of other shadows in peril and torment lifted his soul out of him on curious wings, wings of self-forgetfulness that had not functioned in former days when he and Stella in sober evening finery would attend a Metropolitan production at the Lyceum Theatre, or a Verdi straight from Milan at the Opera House, or a musical play at the Orpheum. Over two decades in the past, he and his Princeton fellow postulates had stolen a holiday from their vows by travelling on trolley cars to Trenton and its vaudeville theatres, but it would have ill become his Paterson role as a man of the cloth to visit even the Empire, which advertised "refined burlesque" and "ladies' matinees." His former station did not now debar him from the nickelodeon turnstile and the space of infinite possibility beyond. Before the lights were lowered there was a murmur of indolent conversation and a crackle of paper bags holding sweets and sugar buns and Polish sausages and cups of ice chips; then came a hush of expectation when the projectionist could be heard moving in his cubicle behind them; his little square windows emitted unscheduled blue flashes and whiffs of smoke that testified to the dangerous spark at the root of his sorcery. Then the projector, turned by hand, began to spin overhead its chuckling whir. There were splinters of daylight at the back of the building which Clarence ceased to see once the great screen came alive. This was a church with its mysteries looming brilliantly, undeniably above the expectant rows. The projectionist slowed or speeded up the reel like a conductor regulating a symphony's tempo, and the piano player in the corner, huddled beneath his sallow lamp like a monk at his candlelit prayers, sought to inscribe the silent images with thunders and tinklings that channelled the unified emotions of the audience into surging indignation, distress, suspense, and a relief that verged upon the comic in the violence of its discharge.

The pictures transported the audience everywhere but to workaday places like Paterson: the Wild West, Manhattan slums, lumber camps in the far Canadian north, Chinese opium dens, English castles, deserts of the Holy Land, and the Roman amphitheatres of the first Christian centuries. There were kidnappings foiled by faithful dogs, and brawls amid furniture that smashed like pastry, and chases in which one was miraculously present first with the chased and then with the pursuers. For the female apparitions there were delicious and languid descents into sexual temptation that ended in abject wantonness and a welcomed death, and for the indestructible male spectres the camaraderie of battle, the thrill of vows redeemed and triumphant rescuings achieved, with the new art's dazzling nimbleness, in the very nick of time.

There was still much vaudeville in the cinematic art; magic and illusionism that once depended upon physical sleight-of-hand now could be managed by manipulation of the camera. Two men serenely ate dinner on the ceiling, while their discarded jackets were pulled upward by invisible wires. Strange and marvellous confections of satin and papier-mâché cavorted before backdrops painted as carefully as pages from a children's book, in Méliès' copious fantasy factory. Freed from the barriers of language, silent films arrived from France, Italy, Denmark, and Germany, their influx bringing with it the first recognizable stars, Max Linder and Asta Nielsen. At first, stage plays and music-hall routines were filmed as if through the eyes of a rigid front-row theatre-goer, but from year to year the camera had grown in cunning and flexibility, finding its vocabulary of cut, dissolve, close-up, tracking and dolly shot. Eyes had never before seen in this manner; impossibilities of connection and disjunction formed a magic, glittering sequence that left real time and its three rigid dimensions behind. Books rose up like radiant thunderheads out of the gray flatness of the printed page: *Uncle Tom's Cabin, Ivanhoe, A Tale of Two Cities,* with breaks between the reels, where the audience could take relief from the burden of enchantment. The world was being created anew, Clarence saw: last year's sinking of the *Titanic,* sounding the absence of God to its very bottom, was recast as a flaming disaster in a Danish film, and Queen Elizabeth was reborn as an aging Sarah Bernhardt. One young swooning, black-browed young woman after another was kidnapped into white slavery—a trade controlled by evil, pigtailed Chinamen in robes and boxy hats. Clarence's companions in the afternoon theatre were by and large of the humbler classes, furtive exiles from the day's work or, like himself, from the disgrace of joblessness, and he suffered with them the perils, temptations, and passing joys of elemental humanity; the films lifted the skirts of the supposedly safe, chaste, and eventless world to reveal an anatomy of passion and cruel inequity. Men in top hats were invariably villains or clowns; a girl attracted to a man from a superior class was usually ruined. Agreeable middle-aged women were courted by slick young men in checked suits, with inevitably unfortunate results. A young pioneer woman loved and married an Indian, with similar results. A Mexican girl was rejected by an American lover and tried to gas him. An impoverished boy was spurned by his sweetheart's wealthy family and finally won her when by the ironies of capitalism their financial situations were reversed. Vile and treacherous Indians attacked covered wagons and kidnapped an infant who survived the flames and tomahawks. A station-master's daughter saved a train from sabotage. These one- or two-reelers unwound their stories with a dizzying speed, and when laid end to end for the length of an hour left Clarence blinking and slightly headachy as he stepped out into the daylight of Main Street, beneath the glaring pewter sky of a New Jersey August. Watching the "movies" took no strength, but recovering from them did—climbing again out of their scintillating bath into the bleak facts of life, his life, gutted by God's withdrawal. He felt himself fading away, but for the hour when the incandescent power of these manufactured visions filled him. Those black-lipped heart-shaped faces, those shapely and agitated eye-whites ringed in kohl, those imperilled round-limbed actresses in glittering pagan undress. Those Babylonian temples, their papier-mâché façades blending into painted images of their rear porticos and extensions. Those rough men combative and ready to die in their shaggy chaps and ornately stitched boots. Those exotic places where life occurred and where he would never go. When the film was over, and the pale lights of the world came back on, he stood and looked kindly upon the dazed and sated faces of the others in the audience, who had been motionlessly pursuing the same adventures as he, and who now awoke from the same dream.

Feeling faint in the stale late-summer heat, beneath a white sky like a blank screen, Clarence carried his briefcase down from Main along Market into the Riverside district, where the houses were thickest, on the remote chance of salvaging the afternoon with a sale. Now that the strike was over, another noise had replaced that of policemen's whistles and defiant shouting and singing in the streets: the insistent rhythmic clatter of the reactivated mills, along Van Houten and Ellison, Prince and McBride, hundreds of unravelling shuttles slapped back and forth in their wooden boats by the snapping levers, hundreds of harplike reeds beating in the weft, beating in, beating in, as the heddles lifted and lowered the alternating halves of the warp, lifted and lowered, twenty picks to the minute as the silk cloth accumulated thread by thread, yard by yard. Clarence struggled to breathe in the day's stagnant heat. Though he still walked erect, with a touch of the Wilmot panache, his sandy mustache was so whitened as to scarcely show in his face—the drained face of an addict enduring his days for the one hour in which he could forget, in a trance as infallible as opium's, his fall, his failure, his disgrace, his immediate responsibilities, his ultimate nullity. Have mercy.

ii. *Teddy*

WHAT HE COULD NEVER STOP REMEMBERING was his father coming home to the house on Twenty-seventh Street after a day of treading the sidewalks for nothing, not having sold a single subscription to the encyclopedia and looking drained, as if humiliation were a worm inside, a parasite growing larger and larger, drinking Father's blood. Thirstily taking the tea that Mother would set before him in the little narrow kitchen at the back of the house, his father in his huddled humiliated body would convey the impression of a terrible storm blowing outdoors, a chaos of pressure and motion which might bear in upon the dirty-green house's wooden walls and sweep them all away. Unlike the solid brick parsonage they had left, with its spiky dark woodwork inside and a feeling of everything polished and tight as on a ship, this wooden house they owned, or that the bank owned thanks to Mr. Dearholt, was leaky and frail; Teddy could see daylight along the attic eaves when he explored up there, and hear squirrels or rats scrabbling in the walls by his ear at night, and feel the cold whispering and pressing in along the edges of the loose rattling window sash in the winter, when he sat in his room trying to study or to arrange the baseball cards (they came in Tip Top Bread and Cracker Jack and cigarette packs) or foreign stamps in one of the little sheltering worlds of papery order he tried to make, though he got up so early for his paper route that he was often too tired to make much sense of anything and more than once fell asleep in his clothes, surrounded by the little tinted faces of Ty Cobb and Simon Bolívar and Christy Mathewson and King George V and Frank Baker and Prince Albert of Monaco and Jake Daubert, slugging first baseman for the Brooklyn Robins. Noises from the Wilmots' neighbors—families quarrelling and slamming doors, a pleading child being beaten, a burst of laughter that yet had something skiddy and out of control about it meaning there was liquor involved, men's and women's voices falling away to a self-engrossed murmur, or a song like "Peg o' My Heart" or "There's a Long, Long Trail" or "You Made Me Love You" being sung by two or three to the jangling notes of a hesitant piano or "The Aba Daba Honeymoon" in a scratchy voice on somebody's cranked-up Victrola—came in through the walls, in this cheap neighborhood where a lot of the people hadn't even been born in this country, let alone going back to near the beginning like the Wilmots. Mother said the people were common but good-hearted, yet the impression Teddy received from the noises he could hear through his walls was of lives at the mercy of passions, people who shouted or sang or cried aloud or fought with each other for no reason, as senselessly and suddenly as accidents and murders happened in the newspapers. He delivered his papers to the stoops and porches of these people when they were still safely asleep, but his father went out into the daylight wilderness of their appetites and rages and tried to sell them books, books that weren't even adventures but dry and nothing but facts, in two columns, with spidery illustrations, and Teddy knew it was hopeless and that his father would die of it. Die of it or of the bloodthirsty worm that was eating him from within.

The worm got a name, eventually: tuberculosis. His father had tuberculosis. It was the year a ship called the *Lusitania* was sunk in big headlines. Teddy always glanced at the headlines on the bundle of papers, the Paterson *Morning Calls*, that awaited him on the corner of Market and Madison, rain or snow, sleet or shine, in the freezing dark of winter or the misty dawn of summer while all the little lawns and their cobwebs were iridescent with dew. The news—news of the European war, in those days—rubbed off on him as he made his way back and forth along the numbered streets that led off Market diagonally. For years he walked on foot, delivering seventy papers for half a penny apiece, and then, he remembered, there was a long family discussion as to whether he should be allowed to buy himself a bicycle so he could skim through his route in half the time. His mother really didn't see how they could afford it—the important thing was not to skimp on food, to keep their strengths up, already there was this dreadful shortage of sugar and bananas thanks to the war and the danger to shipping; but his father said the boy was exhausted from rising so early, he was getting to be a man and needed his sleep, and Esther came through with a couple of dollars from her job as a secretary. The bicycle, a Pierce, cost eleven dollars second-hand; it had some rust on the spokes and a rattling chain guard and had lost some red paint and was stiff pedalling uphill, but Teddy loved it as if it were a loyal pet. In the mornings, getting the Pierce out of the shed in their little backyard, he talked to it; in his mind it was, with its mottled red fenders, a faithful pinto pony. "Faster, faster, the Comanches are right behind us!" It had coaster brakes that could make it skid and a bell he could ring with his thumb and a wire-handle basket he could load his papers in. He got so he could steer without his hands, leaving them free to take the paper from the basket, fold it, and toss it, sometimes a little wild of the porches. He liked tossing the folded paper right where the person opening the front door would see it, and then pedalling on, his sack getting lighter with each toss and behind him the columns of print dropping down through the eyes of the customers into their brains. Always he loved this sensation, hard to describe, of *delivering*, and then moving on. It satisfied the same side of him as arranging stamps on the album page or trading cards to get all three Detroit outfielders, or the full Pittsburgh infield, not just Hornus Wagner. Delivering the *Morning Call* was an orderly procedure that ended with an empty sack and another thirty-five cents to his credit with the distributing agent, Mr. Larsen. Six days times thirty-five was two dollars ten and some of the people gave him a dime extra when he went around to collect on Saturday mornings. The bike meant he could sleep a half-hour longer in the morning, until quarter of six, when Mother stirred and poked him awake, teasing the way she did. His getting to be bigger and stronger and needier embarrassed him. He sensed his mother and sister holding off at the table so he could have seconds. Teddy felt heavy at home but out in Paterson, delivering papers with the morning dew and the rows of houses just stirring and showing their upstairs lights, he felt weightless, free, happy, a little significant cog in the works, spinning and whirring along.

The doctor—who had been a member of their old parish at Fourth Presbyterian—said Father had tuberculosis of the esophagus and the only cure was to stay in bed utterly still and quiet and let the body fight the disease. So there was no more encyclopedia-selling, though his commission on the few sets he had sold kept coming in for a while, in envelopes from St. Louis whose toasted pale brown Teddy associated with the flakes of falling manna in the Bible. Teddy no longer went to Sunday school, it somehow would have been disgraceful for him to go, and he remembered some of the lessons and stories with a kind of horror, as if back there in ancient Hebrew times, those strange Elijahs and Elishas and Joshuas and Judases in their crayon-colored robes, lay the gnarled roots of his family's present trouble. The money had dried up, but he helped with his three-fifty or so a week, and his mother did sewing piece-work, since before meeting Dad she had attended a school for young ladies back in Missouri that had left her clever with a needle and thread, and Esther was a secretary in the offices of the great Weidmann plant down along the river. She could type without looking at the keyboard and write Gregg shorthand, and still lived at home and gave her salary in, half of it, keeping the other half for her clothes and what she called "mad money"—movies and ice-cream sundaes and the little luxuries that women need, unlike men. Jared was at Rutgers, down in New Brunswick, and Mother said his duty was to stay there and get an education, but then in Teddy's impression everything mysteriously darkened; there was some trouble with a girl who thought Jared should marry her, he had abused her trust somehow. Suddenly Jared wasn't in New Brunswick, he was in New York City, and he didn't come home for months. Dad lay in his room quiet all day. When Teddy looked in, after school, there was his father's back, with no way of knowing if the man's eyes were open or shut or if he was alive or dead. When his curiosity got too much and Teddy went in and around the bed, the mahogany fourposter both his parents used to sleep in, his father would wink at him with his head still flat on the white pillow.

"Well, I hope your day has been more interesting than mine," he would say, in that soft voice that seemed to be sifted through some kind of mesh. He would lift his head and hold it there until Teddy took the other pillow and put it under. His father's breath had the faint brown sweetness of soothing syrup.

"It was O.K."

"School is more than O.K. It's a positive pleasure, isn't it?"

Was it? Teddy was no athlete, and no tough guy, the kind that girls somehow like, even though they mean them no good. Girls didn't notice Teddy; by the time he turned fourteen he had grown bigger but was still soft and square in shape, with the beginning of whiskers. He was quiet in class and his grades were good but not the best, not so good as to make him a star that way either, a future millionaire. He enjoyed being one of the bunch, swept through the halls and the day on the tides of young bodies, the others indifferent toward him but accepting, since he had met the basic requirements of the club, by being the same age as the others and being born in Paterson. He felt carefree, a harmless cog, doing his assignments, taking his place at the desk assigned. At home, sickness and worry ruled, and a sense of waiting, waiting for some second, even bigger blow to fall. This blow hung trembling in the faintly sweet bedroom air. "Yeah. I like school."

"I was very fond of school, when I was your age. It seemed to me such a satisfactory place. I excelled, and never knew why I excelled. My mind could just take things in without any effort, it seemed. I fooled myself. Things should never be too easy."

"I guess not," the boy responded, wondering why not. He would never be as clever as his father, or as popular and exciting as Jared—he had accepted that. He was even grateful, since both, through these qualities, had gotten into trouble.

His father strove to elevate his head on the pillows, alarmingly; the bed groaned and heaved with the effort and his head, lean and pale and waxen, seemed bigger than real, with its drooping, elongated, almost-white mustache. The unbuttoned neck of his nightshirt revealed some lank pale chest hairs. It seemed to Teddy at times that but for himself his father was being forgotten, in his quiet room, as Mother and Esther busied themselves with survival. His father was like an untended plant sending out yellow shoots in a dim half-light. "There's some things you ought to know," the invalid's mouth pronounced.

Teddy was so afraid of hearing them that he merely nodded.

"Everything passes," his father said, huskily. " 'This, too, shall pass away' are words more comforting than any I ever found in the Bible. Abraham Lincoln said them, in a speech before the War between the States. He was referring to a story about an Eastern potentate who asked his wise men for a sentence that would be good for all occasions, and that's what they came up with. 'This, too, shall pass away.' It's good when you're high, and good when you're low. I'm not low now, Theodore, though I know I must seem so. I'm having a selfish rest, while my family keeps up the struggle. I feel guilty, sometimes, to be having so good a time, lying here on my side watching Mrs. Levi hanging out her wash so it snaps and shines in the breeze, or listening to the O'Brien girls practice their duets, while the rest of my poor little crew carries the weight of the world. But your mother loves the battle; a healthy husband wouldn't give her enough to do." Silence passed, and then the man continued as if Teddy had asked a question. "You'll be fine, son—don't you worry. You have a caring heart and a good level head. If there's any danger, it's that you'll settle too cheap, from not valuing yourself enough. If I'd valued myself more, I wouldn't have let *my* dad scare me into the ministry. He was the one wanted to preach, and instead he ran a gravel pit." He smiled at his son's serious face. "Now, what does that have to do with anything? When you use your voice so little, when you drag it out of its box it tends to run on." He reached out a bony dry hand, which was surprisingly warm. Embarrassed, Teddy took it in one of his plump, square, sweating ones. His father softly squeezed out of his chest, "This will pass, for better or worse. I feel I'm getting better, the curious truth is. How do I sound?"

"Better," the boy lied, feeling breathless himself.

"Well, then. Now run tell your ma I have some business to do." This meant he had to go to the bathroom, and he needed her to help him get there. Such help Clarence asked of the two women in the house, but not of his younger son.

Thus Teddy moved through adolescence, its storms of desire muffled, waiting for his father to die. Like many organic processes it took longer than it humanly seemed it should; the loss that sooner befell them was Jared's, an arm crippled by shrapnel in the battle for the Marne, outside the village of Trughy-Epied, on the 24th of July, 1918. He lay in a Paris hospital for a month and then was shipped back to the state hospital in Newark. Only Mother visited him, since now with the end of this cruel war in sight an influenza epidemic was raging around the globe, killing more than the war had. Right there in the hospital wards men who had survived Château-

Thierry and the second Marne were dying of it, quickly and quietly, after a few days of aching and fever: their spirits just flew up out of their mouths, Mother said. She told Teddy to stay off of trolley cars and out of crowds. The old red-brick high school on Lee Place, which the city authorities declined to close, was one big crowd, buzzing with news of a grandparent or parent or brother or sister suddenly carried off. The desks on both sides of Teddy were empty for several days but the children—Charlotte Weed, Jacob Wyzanski—both came back, gloating at having out-toughed death. When Teddy came down with a fever and dryness in the throat and a feeling of the walls around him being paper-thin and covered with moving designs, he thought of praying that he not die, but this seemed disloyal to his father, somehow. His father had fallen out with God and Teddy would not go behind his back. It was easy, after a while, not to pray. Statistics showed that children resisted the flu better than the old and frail and what a terrible sort of divine punishment it would be if he brought home the illness that killed his father—if he was his father's murderer. But the fever passed, and then the cough, and he was ready to take on the paper route again. Jared, too, survived, lying in the Newark hospital surrounded by dying young men.

Jared had quit Rutgers with one year left to go, in 1916—they never explained to Teddy quite why; it had not everything to do with the girl who wanted to marry him, there was some problem with his grades as well. He had neglected his studies for extra-curricular activities, was how Mother put it. But he had worked as a slip runner and then found a job as a rent collector with a New York real-estate corporation. Supposedly he was doing well. He wore checked suits and a bowler when he visited, and seemed to his brother harder and more remote than ever; when he knuckled Teddy's head it felt like the grip of a knobby, implacable machine. "I'm going to be a soldier man," he had bragged.

"Why? Do you have to?"

"Yeah, they'll be having a draft anyways. All my buddies in

Noo Yawk are signing up. If you don't, you won't get any more pussy, that's what our girlfriends tell us. Over in France, the mademoiselles do it to Americans for free. They *aimez beaucoup.*"

"They do?" He tried to picture what "it" was, and came up with twisted positions like the rubber man at the circus freak show could get into, in the tent with the smelly sawdust.

"Sure. We go over there to save their ass, you bet they do. They slobber all over you. Anyways, like the President says, who wants to live in a world run by Germans? They'd make you eat sauerkraut every day and wipe your heinie with a wire brush."

Teddy laughed, pleased to be talked to this dirty way—the code of a monstrous world that a man evidently grows into. "Aren't you scared?"

"What's to be scared of? They see that old red, white, and blue flappin' away, they'll run, the dumb Huns. They can push the frogs and Belgies around, but they won't push real he-men. Anyway, Ted, you take your chances, ain't that the way of life? You can't live forever, so why try?"

"You said it," Teddy said, at heart disagreeing. You could see in the newspapers every day, there were the reckless and foolish, who sinned and suffered for it, and there were others, who played it safe and stayed out of the papers. Now, according to Mother, they had removed eight jagged pieces of metal from Jared's right shoulder and certain nerves were severed forever. He had been spared amputation of the arm but would never be able to shake hands the normal way or hold a pen to write—he who had always done everything so easily, tossing a baseball or juggling three apples or scrubbing Teddy's head with his knuckles while his left arm was crooked like a vise around his little brother's throat. And all for a war that had nothing to do with us, Mr. Dearholt said, one day when he visited: "The Europeans in Paterson came to this fair city to get away from all the hatreds, centuries of hatreds going back to the days they lived in caves, and here we go over and join in, all to save the international bankers, who are mostly Jewish, as the case seems to be."

Father, sitting up downstairs in his bathrobe and Turkish slippers, did not agree: it had been necessary, it had been successful, and a lasting peace would result. With Europe rid of its royalty, democracy could take hold even in Germany, where the old autocratic ideas had the most stubborn grip—the darkest part of Martin Luther's heritage. "Wilson is right—America can no longer hide from the role it must play in the world. We are, as Abraham Lincoln said, the last, best hope of earth."

Mr. Dearholt just sat there, his glasses and teeth gleaming, not wanting to argue with a sick man, or else still giving him the respect owed a clergyman. Teddy wondered why Mr. Dearholt stuck by Father, when no one else from the church had. There was something in his father worth admiring: the boy held on to that thought.

Jared when he came home, hard of hearing in one ear and his limp arm in a sling, didn't want to talk about the war, or his experiences in it. Teddy asked him once about the French girls who *aimezed beaucoup.*

"They were there, I guess all right, but it was different than you pictured it ahead of time. The froggies had set it up as a kind of industry—they're way ahead of us, with doctors checking out *les poules* every month, for VD—and the officers got the benefit, not your ordinary doughboy. Everything is some kind of business over there, even the church. Nothing's sacred, believe me. Even the priests drink and eat till they're red in the face and fat as pigs. Imagine: the war just a few miles away, their country a battlefield for four years, and these waiters in the bistros hurrying and scurrying making a quick franc on the Americans dragged over there to save their lousy froggy hides. If the Germans had broken through to Paris, they would have hurried and scurried for them too. They don't have our pride, Ted. For all their talk of *gloire* this and *gloire* that from all I saw this glorious war was just a mess of bodies, some dead and some still alive and kicking, and nobody had a notion in hell of what it was all about—why the war had come, or why it was going away. It just happened. Millions died, and it just happened. *C'est la guerre, c'est la vie.* It was weird, the war, how normal it got to be. Guys you know, guys you've been beside day and night, suddenly they're dead—a piece of garbage, like some big white log you step over without thinking much about it, until it begins to stink. I'm not complaining. It could have been a lot worse, personally. At least I kept my sight, I wasn't gassed like those poor bastards in the Toul, fresh off the boat and sent into battle without masks by officers green as paint. Europe, they can keep it—the frogs, the Krauts. I don't ever want to cross the fucking-ass Atlantic again."

Teddy tried to hide his shock at the swear-word, stronger and stranger than any he had heard Jared use before. "So what are you going to do?" Teddy surprised himself with the question; he realized only he could ask it, directly like that—Mother and Father and Esther were too afraid. They were afraid of Jared since he had come back hardened in a fire they would never experience. Teddy had no desire to experience that fire, or any fire really, but he found that now he loved his brother, which he hadn't before. And his brother in his thin-lipped way found something in Teddy that he hadn't needed before—a listening audience before which he could hear himself speak. Wounded people need an audience.

Jared's eyes since he came back had changed; a muddy green, energetically protruding, they had grown a film, a fishy imperviousness beneath the pointy fox-red brows. "Do? Well, for what they call my partial disability I'll be getting fifteen bucks a month for the next year plus the sixty that comes with every discharge. So I'll sit around living on Uncle Sam till I get some use back in my arm and clear up this ringing in my ears. Then go back to Noo Yawk and make a ton of do-re-mi. If there's one thing this war taught me, it's that money is more important than pussy. Money makes the man, Ted, and pussy unmakes him. Money gives, and pussy takes."

Teddy could see his brother's nervous eyes narrow as he shifted into the more personal gear. Awkwardly, perched on the arm of the wicker chair on the little screened-in back porch here on East Twenty-seventh Street, where they had gone despite the November cold to be out of Mother's and Father's earshot—the bedridden man could hear everything, even the tiniest noise downstairs gave him some kind of pain—Jared leaned forward, his head cocked in a new way he had now, to let the good ear hear. "You got to watch it about becoming a mama's boy. You're going to be alone with Mom and Esther once Pop and I pull out."

"Is Pop pulling out?" Teddy still thought of him as "Dad," which had a childish ring.

"He's been pulling out ever since we've known him," Jared said. "Only it's going faster now. Let me finish about women. They want two things, Ted: your money and your nuts. They spend your money; God knows what they do with your nuts. Nothing, I guess—they just don't want *you* to have 'em."

This all sounded a little off-key and flat to Teddy—missing a dimension, though he had no idea how to supply the dimension. His brother talked survival, and that was the name of the world's game. His mother talked love, and that was the game you played at home, in its shelter and shadows.

Coming into his room in the dark just as he had cupped his left hand beneath his balls in anticipation of the loop-the-loop trip he had discovered he could give himself, she would tousle the hair on the top of his head and say, "Now, don't you fret, little sweetheart, your daddy's getting better every day, the doctor says, though I know he looks thinner—his body's just squeezing the bad cells out, that's what's happening—and the way you're growing, and bringing home those fine report cards, is a ray of sunshine in his life, he tells me twice a day."

But she was scared, he could sense it in the quickened way she moved about the house, and in the way she touched him, for luck or reassurance, more than she used to, and in the tension of her hug, the hug a little shy now that he was fifteen going on sixteen. She had begun to clean houses, not the houses of her old parishioners—that would have been too great a comedown—but of those to whom she was recommended by her old parishioners. Her houses were not just on the East Side of Paterson but over in Clifton and up in Hawthorne, so there were long trolley-car rides. Teddy would often get back from school at four and find nobody in the house but Dad, dozing. He couldn't talk now, just lay there with his head held sideways on two pillows and his blue eyes getting livelier, looking out the window at Mrs. Levi's wash, and the fences and backyards beyond like a ramshackle set of stairs mounting into the distance, south toward the inverted rows of rain clouds above Clifton. When Teddy would peek in, his father was lying there motionless. But then his eyes would open with their disconcerting lightness of milky-blue color and his eyebrows—thin and long like a woman's, not bushy like Jared's and their grandfather's in the old photos—would arch in what Teddy knew to be a question.

"Good," he answered. "School was good." He did not say that he smoked a Fatima cigarette with Jake Wyzanski on the mile-long walk home along Grand and Essex Streets and then through Sandy Hill Park to Twentieth Avenue or that he had seen Charlotte Weed's ankle when she reached down and scratched herself in American-history class or how the armpits of Edna Jacobson's frilly blouse were stained wet from running when she came in late after lunch or how Peter McHegan said you could tell which girls were having their period from how red their pimples were or how Maria Caravello had come to the school as a substitute English teacher for the ninth grade. Or—and this he was tempted to tell—how Mr. Loesser, the geography teacher who also coached baseball, had seen him horsing around with four other guys with a broom handle and a rubber ball during recess this March and asked if he wanted to come out for the team; Teddy had pictured himself for a moment as Paterson High's own Home Run Baker and how all those girls would be in the stands peeing in their pants because he was so great, but then he remembered that if he had too much exercise he might not be able to get up in the morning as early as he had to for the paper route even with his faithful Pierce and that he was thinking now that he was bigger he should be helping out with a job after hours, if not with the Nagle Brothers ice wagon like Jared, working in some store as stockroom boy or as part-time apprentice at one of the dye works, which is what some of the other kids had been doing for years, waiting until age sixteen, when they could legally drop out of school altogether. Then they were lost to education, swallowed up in the clatter and the steam of the mills, their hands skinned down to the bone by the chemicals. A Wilmot couldn't do that. But with Father the way he was, a Wilmot couldn't play games after school, either. So Teddy had told Mr. Loesser thanks a lot, but he didn't think he could. The man—not tall but taller than Teddy, with curly black hair receding at the forehead and one of those tan faces with deep loose sad creases in it—had nodded with curt understanding, and even smiled, but Teddy knew a door had been shut that would not open again. He was old enough now to see that life is a bent path among branching possibilities—after you move past a fork in the road you cannot get back.

Well, he could tell his father one of the things from school. "Dad, remember the Caravellos that used to be members of our church?" The long horizontal head, the ends of its mustache both drooping in the same direction, made a sideways motion the boy took to be a nod. It was not the Caravellos but themselves whose connection with the church "used to be," but his father had understood. "I saw her in the hall and she didn't recognize me, then she came into English class because Miss Harriman is sick and she recognized our name on the list and after class talked a little to me. She was much better than Miss Harriman, much livelier, and her English is perfect now—better than ours. Her sister and mother are both married, she said, but she had it in her mind always to be a schoolteacher in this country, where women were allowed to be teachers without being nuns."

His father soundlessly formed a word with his lips and then repeated it with a distant creak of breath so that Teddy heard the word "Wonderful." Then his father said something else, which after a second of trying to understand Teddy made out to be Italian words, "*La bella professoressa.*"

There were languages in that long sallow head—mazes of books, of dead men's words and the mazy tracks they had left in the dust. Teddy had often stood in his father's book-lined study, feeling dwarfed and oppressed. When they had tried to sell the books to raise money, nobody wanted them, not even the Princeton Seminary. His father's long pale head, its fine hair fanning from the semi-transparent top of his pink skull onto the bleached pillowcase, lay there like a giant egg—the egg, it occurred to Teddy, from which he had somehow hatched. He tried to put the weird thought behind him—people coming out of one another like segments of a telescope. His father and he were two entirely different people bound together only by a name and an unspeakable mutual pity. Since the man couldn't talk beyond a whisper or two, and the boy couldn't think of enough to say, Teddy began to read him the Paterson *Evening News,* which would be sitting on the porch when he came home from school in his knickers and billed cap and high-top button shoes he had walked so much in that the damp and cold came through their thin soles. He would get himself a glass of milk and an oatmeal cookie if there were any in the bread tin and read his father the headlines and more of the article if he indicated it roused his interest. The local news, the obituaries and murders and threatened strikes and marriages, interested him less than the international developments in the wake of the Great War—monarchies overthrown, millions starving, red revolutions in Russia and Berlin and Hungary, New Jersey's own President Wilson like a grim worn ghost of high ideals trundling his message of peace and forgiveness back and forth to Europe and being hailed as a hero to his face and behind his back outsmarted by foreigners like Clemenceau and Lloyd George. Roosevelt, Teddy's namesake, died, and then Wilson broke down on a tour across the United States begging the Senate to approve of the League of Nations. Lenin formed the Third Communist International; Charlie Chaplin, D. W. Griffith, Mary Pickford, and Douglas Fairbanks formed United Artists, their own film company. Father was especially interested in this item and made Teddy read every word, and also an item about a horse called Sir Barton that for the first time ever won something called the Triple Crown, and another on the sports page about Jack Dempsey beating Jess Willard, who had taken the title from a black man called Jack Johnson four years earlier. Father whispered close to Teddy's ear, "Never should have had it. Big bum. They hounded Johnson till he took a dive in disgust." Steelworkers in Indiana and coal miners in Pennsylvania went out on strike and rich men called Frick and Carnegie died, but Father was most interested in an item saying that astronomers had observed light bend around the sun during a solar eclipse, confirming some German's theory of relativity. "Relativity," Father pronounced for Teddy, when he tangled his tongue over the word. "The universe is getting stranger. I was told it would." And then it was a new decade, and drinking was illegal all across the nation, and Attorney General A. Mitchell Palmer accused the IWW of causing the railroad strike as part of an international conspiracy and vowed war upon "the moral perverts and hysterical neurasthenic women who abound in communism." His father faintly rasped, "Had the Wobblies prevailed in Paterson, we'd have a different country." Mary Pickford and Douglas Fairbanks were married in a Hollywood dream come true, and Europe twisted and turned with coups and riots and little wars, and the Democrats at their convention put up James Cox and another Roosevelt, and Bill Tilden became the first American man to win at Wimbledon, and the amendment entitling American women to vote was ratified, but with no women present at the ceremony. And Father, Clarence Arthur Wilmot, slipped away one night, one of the first cool nights at the beginning of September, just died without a sound so they found his body like a beautiful perishable statue in the morning, all of a stiff pale piece—his spirit had slipped through their fingers, his and Mother's and Esther's, as if to spare them any further trouble. Yet there also was in his silence a rebuke, blaming them for having been unable to reverse the trend that had carried him off like an unmoored boat on an outgoing tide.

Of the confused, brief period that followed, Teddy remembered mostly Esther, as if Mother, being the widow, encased in a black that included glittering square black stones that had appeared on her wrists like manacles, was too hot with life's dangerous essence, its hidden lava of disaster, to look at. Now twenty-five, Esther had been working for five years in the offices of Weidmann Silk Dyeing Company, ever since the upsurge in wartime orders had revitalized the company. A little strike by the dyers' helpers in 1919, for a raise and an eight-hour day, had been easily defeated. Esther wore her skirts ten inches off the ground, according to the latest Paris fashions. She was like Father in her tall thin physique and she smoked cigarettes, but not in the house, where Mother could smell them. Esther knew that Teddy smoked, too, on the way back from school, and didn't tell. He and she seemed guilty spies crossing the enemy lines into the real, bustling, indifferent world and sneaking back into the terrible defeated hush of the house after Father's death: his room and bed, day after day, unchanging, unslept-in, though sometimes in the middle of the night Teddy awoke as if Father's cough had punctured his sleep—a dry, dragging cough that used to start timidly and become louder and more frantic, as if he were trying to dig out something jagged and tenacious stuck between his vocal cords. But the house was silent. Paterson at night was silent, but for a lone car purring past and the tiniest trickle of music from a gramophone in the neighborhood and, if Teddy listened hard enough, the faraway roar of the Falls merged with the muffled clatter of the mills weaving breadths of silk all through the night shift. These sounds had formed the undercurrent of his life, in this city crowded in a loop of the river at the foot of Garrett Mountain, and now there was talk of leaving. Modest as it was, the house was too much for them to carry, on the slim pickings of her cleaning and sewing, Mother said, and Jared's charity, and Esther's slender salary—for who was to say how much longer Esther would be with them? The thought of Esther marrying put a gleam of sad merriment into her berry-black widow's eyes, even though Esther waved the thought away with a brusque disgust that was more and more her mannerism. "As long as dear Clarence was here," Mother went on, in that sugary voice that had something pathetic about it now, an outmoded appeal to gallantries being swept away by the world's quickening, nervous pace, "we had to hang on, so as not to disturb him, but now it's not fair to Jared, to ask so much to make our ends meet. He's a young man on the rise in New York City, and he needs nice things to wear. He mustn't keep living in that boarding house, with its dubious characters. He needs his own apartment, with a doorman, and to belong to a club, to associate with the calibre of people he must deal with." As to exactly what that calibre was, or what Jared's enterprises were beyond collecting other people's rent, she was purposefully vague. She didn't want to know. Unlike Teddy, Jared had reached that age when young men could have their secrets. "I've been getting the *nicest* letters from your Aunt Esther, down there in Basingstoke." Basingstoke was the small town in Delaware, a few miles north of the Chesapeake and Delaware Canal, where Father's sister and her chirpy, rosy-faced husband, Horace Truitt, lived in a big house right in the middle of town, with a long backyard that when the Wilmots visited in the summer had seemed to Teddy sleepy and sinister, full of droopy-limbed hemlocks and tall flowers like chains of soft bells strung together. Horace, who had been a chemist for the Du Pont Company and who had retired early on the strength of the shares he had been privileged to buy before they soared during the war, took care of the gardens; his especial pride was what he called a gazebo, wooden and eight-sided and freshly painted white and reached by a path winding through flower beds, even though just over the fence there was a busy street of less ample and picturesque homes called Locust Street, and in another block the downtown, which had shaped itself to the river. On its trips there in summer, the family would drive in Uncle Horace's Hupmobile through miles of marshes to get to the beach, a strip of sand bent around a rocky point where the Delaware became wider than a normal river but still narrow enough so that you could see individual trees in the forested shore of New Jersey on the other side. Teddy was always excited when he got there, by the smallness of everything in Delaware and the hovering salt tang of sea air, promising something to happen that couldn't happen at home; by the third day he became bored and cranky, seeing that it wasn't going to happen, and missing his own room, with his stamps and baseball cards and model airplanes and view of the neighborhood's windows; sometimes he saw Deborah Levi in her slip, but she always moved out of sight before coming back dressed in her nightie. "Well, she solemnly maintains that, ever since Horace"—Mother hesitated; Uncle Horace had run away, a few years ago, with another Basingstoke woman—"did his unforgivable deed, she's rattling around in that place and would like nothing better than if we would come stay with her for a time, until we can find a place of our own. Everything costs less down there, and it would be so healthy for little Teddy to get away from the mills and the rough element they attract."

"I don't *want* to go way down there into the middle of nowhere," he complained to his sister one night when he had still been awake, working in his room on a balsa-wood model of a Sopwith Camel—the struts and wires between the two wings were the fussiest part, and the machine guns that fired out right through the spinning propeller. Esther had come in from a night out with a man she knew from the Weidmann office, a sales representative who went to cities all over the Eastern U.S. Teddy came down to the kitchen, where he heard her getting a glass of lemonade from the icebox. She looked a little mussed and exasperated, there in the stark light of the kitchen, in a shimmering green dress that set off the gleams in her strawberry-blond hair, done up in a thick roll all around like Mother's dark hair, though she talked of having her hair cut short—"bobbed." Her dress had a tasselled belt low on her hips but slipped on over her head, he knew from having watched her when her door was ajar one time. It was a November night and she had worn a beaver-trimmed raglan coat she tossed with an impatient grimace onto a kitchen chair. Teddy could see in the hard light that she wasn't exactly beautiful—too wiry, and too flat in front and behind, and her lips too thin and clever and impatient—but with her white skin and quick decisive gestures she was alive in a competent, hard, unapologetic way that dazzled him. He and his parents had this in common: they were all soft. The world pushed them around. "Why the dickens not?" she asked. "What's in Paterson for you?"

"My friends."

"Some friends. You never bring them back to the house."

"There's nothin' to do here."

She laughed, her quick laugh, surprisingly deep, a kind of bark. "As much as in most other houses, I expect. If there's so much nothin' to do here, what've you got to lose going down to Basingstoke? You need a change. We all do. Paterson has nothing left for the Wilmots. Basingstoke's a lazy little town that'll give us a chance to get our bearings."

"Us? You coming with us?"

At his sudden intensity, her painted lips stretched in a thin smile, and she asked, "You want me to?" She moved closer to the kitchen door and opened it, so the smoke from the cigarette she lit would drift out through the screen door.

"Well, sure," he said. "I don't want to be stuck with two old ladies down there."

"You'll make friends."

"They're all rubes—don't pull my leg."

"Tedsy hon, I got a good job here. I got my gentlemen friends."

"Yeah, I guess you do. Any you're real sweet on? How do you like the guy you were with tonight? I saw him when you were heading out. He was too slick by half, if you ask me."

"Slick is good, in his line of work. He could charm the skirt off a dressing table, like they say." She held out her pack of cigarettes—Lucky Strikes, in that green bull's-eye pack, and shook it. "Want one?"

As with Jared sometimes, he was being led out into deep grown-up waters. He took the Lucky, though, and lit up, and crowded closer to the screen door, so Mother didn't get a whiff and come down. Maybe she wouldn't come down. Maybe she cared less than he thought. Dad used to smoke not just his pipe in his study but sometimes a Sweet Caporal—"for medicinal purposes," he once told Teddy with a wink. The inhaling felt like poking something rough down his throat. His head went light, as when he used to swing too high on the swings at the Sandy Hill Park playground.

Esther was saying, "*Too* slick, it could be. He makes a girl feel like she's being sold a bill of goods. On the one hand you want to buy it, and on the other you don't, you know?"

It wasn't really a question; she was talking half to herself. Teddy nodded anyway, as if he did know. He smelled the perfume she had put on to go out and a little sweat, he supposed from dancing, and the smoke she exhaled, which was mixed with a sickly semi-rotten scent that he associated with empty squarish bottles you found on the cinder paths along the river, among the tall weeds. Hooch. Spirits. Illegal but that didn't stop people. Esther lately wore a kind of squint, from typing all the time or smoking so much or just because she couldn't look at the world wide-eyed any more. Father's quitting his job had hit her just at the point when she might have gone to normal school and become a teacher. "Men," she said, squinting over his head. "They're all duds, in a way. I guess they can't help it. But, Lordy, they're a boring lot. It's all 'I did this, I'll do that, me, me, me.' Don't grow up to be a man, Tedsy; you'll be as boring as the rest."

"Where did he take you tonight? To a speakeasy?"

"What do you know about speakeasies, big boy?"

"There're a lot of them now, all up in Riverside, tucked away in basements and so on. A couple of the Italian kids at school, they have brothers and fathers in the bootlegging business."

"They shouldn't make laws people have to break," Esther said. She reminded him of Dad, saying that. They both knew things without even trying hard, and it made them vulnerable, like animals with feelers that stick way out.

He pleaded, "Won't you be coming if we have to move? Please. Just for a year or two. You don't want to stay here getting dragged to smelly speakeasies."

"Don't I?" she asked, squinting and exhaling upward, so her face was half-hidden, and cruel with that carelessness grown-ups have. They don't care about you as much as it seems when you're a baby; they care first of all about themselves, just like the baby does. Teddy felt his own face cloud, tears welling up somehow out of the giddy strangeness of smoking a sinful cigarette here in his own house, and being awake and talking at this late hour, and his sister acting so tough, like a tramp. The model of the Sopwith Camel he had left in his room with its cozy fumes of fresh glue was a piece of the innocence they were making him lose. She asked him teasingly, "What's down there for me in Basingstoke?"

"Maybe you'd meet a nice man. A man who wouldn't be so slick."

"That's pretty slick of you to say, little brother. You want to link me up with some crab fisherman or nice old tanner."

The town had an old tannery in its center, on the little river that managed a six-foot waterfall before it meandered out through the marshes to the sea. "Now that we've got the vote, you know, and collitch eddycations, we girls are supposed to have more on our minds than just catching some critter who wears a pair of pants." When Esther dragged on her cigarette, her thin lips became even thinner—narrow sharp lines of incongruous red. She was talking to him now as if he was one of her man friends, clowning in that angular way she had, and that reminded him a little bit of Father, before he got so sad and when he was still jaunty. When Teddy thought of his father—visualized him in even the most glancing way—he ached inside, with a sluggish rubbing that tasted of shame. Esther was studying his attempt to hide his tears and said, "Seventeen, huh? And you still need to have your big sister hold your hand?"

It all had to do with what she had said earlier: growing up to be a man. He was soft now, he hadn't grown his shell, and if he was left alone in a strange town with his mother and Aunt Esther he wouldn't, or it would grow warped, in a way he couldn't picture but could feel. He knew from school that he was cautious and underdeveloped: all around him in the halls and on the asphalt were the click and flash of real knives, real loves, boys and girls who really did it, kids equipped to play the real game, this game of manhood and womanhood and grabbing your piece of the world. He wasn't equipped, he was still curled inward, collecting innocent things—stamps from foreign countries that gave pieces of paper the power to fly around the globe. The few friends he had at school would give him or sell him for a penny the stamps from their relatives in Europe, even Turkey and Syria, and new countries like Czechoslovakia and Lebanon. The passion of those tiny stamps in the intensity of their colors and engraving and words of unknown languages fascinated him, drew him in, to a safe small cave. Such papery fascinations had descended to him from Father. To become a man, whatever that was, he needed a little more time, a little more space, and his wised-up strawberry-blonde sister's being with them in Aunt Esther's spooky house down there in nowheresville would give it to him. Then she could come back to Paterson and catch a man who was slick but not too, a nice man in sales or management. He had never asked anything from a woman except his mother but now he was; he had matured more than he knew, for like those flashy swarthy boys at school who asked dirty things of their girls he was discovering that females like to say yes, and the more of a risk to themselves the yes involves the mysteriously greater is their wish to oblige. Esther stubbed out her Lucky Strike on the sole of her high-heeled slipper of green leather and cupped her hand waiting for him to stub out his so she could toss the two butts out the screen door over the fence of the Levis' yard. Teddy could tell from the watchful gleam in Esther's squint that he had amused her. "I'll think about it. We'll see what Mom has in mind. My job at Weidmann isn't so great I have to cling to it like it was life or death. As to the guys around here—who wants to spend their whole life in Paterson? All the men talk and think about is when the next strike is coming and if the next turn of fashion from over in Paris will hurt silk sales and whether or not they should move the whole works over to the coal regions where the dopes are too scared to strike. Phooey to 'em, Tedsy. You're my best buddy."

She moved a step toward him and he flinched until he realized she was giving him a quick hug. Upstairs, though they tiptoed, Mother appeared on the landing with her wonderful mass of gray-threaded chestnut hair spilled down across the shoulders of her voluminous cotton nightie. "Heavens above, why do you two keep slamming the screen door?" she asked, in a voice louder and more humorous than any she would have used when Father was alive, lying on his side staring blue-eyed at nothingness.

. . .

Basingstoke was named after a town in Hampshire, England, by homesick colonists who had set sail from Southampton in 1690. The Swedes and Dutch had already been displaced from rule of the New Castle region and the Duke of York had conveyed to William Penn his vast territories, including the three lower counties on the Delaware, their awkward apartness from the rest of Pennsylvania a strain even then. The colonists preferred to profess allegiance directly to the king rather than the aristocratic Quaker whose pacifism left them vulnerable to seaborne attacks by pirates and the French. The entire snippet of a state, with difficulty severed from the great domains of Penn and Lord Calvert, was saturated in English nostalgia, an emotion embodied, it seemed, in the picturesque mists that on many mornings arose from the river and its nearly level, humid, tree-filled valley. The river was named the Avon, though an old Nanticoke name, the Manito, had been recorded.

Teddy was eighteen his first summer here; awakened early by the unaccustomed quiet, marred by cries of roosters from their neighbor's little poultry-yards, he would watch these mists burn off under a golden sun, or as it were sink back into the marshy, verdant terrain that surrounded the seven hundred houses—many wooden but more of brick, with some laid up in courses of alternating headers and stretchers in a style characteristic of old Delaware—that were home to Basingstoke's more than three thousand residents. The town had been built densely, since the local farmland was rich and precious. Two grist mills had been turned by the Avon's gentle current, less powerfully and prosperously than the flour and gunpowder mills drawing power from the swift-running Brandywine to the hilly north, and had yielded in the late eighteenth century to a tannery. In less than a century this industry had drained the local forests of oak bark and ceased to pour its acids and chromium salts and dyes into the Avon, which gradually recovered its clear color and its fish, its trout and perch and those bright little spiny, vicious catfish called madtoms. Now the only sizable mill in town made, a newish thing, metal "crown" bottle caps, replacing the old stoppers of wire and cork. The mill accepted thin sheets of enamelled low-carbon steel from Pittsburgh at one end of its loading platform and after a clacking, banging, hissing maze of procedures inside set out on the other end of the platform neat wooden cases, which made a musical metallic sloshing noise when moved, full of crimped discs imprinted with the florid scripted logos of manufacturers of root beer, birch beer, sarsaparilla, and other beverages concocted of carbonated sugar water. The bottling plants were at other sites, some as far distant as Atlanta; there the stacked caps were fed downward and jerkily popped, many per minute, over round glass lips by an automatic vertical hammer to which the tensile strength and elasticity of the crown caps were precisely adjusted against the eventual day when a consumer would lever one free, releasing a fizzy hiss of long-captive carbon dioxide. The plant producing this innocent product, and a few back-alley gun shops and automobile garages, and a single large but porous shed in which the last of a once-flourishing tribe of shipbuilders hammered and planed away at about one gaff-rigged oyster boat a year, constituted the visible local industry. Otherwise, the citizens of Basingstoke seemed to survive by supplying each other's needs, and those of the farmers of the land around it, whose peach orchards and chicken houses and produce gardens and cornfields helped feed Wilmington and Philadelphia. The prosperity propelled by the Du Pont Company's war profits on the sale of explosives and its post-war expansion into all aspects of the chemical industry reached far enough south to create, in Basingstoke, an economic sufficiency. Little changed; few new buildings went up, and those that existed were occupied and maintained. Picket fences were now and then repainted white; the most doddering widow contrived with the help of a neighbor child or colored boy to keep her bushes from overflowing her yard. The stores along Rodney Street—the main street, shaped like an elongated S to fit the river and named after Caesar Rodney, whose midnight ride to vote in Philadelphia for independence was Delaware's most famous historical episode—sold their groceries and farm tools and clothes and watch fobs and birdseed and ice-cream sodas and patent medicines in steady quantities. It was a far cry from the economic violence of Paterson—its peril and passion, its laboring masses pitted against unseen, implacable proprietors. In Delaware, the situation was so different that T. Coleman du Pont out of his own pocket was building a highway for everybody, right down the middle of the state.

Teddy at first knew only that he was in a new space, awaking to different, more distant sounds, on the third floor of Aunt Esther's big house on Willow Street. The atmosphere was sleepier, more Southern. The people showed none of the European variety and pushiness he was used to. Everyone bore simple English names; the only different people were the colored people, who lived in back alleys or shanties where the paved streets gave out and who seemed as shy and watchful and cautious as Teddy himself. A colored maid, Edwina, came to the house like Mavis used to, but when he tried to talk to her, she turned her face—the grave and lusterless color of a cast-iron stove—away from him, as if he was potent to a degree he didn't realize. When she did respond, it was in a voice so slurred and entwined with nervous giggles that he couldn't understand her. Beyond the walls of this house, he knew nobody. With Mr. Dearholt's help, Mother had sold the house—to the bank, at no profit—but they stayed on in Paterson until he graduated from high school, fifty-first in his class of three hundred twelve. He had begged his mother to stay until graduation, yet it had deprived him, he saw now, of making friends of any Basingstoke classmates. People his age moseyed back and forth along Willow Street, or roared by in their tin lizzies, as if he were a fish in an aquarium, helplessly staring out. He had passed the age when a child can linger at the edge of a game of kickball or baseball and be, with scarcely an exchange of words, assimilated. Awkward in his new manhood, squarish and soft in build, Teddy walked the town, that first lonely summer, hoping to become part of it, taking the measure of its shady blocks, its ragged curving downtown, its little Greek temple of a town hall, the sprucely painted churches where the Presbyterians, the Methodists, the Baptists, and the Episcopalians entertained their bearded God in His several shades of Protestant doctrine, the close-set deep-porched homes of the not uncomfortable, and the surprisingly stark rowhouses, with piebald asphalt shingles and sagging porches one step up from the pavement, tucked between the empty, hollow-eyed, rose-colored tannery and the busy bottle-cap factory, which had been built recently, of cinder blocks with a half-heartedly ornamental façade of glazed yellow bricks. The downtown turned its back on the river; but for slots between the buildings through which the shuffling glint of sunlight on water-dimples flashed through to his eye, the river was invisible, as it carried toward the sea the suds of brown foam churned up by the six-foot waterfall there by the ruddy ruin of the old tannery. The river was freshwater for several miles more, until it met the saltwater tides. Teddy walked to the edges of the town, to the Negroes' scattered unpainted shacks and their swept dirt yards where dusty hens pecked and shuffled and submitted to the rooster's hasty mounting, and to the lush, buggy, buzzing cornfields and receding pruned orchards and ragged vestiges of hardwood forest that marked the limits of Basingstoke. It would all have fit between the two railroad lines that ran through Paterson; Teddy got so he could hold a map of it in his mind.

What he had trouble holding in his mind was his father's death, his eternal absence. He kept half-expecting time to be reversed and Father to walk in the door and take charge again, in his wry, slender, soft-spoken way. The completeness with which his father had been erased from the earth bore for Teddy the force of a miracle. A numbness of incredulity surrounded the erasure—the daily willful absence and silence—and a sense of injustice, which was absurd, since there was no one who had promised justice. Teddy felt that some critical business between the two of them had been left unconcluded, and some instructions that greatly mattered left undelivered. Had he, in walking the lonely streets of Basingstoke, reached down for a scrap of paper that had caught his eye, and found it to be a loving letter from his father, he would have been startled but satisfied; it was his due.

Aunt Esther and her runaway, unmentionable husband, Horace—Teddy remembered him, a pink-cheeked bald little man who sucked on his pipe and cackled like a woman when he laughed—had laid out a truck garden along the sunny side of their half-acre, including a big asparagus bed, and the first summer that Teddy lived in Basingstoke the women could think of nothing better to do with the sole man of the house than have him dig up several summers' worth of weeds, break up the sod and shake the grass roots out of it, plant leaf lettuce and radishes and whatever other above-ground vegetables could come in after a late start, keep these rows hoed, and weed and harvest the asparagus bed. There was a little art to asparagus, knowing when the tender purple-tinged nose, its leaflets overlapped like fish-scales, had poked enough inches out of the ground to be dug with the asparagus cutter, which was shaped like the tail of an arrow. Bunches of a dozen or so stalks were to be peddled fresh in the neighborhood in the evenings. It was not unusual for the citizens of Basingstoke to sell each other produce; the dimes accumulated pleasantly in the pocket, and even some of the colored households—the better off, who lived closer to town, in painted houses—were willing to buy. But the experience of going door to door reminded Teddy of his father's miserable year of encyclopedia-peddling, and his aversion to suffering such fatal humiliation would set off panic in him as his mother and aunt sent him out the door with his loaded basket of perhaps a dozen bunches, each tied prettily with a bow of red string. When a person came to the door he would sweat and stammer as if there were something deeply shameful in the vegetable itself, with its close, sour, secret fragrance and purplish head—as if he were trying to sell a part of his own body. His mother, seeing how deeply these innocent expeditions upset him, took mercy and would carry the asparagus herself, with an evident gregarious pleasure. She introduced herself to neighbor after neighbor; her Southern accent sounded at home here. It rarely took her more houses than there were bunches to empty her basket. Silently trailing along, he watched her do it but could only envy her simple confidence at putting herself forward, her lack of embarrassment about basic human transactions. Happily, the asparagus season didn't last; by July the beds were clouded over with the feathery forms of stalks gone to seed. As the gardening season tapered into August, and the supper hour impinged on twilight, his mother asked at the kitchen table, in the slightly loud voice of a formal announcement, "Now, what can we all do about finding our Ted some real employment, that will take him out of himself?"

"The factory might take him on, but that doesn't seem suitable for the son of a man with as much education as Clarence had," Aunt Esther said. She was slender and sandy-haired like her late brother, her hair pulled back from a central parting to a strict-looking bun. That quality in her brother, handsomeness's pale afterglow, which had made him seem fragile and misplaced, had imparted to her the strength of vanity. Before marrying she had given piano lessons but had never thought to work for a living since. Teddy tried to see what had attracted the unmentionable Horace, and what had eventually repelled him. Her features were regular and when she was young must have been fine, but her mind didn't rise an inch out of her own skin and see beyond her immediate selfish needs, even to the extent that Mother's did. Mother had enthusiasm, at least. When he asked her why Aunt Esther had never had children she answered carefully: "Well, I can't absolutely say, but she was always vain of her figure and I think she didn't want to be put to the inconvenience. Though Horace has done her a dreadful wrong, he had his provocations, the people around here let it be known." Teddy did not imagine that from Aunt Esther's standpoint he was more than a voracious boarder who should be put out into the community to bring back money. "Guilt checks" now and then arrived from Horace in envelopes without return addresses, and Jared spared them something every month from his expanding enterprises in New York, but the household was cash-poor, and not cheap to keep up, even with but one colored servant. Aunt Esther's comfortable past, as the middle daughter of the righteous gravel-pit proprietor, floated on the merest excuse to her tongue. "He was the strangest boy," she said of her brother, "his nose always in a book, and teaching himself foreign languages as if he was going to wander the globe. Then he never went anywhere, as it turned out. Like father, like son, it appears."

His mother took up the challenge to her son, saying with a proud and wistful smile, beneath the liverish shadows that had come to stay beneath her eyes, "Teddy does take after his papa, in being able to amuse himself so easily, quiet in his room for hours. My dearest hope is in a year or two we might be able to scrape up enough to send him off to college. Wouldn't he make a striking professor, with that wide brow and his solemn manner?"

Watching his father's horrifying collapse had left Teddy with a number of aversions. The idea of his venturing out to the factory every day, with a tin lunch pail, sickened him, and so did the thought of teaching. In both factory and college, there would be all those probing, thrusting, jagged-edged other people to fit himself into, somehow, and compete with. He didn't want to have to compete, and yet this seemed the only way to be an American. Be stretched or strike.

"*Mother*," he protested. "We hardly have enough to eat on as is, you can't go wasting it on me and college. What good did college do Dad and Jared?"

"Oh, it did your father no end of good. His education made his life and work possible."

"And then made them impossible. If he hadn't known so much he wouldn't have had to quit the church."

"He had to quit because his body failed," she said, turning her impressive head, with its symmetrical pile of shining hair, to include the others in this reassurance. "His mind stayed clear to the end."

"Too clear, that was the trouble, don't you remember?" Teddy said. "He lost his *faith.*" It exasperated the boy to the point of tears, the way she was always remaking the truth, so the simplest facts of their family history kept sliding around underneath them. He used to wonder how the stories of Jesus' miracles and Resurrection could have been spread across the world if they were not true, but his mother had showed him how.

"He didn't lose his faith, he lost his voice," she calmly informed her sister-in-law. Esther, like her brother, was a Presbyterian, and unlike him had remained staunch.

Young Esther, as they had to call her here, said to Teddy, "Hey, you can't say Rutgers didn't do Jared any good; a lot of the business connections over in New York come out of friendships he made at Rutgers. College men have a bond, even when they don't finish."

"Well, I'm not even starting."

"Oh, little darling, don't say that," his mother urged him. "You have a brain it would be a sin to waste. Remember the parable of the talents."

"My brain isn't much, really," he said. Nor was his stubby, plump body. He knew himself, and was willing to leave the aspiring to others; that should make things easy. "Look, I'm willing to work, I want to work. I just don't know at what."

"That was what high school was supposed to tell you," Aunt Esther said. "Which subjects took your fancy? Chemistry? There's a lot of talk about chemistry in this state."

"Accountants," his sister chipped in. "The accountants up at Weidmann pulled down their twenty a week and never got their hands dirty, and skipped out early on Fridays. There's always going to be a need for men who can handle numbers in this society. That's all everything is getting to be, numbers."

Teddy volunteered, "I don't want to sell anything, and I don't want to teach anything."

"Well, that knocks down two big Indians," Aunt Esther dryly commented, taking some satisfaction from the hopelessness of the case.

"And I don't want to *make* anything," he added, thinking of those poor micks and wops and polacks and honkies stuck back in the mills, and their children, his classmates, stunted before they could straighten up, their places at the looms or dye vats all ready for them. Hands rotted, ears deafened, lungs clogged all so Milady could wear a silk ribbon in her hair.

"Well, boop-boop-a-doop," his sister said, with a jab of sarcasm. "You're not leaving much." She had found a job right away, as secretary to one of the two local law firms: Pulsifer, McReady, and Bundy. "How about becoming an airplane pilot?" she joked. "Flying's all the rage. I see where they're talking of carrying the U.S. mails by plane."

He liked something about this suggestion, but not the danger, the terrible height from which one could fall, like that boy in the Greek story the wax in whose wings melted when he got too close to the sun. Teddy was beginning to enjoy this, being at the center of attention, and his power over these women expanding with each negation.

"You've done a nice job in the garden," Aunt Esther offered. "Some of the old farms are turning into nurseries, supplying the landscapers for the estates up north of Wilmington."

"Auto mechanic," the other Esther said, squinting. "You've got the patience—the way you used to put those models together. Automobiles, there's going to be no end of them in this country, they're making paved highways everywhere now. You could eventually own your own garage, like Mr. Schwarzkopf over on Twenty-sixth and Market. He was hiring eight or nine men and had a girl full-time in the office by the time we left."

"Clarence wouldn't want his son under a lot of greasy cars all day, inhaling that unhealthy exhaust," Mother said. "And then it's dangerous—the gasoline explodes."

"I guess that rules that out," Teddy said.

"Well, my goodness, whatever *can* the boy do?" Aunt Esther asked, getting impatient with this game. "He's too fine for this world."

"Back home—I mean in Paterson—I had a paper route, and would get up in the pitch dark, when it was below zero."

"Around here, there's only the weekly, and that doesn't always come out, if Ben Radford has gone on one of his binges. You buy it down at Pursey's store, or not, as you wish. Nothing in it, it seems to me some weeks, but weddings and the tides."

"I don't want to work indoors," Teddy said, trying to help them now, since they were trying to help him.

Young Esther laughed. "That's where the jobs all are, except the brute work you're too swell to do. What a brat, if I may say so. I won't do this, I won't do that. Living off a batch of women."

"Now, now," his mother intervened. "He just needs time to feel his way. Clarence hasn't been dead a year, and we're all still mending."

"No law says you can't work and mend at the same time," remarked Aunt Esther, pushing herself up from the table with her two long hands, which were dotted with little freckles and red sunspots like Father's but without blond hair on the backs. "I hear the cap factory's putting on a second shift. These are boom times, now the Republicans have restored normalcy. Young Theodore, there's no excuse not to find a bit of work somewhere, and better for the spirit too. Maybe," she said, darting her nephew a glance from those cool-blue Wilmot eyes, a shade less milky than Father's, "up at the bottle-cap plant you'd meet a nice Basingstoke girl."

He kept to himself his impression that Basingstoke people were all rubes.

"Oh, Teddy isn't ready for *that,*" Mother said.

"I'd like to know what he *is* ready for," his sister said. She asked him, "Where's your old-fashioned Christian gumption? Don't you have any wish to serve your fellow men?"

"I *do,*" he said, surprising himself. "But I'm only eighteen, what's everybody's hurry? Does everybody have to do *something* all the time? Isn't it enough, sometimes, if you just don't make things any worse?"

"Oh," his mother exclaimed in delight, "I can hear Clarence saying that!"

But Teddy was shamed into enterprise, and in the fall did offer himself at the bottle-cap factory, where they gave him a place on the line, toward the end, watching the machine that applied, with a grid of hollow copper tongues fed from above, water-resistant adhesive to the discs of cork that were inserted, by a host of nimble female hands next down the line, into the river of inverted caps that incessantly spilled onto a broad canvas belt from the machines that printed and stamped and crimped. The glue tended to thicken and harden in the tubes and it was part of his job, at the end of his shift, in the half-hour when the line shut down, to clean the machine with a solvent that would burn his hands if he didn't wear rubber gloves and that in any case scorched his nasal passages and made him dizzy. The noise and monotony and messiness seemed a deliberate attempt, by the forces that had slain his father, to drive him mad. He felt his spiritual being was itself a thin tube filling up with a kind of hardening adhesive. The girls—fat and pasty, most of them—who inserted the cork discs giggled at his clumsiness and the miserable daze he moved through, and disliked his lack of responsiveness during the workday's two fifteen-minute breaks, with their precious opportunities for flirtation. One winter day Teddy was just too sick to get up in time for his shift, and Aunt Esther's doctor when he came—Doc Hedger, who in fair weather still used a horse and buggy to make his calls—could find no name or exact location for the boy's incapacity except a horror of his daily job. To save his health, then, Ted quit.

Always, in that uncertain period, Teddy felt the three women, Mother and the two Esthers, whisperingly conferring about him, seeking with an almost inaudible rustling readjustment of feathers and a steady warmth of daily attendance to make him grow. His sister Esther protected him by persuading the two older women that her brother was too intelligent and sensitive to be cooped up in the bottle-cap factory or indeed any local drudgery. With her own crisp success in the secretarial profession an everyday satisfaction for her, she suggested that, though a liberal-arts college was out of the question, he should be put in possession of enough business skills to find work in an office. He had always done well in school, and his ability to sit an evening through with a book, or contemplating and rearranging one of his collections, when other boys his age were out playing pool or hooting at girls, showed an orderly temperament. He could become an accountant. So, after another summer spent in the asparagus bed, and hiring out as an extra hand with the farmers around Basingstoke when there was a haying to do or berries to pick, Teddy began to go up to Wilmington three times a week by electric streetcar, with a transfer at New Castle, to take courses at O'Connell's School of Practical Business. The institution had been founded so recently that red-faced Mr. O'Connell was still actively in charge. He would walk into a typing class and start bellowing, in synchrony with the teacher but drowning her out, "F, J, G, H; F, J, G, H!" Nothing made him madder than to see discarded paper balled up to be tossed away; it wasted space in the wastepaper baskets and indicated a frivolous attitude. "Rip the paper in half, *once,* once and only once," he would insist in his apoplectic voice, "and *deposit* it so it lies flat in the container." He would demonstrate, tearing a piece of yellow practice paper with a ferocious transfixed expression on his face, and then, in a sudden swoop that made the girls behind the rows of black Remingtons titter, laid the pieces softly to rest in the wire basket. If he could spot the girl who had tittered he came and lowered his red round face close to her. "Business is not basketball," he would tell her, grinding his large square teeth, which reminded Teddy of the teeth of Mr. Dearholt back in Paterson. "Business is not baseball. Business is not *fun.* Business is not"—he would stand erect to deliver this truth to the primarily female class—"a chance to gather and giggle about boys. Business is—and I know you young ladies are all dying to hear this—it is scrupulous method and faithful repetition. Scrupulous method. Faithful repetition! F, J, G, H! D, K, S, L! Fingers curled, wrists flat, back straight! D, K, S, L! L, S, F, J! Aha! Tricked you, didn't I? Pay attention! *Pay attention!*" He seemed for a second to forget what it was they were to pay attention to, and then said, "Anyone I ever see crumpling wastepaper into a little ball, it's out on the street, where they have lots of games! Out on the *streeeet,* and no certificate!"

The school awarded a diploma but also certificates, for individual courses passed. It offered typing, stenography in both Gregg and Pitman systems of shorthand, machine shorthand on the stenotype, filing techniques, and a number of accounting courses, of which double-entry bookkeeping was the basic. Debits on the left, credits on the right, like hot and cold water. A − L = P, for proprietorship or equity. Revenue minus expenses equals profit. One side of a balance sheet must equal the other. It was all tediously, soothingly obvious, until they got to bonds payable, which are long-term liabilities, and in the maze of borrowing and hidden assets and leveraged debt which is the digestive guts of capitalism Teddy began to feel confined and squeezed again, and a little panicky. He began to take the trolley up to Wilmington and not always go to the class; instead he would wander the streets of this tidy city, a kind of daintier Paterson, with more colored citizens, and more colonial buildings of fieldstone and white-painted woodwork, with everything tuned to a slightly smaller scale, or so it appeared to his larger, adult body. As in Paterson, the movie theatres were grouped on a street called Market. There was the Grand, originally the city's opera house, with a ten-thousand-dollar Wurlitzer organ; the Garrick, where Keith vaudeville acts also played; the Rialto, once the Lyric; the Majestic, with its massive marble marquee and Grecian decorations; the Playhouse; the New Arcadia, whose decor included caged canaries and goldfish swimming in a fountain on the way to the balcony; and most sumptuous of all, the Queen, housed within the renovated shell of an old hotel, Clayton House, which had been put out of business by the Hotel du Pont. Seated inside the Queen, Teddy marvelled at the towering proscenium arch, the murals representing Science and Music and Beauty and Sculpture, the Japanese garden forming a backdrop for the stage, and the great gold dome whose concealed electric fixtures illumined walls of bluish gray and ivory and old rose—tints meant, a handout explained, to take you back to the time of the French kings. He had never seen anything in Paterson, even the scrolling Flemish façade of the Post Office, like the vast ethereal sweep of the balcony rail, between the relief-encrusted boxes. There was also, in downtown Wilmington, a theatre for the colored people, called The National, to which whites were admitted, though Teddy never went.

He was not quite the betranced moviegoer his father had been. The speckled and jerky but effulgent flickering that had lifted Clarence Wilmot up from the dark pit into which his life had fallen seemed to his son a bit menacing, an alarming and garish profusion. The motion pictures, all made now in California or Europe, three thousand miles away in one direction or another, embraced the chaos that sensible men and women in their ordinary lives plotted to avoid. Sickeningly, while the audiences around Teddy shrieked with perverse pleasure, and the piano player's fortissimos whipped their frenzy even higher, the figures on the silent screen hurtled to the rim of destruction and beyond. Men in top hats drank and gambled away their fortunes; women in pearls and shimmering dresses threw away their marriages and lives for a moment of white-limbed ecstasy eclipsed by a falling bed curtain; reconstructions of the recent war tossed helmeted actors into the muds of exploding trenches; the misery of an Eskimo in the barren snows of the north was exposed to the camera's stare. Always these films were trying to get you to look over the edge, at something you would rather not see—poverty, war, murder, that thing men and women did when they were alone together. Even the comedies—Teddy sat through them wincing at the brutal slaps and tumbles, the terrifying teetering on the skyscraper ledge by the nice man in the straw hat and big glasses. There was something sinister about these constant clowns—the college boy with the straw hat; the man whose expression never changed however wildly his legs were churning; the little tramp with the white face, unreal square mustache, dusty bowler hat, and big floppy shoes. When Chaplin smiled, it was a nervous worried smile. No wonder, when his film life was a constant barrage of miscues and misunderstandings, pennilessness, police harassment, frantic chases, and failures to get the girl. It was all more depressing than funny, except for the rapidity with which one peril and misapprehension succeeded another, giving these sad-eyed men no rest, subjecting them to fresh bouts of abuse and punishment and frustration while the audience around Teddy incomprehensibly howled with laughter. Well, comprehensibly—these apparitions in their baggy clothes and flattened hats acted out our nightmares, and in burlesquing them momentarily banished them. But the nightmares were accurate enough: we are like a swarm of mosquitoes, crazy with thirst and doomed to be swatted. Life was endlessly cruel, and there was nobody above to grieve—Father had proved that. And life's central event, propelling men and women through their days and nights, was an unthinkable collision of slimy, hairy parts that should be kept forever hidden. The cinema wished to leave nothing hidden, to throw nakedness up on the screen, and grief, and fistfights and explosions and violence, and even corpses and monsters, played by Lon Chaney. Terror would attack Teddy even in the middle of hilarious and romantic sequences, as he realized that these bright projections were trying to distract him from the leaden reality beneath his seat, underneath the theatre floor. Death and oblivion were down there, waiting for the movie to be over. Not so, these movies tried to say. Life was not serious; it was an illusion, a story, distracting and disturbing but at bottom painless and merciful. These familiar stars, who suffered and died on the screen yet returned a month or two later differently costumed but unchanged—the man with round pleased-with-himself cheeks who was always leaping off parapets and sliding down banisters and slashing Z's in men's chests with a rapier; the woman with curly hair who was always playing children, even a boy child and his mother at the same time; the stern-faced thin-lipped man with slicked hair who dressed up as a sheik and matador and gigolo (evidently a man whom women paid to make love to them, you didn't see too many of those in Paterson or Wilmington); the bald German with the monocle that the audience hissed when he appeared on the screen in his uniform or tuxedo—these stars led up there a life that was always renewed, movie to movie, without permanent harm, whereas Teddy knew that harm was permanent. The reel of your real life unwound only once. And now the sordidness of illusion was leaking out of Hollywood itself, with the Fatty Arbuckle murder trials, and the murder of the director William Desmond Taylor, an unsolved mystery which touched on Mary Pickford's rival Mary Miles Minter and even on Pickford herself. "America's Sweetheart" was no angel, as the public had learned with Pickford's cynical Nevada divorce and her unseemly rapid marriage to Douglas Fairbanks. Behind the screen's glowing, preachy outpour were orgies of sin like none seen since Nero's Rome.

"How many more certificates you want, for cry-eye?" his sister asked impatiently one day, in Aunt Esther's seldom-used living room, the September after President Harding died on his way back from Alaska, amid disclosures that his friend Mr. Fall had been cheating on the sale of public oil lands. The diagnosis given was cerebral apoplexy but Teddy knew Harding had really died of a broken heart, as President Wilson had done, and Father. His sister's blue squint had lately grown narrower and had a kind of cutting brightness, there under the bangs of her close-cropped red-tinged hair. It had been bobbed and rinsed with henna. She smoked right in the house now, and wore a lot of bangle bracelets that rattled on her skinny freckled arms. There had been some disturbance or scandal, of which he had heard only whispering and tears in this women's house, concerning an attachment she had formed with Mr. Bundy, of Pulsifer, McReady, and Bundy. He was married and, it seemed, after some indecision, intended to remain so. Esther would probably have to quit her job, to avoid a scandal, and there was talk of her going back to Paterson, or to New York, or Philadelphia, or even out west. She was fed up, and seemed to be tackling Teddy as a piece of unfinished business she should clean up before she went away.

"Well, I don't know. Mr. O'Connell—he's scary until you realize he thinks he's being funny—took me aside and told me if I came full-time and took a slew of other stuff I could get his diploma, maybe even by next June."

"Come on, he's just trying to milk more money out of us, for a diploma no company gives a damn about. It's not like his little outfit was the Wharton School or something; O'Connell just trains the field hands. You've learned all you're going to learn, is my guess."

"Well, it wasn't my idea to be an accountant."

He didn't say that it had been hers. Nor did she say that she was in Basingstoke, partly at least, because of him. He had begged her to come down here to the middle of nowhere, where everybody's idea of a good time was a Presbyterian or Methodist church supper and the only moving-picture house in town, on top of the Oddfellows' Hall, had shows only on Friday and Saturday nights and the nearest roadhouse where you could get a drink or dance was ten miles away and the only man who took an interest in her was married. Father had been too high-minded for the ministry, and Esther was too high-spirited for Basingstoke. She was twenty-eight, dangerously close to thirty, and was getting tougher-looking, her lips ever thinner behind the lipstick and the line of her jaw more set. Still, she didn't seem too mad at him. "So—any ideas, big boy?" He was not big, only five eight, but he had filled in; the farm work he did to bring in some summer money had thickened his arms and squared his shoulders.

He squirmed and said, "Yeah, well, I've been asking around, but there really isn't much except the bottle-cap factory, and the foreman remembers how I quit after just two months on the line. That's about the only place that's big enough so the owner can't do his own accounting in the back room one night a week, and up in Wilmington the thing of it is, men who know how to type and do Gregg aren't really what the bosses want—it's a woman's job. They aren't comfortble dictating to men. Men they think of as salesmen or engineers."

"So, now you want to go to engineering school? Don't ask, Ted. You ask Mom, she's such a saint she'll try to send you, even if she goes blind taking in sewing."

"I don't want to go to engineering school. I've had enough school." His face had heated; she was making him blush.

"Maybe Jared could chip in. He seems to be doing all right, from the way he dresses and that Maxwell he drives, though he's darn mysterious about it."

"I said, I don't want to go. I like it here."

"I'll be swiggered, frankly, if I know why—it's been three years and you don't seem to know a soul."

"Basingstoke kids are all snobs and rubes."

"You got to learn to get out there and mix it up, buddy. Even if you get your knees skinned, mix it up. You're as bad as Pop, wanting to hide in his office all day. Scared of life, happy to die."

But they were all, all four residents of this house, scared of life, it seemed to Ted. Aunt Esther years ago, after Horace had left her, had hung out an Overnight Visitors sign and fixed up two bedrooms with a bathroom between them at the back of the second floor, but few people came, and when they did come they tended to be noisy and unsavory—couples up to no good, a gimcrack wedding ring on the girlie's finger, or old travelling salesmen smelling of whiskey and weariness. They wouldn't have stopped if they weren't looking for a bargain or a hiding place. Once there were two pairs of dark-suited men who had to be bootleggers, scouting the territory for a smuggling point. The world beyond Basingstoke was becoming faster and more hellbent on city pleasures and at the same time more desperate. Gangsters were killing each other, and people were doing dance marathons, and the German mark was worth four trillion to the dollar. Wilson must have been right: the Allies should have been nicer to the Germans.

"If you don't know anybody, they'll only hire you to be a slave," Teddy told his sister. "I'm beginning to understand what the workers in Paterson were so sore about."

She laughed. "And you've learned without even having to go to work yourself!"

This wasn't fair; she had forgotten his paper route, and the way it had cost him a chance to be on the baseball team. After a version of their conversation was relayed to the two older women, Mother told him, at the supper table one night when Esther was out on a rendez-vous, "Teddy, you should begin to go to church again. That's where all the respectable people are, the ones who might have jobs to give. Thanks to our friends in Avon Presbyterian I have more sewing and mending to do than I can rightly keep up with. It's almost getting to be a curse; I have to keep getting stronger prescriptions in my glasses. And there are some very pretty young ladies in our choir, too. The good people in Basingstoke don't *know* you, Teddy. I can't tell you how often people ask about you—they see you out walking, you see, but you never come to gatherings. You seem stand-offish. To them you're a bit of a mystery man. The young ladies, especially, ask after you."

This sweetly intoned speech had been long pent-up, with its several plaintive elements. "Mother," he said, having rehearsed firmness on this score, "I'm sorry, but I will not go to the Presbyterian church. Or any church."

Stella sighingly turned to her sister-in-law, explaining, not for the first time, "That's his way of being loyal to Clarence. But I know your father"—turning back to her son—"never meant those who could gain comfort to stay away. He had just reached a point in his life when he couldn't carry the torch for a whole congregation. If he hadn't been stricken down, I'm sure he would have recovered his beliefs. There were signs, in some of the last conversations we had. When I talked about the Heaven to come, he listened real sharp. He as good as said to me, 'Don't let the children fall away. Especially Teddy; he's the one that needs it most. He's such a sensitive, fearful child.' "

"Mother, please. You're fantasizing." It was a word he had just learned, in a book called *The Mind in the Making,* by James Harvey Robinson. "I was the one who used to go in and read the paper to him, and he never said anything of the sort to me."

"Well, he wouldn't. That wasn't Clarence's way, to be bossy like that. And his voice was entirely gone, there at the end."

"I love you dearly, all three of you," Teddy managed to bring out, "but you're not going to get me to go sing the praises of God, after what He did to Father."

Aunt Esther said primly, "Some would say God did nothing to Clarence. If there was any doing, it was the other way around. My brother turned and ran from the Light, is the sad truth of it."

"The sad truth of it is," Teddy said, with a surge of manly spirit that won his opponents' approval, even as he sought to vanquish them, "you two are a hundred years behind the times. Read some Mencken. Read some Shaw. Read some Bertrand Russell, even." In his room on the third floor, alone night after night, he read, preferring the briskly rational, amusing English to the American authors, who wrote about self-help and mental health and dreary Main Streets.

Aunt Esther said, "We once went to a Shaw play up at the old Lyceum in Wilmington, before they changed its name to the Empire and it burned down. I couldn't exactly follow all the ins and outs of it, but it seemed to come down square on the side of the Salvation Army. He used to read Mencken now and then in the Baltimore *Sun,* and it would make him boil for days." They all knew that by "he" she meant the unmentionable Horace, who had also been half of the "we."

"He calls us all the booboisie," Aunt Esther said, now meaning Mencken. "Well, for all of me he's welcome to his smart set. Let alone what comes after, those folks aren't even happy now—you can tell by the way they poison themselves with rotgut liquor."

Teddy felt sorry for Mother, her loving intentions being swept aside. "Mother," he said, "I love church people," and touched her hand, lying plump and defeated on the lace tablecloth, a wrinkled widow's hand, with one fingertip whitened and shrunk from always wearing a thimble. "They're the salt of the earth. It's just after what Father went through . . ."

"What he put us through," she amended, in listless accusation.

"Like it or not, we all must belong somewheres," his aunt said, "or a person's not a person. Nobody makes it alone."

Teddy had a taste of the floating sensation Father must have had when he realized there was nowhere in mankind where he any longer fit—all around him, smooth surfaces without a niche or handhold. And yet Teddy liked people, even the dumb fat girls on the bottle-cap line and the ferret-faced little Wilmington student stenographers. He was happiest among people, if they weren't crowding him. He loved them but he had to have the right distance.

"Last night at Bible study I heard tell Seth Addison down at the drug store's looking for a young man," Aunt Esther said, out of the blue, but with the smirk of a timely release. "Wouldn't hurt if the fellow knew a bit about keeping records, though the main thing would be the soda fountain. Seth's had trouble: if the boy's too young, all his friends pile in and expect to sneak free sodas, and all the fancy concoctions they can dish up now from behind the counter—it gets to be a party. Somebody a little older and not too popular might just fit the bill. No harm in presenting yourself, Theodore, if you don't think you want to keep riding the trolley car back up to O'Connell this fall. Tell Seth you're Esther Truitt's nephew; he and his wife Amy and Horace and I used to go out crabbing when we first moved here, back in ought-eight, in old Noah Watson's orange dory. Mention old Noah to him—only one I ever knew who could get Seth to loosen up."

Addison's Drug Store—Tobacco, Perfumes, and Sundries—was at the center of town, where Rodney Street, curving a bit to parallel the river's curve, made a T with Elm. Across the street stood the slate-shingled business block in two-tone brick, four doorways long and four stories high, that held Pursey's Notions and Variety Store and Krauthammer's Hardware and Seeds, with a barber shop and a dry cleaner in between. The drug store's big plate window displayed above a pyramid of sun-faded goods two ornamental suspended globes, one holding iodine-red fluid and the other a blue liquid like watered-down ink. Entered by a door cut into the corner, the store had a magazine rack to the left of the door and on the two sides to the right a series of five-foot slant-faced display cases; attached to the case holding cigars and snuffs and cigarettes, a little flaming gas jet was cupped in chrome; the flame was lit at seven-thirty in the morning, when the store opened, and turned off at nine at night, when it closed. There was also, screwed into the wood like a pencil sharpener, a cigar cutter—a miniature guillotine where children were always wanting to insert their fingers. The cases at a right angle, across from the soda-fountain counter with its revolving stools, held candies and boxes of chocolates and also perfumes, which were kept in large glass-stoppered bottles usually dispensed, into little vials, by Mrs. Amy Addison; she, a wispy, iron-haired woman of non-committal comportment, was in and out of the store all day, as her domestic duties permitted, since women coming into a drug store on a matter of delicacy would rather consult another woman. The soda fountain was a new thing, installed in 1919; the therapeutic effects of soda water had been long advertised, but with the enactment of Prohibition there arose a need in towns all across the country for a place where law-abiding people could come in and sit on a stool and put their elbows up.

At the back, beyond an area of the floor given over to round tables and wire chairs, up one step on a kind of platform, was the pharmacy itself; here Seth Addison and his assistant pharmacist, Charlie Wainwright, performed their mysteries of measurement and dispensation, pulverization and tincture, rolling as many as six or seven powdered herbs and chemicals into pills or dissolving them in diluted alcohol to become "tonics," behind a high counter that hid all but their faces—the top of Mr. Addison's head bald and gleaming and that of his young black-haired assistant shining with brilliantine as they nodded and bobbed at their tasks. Behind them receded into shadows three sets of shelves crowded with potions new and old, some of them as ancient as Hostetter's Celebrated Stomach Bitters, Lydia Pinkham's Herb Medicine, and Dr. Kilmer's Ocean-weed Perfect Blood Purifier Heart Remedy. Beyond the shelves, Teddy in his capacity as employee soon discovered, lay a small room with a worn leather couch and cupboards full of mysterious metal harness where Mr. Addison fitted people with trusses, and a larger room where empty cartons were kept and full ones waited to be unpacked and their contents marked with price labels. Down a brief hall lit by the dimmest and dustiest of bulbs was a tiny brown-stained washbasin and toilet with a wobbly seat for the employees' use and a back door exiting into the glare of a small dirt parking lot, where Seth Addison parked his Packard and Charlie Wainwright his Ford flivver, and the pebble-strewn back street called Fishery Way, though nobody knew quite where the fishery had once been, back in colonial times. The drug store was comforting in its abundance, its stocks of head anointments from Tulepo Hair Restorer and Dandruff Cure (with a haunting insignia, of a profiled woman whose long hair was twisted to form the horns of a crescent moon) to Wildroot Cream Oil and Fitch's Shampoo, its foot-soothers from Fairyfoot (Stops Bunion Pain) to Dr. Scholl's variously shaped pads mounted on yellow cardboard, and its solemn ministering to the nether parts with Ex-Lax and sanitary napkins and belts and red rubber douche syringes, anti-itch powders and—a new thing—Trojan prophylactics, made in New Jersey and stored well out of sight, in their little tins like those that housed Zymole Trochees. They were available only to those men of a sufficiently adult age who, gathering up their courage, murmuringly requested them. The customers blushed but Teddy soon learned not to; his face as he waited to hear their requests remained as astutely blank as a lawyer's.

Whatever physical puritanism he had inherited was worn away by the passage of enough creams and palliatives, pastes and plasters through his hands. He was allowed sometimes to make the suppositories, in a black-painted cast-iron machine whose handle you turned like a vise while the suppository wax, based on cocoa butter and mixed by Mr. Addison, was forced into bullet-shaped chambers; when summer temperatures rose to body heat, however, the wax melted, as it was supposed to, and could be firmed up enough to shape only by holding a bag of cracked ice to the top of the machine, as if the machine had a headache. The poor hot, semi-liquid, ailment-prone human body stood exposed, scattered and flayed, all about Teddy in these walls of multicolored packages that in sum would erase every blemish, ease every pain, satisfy every need, cleanse every cavity. Olivilo Soap 7¢, Marrow's Boudoir Talc 52¢, Sodiphene 21¢, Terra-Derma Laxative 89¢, Ever Ready Shaving Brush 49¢, Ovaltine 42¢. There was much here, too, for the healthy: cigars behind glass with all their pomp of label and gilt and tinted views of Cuba and Spain; candy and chewing gum, Life Savers and Black Jack and Chiclets and Baby Ruths and

Whitman's Sampler's boxes of chocolates; soaps from Ivory, which was $99\frac{44}{100}\%$ pure, to Lava, which scoured away grease with a stony abrasion, to the ferocious 29-Mule Team Borax; and magazines, on a rack just beside the diagonal entrance, *Liberty* and *Collier's* and the *Post* and *Ladies' Home Journal* and *McClure's* with their eager female faces glistening on the covers, all piling in from New York and Philadelphia in glossy slip-knotted bundles heavier than any he had had to shoulder in the days of delivering the Paterson *Morning Call.* These magazines had the fresh smell of slick quality paper, and in the idle troughs of the day, mid-morning and mid-afternoon before school let out, he would take one behind the soda fountain and leaf through the pages, admiring the advertisements for fancy electrical appliances and looking at the illustrations of ideal families—ideal except for the one small, never irremediable mishap which the story described—and the cartoons, most of which he "got." These magazines emanated from a remote height of human sophistication and glamour, from those aspiring Manhattan towers you could see in silhouette from Garrett Mountain, and there was something wonderfully gracious and kind about their descending upon a town like Basingstoke, where otherwise people would know nothing except what the local parsons and county politicians told them. The movies were like that, too, showing up at the little local Bijou upstairs in the Oddfellows' building, and now there was the radio, which broadcast mostly music in the evenings—dance music by the orchestras of Meyer Davis and Elmer Grosso, harmonica players and birdsong imitators—but also baseball scores and market reports and weather forecasts and nature stories by Thornton W. Burgess read aloud. He had been begging Aunt Esther and Mother to get a crystal set. Mr. Addison had one in the back room he used as an office, and when Teddy worked to nine o'clock three times a week he could hear its crackling musical whisper as he moved around in the store, much as he used to hear the neighbors' phonographs back on Twenty-seventh Street. "Indian Love Call,"

"Somebody Loves Me," "Fascinating Rhythm," "I Want to Be Happy": those were the hits, sung by men with reedy, solemn, bleating voices and women with tiny, bouncy voices squeezed out through the nose, like they were deep in some smoky speakeasy. How did those glowing tubes pick them out of the air like that? How come you didn't feel these invisible radio waves pass through you? The Basingstoke post office, a narrow half of a small brick building in the block of Rodney beyond Elm, also had a radio in it, somewhere on the other side of the grated window where Mr. Horley sat. The postmaster had a hunched, buckled, grimy look, a pencil behind his ear and lots of nostril hair, and he wore old-fashioned striped shirts with sleeve garters, under a gray-blue vest that seemed to be, winter and summer, his uniform. He kept his radio turned to staticky, inaudible ships out in the ocean or the two great bays that surrounded the Delmarva Peninsula. Until late afternoon, that was all that was on. Still, Teddy, doing the daily mail run for the drug store, liked to linger and listen, in case a ship suddenly started to sink like the *Titanic* or the *Lusitania,* with an SOS sent out by a brave radio operator up to his knees in sloshing bile-green water.

There was a tranced rhythm to the day that ate up the years. Mornings in Addison's were a rushed time, with the papers from Wilmington and Baltimore having arrived and working people of Basingstoke settling at all the stools for a hurried coffee and fresh doughnut or raisin bun from Mrs. Brindley's Bakery down the street, and then there was a slackening off, the customers mostly female shoppers doing their rounds of the downtown, and then a lunch flurry, when the schoolkids stoked up on candy bars and ice-cream cones, and then, until school let out, a long lull, in which Teddy sometimes felt his entire life draining from him, without any raise or change of prospect. The ice slowly melting in the cold chests that kept the ice cream firm audibly dripped away into the pans underneath, next to the canisters of pressurized carbon dioxide for the sodas and nitrous oxide for the whipped cream.

When Charlie Wainwright went off to be the head druggist for a new Rexall's in Dover, Mr. Addison asked Teddy if he had ever thought of going to pharmaceutical school, but Teddy couldn't face another spell of riding the interurban electric cars up to Wilmington, or of begging the tuition from the women he lived with. Aunt Esther had been having some problems with her health—nervous complaints, Doc Hedger called them, though they kept her up all night, going to the bathroom. Mother could only do so much sewing without blinding herself, and her attempts to train an assistant ended when the girl got pregnant or proved hopelessly unable to absorb the meticulous ethics of dressmaking—"I declare," she once said, "they just don't make girls as conscientious as they used to; all they want is to get off work and dance and drink and ride in roadsters. Whatever happened to old-fashioned right"—*raaaht*—"from wrong?" In turning Mr. Addison down, Teddy had forever diminished, he knew, his value in his eyes, just as he had with the baseball coach at Paterson High. Teddy wondered if his entire life was to consist of guarded refusals. In America opportunity doesn't keep knocking. His sister, who never did leave Pulsifer, McReady, and Bundy, since her quitting would have seemed to confirm the rumors about her and Mr. Bundy, pulled a surprise in 1925, the summer when everybody was interested in the Scopes trial down in Tennessee. She and Peter Pulsifer—not Bundy, who hadn't been ready, or McReady—were going to get married, as soon as he could divorce his wife. In the meantime, to get away from the scandal, she was moving to New York, to stay with Jared and *his* wife, Lucille, the pert slim platinum-blonde daughter of the man he used to collect rents for, who was now very big in the realty *and* investment businesses. She had come down to Basingstoke to meet the family but the newlyweds hadn't been able to stay the night. "Blonde with black-Irish roots," had been Aunt Esther's dry remark after they had left.

"How do you know," Teddy asked Sister Esther, "Pulsifer'll hold to his promise and go through with the divorce?"

Always, he felt how dangerous adult life was, how fraught with gambles that could go sour.

"Well," she said, and squinted through a plume of smoke from her new brand, Chesterfields, "if he doesn't, I'll have some new information. I can't stay another day in that office; Frank Bundy keeps looking daggers at me, as if I'm the one who weaseled out. The sap. He had his chance."

"But what will you *do* in New York?"

"I don't know—go to shows and museums. Sit in Washington Square and write po-ems. Jared says they'll take me to all their favorite dives. He and Lucille have an apartment right on Fifth Avenue with four bedrooms—I can stay as long as I like. I need a dose of them bright white lights, Tedsy. Hey—I never said I'd stay down here forever. You're pretty well settled in, isn't that so? I got you through the transition, right?"

"Right," he said bravely. "It's just—Mother and Aunt Esther are getting *old.* You were the only live wire around here. You were the only one I could talk to."

"Find someone else, then. It's not so hard. Hell, you're twenty-two going on eighty-two—what's happened to your glands?"

She had a way of making him blush. "Nothing's happened, but to the proper girls around here, I'm just the soda jerk. And if I got a serious girl, wouldn't it upset Mom?"

"*Au contraire,* kid. What do you think, everybody in Missouri was an immaculate conception? She wants *fam*ily. Loosen up. Start going to church socials, or something."

"Church doesn't agree with me. You know that."

She hesitated a second, without a ready answer for once. "Church is where the action is, in a one-horse burg like this. Lick 'em or join 'em's the way I see it." She shrugged. "Suit yourself. I got enough mess living my own life. Maybe you're right—sit tight and wait for the undertaker." And with these breezy words she leaned forward, there in Aunt Esther's gloomy kitchen, with its ceiling of brown-painted pressed tin, and gave her younger brother a hard little kiss on his broad forehead, with her thin painted lips.

It did seem the world was turning sexier. In the movies, the Mack Sennett girls showed more and more leg in their bathing suits, and there were "vamps" played by foreign actresses with names like Pola Negri. In the real world the young women were called "flappers" wearing just little slips for dresses and doing a wild dance called the Charleston. Some guys in the drug store the other day had gone up to Philadelphia to see a burlesque star called Carrie Finnel, who twirled tassels from her breasts and buttocks. Only they didn't call them breasts and buttocks. The country's tough, "fast" currents were picked up by the young set around Basingstoke—the girls in their tubular little dresses and rolled stockings, the guys in their white wide-bottomed ducks. Teddy marvelled that even the children of people working at the bottle-cap factory were able to buy the clothes that imitated the rich youth of Long Island and Chicago and Grosse Pointe. Hungover on bathtub gin, Basingstoke's young blades would come in in the morning for bicarbs and Pepto-Bismol at the counter, and the young women, desperately conferring with Mrs. Addison over by the perfumes, looking to erase the possibility of a pregnancy contracted in a drunken daze. Working in the drug store was like standing on the corner of Rodney and Elm watching the town's woes go by. Tremulous and breathing hard and blue around the edges, the old came in and took away digitalis for their hearts. The young mothers came in and purchased milk of magnesia to speed up their kids' bowels and paregoric to slow them down. The middle-aged bought iron and liver extract for pep and bromides and barbiturates to settle their nerves. Morphine and aspirin eased pain. Cough syrup loosened catarrh and soothed sore throat. Ipecac got you to vomit. Colchicum cured or at least discouraged gout, iodine goiter, insulin diabetes, quinine malaria, Salvarsan syphilis, and vitamin C scurvy. But the last three were rare in Basingstoke.

Belladonna, sassafras bark, sarsaparilla root, cascara, mentholatum, antiphlogistene, Seidlitz powders, Rochelle salts, vegetable simples by the dozen—it was hard to say if any of it really worked. The purpose was to make people feel attention was being paid and something was being tried. Aunt Esther's Doc Hedger had a standard prescription he had made a rubber stamp for—Elixir of I, Q, and S, which consisted of minute amounts of iron, quinine, and strychnine dissolved in an alcohol solution about as strong as bourbon whiskey. It was the alcohol that probably did the good. Life basically had to be endured. Nature fought for you until it turned against you.

Among the chronic customers Teddy began to notice, in the damp, late-arriving spring of 1926, a newcomer to town, a lame girl who generally appeared in the drug store under her father's protection. He was a tobacco farmer who had sold his acres near Lewes and moved to Basingstoke to buy the old Culver greenhouse two blocks along on Fishery Way, with half its windows broken from all the years when Jake Culver was drinking himself to death after his boys declined to come back to Delaware after serving in the Army overseas. Teddy had lived in Basingstoke five years now and knew most of what happened in town, from conversations at the post office or at the soda-fountain counter. It was a pretty sight to see the new panes of glass filling in the greenhouse's rusty iron ribs, though everybody agreed the town never could and never would support a flower business. The answer to that was that Daniel Sifford didn't need the money; he had made a killing selling to a real-estate speculator seeing a great future, comparable to the southern-Jersey resorts, for the area around Rehoboth Beach. Sifford wanted the greenhouse, and the two acres and 1880 farmhouse that went with it, as a hobby, to keep his hand in the dirt. He was a big-boned shambling man whose clothes hung on him like bib overalls; his face was so creased it looked to be in overlapping pieces, as in some breeds of dog. There was a wife, but she never came into the drug store, and was hardly seen out of the house at all—just sometimes hanging out wash in the yard and scuttering away if anybody looked like they might try to talk to her. For children there were only the lame girl, and a much older boy who had gone west somewhere, Indiana or Nebraska, where the farmland was sold six hundred forty acres at a time.

The girl dressed in a slightly off-key way, by Basingstoke standards—a little too fancily for everyday some days, her hair done up behind in an old-fashioned ribbon, and then on other days too plain, with potting soil besmirching her gingham dress and her stockings speckled with bits of mulching hay. She had to order a new leg brace and orthopedic shoe, a high-top with built-up sole, through the drug store, and it had to be sent back to an address in Camden several times before it fit well enough to satisfy Doc Hedger. She had fallen into his hands, and the prescriptions of his that she brought in—APC, morphine sulfate, rubbing alcohol, pain-easing liniments—told a sad story of discomfort that her lovely clear eyes and cheerful factual manner concealed. Her eyes had bigger whites than those of ordinary girls: they were like the eyes of the movie stars Gloria Swanson or Lillian Gish on posters outside the Roxie, an every-day-but-Sunday, specially built movie theatre, with long blank brick sides and a triangular marquee, that had replaced the Bijou upstairs at the Oddfellows' Hall. Her figure was countryish and plump but her skin had an unblemished satin luster, as if all the suffering and embarrassment of her deformed right foot had made her spirit glow just as preachers say suffering does. Having studied the exact measurements of her brace and special shoe on their way back and forth to Camden gave Teddy a curious intimacy with her that he was surprised she didn't feel reciprocally. He knew her name, from the drug-store records: Emily Jeanette Sifford. She was very shy but had a soft spot for ice-cream sodas with a scoop of butter-pecan ice cream. When she was sitting at the counter with her plump white forearms and pink elbows dimly reflected in the veined green marble, one of her hard-working little hands, the fingernails outlined in dark dirt from helping her father in the greenhouse, would brush back a strand of her fine brown hair—hair so fine the individual hairs straying from her ribbon seemed colorless—away from her face as her puckered lips pushed forward around the straw, slightly greedy, sucking with a subdued gurgle the last bit of soda before digging at the ice cream with the long silver spoon. She wore no make-up. She had pretty well discounted herself as a courtable female. Her manner was short on airs and graces. When she finished the soda she would wipe her knuckle across her lips and stare out with a blank, almost burpy look of satisfaction and he would see that indeed, compared with the shimmery hard women dancing across the movie screen and the Wilmington society pages, she was plain and bland. A high forehead, and a bit of a double chin, young as she was. But then her eyes might light on him, sensing his staring; their blue was not milky or icy like that of Wilmot eyes but velvety, a somehow flowering, layered blue, taking green from the countertop and sparkle from the scintillating fixtures and products and advertisements that cluttered the soda fountain. There was a mirror behind him which reflected the customers, wherein she could see herself and the back of his head. "That was right good," she said one day, when there was no one else at the counter.

"What was?" he responded, startled, though he had overheard her slow, careful, down-home voice before, in conference with Mr. Addison and her father. It might have been the slowness that made everything she said sound musical.

"The soda. You cook up a good ice-cream soda."

"Well, I been at it a while," he said, feeling clumsy, in his soiled white jacket imitating that of a real druggist. Mr. Addison wanted him to wear it because the white outfit made people feel they were in a clean, germ-free place; but then he was too cheap to get it laundered often enough, so it looked toward the end of the week like Teddy was wearing a wiping rag. "There's no big trick to it," he said. More seemed required. "The banana split, now, that takes something, and even a chocolate sundae, so it looks like the pictures they give you." With a jerk of his head he indicated the stand-up cardboard advertisements behind him, propped up in front of the mirror, supplied by the ice-cream company, in full and tempting color, of the structures—boats, mock-mountains, snowman-shapes—that could be made with ice cream and whipped cream and crushed nuts and chocolate and caramel syrups. "You should try a banana split sometime," Teddy said, beginning to blush as he felt his topic dwindle under him.

She felt it too, and reverted to his first statement. "How long a while?"

This was 1926. The year he quit going up to Wilmington to business school, President Harding died; then the next summer President Coolidge's sixteen-year-old, Calvin Coolidge, Jr., died, so the whole nation was supposed to mourn; and the third summer Scopes was found guilty of teaching evolution and fined a hundred dollars but the famous witness and speechifier against him, William Jennings Bryan, right away upped and died. So much for defending the Lord's Word. "Three years," Teddy admitted. She was looking at him so curiously that he joked nervously, "It beats making bottle caps." This was a local saying, invoked whenever any dubious activity was questioned.

Surprisingly, this lame girl from below the canal stiffened a bit on her stool and pronounced in a voice faintly pugnacious, "Well, it's not for me to say, but I would think a nice clever good-looking man like you could find something more challenging to your talents than making banana splits that look like the pictures on cardboard."

Clever? Good-looking? Man? But all he said, stung, was, "Oh, yeah?" He went on, "That may be right, but who says it's for you to say? I don't see you doing much, except poking in your old man's greenhouse dirt."

As if conjured up, her father in his saggy gray clothes appeared at the entry door between the magazines and the cigar case; she slid from the stool with an offended face and tried to glide, suppressing her limp, out the door, leaving two dimes behind on the green-marble counter.

That was probably that. She didn't come in for days, but he didn't see how she could escape seeing him forever, the town being so small, and the greenhouse just two blocks away. Several times he walked home to Willow Street by way of the greenhouse, and failed to see her. As casually as possible he asked his mother at supper, "You know that man Sifford, who bought the Culver greenhouse?"

"Why, no, Teddy dear, I don't believe I do. My steps don't often take me up Fishery Way."

"I thought maybe from church, or something. . . ."

"He hasn't shown his face in the Presbyterian church, of that I am sure. What is it you were wanting to know, darling?"

"Oh, nothing."

There was a pause while she tapped out, without asking, another spoonful of mashed sweet potatoes onto his plate. "Perhaps your Aunt Esther would know what you want to know. When you take her chocolate pudding up, you can ask her."

Aunt Esther spent much of her day in bed. Doc Hedger couldn't put a name to her illness, but its stubbornness made his bald head shake to itself as he would come down the stairs. His cheeks wobbled, his watch chain swung across the belly-swag of his dark-blue vest, and the shiny black shoes on his feet seemed to have more creases than anyone else's shoes. Aunt Esther's room was getting to smell like the back shelves of the drug store, of camphor and crystallizing old syrups, mixed with a sorrowful musty human scent that was her body. But she had recently installed an upstairs telephone, in the most modern black Bakelite style, and there it sat on her bedside table, next to her boxes of Blaud's Pills and Eskay's Neuro-phosphates for Nerves, like a thick flower, a black daffodil, its bell to talk into facing her thin yellow head, which was propped up close by on three pillows. "Methodists," she said. "Those Siffords go over to the Methodist church. He goes alone, never brings his wife. The older boy headed west, and then there's the unfortunate girl. They're not what you'd call jolly people."

He asked her his question, and like his mother she looked sharp and asked him, "Now why would you want to know?"

"No reason. I see her hobbling into the store with her dad, getting her medicine and braces. I guess I feel sorry for her."

"Don't feel too sorry. Her dad got a pretty penny for his land, nobody knows just how much." The invalid thinned her lips and answered his question: "Some say it happened in the womb, but others say the mother is a tippler and dropped her as an infant. The mother is certainly strange, keeping to her yard and staying upstairs when anybody comes to the door. Whatever happened to the girl, it happened a while ago, and I suppose she's resigned."

When Emily came into the drug store next, she didn't look so resigned. She sat up to the counter and without a word of hello said, "In response to your rude remark, about digging in my father's dirt, our cases are not parallel. You're a man, I'm a woman. A man has to go out into the world. A woman doesn't have to do anything, except what men tell her to do."

A woman. Innocent and unkempt as she looked, she had men and women on the mind. He perceived that one way she had developed to cope with her lame leg was to say provoking things that showed she didn't care for your opinion. He was not as taken aback as he might have been with somebody else, figuring this was her style. He said, "Being a woman is that bad, huh? Anyway, I'm sorry if I hurt your feelings. You poke around in whatever dirt you want."

"That's rude, too."

"Well, Jeez. You're not so easy to talk to, it turns out."

This made her smile—a quick dimpling in the softness next to the corner of her mouth, a slight pinching shut of her lids over her eyes with their vivid whites. "Did you think I would be?"

"I guess I did. Foolish me. I must have been dreaming."

Another customer sat down at the counter, taking his attention, and then a third, and by the time he returned to her the tulip dish that had held her pistachio ice cream was melted down to a pale-green stain at the bottom and she was gone. A dime on the counter dismissed him. After a week of her not appearing he wondered if the Siffords were using the other drug store in town, the Liggett's across the street and one block up toward the tannery ruin. Liggett's shaved a penny or two off most items but the floorspace was half that Addison's had, with nothing like the selection of cigars and magazines. Addison's stocked the newest magazines—*Time* and *Reader's Digest* and even *The American Mercury,* which was said to be radical and God-mocking. People were always sneakily turning it in the rack so you couldn't see the cover, but Teddy would turn the copies right side out. He liked Mencken, as the closest thing America had to Shaw and Wells.

One of the days when he got off work at five-thirty he walked home to Willow Street by way of Fishery Way, along the alley past its garages built of concrete blocks imitating real stone with the same rock-rough shape out of a mold, over and over, and its gun shop emitting the sound of grinding and the smell of hot metal. It was fall in Delaware, with a harder drier sparkle on the blue tidal stretches of the Avon and the marsh grass turning the color of an orange tomcat and the trees overhead yielding up chlorophyll. Parched leaves littered the lawns, which except where watered by a fanatic householder or directly over a septic tank had given up growing, becoming as flat and dry as dusty carpet—a matted look that merged in Ted's mind with the chirring of cicadas, a song that crept upon the later summer as the sound of peepers crept upon the spring. All the panes of glass in the rusty greenhouse frames had been replaced, and spattered inside with a kind of whitewash, so it was not easy to look in. Hanging across the alley by one of those fake-stone garages, near an oil drum that had been punctured to be somebody's burning barrel, Teddy studied the flickers of activity behind the spattered panes, and decided that the dark flickers were the father and two hired Negro helpers. The pale pieces of cloth that came and went with surprising nimbleness were Emily. Emily Jeanette. Her name in his mouth, even when he didn't speak it, was like one of those mentholated cough-drop lozenges that fill your mouth with an almost painful fullness of taste. Yet she was two unfortunate things: she was a cripple and a rube.

He began to worry that Mother and Aunt Esther would be anxious about him. They liked to eat dinner earlier and earlier, and had their radio programs they listened to without fail, beginning with something called dinner music, with featured musicale singers, at six o'clock from WEAF in New York, followed by baseball scores at 6:55, which only he cared about. This year Babe Ruth was obeying doctor's orders and the Yankees looked like a shoo-in for the pennant, except that Tris Speaker's Indians were closing in; in the National League, Rogers Hornsby's Cardinals looked likely to beat out the Cincinnati Reds. Teddy cared but not as much as he used to. As he was about to turn and run home Emily came out of the greenhouse door, which was so low she ducked her head. Her hair was covered in a checked blue bandana. The oval of her face turned right away to his, as if by some electricity-carrying ether in the air she had sensed his gaze. She took a halt step or two toward him but to spare her walking he swiftly—too swiftly?—trotted across the alley to face her, there on a white path that had been refreshed with new crushed oyster shells. "Who are *you* spying on?" she asked him, with her defensive edge of pugnacity, which he knew she didn't mean; it was just her way to compensate. In the softening light of a September six o'clock, her face, wrapped in the bandana, was plain, perhaps, but each feature had its electricity—her rounded eyes with their wet gleam, the inquisitively lifted brows, her small nose with her bump at the bridge and pink nostrils smudged where she had wiped one with a dirty hand, and her rather full lips, all their curves nestled into one another with a complacent, challenging precision.

"Nobody," he lied. "Just walking home at six o'clock, minding my own business."

"Walking home the long way."

"Maybe. Maybe I have some business up there"—he gestured toward the end of Fishery Way, which in a quarter-mile gave out in the weeds along the river, where a few tarred shreds of a long-abandoned dock were rotting among goldenrod and blue mussel shells that gulls had broken.

"You want to see the greenhouse?" she asked, seeing him at a loss for further words.

"Oh sure. Sure."

"Be careful. You step down a step." Inside, the spattering on the glass smoothed the light to an even gloom, in which Mr. Sifford—his bulk magnified amid so many tiny potted seedlings, under this tilted artificial sky—moved with a silent watchfulness, having given Teddy a brief, suspicious greeting. One colored boy was lugging flats of potted seedlings around, and the other was painting white the wood of the newly built raised beds, which were crude tables. Everything was painted white that could be. "It reflects light," Emily explained. "Plants need four things to grow—light, warmth, water, and carbon dioxide."

"I know about carbon dioxide," he said, thinking not just of making sodas but of biology class back in Paterson.

"You breathe it out," Emily said, "and plants breathe it in. That's why greenhouses like to have people in them." Her voice quickening, she explained what they were setting out, poinsettias in time for the Christmas trade, and gladiolas and chrysanthemums and long-stemmed roses. She showed him a big icebox where the harvested flowers would wait for their buyers, and the steam pipes running all along the walls and under the tables, fitted to a new coal furnace at the far end. There were fans to move the air around, and levers and chains to open sections of the glass overhead, but he was hardly listening, thinking of the awkward position this unplanned visit placed him in. He had been host of a sort to her at the drug store, and now she was playing hostess to him in her place of business; then it would be his turn to do something. What? Awareness that his mother and Aunt Esther were impatiently waiting supper for him tugged at his stomach; he made several nervous motions toward leaving while she was still talking on, excited and fluent, in her element. The sheltered bright stillness brought to an animated focus the life in her; the heavy fragrant atmosphere within the glass walls dragged at his limbs.

At the end, back outdoors, sorry in a way he had come, he said impulsively, to put an end to the encounter, "You ever go to the movies?"

Her satiny face, with its touch of a double chin, took on a tension, as of an oval raindrop about to break and run. He felt he was frightening her. Her voice had turned careful and slow. "Why, no, I don't, not often," she said. "Father doesn't believe in such things. We're Methodists, did you know that? But once years ago when we were visiting over in Cambridge, Maryland, a girl cousin and I peeked into this dark lobby and could see people doing things on the screen until an usher came and told us to pay up or get out." She trailed off and, Teddy failing to speak up in the opportunity she had given him, went on more brightly, "But I *can,* now. Our branch of Methodism has lifted the ban on theatre-going and dancing—going with the times, I suppose. Now it's just smoking and cardplaying and of course drinking we can't do." She added, when he again failed to speak, "But, then, it's all rather silly, isn't it? All these prohibitions old people think up. I think people should be free to do what they want unless it's hurting someone else."

He cleared his stuck throat and said, "Well, let me look and see what's coming to the Roxie the next couple of weeks." And he discovered himself, with a little glide into the receptive, glowing presence opposite him, able to tease: "Some of these foreign pictures are pretty strong stuff, we wouldn't want anything shocking for a nice Methodist girl."

He ran home to Willow Street; his mother said, "My goodness, child, where have you been? The pork chops are so overdone it will be like chewing shoe leather, and the mashed potatoes are cold as mud."

"Sorry—he kept me a little late."

"Well, that is strange, because your Aunt Esther telephoned the drug store and Charlie Wainwright said you had left an hour ago."

"Say, don't I get any freedom around here? Holy smokes, I'm twenty-three years old."

"Don't tell me, dear, I was there the day you were born. You can be any age and it doesn't absolve you from common courtesy to those you live with. Now, you let us know henceforth if you're going to be delayed by these mysterious person or persons."

"It wasn't persons, it's just a—"

"Don't tell me," she said, rather girlishly, clapping her hands over her ears so a wooden serving spoon between her fingers became a tall horn sticking out of one side of her head. "You said it, you're twenty-three, Heaven forbid your mother be guilty of intruding! Now you sit down and chew slowly while I bolt my food in five minutes to catch what's left of this lovely contralto, Roxanna Erb. I've already served your aunt in her room, up and down the stairs. And to think I went to the trouble to make your favorite, peach pie all crusty with sugar on top. You'll have to do without your baseball scores."

As he hurriedly sat down to the meal, its heavy sweet smell rose around him possessively; but compared to the spicier, more uniform fragrance of the greenhouse, it seemed faintly disgusting—dead cooked plants as opposed to plants living and growing.

It began his pattern, those days when he didn't work until nine, to come home for dinner a little later than he used to, or if he came home on time to wander out afterwards, into the late-summer dusk, and return in the dark, when all the downstairs lights but the porch light were switched off. He could feel his mother and aunt curbing their curiosity, giving him the privacy due a man, but the night he had arranged to take Emily to the movies and was trying to sneak out quietly they couldn't restrain themselves. "A fresh white shirt!" his mother cried. "It's as if you never sat and watched me starch and iron a shirt and didn't know the labor that goes into it."

"I had to come downstairs," Aunt Esther announced, rather erect and elegant in her Chinese bathrobe. "The smell in the house was so strong I thought the oil stove might be about to explode. But I guess it's just the amount of hair oil Theodore has poured on himself. What an aroma! Just don't you stand too close to any open flame!"

Being teased, like teasing, was not as yet a comfortable sensation for Teddy. "Take it easy," he said helplessly. "I'm just going out."

"That we can see," said Aunt Esther.

"To the movies."

"The way you're slicked up you're setting to be downright *in* the movies."

"I think he looks absolutely handsome," his mother said, as if she were on his side. "I can see his daddy in him tonight, the way he'd come to Saturday Night Sodality back in Jackson Bluffs. Now," she went on, her voice thickening like chilled syrup, "who might the lucky young lady be?"

He wanted to protect Emily from his mother, and his mother from Emily. "Nobody," he said. "Just a bunch of us are going."

"You never made much mention before of a bunch. Who are these new friends?"

"Oh, you know," he lied, picturing the young people his age he had observed in the drug store and on Rodney Street but who had never given him more than a flip greeting on the street and some condescending kidding in the drug store. "Angus Whaley, Judith Phillips, Ann and Ken Gordy, Harry Lowe, some others I guess. They said why don't I come along? It's that new Swedish actress who's been in the papers."

"They say she's the female Valentino," said Aunt Esther. "And look what happened to *him.* Too much adoration isn't healthy for a man."

"Oh dear," his mother said. "I hope she's not *too* advanced. These Europeans don't think the way we do about certain matters."

"You can't be too advanced these days," Teddy said, seeing an opening in which to joke his way out the door. "Haven't you ladies heard of flaming youth? And, hey, aren't you both missing the *Maxwell Coffee House Hour*?"

He hurried along Willow and cut down the shaded gloom of Elm to Locust Street, a half-block up from Fishery Way, and the street on which the Siffords' house had its address, with its greenhouse behind. Emily was waiting in the brightly lit front parlor. Mr. Sifford, at the far end of the hall, gave Teddy a wordless wave of recognition, but there was no sign of the mother. A moist gleam of nervousness added to Emily's glow. She was too dressed-up, he thought, in a bulky old-fashioned silk dress with too many pleats in the front of the blouse and the skirt too full and long for today's styles, so it almost covered the ugly metal-and-leather brace on her leg. He might have imagined a touch of make-up around her eyes, emphasizing their whites. Her light-brown hair was cut shorter than when she came to town last spring, and a curling iron had induced a shiny waviness that disconcerted him, making her look years older than with the long straight hair simply tied behind like a girl's. As she walked beside him down past the shop-fronts of Rodney Street he was conscious of the irregularity of her gait, jerking her head up and down in the edge of his vision, and he stopped hurrying, though he always had this fear, ever since the paper route had overcrowded his mornings back in Paterson, of being late. But the crowd—a dozen or so, including Angus Whaley and Harry Lowe, whom he had lied to his mother about—were still wandering up to the ticket booth, under the marquee whose lights carved a bright space from the silvery gloom of early evening. A multitude of moths fluttered around the rows of marquee bulbs surrounding the title spelled out in detachable letters. "Oh my goodness," Emily said, though she must have known what movie was playing.

"*The Temptress,*" he read. "Gee, I hope it's not too strong for you and gets your folks upset. I'd rather it was something with more adventure, like *Beau Geste* that was here last month, but Saturday night only comes around once a week, and I didn't want to wait forever—did you?"

"Oh, no," she said, "this I'm sure will be fine," but in a rather preoccupied tone, he thought, as if her mind was already hastening ahead into the lobby with its red carpet and velvet ropes, and then out and home again. It occurred to Teddy that perhaps like her mother she was shy out of doors; her smile—her nice, plump, confiding smile—gleamed only when they had found seats inside, in the near-total dark. He offered her a horehound drop; he had supplied himself with a paper bag's worth from the bowl of them free that stood on the cigar counter by the cash register. "Thank you," she whispered. "But not yet."

The heavy purple curtains drew back and the orange side lamps dimmed and in the air above their heads, with a racheted whir, a shuddering shaft of light surprised a few winged bugs, suddenly turned into darting, looping stars. The movie began at a masked ball. The tall, glacially beautiful heroine, with her languid, hesitant motions, and the dark Latin lover fall in love, and are seen after the ball in the garden at dawn, in besmitten profile. The Swedish actress's expressions are so exquisite, her passions so evident, that the intertitles are scarcely needed. It turns out she is married, and her lover is a friend of her husband. The temptress has shown herself to be heartless in the past, ruining her husband and driving others to suicide. She follows Antonio Moreno, the actor playing the lover, to South America, where he is trying to build dams. More men fall in love with her, to their ruin. By this time Emily is ready for the horehound drops and as Teddy passes them to her one by one he can feel the silky texture of her palm.

The film's disasters gather momentum, with flashing lightning and a tumult of waters from the screen; she transfers a cough drop to her other hand and lightly seizes his fingers and lowers their two hands, linked now, to the wooden armrest between them. Greta Garbo's husband is shot, and in a terrible storm the dam collapses. Teddy can see that the dam is miniature, a model, disintegrating in a giant tub of agitated waters, but it doesn't matter, his throat is clenched anyway. The lover vows to rebuild. At the dedication, as he extols the woman who inspired him, she shows up and claims him at last. Fadeout. The hard-working pianist lapses into a dismissive, fading waltz. The audience rises into the bewildering light. Shouldn't she have been punished more, or at least condemned to loneliness? If women as wild as that are permitted to roam the world successfully, what is sacred?

Emily's limp seemed to have been made worse by the hours of sitting. In the corners of her lips there were amber traces of horehound-drop juice, of which she was unaware as she smiled up at him, taking his arm under the bright marquee. He didn't know how to shake her off. Angus Whaley and Harry Lowe had preceded them into the warm evening, and stared toward Teddy with tentative mockery on their faces. In the corner of his vision, as he turned deliberately away down the sidewalk, causing Emily to tug awkwardly at his arm, he could see Angus begin to imitate a limp, and Harry bend backward in laughter. He tried to slow his pace, so she didn't pull at him so much. Moths swirled and bumped at the lit plate-glass window of the other emporium open in the town, the Blue Hen Ice Cream Parlor. "Want to stop for, oh say, a vanilla soda with a scoop of butter pecan?" he asked. Inside, beyond the window where wooden slats in ladder form listed the available flavors, a mob of the town's young was gathered beneath a ceiling of cigarette smoke. Shrill rays of female laughter shot out from the cluster up at the counter; he saw Ann Gordy looking swell in a close curly bob and flapper dress up to her knees, her bare arms flashing in agitated angles like lightning strokes.

His invitation had been friendly enough, with a little tease in it, since he knew her tastes, but something in his tone warned her off. She said, "Thank you, Ted, but my parents aren't used to my going out at night and I don't want them to worry. Some other time?"

"Sure," he said, relieved not to have to tow her, in her voluminous country-girl dress, into that jagged loud gang who knew him only as a soda jerk. On the quiet of Fishery Way, passing the garage doors and empty burning barrels behind the stores along Rodney Street, he asked her, "What did you think of her?" Greta Garbo, not Ann Gordy.

"She *is* very beautiful, though if you notice she moves rather awkwardly, with her big feet and hands, so they never show her full-length, just in close-up or from far away."

"I meant the character, I guess, not the actress."

"Oh, I *liked* her. I liked the way she went after what she wanted. Women can't really do that yet, but it's nice to think they can some day."

"You think an awful lot about women," he said.

"Being one, I have to."

"I mean, you *got* the vote. There're two lady governors out west now, and this Gertrude Ederle just swam the English Channel. What more do you want?"

Emily thought for some steps, as her head bobbed up and down and her grip tightened on his arm. "Respect," she said. "We want respect and equality."

Her house frightened him a little, with her spooky mother inside. The porch light was on, and in that glare he didn't dare try to kiss her. His chance had been back in the shadows along by the greenhouse. But he squeezed her hand, as she thanked him for the movie, and she squeezed back. He turned at the end of her walk and saw, through the clear part of the engraved and bevelled window-glass in her front door, Emily's face, in profile, mouthing some words he couldn't hear to someone he couldn't see. She carefully took a pin from either side of her hairdo and tossed her head as if to say, *Well, that's over.*

His family discouraged his relation with Emily, and he did not find in himself much heart for combat. "It's not that she's not a *nice* girl, Teddy," his mother said, in her utmost tone of Christian sweetness. "I have no doubt she is, with her handicap and everything. But her people don't seem to be quite the Wilmot sort of people, and her mother would appear to be definitely *odd.*" Teddy sensed how alone Father must have felt; all Mother really cared about was how things looked to the neighbors.

"I don't want to argue, Mother—but who *is* the Wilmot sort? Poor Pete Pulsifer living above Krauthammer's Hardware and Seeds while his wife stalls the divorce and tells everybody what a rotter he is? Or Jared's little tootsie, acting so hoity-toity, as if her maiden name wasn't McMullen and her father's money didn't come up out of Irish bars and the bootleg business?"

Stella's bright-black eyes flared a little but this sort of brawling challenge didn't shake a girl raised among Missouri Baptists. "It was Mr. McMullen's *father,*" she said, "who owned the saloon on Ninth Avenue. Lucille's father owns rental properties and operates an investment house for well-to-do clients; he has been *very* kind and helpful to your brother. Nothing is ideal under Heaven, dear Teddy, and it doesn't do to look down on people because of their origins."

"But you just said—"

"It's where they're *going* that matters in this country. I never heard your father say a harsh word against anybody of another race or creed, even when Father McNulty over at St. John's seemed to think he was the unelected mayor of Paterson. My opinion is, going out with this crippled girl embarrasses you, and that's why you're being so testy."

"Well," he muttered, wanting to leave the subject alone, "I wouldn't call taking her to a movie once in a blue moon going out. We neither of us have any other friends to speak of."

"You shouldn't take out a girl for reasons of charity," his mother instructed him. "It confuses their heads. You may think you're just being kind, but they can't help but think you have intentions."

"Yeah, what *are* your intentions?" his sister, Esther, asked him in private, on one of her infrequent visits home.

"Does a body always have to have intentions? She's fun to be with. She has more ideas than you'd think. She thinks women need to stick up for themselves, and she admires the way you thumbed your nose at everybody when you broke up the Pulsifers."

This was putting it too bluntly, even for Esther. "I didn't break anybody up, snooks. They were in lousy shape for years. They hadn't slept together since the Armistice. She said it was a filthy business unless you were making babies."

Teddy wasn't sure he should know this. He was embarrassed, and in over his head. "Well, you know what I meant."

"It's what they say around this small-minded town, sure. I just don't need to hear it from my own kid brother. Anyway, for your information, and strictly between us, she's giving him such a hard time over the divorce I'm not sure he's going to stick with it. She uses the kids on him, and the money. She's squeezing the poor bastard six ways to Sunday, and if she gets him into court he'll have a hard time ever practicing law again in Basingstoke. Hell, what do I care? There's plenty more fish in the sea, it turns out. I've been going out with some pretty nifty gents in New York." Seeing the shocked look on his face, Esther reached into her gold-beaded purse and asked, "Want a Chesterfield?"

"No, thanks."

"What is it, against Emily's religion?"

He blushed. "She doesn't like my breath when I smoke."

"Oh boy. Getting close enough to smell each other, are you?"

No matter how long he let it go before asking her out again, Emily always accepted calmly, without reproach. He was her only suitor: this was comforting as well as frightening. She didn't come into the drug store as often as in the summer;

winter brought the dance season, and Christmas, and the greenhouse was busy with poinsettias and corsages and long-stemmed roses. Its tropical warmth and all-white woodwork were like nothing else in town, and Emily was getting known as the girl in the greenhouse. When they went to the movies now, people said hello to her, limp and all. After the movies, in the dead of winter, they would walk home hurriedly, with stinging cheeks, and she would invite him into her front parlor, and give him a cup of Ovaltine and some Cameo cookies. On the old-fashioned settee of crimson cut plush there, with the streetlight throwing a dim diagonal copy of the window lace on the floorboards, they would expand on that touch of his fingers on her silky palm when they had seen *The Temptress* together. The radio in the corner—a six-tone Silvertone mahogany console, ordered from Sears, Roebuck—would be turned on to mask whatever sighs and sounds of friction they emitted. Somewhere off in Manhattan or Chicago a hotel band would pump and chuckle and wheeze away at "In a Little Spanish Town" or "When the Red, Red Robin Comes Bob, Bob, Bobbin' Along" or "Someone to Watch over Me." Supposedly they were playing cards, cribbage with a Rook deck, since the colored pips and kings and queens and jacks with faces were thought by the Methodists to be sinful. Most evenings, her father in rumpled gray trousers and a work shirt and suspenders would look up from reading the newspaper to greet Teddy and then after a few awkward words retire, first into the kitchen and then upstairs, to where he and his wife could be heard talking, and then making the floorboard squeak above the ceiling as they settled to bed. Teddy even met her mother a few times—a small woman, so short that Emily looked pleasingly tall beside her. Mrs. Sifford had a taut square-jawed face the color of a hazelnut shell; her hair was as dark and dull as lampblack and she couldn't look him in the eye, but there seemed nothing too odd about her except the way her hand kept nervously lifting to cover her mouth, which had that caved-in look of not many teeth. So maybe her shyness was based on dental problems.

There on the sofa, as the other inhabitants of the house, including two beagle dogs and a calico cat who was always producing kittens, settled into their places, Emily, to his surprise, knew pretty much what to do. Wherever could she have learned it? Calmly, with a shy smiling wordlessness, she led him on as if deeper into a humid white warm great flower, of which their two bodies side by side on the sofa were some of the petals. The flower opened very slowly, while she emitted slight sighs and murmurs and her parents' feet made the floors squeak above their heads. Emily liked to kiss even more than he did; after a while, he would need to breathe. Her face would get rubbed-looking and vague and she would touch the side of his face wonderingly after a kiss long enough, backing off so he could see the brilliant whites of her eyes surrounding the layered blue irises. She began to kiss with an open mouth, like Greta Garbo with John Gilbert in *Flesh and the Devil.* One night she didn't push away his hand when it rested on her breast, but let him test its resilience, its surprising heft beneath the clothy thicknesses of blouse and slip and brassiere. So they added his holding her breast to what they did, to kissing and hugging and stroking faces. Later still—weeks would go by before his need for her would build up enough for him to brave family disapproval—she allowed him, after her parents' footsteps overhead had grown silent, to unbutton her frilly white blouse and lower the slip straps and unhook the bra at her back, all three of its catches; all this manipulation, awkward and stealthy, did not harm the simple wonder of her bare breasts, the radiant breadth of a woman's chest never touched by a moment of sun, the faint blue veins on this finest so sensitive skin, the rosy round little nipples she let him suck, if he didn't do it too hard. They were like kitten's noses. She would grow slick with his spit and dewy with excitement, her face flushed pink and the caves on either side of her neck becoming damp and tangled nests of straying hair. And then she would touch him, at first very shyly and then more confidently and curiously, where his fly was bulging, his body's pleasure rising to this explosive peak. There was nothing lame about Emily as her hands moved exploringly among the bulges of these fleshly mysteries; she seemed intent and matter-of-fact, as if she knew that the opportunity to love would be rare for her and she must not waste it through false coquettishness. Yet she did not let him touch her below the waist, and whenever in their heated tumble a knee or shin of his encountered the hard rods of her leg brace she would stiffen and cool all over.

"Sorry," he would murmur.

"No, *I'm* sorry, Teddy. You know I want to give you everything. But I can't. Yet. Not with things as they are."

He knew what she meant. With him sneaking, and him not ready for marriage, and her not suitable anyway, too lamed and strange for his family. He was straining toward her but it was like his hard-on behind his fly, which she stroked and pushed at, so that he came off, but had never seen. He was buttoned in, by a fear that like his father he would go too far, beyond the boundaries society had set for everybody's protection. He would return home feeling guilty and drained and almost at peace, sneaking along past the picket fences, leaving tracks in the inch of fresh snow that had fallen, the sparkle sweeping like wind on water as his head travelled in relation to the streetlamps, and the few lit windows of the houses in this neighborhood making golden fans on the pristine white yards. His mother's window would be lit as he came in sight of the house. His shoes scuffling on the porch, stamping off the snow, seemed to strike a great hollowness that amplified the sound.

In March of 1927, Clara Bow created a sensation as the irrepressible shop-girl Betty Lou, who wows her boss, played by Garbo's former screen lover Antonio Moreno, in the film adaptation of Elinor Glyn's *It;* in April, Mae West was found guilty of indecency by a New York municipal court for her good-hearted improvisations in the Broadway show, of which she was both star and author, titled simply *Sex.* Early in that same April, Jared, who had not been able to come down to Basingstoke for Christmas—he and Lucille and her parents and little brother had taken the train clear to Florida, where there were quick fortunes to be made in real estate—paid a visit with his petite wife, who had stopped bleaching her black-Irish hair. Lucille was four months pregnant but still wearing the boyish fashions—hipless, bustless, above-the-knee tubes with a wide belt draped low across the middle, so women looked like slender gunslingers. She tried to amuse herself shopping but after a morning strolling on Rodney Street had to report that she didn't know how people survived down here, there was nothing whatsoever to buy. "All you people must be *rich,* the way the money saves itself!" Lucille's mouth was a little rosebud—almost purple, the lipstick was so dark a red—and she had trained two spitcurls to point right at her cheekbones, which were emphasized with brushed-on rouge. Her hair was like a slick black helmet, and if Teddy hadn't known her maiden name was McMullen he might have thought she was French, or purebred Spanish, until she opened her mouth. She was nothing like that pale freckled Irish girl who had helped with the housework when he was a boy. He liked her. She was so bored, even though she was only here for the weekend, she kept begging him to play gin rummy with her, or play quoits with her in the backyard. When Jared took them all in his long tan Stutz convertible to the beach at Woodland her bathing suit was way lower in the back than anybody else's. The water was much too cold to go in but it was warm back in the dunes away from the wind. She was worried that her "baby tummy" was starting to show and she more than once asked Ted's opinion. With a comic judiciousness he sized up the profile of her abdomen as she posed, there in the hollow of the dunes. Something about him now let it be known that he could handle such a delicate feminine issue. Mother at last exclaimed, "Lucille, you let that boy alone—he has girls enough on his mind!"

Jared took him aside on the porch the second evening, while the women finished the dishes and listened to a string quartet on the radio, followed by Emlyn R. Edwards, baritone, on Station WOR from Newark. Teddy guessed, from the determined depth of Jared's own baritone, that Mother had ordained the topic, which was perhaps the point of the visit. Jared took the wicker rocking chair. "Ted," he said, offering his brother a La Palma cigar to accompany his own, which he had already lit, "remember what I told you about pussy?" He turned his face, giving his brother the benefit of his good ear.

"It unmakes a man, and money makes him."

"Did I say that, flat out? I must have known everything, when I was a young squirt. Ted, my friend, your mama's not happy you're seeing this girl. She says her mother's a nut and the girl herself is gimpy."

He said this as if his arm did not hang pretty useless from his shoulder and he did not have to offer people his left hand to shake. "Nobody's perfect," Teddy simply said. "I don't see her all that much. Just once in a while, for laughs, kind of."

"Who else do you see?"

"Nobody."

"Well, then. Those are pretty serious laughs. She must think she's got you sewn up. You're not doing her any favor—forget what your mother wants."

"What *does* she want?" Teddy exclaimed, months of quiet frustration finding vent. "I gotta see *some*body, I can't spend my whole life just hanging around the house and whipping up banana splits down at Addison's."

"That brings me right to the point. How'd you like to work for me?"

"You?"

"Me, kid. Come to Noo Yawk with the rest of us slickers. Lucille's dad and I have a place all set out for you."

"What would I *do?* Nobody exactly understands what *you* do."

"Some days I don't understand it myself. I oversee rent collection on properties some of which I jointly own. More important these last years, I invest, for myself and others—Jimmy has connections with some guys who have more money coming in than they know what to do with. Stocks have been going through the roof lately, if you read the papers. A moron could make money on Wall Street right now, believe me. Come along and I'll teach you the ropes. We'll start you at thirty a week and you'll be making double that within a year."

Teddy took a deeper puff on the La Palma, trying to hold the smoke in his mouth the way Jared did, releasing it slowly, scarcely exhaling, and said, "A moron could do it, even me, huh?"

"Don't get touchy. You know what I meant. Land of opportunity, that's still the good old U.S. of A. And that town—boy, it has everything. Shows, clubs where you won't believe what you're seeing, girls—not that I'm not out of that particular action, being hitched to Lucille and she ripe with child as you saw today. You get along with Lucille, I notice—that's nice. She's a New Yorker, through and through. You like her, you'll like the millions. This little burg was maybe what you needed six years ago, after Pop checked out, but it's dead on its feet, basically; basically it's just a hatchery for chicken farmers and bottle-cap makers. You don't want to get stuck here—Christ. A Wilmot wants more than that. You want more than that. This girl, what's her name—"

"Emily. Emily Jeanette Sifford."

"She'll hobble you so you'll never move. You'll be married to this one-horse burg. That's what frightens your mother."

"Mom wants me to leave Basingstoke? You'd never guess it."

"She does. She wants it with all her mother instinct. She wants you to get the hell out and make something of yourself, the way I'm doing, the way Esther would be doing, if she weren't a skirt. The thing about Esther is she has more brains than either of us—it's driving her wild, knowing that."

An unwell feeling was rising up under Teddy. The porch

rail appeared to sway, to swing, like the rail of an ocean-going ship as he had seen them in the movies. A sickly sallow light lay on the rail from the single overhead porch light, its glass shade dirtied by bodies of dead flies and the stains of moths that had battered their soft heads against the glare. Something was awry with his insides, like a rug was being slowly pulled out from under them. His mouth was suddenly full of unwanted saliva. The end of the cigar was coming apart in his lips, and the cry of the spring peepers from the backyard pond that Horace Pruitt had dug and that was now sludging in sounded like a beam of sound itself swaying, surging, in waves. He closed his eyes and thought of being with Emily on the red sofa but that didn't help; he was sliding into a weakness where even uttering a word was an effort. "I don't know," he managed to say. "I hate to be dependent . . ."

"You wouldn't be," Jared snapped, with a barking quickness that afflicted Teddy's tender, off-balance state. "Everybody's dependent. Everybody does favors, especially for kin. You'd be an asset to us, honest—didn't you study accounting?"

"I've forgotten most of it. The rest was just common sense." He had located the trouble: the cigar. Its blue smoke scraped against his face, which had begun to sweat.

Jared's red cigar tip circled dizzyingly in the center of his own cloud of smoke, through which Teddy could fitfully make out his brother's face, with its wide mouth that talked too easily, its reddish hair so thick it tended to stand on end, its canny slant eyes with the puffy lids, half-closed like a gangster's. "Sure, it might take a little time for you to find your niche. We run a many-sided operation. You want to be where the advantage is; you got to play the angles. We'd have to find you somewhere to live. There are O.K. places not too expensive over on Murray Hill. Maybe you and Esther could move in together. Between us"—he leaned forward to lower his voice, and the whole porch seemed to be pitching with this sudden motion, out of the rocking chair, his limp arm swinging—"having her with us is getting on Lucy's nerves. In a family way like she is, she flies off the handle. You and Esther could be roomies till this chump Pulsifer gets it up to marry her, if he does. She'd show you the ropes around town, and wouldn't be there when you didn't need her, if you know what I mean."

Teddy didn't, exactly, and he felt too sick to figure it out. He knew that the time, after Dad's death, when he begged Esther to stay with him was deep in the past, buried, mulched in, as they said at the greenhouse. He threw the cigar over the porch rail and tried to find a spot somewhere in the woodwork—porch boards, lathe-turned wooden pillars, jigsawed ornamental brackets with shapes like diamonds and hearts in them—where his eyes could rest and give his stomach a place to settle. Always Jared was leading him out a little further into life than he was quite ready to go. Teddy looked at his palms in the sallow light and they were damp and mottled as if with a message too worn away to read. "I think the cigar is making me sick," he confessed to Jared.

"They'll do that, if you suck too much in. The thing about a cigar is you're meant mostly to hold it, and take a sip now and then. It's like brandy—gulp it, and you're done."

"Jared . . ."

"Yeah, Ted?"

"Thanks. You're generous to ask, even if Mom did put you up to it."

"Hey, don't go getting that idea. It's strictly a selfish deal. You have a lot to offer, we get you in the right slot. You don't have my hot head and run-on mouth. My trouble is, I have something on my mind, I have to say it. I can't keep it bottled up like you can."

Teddy burped, and swallowed, feeling his insides wanting to climb up through his throat. He willed them back down. "I can't think about it now. I can't think about anything." The picture of a banana split, chocolate syrup oozed over the three flavors of ice cream and the slimy long sides of the bisected fruit, came unwanted into his mind. He said, "I wonder if I walked around the yard. I think maybe if I could see the moon." The white moon like a bare breast, a little short of full.

"Help yourself," Jared said, taking a billowing puff on his own cigar, and rocking so sharply back in his rocking chair the wicker cracked explosively. "Fresh air never hurts. Look—Lucille and I gotta head back early tomorrow, to get ahead of the traffic; we have a luncheon date out on the Island. Oyster Bay. But you think it over, my man. You let me know. I'd love to have you join us. You, me, and Es together again—it'd be like old times back on Straight Street."

But from the flat, hurried way he pronounced these urgings Teddy perceived that his brother had decided his offer was rejected, and that Jared was relieved. Even so, he kept selling the family line, in his terms. "Come up to Baghdad-on-the-Subway and branch out. Make some new connections. You know what they say about a woman, don't you? Why buy a cow when milk's so cheap?"

Teddy couldn't even smile. He was afraid if he stood up to leave the porch the little test of his equilibrium would spill everything. It was like one of the square pans of water from underneath the soda-fountain ice chests: the water started to sway and slop over when it was too full. How can men poison their systems like this every day? He begged, "Let's not keep talking about it. My instinct is New York is too rich for me."

"There can't be *too* rich, kiddo. Whatever the traffic will bear—that's the philosophy these days. See how you feel tomorrow, when you don't look so God-damn green. Talk it over with your near and dear."

"With Emily?"

"Jesus, no. It's the last thing she wants, you getting out of her clutches." His brother leaned forward in the rocking chair and, without knowing how pathetic the gesture looked, caught his inert arm from swaying forward by pressing it back with his good, his left, hand. "You know what *my* instinct is? My instinct's been telling me this is going to be a great year, for the Street and for the Yankees. The Babe is going to hit sixty, if Gehrig doesn't beat him to it."

His mother, when Teddy described Jared's invitation to her, seemed uncomfortable, though he suspected it had been her idea. "Oh, I just don't know, sweetheart, what's best for you—if only your daddy were here to advise. It seems to everybody I talk to who knew him that your father would want you to get out into the world now, before it's too late and you end up a hopeless Basingstokian."

"What's so bad about that? You and Aunt Esther—"

"Ah yes, darling, but we're women, and women short on prospects, without much of a penny between us. Furthermore, your Aunt Esther is far from well, and I—"

"What, Mom?" he said, suddenly alert and scared.

"I'm not the girl I used to be," she concluded, as if sugar-coating some secret woe.

"Have you been feeling poorly?" A worm of panic turned within him, at the thought of her drifting into death the way his father had done.

"No, dear. But I've been feeling every minute of fifty-nine." She was going to turn sixty in May. She had been old, thirty-six, when he had been born. He couldn't picture it, at the age of thirty-five Dad and Mom— "I pray about you, Teddy," she told him abruptly. "Oh, how I strain to hear the answer! You were always the child your father worried about. You seemed so timid of the world, somehow."

"Well, I remember how he used to look when he'd come back from trying to—"

"Oh, but we mustn't make excuses not to *live.* That's the worst sin of all, turning your back on the opportunities Heaven sends."

It made his skin crawl when she talked about prayer and sin. "Yeah, yeah—but who says New York is the place to do your living? It's a heap of maggots, Mother—a ton of greedy people living all on top of each other." Yet, when he was with Emily, her parents' footsteps stilled upstairs, the radio in the corner murmured its music from New York, the Waldorf-Astoria ballroom or whatever, and the cluster of tall tubes in the back of the console seemed a magical miniature city where the filaments glowed like fiery snakes. That was New York to him, that insinuating faint dance music.

"It's one of the wonders of the world," his mother told him. "It's the wonder of our *New* World." Her voice became Southern and singsong and emphatic. "It would be a *ter*rible loneliness for your aunt and me, but I *do* think when Jared has been *good* enough to offer you *such* an opportunity it would be *wrong* not to give it a *try.*" She pronounced it *traah.*

Seeing him still hesitate, she said something he could never quite forgive her for afterwards. "If it's that little Sifford girl you're worried about leaving, she'll still be here. Nobody else is going to carry her off, believe you me." She said it rapidly with almost a sneer—the sneer of appraisal which women secretly give other women.

But his mother had asked so few things of him in his life that he could scarcely deny her. He did go to New York to live with Jared and work for the McMullens. Seth Addison, balder and more wiry as he hunched over his potions than he had been four years ago, expressed regret at seeing Teddy leave, but in the same breath confessed that he had never expected him to stay behind the counter so long. Emily took his news bravely, and accepted his reassurances as more sincere than Teddy felt as he pronounced them. But she didn't let him unbutton her blouse on their last night on the cut-plush settee together. Only a roughness in her voice as if from a cold and, from the side, an unshed tear in her eye like a second lens, betrayed the sense of desertion she otherwise did not declare, lest it make a total breach where only half a breach existed.

Thus liberated, he tried to enjoy New York that spring, and for moments would lose the sore tug of fearfulness nagging his stomach: the music from the orchestra pit swelled to lift higher and higher the kicking long legs of Ziegfeld girls dressed mostly in pink feathers and tight-fitting sparkling white caps, and from the top of a double-decker bus he felt sheer space pour down from the man-made heights and cliffs. A certain death-defying splendor was posed here on purely human terms, in this tirelessly active pile of bodies and aspiration. Teddy marvelled at the multitudes that pressed through the canyons at twilight, while a daytime blue still ruled above and wheat-colored lights came on erratically in the upward-receding windows. Slim women with pale faces cupped in cloche hats and with trimmings of fox and mink on their coats strode along the grid, the flaunting north-south avenues and the intimate side streets, like an army suited for passion, but none of them attached to him, a chunky bland pedestrian ill at ease and unworthy of a second glance. In the crush of identities his own seemed imperilled, more fragile than he had ever felt it, even in those last years in Paterson, witnessing his father's suffering. The great iron-fenced mansions along Fifth and Madison and Park were to him sealed tight as Pyramids, though a traffic of limousines hinted that live slivers of flesh still inhabited these massive brownstone shells, while taxis and immigrants jostled for space. There was a snowfall, late in April, and Teddy saw the city hushed under a veil of enchantment; but in a matter of hours the snow turned dirty and melted, arranging the gutter filth—coal dust speckled with bits of paper and cigarette stubs—in newly eroded patterns around the choked iron grates at the curb.

The life he saw Jared and Lucille and Esther leading seemed fuelled on tobacco and bootleg hooch, and jangled to a desperate rhythm imported across the color line—jazz. Teddy went with them, the three of them and sometimes a too-slick associate of Jared's who served as Esther's date, to the speakeasies and nightclubs and Greenwich Village parties where they had what they called their fun, and smoked and drank along with them, until he attained that state where the onrolling Negro music seemed his, defining with its clarinet and cornet and drums and driving, tinkling piano some inner shape of bliss and final arrival that had been his from birth. Lucille's "baby tummy" unmistakably showed now, and rendered her wide-eyed volubility vaguely comic, as if she were straining to make herself heard above the head of a second presence, who had attached itself to her without her quite knowing it. Her silhouette had a perverse elegance, slouched into her protruding abdomen, which hoisted the front edge of her skirt an inch or two higher, up to her knees, and provided a little ledge where she sometimes unconsciously rested her cocked wrist as she held a smoking cigarette. She was all outthrust angles, in her tight-fitting black helmet of hair. Teddy thought she might soften her behavior at a party her parents gave, in their penthouse on East Fifty-second Street, but in fact she was shrillest and most recklessly animated there, while her parents—he in a tuxedo, both his shirtfront and face looking boiled, and Mrs. McMullen in a sleeveless gown of green lamé that exposed limp pouches of flesh above her elbows—looked on beamingly, proud to have produced so luxurious an American product as this perfect flapper in her swinging ropes of imitation pearls. At such parties Jared and Esther underwent an electric transformation, flying from one buzzing group to another, recognizing acquaintances on all sides, and feigning, with flushed cheeks and piercing voices, a hysteria of happiness and indiscriminate affection. Sometimes they dragged Teddy with them into their mood, but he invariably awoke the morning after with the small sore scared spot in his stomach enlarged. His mouth parched from the night's excess of liquor, his eyes still watery from the smoke, he felt, in the back room Jared and Lucille had set aside and starkly furnished for him, imprisoned, for some crime he could not remember but did not doubt. Ten stories below his towering curtainless window the city's traffic had already begun to rumble and bleat; in fact it had never stopped, and only his drunken fatigue six hours ago had muffled the noise, a metropolitan surf as incessant as the sea's. The day's duties yawned before him with a glassy blankness, like that of the cloudless blue sky which hung ignored above the city's skyscrapers, with their topping of gilded gargoyles and rural-looking wooden water tanks.

To Teddy had fallen the job with which Jared had begun to serve the McMullens' empire, that of rent collector. Far from the glamour and hurry of Manhattan's central avenues he ventured, with his leather collection-book and tablet of receipts, to low brick rows on Ninth and Tenth, to noisy neighborhoods of Italians and Slavs south of Washington Square, and over to the East Side, where the avenues were designated by letters of the alphabet or else dissolved in a skewed welter of streets with homely names like Henry and Hester, Water and Broome. He crossed the East River, more customarily by claustrophobic subway tunnel rather than on the soaring bridges visible from Manhattan's edges, to the boroughs of Brooklyn and Queens, where more rents waited to be pulled from the balky backroom drawers of tenants perched in their rooms like pigeons on a ledge. Teddy, homesick for Basingstoke's wildlife, from his Fifth Avenue bedroom studied the pigeons rotating anxiously in their drying offal, leaking a throbbling noise out of their gray rainbow throats, flying off with a battering of verminous wings when he tapped on the window.

The renters were workers, strugglers, many of them immigrants not long removed from Ellis Island, where the wide-open gates had been finally lowered six years before, with the Emergency Quota Act. The sounds of conversation in an unintelligible tongue would come from unseen rooms, and the odor of potatoes and turnips and onions and mutton scraps stewing. A woman, usually, came to the door, with a thin-faced child half-hiding behind her skirt, and on her lips a scarcely intelligible explanation as to why they could not pay now, but next week, promise to God, her man he too sick to do job, getting better, go out tomorrow, promise to God. Teddy was reminded of Paterson, but that polyglot population had appeared healthier, more hopeful, the American mood more fertile then in its promises, and the streets of Silk City with their little yards holding a fuchsia bush or a blue-robed plaster statue of the Virgin more livable than these stacked, stinking, ill-lit dens. He had been a part of the population then, a schoolboy immersed in its details of competition and expectation and childish collusion and hierarchy, alive in its struggle and too absorbed to judge or pity, whereas now he came upon it from outside, from above, as an agent of power and ownership, an enforcer and avenger, the representative of the system which squeezed the lowly by the same iron laws whereby it generated profits for the lucky and strong. Teddy was reminded of his father's fruitless canvassing on behalf of an encyclopedia few could understand and fewer could afford; but his own canvass, though at many stops fruitless, drew upon fundamental capitalist sanctions and represented an orderly progression of the addresses in his rent book. He liked finding the addresses, and day by day extracting from the human morass of the city an exact, accumulating mental map. But his collections lacked righteousness and ruthlessness and Jared would audit his weekly report with an impatience he less and less troubled to hide. He would cut short Teddy's attempt to paraphrase this or that non-payer's excuse, saying, "Everybody has a hard-luck story. I have a hard-luck story, you have a hard-luck story. We're dealing here with numbers. McMullen Investments is paying us to bring the numbers in, so things add up. Jimmy has his expenses, don't forget—taxes, mortgage payments, maintenance. The banks aren't interested in *his* hard-luck story. They want *their* numbers, we got to get *our* numbers. We're suppliers here, and these starving kikes and wops you feel so sorry for are takers. They're taking from *us.* They're robbing us, and they know it. You're dealing with con artists, and don't forget it. Without us, kiddo, they'd have no roof over their heads or steam in their radiators or glass in their windows. There are no free rides in America—didn't you get that message back in Paterson? So it stretches them to come up with the rent? That's what it's all about, stretching. Jimmy himself is stretched to the maximum, and me along with him. You borrow from the bank and buy on the least allowable margin—you got to get every dollar doing the work of three, because that's what the next guy is doing. Or have I given you this sermon before? Stop me if I have."

Teddy had in truth not been quite listening; his brain was worrying over what Jared thought his, Teddy's, hard-luck story was. Jared's was plain—his wound, and maybe his mysteriously blighted Rutgers career before that, a mismatch of aspiration and follow-through that somehow was at work in his marriage, giving Lucille her slightly frantic edge. But Teddy? Where was his hard luck? He had been lucky in life so far, he felt. He had dodged the lightning bolts. His only trouble was that he missed Basingstoke, and Mother's sugar-topped pies, and Emily. At night, when he lay down in his stark back room, the sheets warmed into a remembering of her body—the damp nests of hair beside her neck, the dewiness her skin would get as she with studious calm concentrated on how to touch him in the spot where his capacity for happiness had gathered itself into a tender peak, so that he whimpered and came, there on the plush sofa then and now here in the narrow New York bed.

They didn't want him here forever; Lucille wanted his room for the nursemaid when the baby arrived. Jared's suggestion that he and Esther find an apartment together didn't sit well with Esther. She squinted at him across Jared and Lucille's glass table—the newest thing, all bent tubes and plate glass, in a design imported from Germany—and said, "I don't know about your style, but it would sure as hell cramp mine."

"I'd stay out of the way," he offered. "You'd have a room you could shut the door to."

"Yeah, yeah. Spare me the pictures. Even if that weren't a problem, what about the cooking? The housework? You'd expect me to do it all, right, just like Mother?"

"No, I'd help. You'd tell me what to do."

"I'm not your mother, Tedsy. I'm not sure I want to be

anybody's mother, and anyway you've got one. You've got a honey of a mother and my whole life is on hold. I still don't know which way Pete is jumping, or if I care."

"Yeah," he said, glad she had brought it up. "What's the story?"

She exhaled humorously, a long hissing plume straight out from her puckered lips like a dragon's jet. "Beats me. He still writes. Mrs. says she's reconciled to the idea of divorce, but my suspicion is he still screws her now and then, up above the hardware store. Let's face it, he's a cute but weak guy who fancies himself as upper-class, and professionally he's tied to the town. His letters are still lovey-dovey—these lawyers, they can make the language jump through hoops, that's their business."

"Does he know—?"

"I'm going around with other guys? He knows it, and doesn't like it. But what can he do?—he's in no position. What else do you want to know? When I had my last period?"

He blushed, and guffawed, though he was interested in these mysteries of a woman's tummy. His sister told him, "You need to get laid, Ted. You should be nice to some of these girls Jared tosses your way. Emily doesn't know you're being faithful, and probably cares less than you think."

The thought astounded him; but, as often with the wisdom of his older siblings, he felt there was something a bit off, a bit glib, a bit harsh, that misstated the delicate nature of reality as he needed to grasp it for himself. He did not want life to shatter in his hands as it had for Father.

Esther told him, "Emily wants what we all want—you to grow up and be a man." He was flattered, to think of himself as an object of such desire in several women's minds, but doubted that Esther had it quite right. Her oracular power over him had been diminished by the years, and by her evident inability to foresee and shape her own future. She was drifting on America's sea of appetites and easy money and jazz.

In late May, a young Minnesotan named Charles Lindbergh, munching some sandwiches he had made and dipping as low as ten feet above the whitecapped surface of the ocean and then climbing as high as ten thousand feet, achieved the first non-stop solo flight across the Atlantic. In June, watching Lindbergh's ticker-tape parade from the windows of the McMullen Investments office on lower Broadway—the snow of torn paper and spiralling ticker tape flickering down upon the rectangle of open limousine and the parallel bean-shaped backs of the mounted police—Teddy felt blinded by a surge of inspiration: such feats of daring and perseverance are what the world asks of young men. Teddy was twenty-four, Lindbergh was twenty-five. Lindy had left Roosevelt Field in New York so overloaded with gasoline he had barely cleared the treetops, and by ten o'clock the next night had sighted the lights of Paris. Appalled by the sheer drop of corniced brick wall, yet to test his nerve leaning further out of the window (one of the little sharp-faced stenographers clutched excitedly at his arm; blobs of sun twinkled on the nickel-plated instruments of the marching band far below), Teddy in a great inner leap decided to leave New York, return to Basingstoke, and ask Emily Sifford to marry him.

She was not as surprised and overwhelmed by joy as he had thought she would be. She explained to him, walking in the June heat down Fishery Way to as far as the old pier, "You had to *see*, Teddy, what that world was like. You had to see if that's where the answer was."

"It was boring, among other things. New York looks like there's a million choices but in fact everybody wears a little rut and sticks to it. Every day, you do the same things and run into the same people. The only one I thought really belonged there was Mr. McMullen. He didn't have much to say to me but I liked him. When I said I was quitting, he said he thought I'd come to the right decision. He was the only one who said that. Nobody around here says it, I tell you that."

She avoided this last sentence, with its hint of challenge and blame, and asked, "Is he really a big bootlegger, like everybody claims?"

It all seemed far away already. Teddy's most vivid memory of Jim McMullen was taking his spring overcoat one time when he came to Jared and Lucille's apartment and being startled by how light, how soft, how *expensive* it was, as if conjured from the wool of angelic black lambs. "Beats me, Em. I don't know if he does the dirty work himself or just knows guys who do. He gets a lot of money from somewhere to invest, I know that. Jared's so flush he's talking about an estate in Connecticut, to give his baby fresh air to breathe. I guess he would have made it worth my while, if I hung around, but I'd always be the little brother. Like I said, I had this flash when everything unimportant fell away, and I could see down this sudden straight road. With you at the end of it." Shining like the lights of Paris for Lindy. It had been the closest to a religious experience Teddy expected to have.

She absorbed the compliment without surprise but asked with a grave intonation, "Did you really miss me?"

"And how."

She gratefully squeezed his arm, with both hands, a gesture she sometimes used to slow him down when he was walking too fast. But since he had, on the cut-plush sofa, with the radio turned off so as not to distract them from this high moment, asked her to marry him, she had moved more lightly, her limp become a kind of skip at his side.

"I'm so glad, Ted. I was afraid, there with all those fashionable girls . . ."

"There were girls there all right, but they didn't have anything to do with me. They slid by on the street. The stenographers at McMullen's were silly twits with boyfriends back in Flatbush."

"You have to reach *out,*" Em said, almost scolding. "You can't expect girls to come running up to you like yellow jackets to a jam sandwich. I know you're shy, that's one of the things I'm crazy about, about you, but I was afraid that Jared, he's not so shy, would find a girl that . . ."

He realized she wouldn't finish. "Well, I guess he would have, if I'd been more interested. But I felt—I can't say exactly frightened, but—do you ever get that feeling of being someplace you shouldn't be? And waking up with this empty taste in your mouth?"

"Oh yes. I've had it ever since we moved to Basingstoke. My mother has it even worse."

"Now that we're sort of set I should ask you, is anything the matter with her? One of the things my folks bring up about you is that she seems a bit, well, out of the ordinary."

"My mother," Emily said, hardly hesitating, matter-of-fact like a wife, "is a Moor. Have you been in Delaware long enough to know what a Moor is?"

"Well . . . sure."

"I can tell you don't. There used to be a lot of pirate ships off the coast, up and down Delaware Bay in the colonial days, and one story is that a ship from the north of Africa shipwrecked down in Sussex County and they came ashore and began to farm and so on. There used to be quite a prosperous community of Moors near Cheswold, in Kent County. Another story is that in the days of slavery a captured Moorish prince was being auctioned off in Lewes and was bought by a beautiful Irish woman who lived near Angola Neck nearby."

"I like that one," Ted said, teasing, since Emily was being so solemn and instructive.

"And some say the Moors are just mulattoes and belong with the Negroes as far as schooling and everything goes. It's very old-fashioned Southern down below the canal and one of the reasons my father was willing to sell out and come up here was he was always having to protect my mother. One time I remember them talking about was they wouldn't let her into a revival meeting with him and he turned away rather than sit way back on the colored benches with her. You can understand how such experiences would make a person keep to themselves."

"I sure can," he said, already loyal to his future mother-in-law, but excited by this suspicious revelation. There was something unusual about Emily's own skin, a glow to it that wasn't a pink glow.

As if reading his mind, Emily said, "She doesn't have a drop of Negro blood. The worst you can say about the Moors is that they might be related to the Delaware Indians."

"Honey, don't look so *serious,*" he said, and stopped her walking and hugged her, here on the path that straggled on beyond the end of Fishery Way, along the marshes that flanked the broadening Avon. "You're my sweetheart for life and that's all that matters."

"I have a horrible deformed foot but no black blood," she said, with a child's petulant insistence, twisting her head to avoid looking him in the face as he held her in his arms, fighting and holding the moist elastic bulk of her torso in its wide-collared sailor-blouse. It was a June day of oceanic splendor, with a few silent seagulls etched in feathered wingspread on a sky purer than glass. Heat and light poured down and the tidal marsh that stretched to the low horizon revealed with intermittent furtive sounds the suck of ebbing water and the movements of the invisible lives—crabs, birds, muskrats, turtles—that its mud and reeds harbored. A half-mile away, a dory was being rowed up the Avon, its oars rhythmically dipping. Emily in his arms was shuddering with tears.

"Honey, honey," he said, "I don't care if you do or don't."

"How can you not?" she ungratefully sobbed. "What's the matter with you?"

"Nothing's the matter with me," Teddy said, "that a little cuddling won't cure."

This made her laugh, through her snuffles. They found a little privacy by climbing over a rotting rail fence and settling beneath an old apple tree where the grass had been allowed to grow long. He leaned his back against the tree and let her curl against him; he caressed the side of her neck with one hand and with the other undid the buttons of her blouse and traced the tops of her breasts along the line of her slip and bra. Her fine pale-brown hair, mussed by their walk and her crying, had the sunstruck hayey smell of the grass going to seed around them. He tugged loose her hairpins, without asking. In the confident mood swelling in him as he descended deeper into this other's docile presence, he teased, "Weren't you afraid I wouldn't come back?"

"I was," she said, "but—what could I do?" Her shrug twitched his body. "It was in God's hands. If you didn't, I was no worse off than before, and we'd had our nice times together."

"You believe God has hands?" he asked, idly watching a bee move back and forth in the air, looking for flowers. Teddy's happiness, as he lay here idly touching Emily, as she played with a button of his shirt, was gathering like a sweet fist behind his fly. How strange to feel another person is yours—to play with, to talk to, to expose your self to in all its shame.

"Oh yes," she said, a bit combatively, the way she could be, but her voice still lulled within the same mesmerized doziness he felt, all his decisions behind him. "Why not, to make—all this?" The flat lush Delaware landscape around them. In a far field a dozen Holstein cows grazed along the horizon of a green ridge that might have been the edge of the world.

"I mean, you believe what they tell you in church?"

"Yes. Yes, Ted, I do. I know you don't, or think you don't."

He sighed. "That's right. I think I don't. I get that from my father. My poor dad wanted to believe and needed to believe and God just stayed silent."

"He's not silent with me."

"What does He tell you?"

Her hand had gone to the sensitive bump behind his fly. "To love you with all my heart," she said. "To serve you, in the faith that you'll serve me."

Her words, and her voice, and the day's buzzing impervious beauty, with the distant cows on the world's edge and the soft steady chunk of oars coming from far in the other direction, brought him to the point, as she had been earlier, of crying. She was so good, her hand so white and quiet resting there.

"Do you mind?" she asked, so softly only an ear inches from her mouth could have heard.

"Mind what?"

"My believing still. I know all the arguments against it."

"No," he said, his heart's blood feeling to leak away in the gush of the realization, "I don't mind it. I love it." More urgently: "I want you to."

That day for the first time she took him, the grotesque helpless core of him, out of his pants—a strong smell came to their nostrils, like that of a crushed bug—there in the sun. They looked together as she moved her perfectly shaped hand up and down on the loose skin until he spent his white spittle of human seed. He shut his eyes, but knowing that she was still steadfastly looking gave him courage to open them at the moment of ecstasy. They were both surprised by the sight, which neither had ever seen before. "How high it jumped," she murmured, wiping her hand on the grass.

He tucked his milked self back into his fly while she heavily relaxed back against him, her hand giving off the crushed-bug smell as she moved it to his shoulder. He should have felt grateful for the gift of her act but instead felt faintly disagreeable. "Wasn't that a sin?" he asked her, teasing her professed faith.

But she wasn't to be put off, here in this sun-warmed meadow, awash in womanly confidence. "Not if you marry me," she smiled.

Now came a time of changes and decisions, events that tumbled together confusedly in the family memory—a quick avalanche settling into the static decade of the Depression.

Very well, Teddy was to marry Emily Sifford, there was no stopping it; but what was Teddy to do? He couldn't go back to being a soda jerk, even if Seth Addison hadn't hired another boy, Charlie Wainwright's younger brother Bob, on his way to being a registered pharmacist himself. Education didn't seem to take with Teddy, though he was bright enough; his brightness was something he kept hidden, as if it might get squelched in the open. He needed something respectable, because he was a Wilmot, and yet not too demanding, because he was Teddy. Once again the answer came from Aunt Esther, immobilized though she was in her upstairs room. On her chunky black Bakelite daffodil of a telephone she heard that Jeb Horley down at the post office was looking for a new mail carrier. With the bottle-cap business flourishing and Wilmington and Philadelphia needing ever more oysters and peaches, corn and crabs, the town had grown enough so that the crowd calling for its mail at the post office, in its narrow half of the downtown brick building it shared with a new sweetshop opened by a middle-aged couple moved down from Chester, had become unmanageable in the mornings, while the mail was still being sorted. The Postmaster General in Washington wanted to expand rural free delivery, and Basingstoke was to be divided into an auto route on the outskirts and a walking route in town, including the colored shantytown in the west end, along Beaver Road. Old Wes Freeman had been doing it all, in and out of his canvas-top Model T until he was bent over permanently in a crouching position, and they needed a young man to take on walking three miles twice a day, six days a week, for a thousand dollars per annum, payable twice a month, with consecutive raises of one hundred each for the first two years and fifteen days annual paid vacation. Applicants had to take a Civil Service examination down in Dover, and then be appointed by the Postmaster General, on the nomination of the postmaster. Jeb Horley had the applicants read off a batch of handwritten names and transcribe some strings of numbers—child's play to Teddy, after the rigors of

O'Connell's School of Practical Business. It was also necessary to have a physical exam, and Doc Hedger gave him a good bill of health. "You children got your mother's constitution," he concluded wheezily, as Teddy dressed himself again. "Missouri mules. You'll live forever. The Wilmots, now, seem to be a little too fine-spun."

This left the matters of attitude and aptitude, and Teddy surprised himself with his passion when he told the grimy postmaster, in his sleeve-gartered shirt and tired blue-gray vest, how much he wanted the job. He was about to take a wife, to whom he owed the security of dependable employment, and what more dependable than the U.S. government? What more honorable, for that matter, than knitting together your society by carrying the mails? His brother had been a soldier wounded in the Great War, Teddy perhaps unnecessarily told Mr. Horley, and though he himself had been too young to serve he liked the idea of serving the country somehow. As a boy, he added, he had collected stamps, and still had his collection, somewhere in his Aunt Esther's attic. "Knew Esther when Horace first brought her to town," Mr. Horley unexpectedly volunteered. "Wondered how he'd ever talked such a beauty into being his bride. And here you're about to carry off the Sifford heiress. There must be more to you little roly-poly fellas than meets the eye."

After this gruff pleasantry Teddy knew he would get the job. And so it was that that unseasonably warm September, as the locusts and poplars and willows and lindens along the streets of Basingstoke turned yellow and slowly dropped their variously shaped leaves onto the buckling sidewalks—blue slate slabs in the oldest section of the town, three-foot concrete widths most elsewhere, and in the less developed districts dirt paths trod in a wavery line beside the roadway—he resumed the walks that he had taken through the town in his earliest days there, only now he leaned against the weight of a leather carrier's pouch and wore a gray-blue uniform and shoes black and thick-soled like a policeman's. The carrier himself paid for the uniform—the coat wool worsted and double-breasted in winter, and single-breasted and cotton serge in summer, with black mohair braid piping and ten brass buttons each of them showing a tiny carrier with a mailbag and an uplifted letter. There was broadcloth piping down the outside seam of the pants. For cold weather, regulations offered either a reversible cape or an overcoat, and Jeb Horley didn't think a cape would be Basingstoke style—though there were stories of highwaymen in these parts in the colonial days.

More houses than Teddy had ever noticed were set well back from the street, with cement or flagstone walks that in sum added a mile or two to the route, and front-porch steps that amounted, he felt, to climbing the Washington Monument twice daily. Some of the larger old houses, dating from before the Civil War, and built by money derived from slave plantations, had been broken up into apartments, and these changing names and backstairs addresses had to be sorted out. He walked Beaver Road, though the mail volume was slight, striding his way through the stray chickens and snarling coon dogs and barefooted, even bare-bottomed pickaninnies. Houses, as he stepped up to their mail slots, seemed to hold their breaths in expectation: the humming of a Hoover was shut off, the crying of an infant ceased, the braided voices of a strident quarrel broke off. On rainy days, he wore a black slicker with a fisherman's hat that poured the water down off his back; the colors of the town seemed dyed deeper, green lawn and black asphalt and red-brick wall all speaking to him with the intensity of his ambulating solitude. The only man out in the rain, he moved in and out of the shelter of porches as if down a long broken tunnel. As cold dark mornings brought in a November chill, he wore knit underwear beneath his uniform, and a wool liner that Emily made for his black-billed carrier's cap. He liked to be at the post office by seven-fifteen, when Wes Freeman brought the mailbags up from the Canal station four miles away in the back of the Model T, from which the buttoned-leather seat had been removed. Teddy had generally come back from his second, lighter route by four or four-thirty. His bag as he shouldered it by nine-thirty had the satisfying weight of responsibility, and the empty pouch he slapped down on the sorting table at the end of the afternoon had the lightness of freedom. Fridays, when the magazines came in, and Mondays, with the delayed Sunday load, were the heaviest days; after Christmas, volume dropped to half. Some December days it seemed that Baby Jesus was personally trying to break his back.

Teddy and Emily were married two weeks after Christmas, in the Methodist Church on Third Street, just off Rodney, on the afternoon of a quick and wet Saturday snowstorm. It was strange, to be again in a church—its spiky varnished woodwork, its warm haunted smell of flowers and wax and coal-gas and dust. The vows went through him like wind through a window; Emily in the corner of his vision appeared expanded by the white veil and the quaint redundant words "wedded wife." Her hand trembled so much as he fitted the ring to her finger that she half-laughed, there up at the altar, at their mutual clumsiness. Outside, on the church porch, sleet slashed their faces and a few handfuls of rice rattled off their flinching shoulders. The guests had hardly filled the three front pews. Aunt Esther had hoped to attend but in the end just felt too frail and nauseated out of bed. Lucille was too pregnant to come but Jared had driven down, and acted as the chauffeur for the bride and groom. The church lawn was hard as iron, and slick; on her good foot Emily wore a white silver-brocaded slipper with an English penny in it. The slipper, which was a bit roomy, had come from his mother, and the old penny from her father, who had turned it up with the plow in the tobacco fields years ago. Her husband of five minutes, seeing her hesitate fearfully at the edge of the curb with its inch of wet snow, reached down and carried her the two strides into Jared's long tan Stutz convertible. She was heavier than mail but deliciously smooth-bottomed in her simple gown of white silk charmeuse, with a headdress and veil but no dragging train.

Jeb Horley had given him the day off but he was too newly hired to be given leave for a honeymoon, so they took the five o'clock express from Wilmington to Philadelphia and stayed in the Bellevue-Stratford Hotel, which could have put up every citizen of Basingstoke in its rooms and held all the churches of the town in its lobby without their steeples' touching the chandeliers. Teddy had been told by Charlie Wainwright, that know-it-all, that it was an easy walk from the Broad Street Station, but Charlie hadn't figured on the cold and the dark and having a lame wife. Nevertheless, warmed by the spectral jostle of so many people, and by the sensation of being alone together in a world where no one knew them, the couple made their way across City Hall's brightly lit courtyard and three blocks down South Broad Street. Twice they paused so Emily could get her breath, once to look up at William Penn high above them like a staid spotlit angel in a broadbrimmed hat, and again to lean a minute against the stone banister of the Union League's curving double stairway. The trip inside the hotel corridors to their room was itself lengthy, Teddy desperately worrying all the while whether a quarter was enough tip for the jaunty bellhop carrying their homely old suitcases, scuffed pale leather left over from Clarence and Stella Wilmot's travelling days in the Midwest. Shyly keeping the bathroom door closed, first Emily, then he, took a bath in the vast tub. Water pounded from the long-nosed faucet with the force of a geyser and the heat of a volcano. The cabinet mirror steamed; vapor turned to frost-ferns on the bathroom window, at whose edges Teddy's hand felt the whisper of January wind. Dry spatterings of snow appeared in the windowlight and fell away, down into the dirty city. On the big brass bed the hotel provided, with fringed pillows and a quilted coverlet smelling of crushed lavender, Teddy and Emily, fumbling and wincing, devirginated each other, then fell asleep with odd speed, hardly giving themselves a minute in which to discuss the events of a day so momentous and active.

Church bells woke them, amid these January cliffs of stone.

But from where? Emily had read, in preparation for this brief honeymoon, about Rittenhouse Square, with its elegant townhouses and an Episcopal church whose rector had written "O Little Town of Bethlehem" during the Civil War. She expressed a shy wish to attend service there, since not only its former rector but its interior architecture was famous, but Teddy begged her to come back to bed from the window, if she wasn't too sore from last night. The sky in the top of the window was that impossibly distant cold city sky he had found himself awaking under in New York but now she was with him, her shape touching her thin nightie with shadow from within as she limped toward him, in the high-ceilinged room with red velvet drapes, which they drew shut so the sight of each other wasn't too intense. Afterwards, while she was in the bathroom cleaning herself, he took the bedside telephone and ordered breakfast to be brought up to them right there. Fried eggs, toast, and scrapple with syrup, all served under big domes of plated silver by a uniformed colored man with kinky gray hair, tiny white circlets, above his ears. Teddy tipped him a whole half-dollar, as he had seen Jared do in New York; the old man's eyes widened, it had been too much—what a rube would do.

When at last they stepped out onto the southern side of Walnut Street—he in his one dark suit, she in a new moss-green all-wool poiret sheen dress that fell straight from her hips and whose high hem exposed the leg brace attached to the thick-soled shoe—it was nearly noon. Sun reflected back at them from the brick façades of the houses, packed one against another like stripes, as they walked west toward Rittenhouse Square; the newlyweds mingled in the park with the fur-clad, top-hatted Philadelphians who had been to church. Diagonal paths crunched past a dry fountain, with a wading pool. There was a statue of a billygoat, much burnished by being mounted by children. The twigs of the graceful bare trees gleamed in the winter sun as if with ice. Yesterday's flurry of snow lingered as white shadows beneath bushes and at the edges of things, wherever real shadows were cast. Nursemaids in mousy dark coats and felt hats trimmed with a feather or a silk flower were sitting on benches beside big-wheeled baby carriages each heaped with crocheted blankets all but burying a set of red cheeks, a pink nose, a frilled bonnet. On the far side of the square, the famous Church of the Holy Trinity was smaller, Teddy thought to himself, than St. John's back in Paterson, and its tower didn't compare to that of Paterson City Hall. The day was so bright it seemed warm; Teddy, whose legs were hard from carrying the mail, would have stridden all over the town, but to spare Emily more walking they hired a taxi, which took them at a sightseeing pace back down Chestnut Street to Independence Hall, where the signers signed the Declaration of Independence and the Liberty Bell was rung before it cracked. The driver stopped the cab long enough for them to get out and cross the sidewalk and view the bell from close up; it hung from an ornately supported squat beam; the crack had been touched so often by curious or reverent hands that the metal shone a coppery golden color. Strange, Teddy thought, that the crack, the imperfection, had become the important thing. He was more interested in the offices of *The Saturday Evening Post,* since he had carried so many copies; the Curtis Building happened to stand next to Independence Square. The taxi driver, an old man who had not shaved that morning and who seemed bleary from the miles and miles that had taken him nowhere, suggested they look in the lobby: there was something there to see, "something wonderful." They got out and looked in the vast building's marble lobby, which was open so that even on a Sunday people could admire the unearthly Maxfield Parrish "dream garden" worked out in a mosaic of Tiffany glass, the colors as if from another rainbow than our own, a rainbow arching on another planet. Emboldened by this marvel, feeling the hour drawing nearer when they must return to Basingstoke, Teddy asked if the main post office was far away, and the driver said No, it was just a few blocks away, at Ninth and Market.

"I work for the Postal Department," Teddy explained to him, giving Emily's thigh a squeeze through her shiny green dress. A job and a wife: he had become a man. He climbed from the cab and basked a moment in the block-long post office's splendor—its four heavy cornices, its mansard-roofed central tower flying the American flag. The majestic portals and uncountable windows all presented the grave shut face of a nation's Sunday rest. "Thank you," Teddy said to the driver, getting back in, and to Emily, "Anything you want to see, or shall we have a quick lunch at the hotel before the train back?"

Leaning forward in her seat, the color of her face somehow higher than before he had made her a woman, she cleared her throat and spoke up to the driver: "Where are the museums?" To Teddy she said, with a shy upward glance that displayed her luminous eye-whites, "Darling, do you mind? I want to see something lovely, to take the memory back." Hadn't there been enough loveliness, losing her virginity and seeing the Curtis Building lobby? The grizzled driver also did not quite understand, but assumed she would want to see the museum whose lavish construction had been in the papers for years. He continued along Market and around what they now recognized as City Hall and up a broad diagonal boulevard, past a big fountain holding three naked Indians and a swan, toward a little mountain where a great wide many-pillared temple, its granite and marble shining with newness, waited above a multitude of steps. But the museum, which the driver called "the Museum at Fairmont," was too newly constructed to be yet open to the public, though it had been recently open to the press; a rubble of lumber, worked stone, scaffolding, and ungrassed frozen earth muddled the base of its grandeur.

Teddy looked nervously at the woman at his side, in her shiny green dress that exposed the metal brace on one foot. "That lovely enough?"

He was not surprised by the tears that had started to her eyes. "It's like us," she said. "At the beginning. I want to see something complete and perfect." She was beginning to sound unreasonable. He had heard about women's fits of unreasonableness but had never been in charge of one before. The grizzled taxi driver, too, was beginning to worry, perhaps thinking that his fare was growing beyond the capacity of this young couple to pay it. He turned left off the Benjamin Franklin Parkway onto a street called Cherry and stopped before a many-textured, Turkish-looking building with PENNSYLVANIA ACADEMY OF THE FINE ARTS above a pair of cavelike doors. Teddy paid the driver the four dollars he asked plus fifty cents tip; this time, he felt it was not too much, though the cabby said emphatically, "Thank you, *sir.*" Four dollars was more than Teddy got for a long day lugging the mail. Money makes the man, pussy takes.

They moved through the mouth of the cave and a shadowy foyer and then suddenly space dazzlingly opened into a four-story stair hall lined in gold and silver, bronze and red, tiles and wall flowers, all crowned by an artificial sky sprinkled with stars and holding a great glass square of real sky. Ornate visual luxury crowded every space of floor and wall and stair, up which Emily labored as if ascending, step by painful step, into Heaven. On one side, at the top of the stair, was a large painting called *Christ Rejected,* with a confusion of heads and gestures; facing it across the stair hall was another by the same painter called *Death on the Pale Horse,* even more confusing, with horses and crowned men and falling, desperate figures, all out of Revelation, Emily explained. Teddy felt oppressed by the oily clutter of these visions, as he had by the tall shelves of books in his father's study back in the manse in Paterson. The snake-pit of history bequeaths us its mad dreams. These painters and their models had already sunk into the teeming abyss that will swallow us all. Through pillared and pointed archways, past walls covered with raised diamond-shaped flowers or else painted the bright pink inside an eyelid, the young couple moved into chambers echoing of emptiness, rooms of the palace of an invisible sultan. Yet another big canvas, again by Benjamin West, showed William Penn arranging a treaty with the Indians, using the same expansive gesture with which Christ had been rejected. Statues floated in light admitted from above, angels and goddesses carved as if from the whitest soap, the angels baring but one breast in their loose wrinkled robes whereas the goddesses were quite naked, their faces tranquilly blank and benign above the twin bared breasts. Their nakedness, unlike Emily's, had no pink tinge, and would not yield to his own skin if he dared reach out and, disobeying admonitory signs at the entrance of each gallery, touch. And there were dark naked bronzes frozen tiptoe on the edge of decency, and busts and portraits of Washington and Franklin and those other velvet-clad founders of our freedom, quizzically peering out at these shuffling citizens of a shadowy future. Bobbing along with her crippled gait, Emily seemed to lift her head into a realm where her face glowed and flashed its highlights just like the faces painted on the canvases around her. She called his attention to this and that—a red fox silhouetted on a field of snow with pricking ears, a couple of women hailing a ferry from a reedy riverbank—and he was touched by this appetite in her for beauty, and proud of it, though saddened to foresee how little the life he could give her would feed and satisfy her yearnings.

When they emerged, Broad Street had been warmed into raucous pedestrian life, with peddlers and beggars, fruit carts and street dancers, players of the harmonica and the accordion. Trolley cars rumbled and jangled down the center of the cobbled street, but he was afraid of the trolley's taking an unexpected turn and losing them in the city. He could see City Hall's now-familiar silhouette, the tallest in a chorus of spires, two blocks to the south and calculated that their hotel lay three blocks beyond it. Knowing the layout of streets always gave him pleasure and a sense of control. "Em, can you make it as far as City Hall?"

"Of course, dear."

"The station'll be on the right. You go in and have a soda

while I hoof it on down to the hotel and get the bags and bring 'em back."

"Darling, I wouldn't dream of eating without you. We'll have a sandwich on the train."

Nevertheless, at the bustling station doors, the winter light already dying, he gave her two quarters, making sure he had enough money left to settle the bill and tip the bellhop. That was what being married meant: thinking for two and shelling out dough twice as fast. The responsibility of it made him smile as he hurried along. People laughed, in the years ahead, when they confessed that they had spent their honeymoon in Philadelphia, but in truth the old city had showed them a pretty good time.

They moved in at first with Aunt Esther. They agreed to pay six dollars a week rent. His room on the third floor was fairly spacious, with windows on two sides, one of which overlooked the white gazebo, glowing in its dank neglected garden at the bottom of the yard. Beyond the door was a space of hall at the head of the stairway which, though drafty, could be used as a sitting room. Her parents spared them some furniture, including the red cut-plush sofa. That first winter they bought themselves a little radio and would sit there after supper listening to whatever the dials magically dragged in—the musical program by Major Edward Bowes from the Capitol Theatre in New York City, a bedtime story from Uncle Bob out of Station KYW in Philadelphia, dance music or opera arias drifting in and out of the surf of static. There was no plumbing on the third floor but, with only Mother and Aunt Esther to share the second-floor bathroom with, this was no hardship. The two older women pretended to be thrilled, and maybe they were, to have a younger one in the house; Emily limped nimbly about in the kitchen, but Mother didn't encourage her to take over the cooking: "It gives me so much pleasure, dear, and now that I'm slowing down it's my only way to earn my keep." She gracefully yielded, however, much of the housework—that significant part of it which Edwina never got to—and attendance upon her increasingly bed-ridden sister-in-law. Emily spent hours in Aunt Esther's bedroom, the two of them talking, until Emily knew as much Basingstoke gossip and history as a native. Sometimes of an evening, expansively feeling his role as the only man of the house, Teddy would visit Aunt Esther. He pondered her, this woman who had welcomed them into her house, and who had guided him into one job after another, and who now had taken his bride in hand as if she were her spiritual mother, and yet who had always loomed to him as a prim, cold presence. Esther Wilmot had been a beauty, the May Queen of the class of 1889 at the Hopewell Academy for Girls. Awareness of being entrusted with a treasure had locked her, perhaps, into an attitude of aloofness; those endowed with a splendid self have a duty to be selfish. She sat upright in bed and her face in its slow withering still held its straight nose, its high brow, its lucid frosty eyes, its chin a little square and masculine in the style of long-ago Gibson girls. In the sickroom light it seemed to be his father transparently gazing out at him through those shadowy, sandy-browed sockets. Father had been in that final waning somehow happy, as a child confined to bed on a school day is happy. His sister had less of his wan tubercular helplessness but also none of that happiness; she was supported only by the husk of female vanity and the stiff affirmations of conventional Christianity. Aunt Esther's mouth, habitually severe, had already deserted her face for the reptilian realm of death; her upper lip had become hideously riddled with wrinkles, vertical creases at first and then spidery horizontals imposed crosswise, like the mouth of a mummy. She had pain, and Teddy recognized the patented elixirs Doc Hedger prescribed as thickened, sweetened infusions of alcohol and opium.

Aunt Esther looked at him one day with special keenness. "You're the man around here—what do you make of this?" she asked him.

She showed him a letter she had received from a hotel in

Hagerstown, Maryland, written in a precise slant hand, saying, *My dear Esther, I have been sorry to hear poor reports of your health. Is there any service, personal or financial, you would allow me to perform at this time? Though we had our differences I am still your husband in name and law, and I sign this sincere inquiry with affection.*

"Uncle Horace," Teddy said.

"How about that?" she said, her dreadful dead-woman's lips tweaking in a small smile—pride justified.

By the late spring of 1928, as dramatic fluctuations in the stock market and government reports of widespread unemployment in the textile and other industries were sending vibrations through the nation, Horace had come back to the house, his hair thinner and whiter than they all remembered but his face as rosy as ever, and his voice as chirpy, insistent, and irritating. He had a dozen ideas as to how the house could be brought back up to scratch, beginning with the garden, where he expected Teddy to work every evening, dog-weary as he was from walking his route. He didn't treat Teddy like a man, still, even though he wore the mailman's uniform and everybody said that delivery had never been like this in the days of Wes Freeman, who might keep the bulk mail in the back of his Model T for weeks at a time. Emily, too, felt awkward in the house now that Horace was back, since he took on his wife's care with a vengeance—Stella marvelled at the devotion he showed. "How hard it is," she told Teddy and Emily at the kitchen table, "to judge other people. Away for ten years, and comes back a devoted lovebird, with his whole other life dropped into the void."

Teddy knew that Horace had taken out a box at the post office, a number to which his private mail from that other life could be addressed; letters in a woman's hand from Hagerstown came at least once a week, and there was business mail sent to the box number, and at the time of Horace's birthday several tinted square envelopes addressed in childish writing. Teddy said nothing now; he felt postal information was sacrosanct. But he did say, "Mother, I think Em and I had better be clearing out. This house is getting to feel crowded."

Stella's shiny plumlike eyes, beneath her bushy low hairline, looked at him with much the same mixture of compassion and bewilderment with which she had long ago received her husband's announcement that he had lost his faith. "You'd go and leave me alone here?" she said.

"You won't be alone," Teddy said, rather sternly. "You have one more in the house than when you sent me off to New York. And now Pete Pulsifer has his divorce, Esther may be coming back to town."

For this, too, had happened, that same summer, in the old courthouse in New Castle, just as everybody around Basingstoke was agreeing it never would.

Aunt Esther was sinking; Horace had taken her in his new Chrysler up to Wilmington to consult a doctor, saying Doc Hedger was an old-fashioned quack and always had been, and the city specialist had confided to him that cancer had spread from her uterus throughout her body. Had it been caught in time, an operation might have saved her—who can say?—but now it was too late. She had stopped eating, except for a little chicken broth and dry toast he would take her on a tray, yet she looked imposing, thin as a crucifix, propped up straight in bed, her long hair lovingly combed and pinned by her husband. She gabbled on the telephone in a voice sharper and stronger than ever; her sardonic laughter, as she heard of this or that mishap among her neighbors, echoed throughout the house, which now held its own scandal of impending death.

Emily took word of Teddy's discontent to her father, and Mr. Sifford put the five-hundred-dollar down payment on a little two-story wooden house halfway down Locust Street, on the north side. Her parents' side porch and a stretch of greenhouse glass could be seen from their front-bedroom windows, looking southeast. The mortgage payments—twenty-eight dollars a month for thirty years—were theirs to keep up. The place sat on a quarter-acre lot, tucked between two larger, brick houses, somewhat back from the road. The last time it had been painted, at least ten years ago, the owner had chosen a leaden gray, like that of a battleship, possibly because so dull a color was on sale cheap at the hardware store. Yet, when Teddy, working on weekends throughout that first summer, painted it himself, he chose virtually the same shade. He liked the way the house seemed to hide, to hang back, between its two imposing neighbors. He put all the color into the grounds, where, drawing on the experience he had gained gardening for Aunt Esther when freshly come to Basingstoke, he planted hollyhocks and foxgloves, pansies and geraniums, peonies and phlox, irises and orange daylilies. People always assumed that Emily was behind the carefully groomed splash of flowers, because of her association with the greenhouse, but it was Teddy, bending down in his undershirt in the hour of light that stretched out after their evening meal, who kept up the weeding, the fertilizing, the transplanting. Emily didn't like working outdoors, actually; the bugs bothered her sensitive skin too much, evergreen pollen made her eyes itch and puff up, and the sun on her skin gave her hives. There was something delicious about her, something indoorsy and pampered, a thin-skinned succulence, which everyone could appreciate as the years added a few pounds to her figure, but which Teddy had spotted at the beginning. The couple formed a touching—what one old neighbor called a "quaint"—sight, as they walked along Locust Street and Fishery Way to the Roxie on Rodney Street. The Roxie had installed sound to accommodate Warner Brothers "talkies." Movietone newsreels backed by a booming Godlike voice intoned word of zeppelins and speakeasy raids and the smiling Josef Stalin's newly announced five-year plan.

Esther and Peter didn't settle in Basingstoke, where Mrs. Pulsifer remained, in what had become her handsome slate-roofed, step-gabled house on Juniper Street, with the three small children. The new Pulsifers were married by a justice of the peace in New York City Hall, with only Jared and Lucille standing there as witnesses—Lucille's four-month-old son

James Patrick held in her arms. After a trip to Barbados, they settled into a spacious river-view apartment in Red Lion, six miles away. Pulsifer was a muscular amiable man of thirty-five, his wiry amber hair thinned back high off his temples; the back of his skull showed a bald spot the size of a silver dollar. He had the lawyer's gift for getting along with all types, but when the two newlywed couples arranged to get together, in Basingstoke or Red Lion or at a roadhouse in between, he was clearly uneasy at being in company with a mailman and a farmer's daughter; he would either be facetious and giddy in a condescending way, as if they were children to be entertained, or else stare into space, wondering perhaps why he had ever left his wife and expensive home for these mediocre and depressing relations. Sometimes Teddy saw Esther alone at the house on Willow Street, when they would go visit their aunt and mother. He mildly complained, "That husband of yours's an awful snob. Emily reads books and magazines all day, when she isn't over at the greenhouse, and I'm not as dumb as I look, but he treats us like rubes. You can see his brain shut down when either of us tries to talk."

She squinted a second before answering: "Pete's got problems. His bitch of an ex-wife is always whining for more money than the agreement calls for. And he broods over which clients have dropped him, because of us. I tell him, 'Don't be paranoid—in this day and age? Everybody's playing around, nobody gives a damn. Nobody cares. At least you didn't let your wife burn up in a boarding house like Babe Ruth.' But it's true, Bundy and McReady get a lot more business now than Pete. It'll be a long haul for us, to win back the Babbitts of the world."

"Well, still. He shouldn't snub Emily. She's bright. She just read that novel about the bridge falling down in Peru."

His sister squared her jaw and touched his shoulder with a little push. "Look. Relax. We've made our beds, let's lie in 'em. *Toujours gai,* right?"

It was February of 1929 when Aunt Esther did die; Horace

came in with her breakfast tray—a little toast, a cupful of steaming oatmeal, anything to keep her from wasting into nothing—and found her lying sideways on the pillow, the telephone in bed with her, as if her last thought had been to give somebody a call in the dead of the night. The next week, Mother, on a Sunday morning before church, came rattling at the Locust Street back door; Teddy and Emily had been embracing in the kitchen, and sprang guiltily apart. But Stella was too upset to notice their flushed faces, or if she did waved their embarrassment aside, wide-eyed with her news. "Horace is bent on selling the house and moving back to Hagerstown! He has this second family out there and already's been back to visit, he was bold enough to tell me. He can't wait another week to put the place on the market! I hate to say so, but I do believe he came here not out of any concern for Esther but just to claim the house—to make sure she didn't leave the property to one of us."

"I'm not surprised," Teddy said, feeling guilty that he had known about the letters from Maryland all along. Still, it was hard to believe wickedness of Uncle Horace, who in one of his nephew's earliest memories was giving him a piggyback ride to the glowing white gazebo and back, chuckling and clucking, over a lawn that seemed like an emerald carpet. That chirpy little voice, squeezed out through his nose as if he were imitating a duck, and the pink smooth cheeks that looked like he never had to shave. Teddy had seen him crying, the day of Aunt Esther's funeral, out there in the cold, the family standing around the rectangular hole pickaxed through the frost and an inch of fresh snowfall.

Stella sat down at the table and unpinned her navy-blue churchgoing hat. Her splendid head of hair, streaked with white, seemed less a crowning glory now than a burden—her whole body, in its winter coat of once-opulent beaver bought way back in Minnesota, heavy on her soul. "I said to him, 'Where will I go, Horace?' and he looked at me sly as you please and said, 'You have three kiddies.' But Jared has no place in his fancy life for an old woman, and Esther with the best will in the world is in no position, they're just scraping by for now—"

Emily stepped forward awkwardly, from over by the new porcelain sink they had put in, beside the oak icebox, and said, with a quick helpless look at Teddy that flashed the whites of her eyes, "Ted and I would be *thrilled*, Mrs. Wilmot, if you'd consider moving in with us. There's that big front bedroom upstairs of no use to me except to sew and read in when the natural light is gone downstairs, and the bathroom is between the two rooms so we'd all have privacy, and . . . and it's something we've discussed more than once, knowing that Aunt Esther . . . and Ted's sister with just the apartment . . ." She trailed off, having talked too much in the heat of this sacrifice. Of space and privacy: their six months here had been like six months on the red sofa, the world shut out and nobody to criticize or interrupt their deepening and—they could scarcely believe it—legal and licit pleasure in each other.

Her mother-in-law looked dubious. Her black glance shuttled from one to the other of their faces. Teddy was too startled and conflicted to speak. "Well," his mother pronounced grudgingly. "It's something to consider." Then she decided to smile, and smiled at Emily. "Darling Emily," she said, "you should start calling me Stella."

Emily said, finding her tongue again, "We want you to be with us, Stella. I swear to God."

When they were alone again, the minister's widow having snatched up her prayer book in a black-gloved hand and headed hastily off to Avon Presbyterian, three blocks away, on the corner of Locust Street and Cedar, Emily asked her husband, "Was that all right? It seemed there was nothing else to say. Was I wrong—isn't it what you wanted me to say? I had to be the one to say it."

"Yes, what could you do?" he asked, rising with a sigh and studying the linoleum floor, a pattern that imitated small bricks, in shades of red and yellow, laid this way and that, with imitation mortar. "Honey-pie, I don't want to live with anybody but you," he told her. "But, as you say . . ." He felt invaded, but not unpleasantly. Two women to wait on him, to protect him. "Let's see how it goes. If it doesn't work out, we can work something else out."

"It *will* work out. Your mother has a good heart. She'll try to give us our privacy. I *like* her, Ted, I really do."

But they would have to suppress their noises, and not wander the house as they had done—even the downstairs, the two of them naked as Adam and Eve, and the light from the street lying like long bright tongues on the furniture. Anyone passing on the sidewalk outside might have seen bits of their bare bodies darting up from behind the back of the cut-plush sofa. "You were beautiful," he told her, "stepping right up to the plate like that."

"I had to say it right away—if we'd hemmed and hawed, she would have been hurt forever and never have come. I was so scared you'd be angry, but I had to do it."

"Angry? She's *my* mother, you know. It's you doing *me* the favor."

"I would have kept quiet if I hadn't come to like her so. I know I'm not the girl she exactly wanted for you but she's tried to be warm. She's much more of a mother, really . . ."

She did not need to finish. Than her own.

The property on Willow Street did not sell immediately—money wasn't growing on trees, contrary to what Wall Street might think, now that another Republican had been elected President—and Horace asked Stella to stay in the house until it sold. In April he accepted an offer of nine thousand nine hundred. In May Stella moved in, and by July realized that Emily was not just thick in the waist from eating her own cooking but was in her third month of creating another resident of the little gray house on Locust Street.

Emily liked "cuddling," as she called it. Her directness and passion in bed were more than Teddy had bargained for; he was amazed and flattered and tried to keep up with her, but in his mind lurked the Protestant suspicion that there must be a hook to it, that there was something corrupt and punishable about enjoying your flesh so much. She would come to bed naked when she wanted him to make love; she teased him about her "conjugal rights." At times her entire skin became so sensitive in love's inflammation that she moaned wherever he touched her. But for months after they were married she would not let him see her bad foot, out of its brace and thick-soled shoe. Even in the bathtub, as he soaped her breasts and her throat, she tucked this foot under the other calf, so it vanished in the wobble of gray water. It became a matter of tearful resistance on her part and hurt insistence on his; one night, after Peter and Esther had come by with a shaker of martinis, Teddy with Dutch courage had stripped back the bedclothes and, gripping her kicking right leg while Emily shrieked and sobbed, looked his fill. Her bad foot was small, a child's foot, and set at a turned-in angle to the ankle. He lowered his face to it and kissed it—its smallness, its pallor that had never seen the sun, its sweet little sticky foot-smell from the tight high-top laced specially made shoe she wore. Emily grew still and stopped resisting. He kept kissing and caressing it, the sad weak strangeness of it, the miniature toes, and abruptly she twitched, her hips twisting in the bed, her hands fluttering at her sides. When Teddy returned his face up to hers Emily was blushing, blushing wildly. She opened her arms to him in helpless embarrassment. "I guess I'm every inch yours," she told him, as he drove his penis home into her already wet sex.

In May of 1929, Charles Lindbergh, who had inspired Teddy to seize this happiness, married, at the bride's home in Englewood, New Jersey. In Hollywood, the first Academy awards went to *Wings* and Emil Jannings and twenty-two-year-old Janet Gaynor, who starred in three films that year. In Chicago, Al Capone was jailed for carrying a gun, and in Washington oil tycoon Harry Sinclair was jailed for contempt of Senate, since he had refused five years before to answer questions about his role in the Teapot Dome Scandal. Henry Ford signed an agreement to build a factory in the Soviet Union that would produce one hundred thousand automobiles a year. Bell Laboratories demonstrated a system for transmitting color pictures by "television." Transcontinental Air Transport inaugurated cross-country service; passengers from New York's Penn Station flew by day and rode a train by night to reach Glendale Airport, outside Los Angeles, two full days later, for a one-way fare of $351.94. Jews and Arabs fought in Jerusalem; Chinese and Russians battled along the Manchurian border.

In October, the New York stock market crashed, with little immediate and visible effect on Basingstoke. Few of its citizens owned stocks, and those that did held on and hoped for a rebound. The bottle-cap factory continued to set out its jingling crates on the loading platform, the Roxie showed for the second week running John Ford's panoramic talkie *The Black Watch*, starring Myrna Loy as a glamorous female Mahdi who dreams of conquering India, and Teddy Wilmot continued to rotate through town with a planetary steadiness, delivering the mail.

Jared came down from New York seeming only a little chastened. "We took a licking, no doubt about it," he admitted. "The margin accounts were wiped out, and Jimmy in margin up to his—I won't say 'ass,' because that's only half of it. He was in up to his eyeballs. Some of his clients aren't very nice people, and he and Teresa are taking a long holiday up in the Adirondacks. Least that's where I'm supposed to tell people they've gone."

"How long are you in Basingstoke for?" Teddy asked him. Jared had showed up at the house one evening late in October and they had put him in the little room upstairs they had been readying for the baby when it came in January.

"Oh, not long. I just needed to catch my breath. It was Lucille's idea. She said, 'You're looking wrung-out.' She said,

'You need to see your family and breathe some salt air.' " Jared laughed, in that dry quick way he had, which didn't invite you to laugh with him. He had lower teeth that had come in too fast and overlapped, teeth that said "Paterson" to Teddy.

Jared called out to Emily where she was standing in the kitchen, hanging back so her mother-in-law could sit at the kitchen table with their prodigal guest, "Don't worry, Em—I ain't taking the baby's room over. You look great, by the way. That's something I love to see—a woman making good American babies to hold off the heathen Chinee."

Emily blushed; though her shape was no secret, she wished people wouldn't mention it. "How are Lucille and little Jimmy?"

"Great," he said, but somehow vaguely, "just great. The kid walks and talks like a real little Irishman. In fact he walks and talks like a little snob; we got him an English nurse. I tell Lucille she should spend more time with him, but she loves parties. Now she's interested in modern art. To me it looks like they just threw paint at the canvas, but she swears by it, all these French guys."

"The post-Impressionists," she said, shyly. "Cézanne and Van Gogh."

"Right. They're going to have a whole museum to themselves, and she's been involved in it, raising money, going down to the Village to visit these arty bums, I don't know. You ought to come over sometime, if you're interested in it. Me, they can hang the stuff upside down and I wouldn't know the difference."

Mother broke in, knowing he was hiding things: "Jared, whatever is going to happen? To Mr. McMullen's business and your job and investments and everything?" Teddy could see the fright in her eyes, the same fright as when Dad was out there making eleven bucks a week with Goldman's Clothiers and then going door to door for even less. She knew what it was when you lost your niche, no matter how big a bluff a man put on.

"Don't you fret your pretty head," Jared told his mother, with his left hand deftly lifting a sheaf of her hair to tug at the lobe of her ear. But something had flattened his easy baritone voice. He had taken his chances, and lost. Just the way he held his bad arm was different, more wounded. "The market will bounce back," he assured them. "Every rube in the country's been buying stock, driving up the prices to where it was ridiculous. The smart money knew it, and got out. We needed a correction, and now we're getting it. The big bankers—Morgan and Mitchell and Pierson—will see to it that equilibrium is restored. Hoover's stepping in with a lot of public works. Jimmy and I took our lumps, but he's still got a little tucked away. Can the long face, Mom. It'll work out, I'll land on my feet again. You know—the luck of the Wilmots."

Jared had ventured out too far and couldn't get back. The kidding, the confidence were things he remembered how to do from an earlier time. Something pathetic had crept into his manner, a sickly need to ingratiate himself, even with his younger brother. When the two of them were alone in the front parlor, Teddy refused the offered La Palma cigar, and lit an Old Gold ("Not a Cough in a Carload"). Jared told him, "You got a nice setup here. I wouldn't mind it right now if *my* father-in-law were in the greenhouse business."

"He keeps his nose out of our life, but he's there when we need him. He worships the ground . . ." He trailed off; it would be a mistake to say, *Emily walks on.*

Jared understood, gazed at the ceiling, and spoke of his own wife. "Lucille's a good kid, a great looker, but"—he sighed—"a lousy mother and a damn expensive bitch. And pretty cold, it turns out. I thought Catholics would be warm and loving, you know—wasn't that the line? Or was it only Italians?"

Teddy felt Jared probing at his sex life, trying to nose his way in, and said nothing. Jared felt the refusal and went on, "Now your Emily—you and she are my idea of a perfect match. You've been kind of a cripple ever since Pop collapsed."

Jared didn't stay until the baby came; he went back to New York after a week of eating their food and taking their Chevrolet up to Wilmington to buy *The Wall Street Journal* and running up their phone bill with cryptic conversations. He and Teddy went fishing together, one unseasonably warm Sunday noon, when the broad estuary of the Avon was as calm as glass. Jared even caught a fish, a winter flounder, pulled up from the cold sea there by the old granite breakwater and scattering sunstruck spray in its flipping agony like a flattened angel pulled from a cold blue heaven. The baby, a seven-pound girl, came in February of the new decade, the week of Valentine's Day and the first anniversary of Aunt Esther's death. For that reason and others—homage to his father, somehow, and continuity in the Wilmot clan, which had used the name generation after generation—it seemed right to call the infant Esther. Emily had no name from her side of the family to offer; her mother was outlandishly called Tabitha. Yet her mother now began to appear at their house, to do grandmotherly duty along with the grandmother in residence. Though Tabitha couldn't overcome her habit of turning her small, dusky face away when she talked, she had a more active, tender way with the infant than Stella, who was ten years older and so overweight that one trip up the stairs left her breathless.

Too many grandmothers, Emily sometimes complained. She was besotted with little Essie. The child was perfection. Once, a week or so after they had come home from the hospital, Teddy surprised Emily bent over the child's crib. Her two hands were rapturously clutched around her daughter's bare feet—those tiny, round-soled, puffy-backed, violet-tinged feet, feet just unfolded from the bud, the skin of them wrinkled like dogwood petals and finer-grained than silk. Softly, greedily squeezing, Emily had been taken unawares by her husband; her eyes, with their big movie-star whites, rolled upward to him in a glance of guilty surprise swiftly replaced by a watery plea that he ignore in her worship the something shameful. "She's perfect," she said apologetically.

"So are you," he lied, and she left the baby and came into his arms for her hug, her hard-earned reassurance. But this vision of her, plaintively crouched over the baby like that, was another that Teddy could never stop remembering. Such pain.

iii. *Essie /Alma*

LIGHT HAD FELT ITS WAY in under the dry green window shade above the spines of the radiator and was standing beside her bed when the unhappy tangle of her dream fell away and she dared open her eyes. Like a leak in a great tank of darkness the light had seeped into all the familiar things of her room—varnished pine bureau, painted straight chair, staring doll sitting on the chair with the oval soles of her cardboard shoes showing, radiator (which under its flaking silver paint had ivylike designs in a low raised pattern like a kind of secret), dark-green window shade with its pinholes of light, shelf Daddy had put up with hammer and nails and hitting his thumb so the nail turned blue, framed pictures of Jack and Jill falling downhill in stiff surprise and a lady in white with pink ribbons taking a step toward you. Essie's eyes touched each of them, and then the four corners of the ceiling. The world was intact, it had not been torn apart by her dream, full of yelling and fire and spilled things. The world is like stones: dreams and thoughts flow over them. She looked at the four corners of the ceiling again, in the reverse direction, holding Mr. Bear so his glass eyes with the loose black disk (like a little tiddlywink) in each could look in parallel with her. He was a Teddy Bear but her Daddy was called Teddy and so she called her toy Mr.

Bear. She drew a diagonal with her eyes in one direction and then in the other. The air seemed to vibrate, to have something in it that was moving, finer than any rain. If she didn't do the diagonal in both directions things would be unbalanced and God might be upset. The joy of being herself flooded seven-year-old Essie's skin; it felt so tight she wanted to scream or laugh out loud. Almost the first feeling she could ever remember was this joy at being herself instead of somebody else—one of those millions and millions unfortunate enough to have been born somebody other than Esther Sifford Wilmot of 27 Locust Street, Basingstoke, Delaware.

Oh, she knew there were girls richer and famouser than she, like Shirley Temple and the Dionne quintuplets and those two little English princesses, but fame and riches were things she could always have in the future, which was endless and tremendously large. For now here she was in what she was sure was the nicest and prettiest town in the whole wide country, in the happiest home, that just fit the five of them like a glove for five fingers. She felt such pride seeing her father out in the town in his blue uniform; everybody knew him and said hello, he was like the king of Basingstoke visiting his subjects. And Momma was like a queen in her house and in the greenhouse down and across the street, gliding through all that light, with her chrysanthemums and gloxinias and other such wonderful words, her stray single hairs glowing like electric-light filaments as she wiped her eyebrow with the back of her wrist. Sometimes Momma was tired and her weak leg hurt and once when she was ironing Essie remembered seeing her hand jump to her face because her tooth suddenly gave off a spark of pain, but every morning she was up when Essie was still untangling herself from the sticky dark sweetness of sleep and moving about downstairs making things tidy and cozy and bringing them to life. That was a woman's duty—to keep the house and to be pretty. Momma knew all about how to make Essie feel pretty, brushing her hair seven times seven strokes at night so that it shone as bright as Aunt Esther's blond hair even though it was dark, silky black, not black exactly but a rich shimmering brown, the color his own mother's hair had been when she was young, Daddy said. Though her other grandmother had dark hair, too, nobody mentioned that as much. And then you must brush your teeth and rinse afterwards with yellow Listerine and use the Q-tips dipped in warm water on the folds of your ears but not in the hole where the wax is, you could go deaf puncturing an eardrum. To bring out the rosy cells on the cheeks Momma could be quite rough with the washcloth on her face, and it also felt scrapy down below, where girls were different from boys. When Daddy was the one to put Essie to bed he didn't wash her down there at all.

Next to the greenhouse lived Momma's mother and daddy. He wore old loose clothes that smelled like a flowerpot and tobacco juice and always had in one of his pockets a wrapped nougat or caramel or Hershey's kiss, with the little paper tag you pulled to undo the tinfoil. His face and neck were loose, too, with the whole back of his neck all in X's. In snowstorms and cold snaps he slept in the greenhouse, getting up every three hours to stoke the big coal furnace. He did it himself because the colored boys he paid good money to sometimes didn't wake up even so, and if the furnace went out all the flowers would freeze. Grandma Sifford was quiet and shy with missing teeth so she covered her mouth with her hand but she knew lots of secret things. Whenever Essie was sick she would come over to the house and hold her knobby hand on Essie's hot forehead and make a hot pale-green broth of boiled leaves and twiggy stuff that usually wasn't too bitter and scummy to drink at least some spoonfuls of, to make her better. Then Essie could spend the day in her parents' big bed and listen to the radio right from *Lorenzo Jones* up to *Lum and Abner* and have her dolls and paper dolls and Mr. Bear all in bed with her, her crayons and colored pencils getting lost in the wrinkles of the blanket and trying to hide behind the mountain her knees made. It was important to stay in bed, with the curtains drawn all the way down that time she had measles. And to stay away from the children who lived at the tannery end of town, because they didn't wash and carried germs. And in the summer not swim in the river or go to the movies, because that was how people got polio and were crippled even worse than Momma. Some poor children had to live their whole lives in iron lungs, you saw them in the newsreels before the ushers went around with the cardboard boxes you were supposed to put a dime in. She was so lucky to be herself and not them she sometimes felt dizzy with it; being who she was was like a steep shining cliff she stood on the edge of looking out over everything like a fair-haired girl in a storybook she had about Scotland.

She loved her greenhouse grandparents but even more she loved Ama. She was called that because Essie when she first tried it couldn't say "Grandma." She lived with them and was even busier than Momma, who liked to spend quiet time with books and records on the gramophone sometimes. Ama never wasted time like that but sewed and baked cakes and pies and talked over the telephone to people in the church. She was so important in the church that people were always telephoning her for advice as to what to do. She wore old-fashioned dark rustly dresses and her heap of iron-gray hair was held on the top of her head by a lot of combs and wiggly U-shaped pins made of turtle shells. When Essie was smaller she had let her play with the hairpins at bedtime, after she let her hair down. And she had shown her from the bottom of her bureau ugly long tapered pads of other people's hair that Ama said were called "rats" and she used to roll her own hair around when styles were different. She had silver-backed hairbrushes and an ivory-handled buttonhook and long smooth slivers of ivory she said were corset stays and kept her tummy in. When she was little Essie had thought these things were just for her to play with, like clothespins and spools empty of thread and those red rubber rings Momma and Ama used when they put lots of cut-up peaches and pears in jars and boiled them, filling the whole kitchen with steam. Now she knew that almost everything has a grown-up purpose. Ama had shown her how to hold the big thick knitting needles but it was too hard still, the loops of yarn kept slipping off and unravelling. Even the little loops of cloth in the rag rug in the bathroom had this grown-up purpose attached to them, though as she sat on the toidy waiting for it to come they looked like the tops of the heads of a great crowd of people jammed together way far down below to hear her give a speech, their wonderful princess. Sometimes the world just made her wild, there was so much of it, and all so exciting. Now that she was in the second grade they were letting her walk different places by herself, if she always looked both ways and crossed mostly at the corners. After she told Momma where she was going she could cross Locust Street on a Saturday and all by herself walk down past the different front lawns and the empty weedy lot that Grandpa Sifford owned and then the crunchy stretch of crushed oyster shells and enter the greenhouse, full of sunshine and flowers and leaves and the smell of summer even with snow stacked against the glass outside, with all those cranks and pulleys to regulate the windows and those snaky, rusty steam-pipes breathing out heat down by her ankles, down in the straw-speckled dirt where twice she had found money, once a nickel and then a whole quarter. They had fans that blew air around all the time so the plants wouldn't suffocate or get stem rot and the tables where the plants sat in pots weren't solid wood but of thick rusty grids so the air came through from underneath. Other times Daddy let her come to the post office with its bright new mural of men with blue coats and pigtails that had to do with why Rodney Street was called that and watch him and Mr. Horley sort the day's mail at the end of the day, tossing the letters into different sacks held up on some big pipe frames, for different parts of the country. Mr. Horley could toss letters, twirling them by the edge, so far he could even get it in the sack for California, and never miss. It was all so exciting to wake to every day she couldn't blame the other children for being jealous of her and calling her "stuck-up." She wasn't stuck-up, she just was perfect and so glad of it.

Ama lived with them because her husband, Essie's other grandfather, had died. That was a small flaw in her world, a corner missing. She always looked at all four corners and did every diagonal with her eyes twice, because the other grandpa's absence showed that terrible things could happen. Yet Ama said he was an angel in Heaven looking down and loving them, especially his little raven-haired granddaughter in Delaware. Essie tried to think of having a member of her family in Heaven, just like Aunt Esther lived in an expensive house in Red Lion with Uncle Peter and two rude boys, Peter Junior and Jefferson, and Uncle Jared owned a big piece of a mountain way out in Colorado and mined copper, though Daddy would shake his head as though there was something sad about it. The Wilmots were a very special family even though people in Delaware were always talking about the du Ponts. The du Ponts lived in hills far to the north and were less real to her than God. God was in the clouds and had sent Jesus to earth to make Christmas and Easter, and His love pressed down from Heaven and fit her whole body like bathwater in the tub. The fact that Jesus came down meant that God wasn't just up there but was all around them, invisible, not like a ghost, who would be scary, but like blood in your veins that you can sometimes hear when your ear is against the pillow and that the doctor can feel when he puts his cold fat fingers smelling of antiseptic on your wrist. Dr. Hedger was so old that his tongue drooped out onto his lower lip when he was listening to your chest and thought you weren't looking.

God was in all the different churches in Basingstoke. Momma used to go to the Methodists but seeing Ama go off to the Presbyterians every Sunday she had decided to go there too. That made it much nicer, the two of them setting off at quarter to ten on Sunday morning with Essie between them, in patent-leather shoes she could see the pale blob of her face in if she bent down close, with a little strap across, and white kneesocks that stayed up until some rude boy like Benjy Wha-ley pushed her during the singing march-around toward the end. Except for Benjy the children who went to the Presbyterian Sunday school weren't so rough, though, as those who went to the Methodists and Baptists and the Church of the True Word, which didn't even have a steeple. Even the church for the colored folk out along Beaver Road had a steeple. Of all of them the Presbyterians were the best. Grandpa in Heaven had been a minister, entitled to wear a robe and bless the Communion bread, the little cut squares of it she was too young to eat yet. It was passed along the aisles in low silver dishes by the ushers and one very bad boy once put his chewed chewing gum on the dish as it went by. Ama taught a class of older girls in the Sunday school, and Mr. Horley, so important in town he was even more important than Daddy, taught a class of older boys. Mr. Phillips, who owned the bank and always wore a suit even on Saturdays, was the superintendent. The Methodists for teachers had only Mr. Pursey, who ran the notions store, across from the drug store where Daddy worked when he met Momma. Pursey's sold pointy wax teeth at Halloween and tablets with Irene Dunne on the cover or Dolores Del Rio, who had dark hair like Essie, or Jeanette MacDonald, who sang in a voice so high the movie sound track would skip. The Methodist older boys were taught by Shorty Sturgis, who ran Sturgis's Garage and always had black rings around his fingernails, which just went to show. The Presbyterian Sunday school was in the basement, with little low frosted-glass windows at the top of the walls, so even on sunny days the lights had to be on. Jesus came down to earth and went about healing blind men by pressing mud against their eyes and before that Joseph's brothers were so jealous of the coat of many colors they left him in a ditch for dead. The Biblical people were sheepherders and wore purple capes. They wore sandals and would wash each other's feet. When Momma or Ama washed her feet, especially the bottoms, it was so ticklish she squirmed and giggled and sometimes had to pee.

Downstairs in the kitchen Danny was squalling and squawking over something—the crybaby, probably his morning cod-liver oil, which just took a second to swallow down and protected you all day against germs. He was always fighting and protesting things it was easier to accept, since the world knew what was best for you and was anyway too big to fight. Who would want to be him?—always with a runny nose and scraggly hair and wanting to fight everybody and coming home blubbering because some bigger boy beat him up. Served him right. After Momma had brought him home from the hospital Essie, who was three then, sneaked a look under his diapers and his pee-pee was like a little doorbell only fatter than that, on a fat pink cushion with a line down the middle like the seam on a sock. Who would want one of those? She much preferred her own sleek shape, with everything nasty hidden.

Though by her Mickey Mouse clock on the walnut bureau it was eight o'clock, the whistle at the bottle-cap factory didn't blow. Today was Saturday. No school and no Lowell Thomas, who Daddy liked to listen to, on the radio and, right after it, to *Amos 'n' Andy,* which Ama liked for some reason—it made her laugh, she said, and in these hard times, a third of the grown men in the country out of work, what else does?—and (the bad thing on Saturdays) piano lessons and then tap-dancing class. Miss Reeves came to the house at nine with her sheaf of music and her swollen blue nose that Momma said she had fallen on on her icy porch steps when a girl and had ruined her life by making her too ugly to marry, and she would put a gold star on the page if Essie had practiced her Minuet in G from Mozart or ballet music in F sharp from Gluck and take a cup of coffee and a cornbread muffin from Ama before rushing on to the next pupil, Marvin Gordy, who she said was gifted but nothing like as diligent as Essie. Then she and Momma would themselves rush on to the studio above Krauthammer's Hardware and Seeds, where Mr. Josephs who used to be in something called vaudeville would make the class do shuffle-one, shuffle-two, tap, tap, tap, and twirl. He told them how to hold their heads and hands, as if on strings being pulled from above, so you looked like you weighed nothing and lifted the hearts of the audience. He was a sad man with a raspy voice, when he talked about lifting the hearts of the audience. He had orange hair that didn't go with his face, and the hall had a sad dusty smell, just one big room you came up to on linoleum stairs and with the toilet out in the hall for boys and girls both so you had to be careful who was in there and with chairs along the walls for the mothers while they waited. But Essie had gotten to like it, the game of pretending that there was an audience in front of her, out there somewhere under the tap-scarred boards, and the fact that she was the best, of the eight or so children who showed up for this beginners' class. She could feel she was the best when she twirled, for sooner than any of the others she was back facing Mr. Josephs, her weight on the right foot and her left knee touching the floor and her arms out in a "howdy" motion the way he had showed them. Momma said even if she never tap-danced a minute of her life it would be good for her poise and muscle control and bodily grace. Essie even at seven could sense that Momma wanted her to miss nothing of all that she had missed, being raised on a farm and with her bad foot, that kept her from having "bodily grace." Essie loved her own body, the way it was so taut and flexible, and how the front of her ankle rippled when she twisted her foot this way and that to see it work; some mornings she just lay in bed for minutes holding her hand up into the sunlight and seeing how the red shone through her fingertips and spreading the toes at the end of her legs with their tiny shining hairs on the straight white shins. When she got older, she promised herself, she would paint her toenails so she could wear open-toed shoes with slinky slacks like Marlene Dietrich and Dolores Del Rio.

On the walk home, they passed the Roxie, where ONE HUNDRED MEN AND A GIRL STARRING DEANNA DURBIN was spelled out on the marquee. "Please, Momma," Essie begged. "I want to go."

"But Daddy and I can't take you," her mother told her, in that singing, spaced-out, too-clear voice she used when being a mother. "I have to help Grandpa and Grandma in the greenhouse this afternoon, and Daddy and I are going to play cards with Aunt Esther and Uncle Peter this evening while Ama takes care of you and Danny."

Essie was silent, thinking of how when her parents came back from Aunt Esther's they stayed in bed later, and Momma had to hurry to get her church clothes on, while Daddy hid under the covers some more. He never went to church, except for the Christmas-carol service when she had been a shepherd. For a girl only in the second grade Essie had been to the movies a lot: since before the first grade her parents would take her to the seven o'clock show when there was no school the next day. This year she had already seen *The Good Earth,* about how poor Chinese people are, with a plague of locusts in the sky, and *Lost Horizon,* where the pretty woman's face very frighteningly crumbles into old age when they take her out of their magic valley in the mountains, and *The Prince and the Pauper,* with Errol Flynn, where the dirty boy in the street switches place with the little prince. There were poor people and very rich people in the movies, and not so many like the Wilmots and the Siffords who were quiet in the middle. Being in the middle like that was another reason for Essie to be so happy. Bums came to the back door, some of them with skins darker even than their dirty clothes, and Ama always made up a little paper bag for them—a sandwich, an apple, a piece of shortbread—and gave them a cheerful word and blessed them on their way. They said they wanted work but what work could there be in their little house and yard, where Daddy did all the work? Even Ama was having trouble finding sewing work, with women more and more buying their clothes readymade. Some of these drifting men smelled sour and looked funny at her, but Ama said we were all God's children, and never went to the movies, as if there was something wicked in the dark of the movie theatres. *One Hundred Men and a Girl* was about a girl who sang thrillingly, Essie knew from what Loretta Whaley was saying in school the day before yesterday. Her parents had taken her even though it was a school night. "I'll go see it alone," Essie said defiantly. As she and Momma passed the Roxie doors they were open enough for her to see a boy who was the older brother of a boy in her class, Eddie Bacheller, sweeping up the purple carpet with a vacuum cleaner with its little headlight getting ready for that day's matinee at two. "I'll walk down past the greenhouse and stay on this side of the street," she promised. "I'll tidy up my room before I go and, and everything. I'll do the l-lunch d-d-dishes. Oh please please *please.*"

She blushed, having stuttered. She didn't know why it happened, sometimes it didn't happen for days, and then suddenly she couldn't get her words around something like a ball of air in her mouth. It happened when she got excited because she was pushing out the words too fast; it happened when she overstepped, or felt in the wrong. Not really in the wrong, but when things were hard to explain without a lot of words and nobody would listen, nobody was paying enough attention and there wasn't enough time to get it all in.

"You are too young to go to the movies yourself," Momma said, very slowly and calmly, as if to show her how to talk. She had a lovely smooth voice. You could spell every word from how Momma said it.

"B-boys go," Essie burst out. "Boys go much younger than me."

"Boys can go places and do things girls cannot," Momma said.

"Why is that, *why?* That's not fair and you know it!"

"Women and men are not the same and perhaps that's not fair," Momma said, looking down at her with a heavy smiling expression. "But that's how it is, Esther. Girls are vulnerable in ways that boys are not."

"What's vul-vul-vul—?"

Momma looked away, pained by Essie's inability to get the word out. The pain in her face was the nearest she ever came to scolding. Momma's face had a double chin that didn't use to be so ugly when Essie looked up. "Open to injury," she said, like a prim dictionary, and added, "Boys can run faster."

Essie never had trouble talking around Ama and Daddy. They were Wilmots, she thought secretly, like her. When Daddy came home for lunch at noon, before going back to deliver the mail that came in on the noon train, she told them all at the table how she wanted to go to the movie matinee, how a lot of other second-graders went to the movies by themselves. Daddy smiled. "You've only been a second-grader for a couple of weeks," he said.

"Four weeks, Daddy. Loretta Whaley has already seen it, she's already seen it or I'd ask her to go, it's about a girl who saves a whole b-bandful of musicians j-j-just by her singing."

Daddy shifted his slow careful weight in his chair and after chewing said to Momma softly, "I don't see much harm in it. At her age back in Paterson—"

Momma interrupted him. "You were a boy. You were city-smart."

Momma had come from the real country, way south of the Canal, and Daddy was from a big city up in New Jersey, within sight of New York. It was wonderful how they had managed ever to meet, in the drug store. If they hadn't, Essie often thought, she herself wouldn't exist, and this was impossible. The world without her in it seeing the sun and trees and clouds and hearing all the birds and cars and voices was impossible.

"Oh, no," Ama said, in that lovely big sweet voice of hers that just poured friendliness over everything, "Teddy was a tender soul, always hiding in his room with his baseball cards and a book. Or maybe they came later. At Essie's age, it would have been 1910—oh dear, what nice times they were, before the big strike and then the war and Clarence . . . Clarence took to the motion pictures so, I bet that's where Essie gets it from. She has his way of dreaming off, into another world."

Essie could see Momma's plump lips falter, with the Wilmots against her, and the ghostly grandfather backing them up.

Daddy looked across the table at his daughter, so she could see his full broad face, tan and crinkled around the eyes from being out in all weathers, his pale eyebrows with a few dark hairs making the boundary with the forehead dead white from the hat he always wore, and his mouth changed, like a tiny crack in a blank plate. Out of his manly blankness she felt something like rain you can just begin to feel prickling on your face, walking along the street. He would let her go. He had taken off his gray-blue jacket with the brass buttons, so he sat among them in his shirt and official suspenders. The shirt was gray and even the suspenders were a regulation black. He turned and touched the back of Momma's hand and said to her mildly, "Why not let her go, Em, this once? This is as safe a town as there is. She can't take a step without somebody's eye on her that knows she's our daughter."

"Yes, and everybody knew who the Lindberghs' baby was, too."

"Em, you can't keep her under glass like at the greenhouse," Daddy said, his voice lifting into that soft hardness of warning that men have. "This little bud has to grow outdoors."

"Clarence used to say, 'We learn by doing,'" Ama said. "'God made us free, Stella,' he would say, 'so we could make our own mistakes.' Now *our* Esther used to walk a half-mile each way to the Clark Street Elementary, through neighborhoods packed with every color and creed, and some of the fathers reputed to be out-and-out anarchists."

"I don't want to keep her under glass," Momma argued against Daddy, in a steady way that showed she was planning to lose, "but I don't want to set her out in the frost either." When Momma smiled, even a little bit, her cheeks lifted like little square pads under the skin, making the shadow of a dimple just under them.

Bratty Danny could tell the way the tide was running. His sissyish quick eyes went from one grown-up face to another and he began to whine. "Me, too. I can go with Essie, too."

Ama said, protecting what they all had won from Momma,

"Now, don't you be silly, young man. You're going to stay home with me, and we're going to have a wonderful time making a molasses-and-raisin pie. You can help Ama roll the crust, and sprinkle on the brown sugar."

So Daddy went back to the post office to do his afternoon sorting, and when the lunch dishes were washed and stacked Momma walked her as far as the greenhouse, and by way of expressing love pressed an extra nickel in her hand for a candy bar. Essie felt her mother watching as she carefully crossed Fishery Way, which had recently been tarred and steamrollered like the other streets, instead of being left in dirt and pebbles that would dig into your knees if you fell. Once Essie was on that side, there were no more streets to cross, just the cement walk between the Oddfellows' building and the mysterious brick building with its side windows painted a green-black inside, and a clicking sound inside that was pool balls hitting each other—sharp flurries of them run together like birdsong, and then heavy silences in which she could hear men breathe and say words little girls weren't meant to hear. The light that had felt its way in under her window shade forever ago had turned grayish, with a rainy warmth to it. She imagined that it might be raining when she came out of the movies, the sidewalk dry under the marquee but wet all around, the puddles jumping up with drops and the black street shining; she foresaw how she would have to run from doorway to doorway since Momma had forgotten to make her take an umbrella, and how tomorrow morning if it rained all night the first yellow leaves of fall would be lying on the lawn and pasted to the tarpaper porch roof outside her bedroom window: at these inner pictures happiness squeezed her chest and waistband so tightly Essie almost yelped with the sheer stretching feeling of it, as she stepped out from the edge of the brick building where men played pool behind painted windows, into the safety of Rodney Street.

Today, without a grown-up beside her, the street looked perilously long—a chain of rectangles tapering to nothing. So many shops, awnings, parked cars, people she didn't know walking along like all those Chinese fleeing from famine and enemy armies in *The Good Earth.* Holding her head very still like Mr. Josephs said, and staring straight ahead even when a Scottie with a plaid collar strained at his leash as if to bite her bare leg, she passed business doorways painted various dark colors and with signs she didn't understand exactly, REALTOR and CHIROPRACTOR and PODIATRIST and DIAMOND STATE INSURANCE and BUNDY AND MCREADY ASSOCIATES ATTORNEYS-AT-LAW, which had some connection with her family, a shadow, something about Aunt Esther and Uncle Peter, who drank too much, Momma said. Then there was the Kresge's with the little green-and-yellow birds chirping in cages above the orange boxes of birdfeed and the powerful smell of coconut cookies just inside the front doors, and Mr. Phillips' bank with its two white pillars grooved sort of like coconut cookies, and the Blue Hen Ice Cream parlor where the big kids looked out the window—they were the most frightening, because though they were the size of grown-ups, and smoked cigarettes like crazy and some even drove cars, they didn't pay attention to any grown-up rules, they were as rough as second-graders and would just as soon pull up your skirt and push you into the river as not; in their eyes Essie was no bigger than a bug to be squashed. From just the way their mouths moved and eyes flashed on the other side of the plate-glass window with the little blue hen on it you could see they cared about nothing but themselves, not their teachers or parents or the Lord above or anybody.

But then after the little birthday-card-and-stationery store, which had a children's-book section at the back (but not books as bright and interesting as the comic books at Pursey's or the Big Little Books in Kresge's, beyond the socks and underpants section), and the shop that always had a dusty bride's white dress in the window and a bouquet of cloth flowers and cardboard wedding cake, Essie arrived at the movie house. Already a line was forming and as she got in it and looked around she saw some third-graders she knew and a bunch of very bad fourth-grade boys, but nobody else as small as herself. Momma had been right, and she felt all watery and guilty down in under her dress. She shouldn't be here. The very bad boys were snorting and shoving among themselves and she was terrified they would notice her. She tried to hide between two women, one fat and one skinny, who were talking over her head about the uppity colored people, now that they had a boxing champion again and four of those rapists, it was shocking, had been released from jail down in Alabama. "Next thing," the skinny one said, "we'll be giving the niggers the whole country to cut each other up in," and the fat one hummed so it looked like she agreed, though Essie could tell she wouldn't have put it exactly like that. But then the line began to move and the nice old frazzled lady in the ticket booth took her dime and gave her a raspberry-colored ticket with a kindly smile and inside the lit theatre Essie found a seat over on the side, where it looked like nobody would sit near her and she could eat the box of gumdrops she had bought with Momma's extra nickel in peace. As the lights dimmed and the last people hurried to their seats she felt her aloneness here tremblingly, like one time on the beach below Port Penn she had looked around and couldn't find her family among all the bodies in bathing suits, everybody looking the same with white legs and arms and black bodies. She longed to be back in the bright greenhouse with Momma, who sat surrounded by spools of ribbon in shiny colors.

But then in a sliding gush of the special Disney music Mickey Mouse burst on the screen, those yellow rays coming out from his head with its round black ears and funny sharp widow's cap, and Essie felt safe. She liked Mickey cartoons better than ones with Donald Duck; there was less hitting and angry squawking. She had trouble understanding what Donald was quacking, though Eddie Bacheller could do a good imitation at recess, squinching his mouth shut and getting all red in the face. Mickey though he walked through life alone (like her today, to the Saturday movie) had tender feelings, picking those nice flowers like little platters for Minnie with her blushes and big shoes, and there were even little children, baby Mickeys crawling among the funny round furniture wearing gowns with the ends sewn shut like ghost costumes, with a patched place where their tails came out. She remembered when baby Danny wore nighties somewhat like that but his little feet always showed. Even when there was Pegleg Pete in the cartoons he wasn't really evil, you could tell by his ears, he was just gruff and growly and didn't always shave, like Mr. Horley at the post office. From the pointy ears Pegleg Pete was a cat but from their floppy ones all his henchmen were dogs: that was strange. Today's cartoon was about hunting moose and there was a sadness and cruelty about hunting living things that kept Essie from laughing as much as she wanted to. From getting the *Mickey Mouse Magazine* she knew that by Christmas a full-length cartoon about Snow White was going to come to the theatres but she wasn't sure she wanted to see it if it was too scary, if it had a witch in it as bad as the Big Bad Wolf. Some of these cartoons got into your thoughts deeper than real actors could do. What she loved about cartoons was the jingly-jangly swooping music that hurried things along, that entered straight into your excitement so you didn't even hear it except when you deliberately listened.

At the edges of the screen's rectangle curves appeared and the circle got smaller and smaller and pinched everything shut and it was over with a final comical toot. The travelogue in Sepiatone was about beautiful Thailand where they had fat-bellied Buddhas of solid gold and girls with long black hair darker than her own, in dresses slit up the side and glistening like Christmas paper, and canals with boats woven like Easter baskets floating on them. The newsreel with that great serious voice booming above everything, like God's—even though it sounded scolding, you knew it cared for you—showed running soldiers and explosions in Spain and China and a bridge in San Francisco and a tunnel in New York opening and that stupid Hitler with his tiny mustache saying something angrily you couldn't understand, worse than Donald Duck, and that Joe Louis the women were talking about knocking down a white man in a square ring like a movie screen on its back. The screen showed a factory with men putting cars together as fast as machines and the great voice said how Ford Motors had turned out its twenty-five millionth automobile and then another factory had things like triangular spools in it spinning and the voice said that Du Pont Industries had developed a new miracle thread called nylon that would make the silk produced by worms obsolete. This was right here in Delaware and it made Essie feel proud and loyal. The previews showed Napoleon in one movie and a hurricane in another but she knew Momma and Daddy would want to go to a sappy one about a man and a woman always fighting and then it turning out they loved each other, starring Cary Grant and Irene Dunne. Essie would look over and see her parents holding hands and be humiliated.

By the time the main feature came on she had eaten all her gumdrops, their insides rubbery under the crackling crust of sugar grains. She must remember to brush her teeth an extra minute tonight, otherwise she would wind up with teeth you take out at night and put in a glass like Grandpa Sifford; he showed her one time with a sly kind of pride. When the teeth were in the water they looked larger. This was as frightening as the crumbling face in *Lost Horizon.* One kind of movie she never wanted to see was a horror movie: when the previews came on showing this big man with fine black lips and nuts holding his head together and lightning flashing behind the castle or the creepy big house like the house up on Willow Street before Daddy's Aunt Esther died and they sold it, Essie would slouch way down in the seat and clamp her eyes shut. But now she sat upright, imitating Deanna Durbin's nice fearless posture, and let *One Hundred Men and a Girl* flow through her. Being alone was like being alone on the deck of a great dark ship slowly moving through an unseen sea. She was in ecstasy. The movie made you laugh and thrill. Though what the girl heroine attempted seemed impossible, persuading this great conductor (who really *was* a great conductor in real life, playing himself), you knew it was possible. "Fairy tales never come true," the movie father, Adolphe Menjou, told Deanna Durbin, but when Mischa Auer looked up from the piano keyboard with his frizzy hair on fire in the light and listened to her sing, this cold rod of certainty like smooth metal went through you and you knew every dream of hers would come true, through the power of her pure singing: she put her elbows up on the piano edge and opened her smiling mouth and out came these amazing silvery trills, as Essie floated forward on the great slightly slanting deck above the unseen black sea. She loved being alone in the movies; she could see and hear better, without her parents' hands and breathing distracting her, she could better gather the movie to her own being. When she got home she must ask Momma to get singing lessons for her, so she could open her mouth and have that thrilling pure icy sound fly out of her face, beneath the little hair ribbon Deanna Durbin wore.

Outside the Roxie, the day had gone on being Saturday. Days were so long she couldn't see how people could ever get old, the future was so far away. This day's grayness was several notches darker, and just as she had hoped the sidewalk was speckled with the start of a hesitant rain. Essie loved the feeling of rain: sometimes when it was falling outside and chuckling in the gutter she would crouch there where her window above the radiator was open enough to admit the tingle of it, the woolly smell of it like a big soft not very dangerous animal turning around outside, while she was safe inside. It was not raining enough that she needed to dart from doorway to doorway; she walked along with her head high like Mr. Josephs said, dreaming, enjoying her awareness of the day, the way it had jumped ahead two hours while she was hidden in the movie house. One of the sensations she loved was being hidden, crouching where legs and voices would go by with nobody knowing she was there. People seemed larger and less predictable, spied on. In a way, you were always hidden, inside your head. Her impression of danger glinting along Rodney Street was gone now. The people on the street seemed large and stupid, like cows bunching up the way they do in a corner of a field. Fat motherly women were shaking bandanas out of their pocketbooks to protect their marcelled waves and one or two men had put up black umbrellas they had been carrying. The movie was inside her like a craggy landscape in shades of silvery gray, with deeps down to black and a feeling of dizzyness. In their shining, with their swift-talking barking voices and sharp snapping movements as if by pairs of scissors, the movies took you to an edge but left you safe, all shadows sealed shut inside a happy ending, and sent you out into a Saturday where the actual people bumbled along like shapeless animals, blobs against the daylight that puzzled your eyes. These crags and chasms of danger existed in real life, because people you knew, or almost knew, fell into them—the seventh-grade boy who drowned last year down near Port Penn, a couple Aunt Esther and Uncle Peter knew who crashed their car against a thick old elm after leaving a roadhouse, and in her own family tree the other, older Aunt Esther and the dead grandfather. He was like a ripped corner in the rectangle her grandparents made and at times when she thought of him a bright kindliness like salt or fine sugar seemed to pour out of him into her, urging her on, feeding the silvery song inside her. Her feelings of God came from him.

She almost didn't like movies because of the way they scared you. Even in the funniest of them, somewhere, the chase got so fast somebody could be killed, or the thin man began to hit the fat man really hard. The real world was more muffled than that; there were policemen to get you safe across East Rodney Street at elementary school and teachers inside to keep the mean boys from doing more than pulling your pigtail. At times the movies seemed so out of control and dangerous Momma and Daddy put her between them to quiet her wriggling. Her favorite pictures were those with women who just skimmed along over everything—the one who ice-skated in a sparkly dress and kind of crown and had more dimples than Momma and the one who was always dancing with the skinny man in the tuxedo. She wore dresses that were mountains of ruffles and big snakes of ostrich feathers that came up and covered her chin and no matter how fast he was making her move and twirl on the slippery ballroom floor her eyes stayed level and calm and warm like lamps inside her head: the skinny man with his long chin and little white bow tie amused her. They loved each other but didn't always know it.

Several of the grown-ups along the street looked familiar and smiled down but she was hurrying now to get herself home. Your body is your only one and has a very thin skin over lots of blood going around and around like clock hands only faster. Where little Danny fell and cut his forehead open she could see a white scar that would never go away. If you made a bad enough mistake even if it wasn't your fault it would last forever. Her second front teeth had come in and if she fell and chipped one she would never be beautiful; it would be like Miss Reeves's blue nose. The doorway of the long brick building next to the Oddfellows was halfway open and she could smell tobacco and hear men's voices grating and gnashing together, the pool balls clicking through it all, and before moving into the narrow space next to the windowless wall she checked to see that there was nobody behind her or waiting for her at the other end with a knife. Pirates in movies had curved swords and Arabs had ones even more curved but the swords were straight in *The Prisoner of Zenda,* where the same mustached man as in *Lost Horizon* was this time talked into pretending to be a king somewhere, a lazy king like the English one who went and quit because of some lady from Baltimore, which is how the two little girls became princesses next in line.

But there was nothing at the end of the passageway but Fishery Way, with its tin trash barrels grooved like the pillars at the bank, and a farmer's cart creaking and clopping by with a load of watermelons. Essie liked the way watermelon tasted but didn't like how the seeds stuck to your blouse and how your fingers stayed sticky. She ran the distance to the greenhouse, half because the rain was getting worse and half for the joy of running. Momma was inside working, and even with the rain it was brighter inside than anywhere else. Rain tapped now, every drop loud, on the slanting glass, and the warm long sheltered space inside, with dirt for a floor, seemed trembling in all its leaves, as if the plants could hear the rain and wanted to be up in it. Grandpa was moving pots of baby plants growing from slips to other tables and he let her help, carrying one little clay pot at a time, until she got bored and one bumped and spilled when she was thinking about a moment in the movie, where all the faces in an audience are turned to the heroine like flowers in rows. Momma was up at the front desk making up a bouquet of roses and ferns and wrapping it in a paper cone for some man going out on a Saturday date and Grandma was hiding in the back room spraying something awful and brown on plants to kill aphids and thrips and mites and mealybugs. "*Ooh,*" said Essie, "Grandma, what's that awful, awful stuff? It smells like old cigarettes."

"That's nicotine tea, Esther." She always called her "Esther," unlike anybody else. It was a secret between them, Essie's right to her own grown-up name. "I make it from old cigarettes and cigar stubs." In a Maxwell House coffee can she had brewed a black-brown water with tobacco crumbs floating in it. "Don't breathe in, dear. And keep your fingers out. It's poison."

"But Daddy smokes cigarettes. Old Golds."

"He smokes poison, then. But not this strong. Watch out, girl; I'm squirting. Hold your breath."

Plumes of foul spray fluffed into the wilt-edged and spotted leaves of the sick geraniums. Essie liked this second grandmother because she never tried to overfeed her or pretend that Essie was sweeter than she was. A tawny strength moved through the shy old lady's stained fingers. When Essie was with Grandma Wilmot she became soft and frilly, and wanted to eat lots of dessert and be cuddled; when she was with Grandma Sifford she felt harder and older, as if women were partners in a world full of danger and little secrets to know. "Another bug-discourager we used to use down home was garlic," the old lady said, not raising her voice as if Essie just because she was small was deaf, the way the other grandmother did. "Six or so cloves boiled in a quart of water for twenty-five minutes. But people buy flowers for pretty, they don't want them smelling of garlic. If a girl eats garlic every day," she went on, and turned on Essie sharp deep honey-brown eyes that made the child tighten her lips, "she will never catch a cold. But then the boys will never kiss her."

Essie laughed, and Grandma, covering her gappy mouth quickly with a bent brown hand, laughed too.

The light changed, because Momma was there in the doorway to this back room, frowning. "Mother, you'll poison her," she said.

"I told her not to breathe in," Grandma Sifford said humbly. She never argued with Momma and seemed afraid of her, or at least never to look at her. It was time for Momma to take Essie home and see what Grandma Wilmot had cooked for their supper. The rain was thinner than when it drummed on the greenhouse panes and there was still light left in the day, though the day in September when the day and night were equal had come and gone and now every day would be a little bit shorter. Toward Christmastime it was dark when she went to school and dark again before Daddy got back from the mail route. "Now how was the movie?" Momma asked.

"It was nice. The girl saved an entire orchestra from not having a job. Momma, I want to l-l-learn how to sing like her."

"Oh, singing like Deanna Durbin is a God-given talent. Only one in a million can sing like her. Not even that many."

This hit Essie in the same deep place that the woman's face crumbling into old age in *Lost Horizon* had. It meant a terrible limit to things, a damp weight pressing down on her. "Why wouldn't God give it to me, too?"

"God has given you many good things already," Momma said primly, her body and head dipping in that embarrassing way she had, like there was a hole that kept appearing in the ground.

"What, Momma? Like what?"

Momma smiled. "He has given you a perfect body and a hopeful nature and a lot of nervous energy."

"That's all?"

"Some would say that's a lot, and little girls who want more are being greedy." It scared and offended Essie, slightly, when her mother talked to her by spacing her words in this solemn careful way, as if teaching her how to talk. Momma softened her tone. "Some day, maybe, if you've done well with your dance lessons, we could look into singing lessons, if Daddy can afford it."

"G-Grandpa can afford it." This was overstepping.

"Daddy and I don't want to ask favors of Grandpa. He's been too good to us already. And Danny will need his lessons, too, and his education. Anyway, you're not old enough for singing lessons. You still have your baby voice."

All this ran counter to the mood Essie had brought out of the movie house, and rather than hear more she began to skip, partly in the excitement of being out in the misty rain without her rubbers and her stiff slicker that smelled so funny and rubbery, and partly in exaggeration of her mother's limp. She skipped ahead of her and then back on the other side, as if encircling some clumsy animal caught in a lasso. *Baby voice.* She'd show her. "I'm going to go to the movies all alone all the time from now on. I loved it without you and Daddy there."

"Oh my," Mother said, slowing and seeming to exaggerate her limp herself. "Such ambition. Such *pep.*"

In reconciliation Essie took her mother's hand, pretty and white and perfect and moist, and stopped skipping. There was no car in sight either way but she had been told to be careful crossing Locust Street and always was. Daddy was still out in the yard, finishing up, carrying a wheelbarrow-load of weeds and dead peony stalks away to the heap next to the fence, behind the wire trash cage where he burnt newspapers and Ritz-cracker boxes and envelopes that had been slit open. His little red fire was smoking blue in the rain. The kitchen lights were on, and Ama's hunched shape flitted past, on her way to the stove holding a pot, taking tiny hurried steps because it was hot. The set-back gray house, with her father in the yard and her grandmother in the kitchen, and Mr. Bear upstairs waiting on her bed, where the day's light was leaking away above the spines of the radiator with their secret pattern of twisting ivy, struck Essie suddenly as sad, and insubstantial, a ghost house, seen by the light of the silvery movie world whose beautiful smooth people rattled all those words at each other and moved through their enormous ceilingless rooms with such swiftness and electric purpose. The day was still Saturday, every day lasted and lasted, and tonight if she begged she could stay up to eight and hear Professor Quiz, though sometimes Daddy wanted to hear Ed Wynn at the same time. He made him laugh, he said, and forget the world's misery, and this seemed sad, too, and shabby, like the places at the corners where the kitchen tablecloth was wearing through so the shiny checked pattern flaked away to reveal the tan burlappy cloth under the shiny layer. Black came off on your finger when you touched the oil-stove grates, and the wooden icebox held a great crazed whitish block sweatily melting in its belly, getting smaller and smaller on the metal slats. Essie saw her home by a light as if from above the clouds and realized that at some incredible time in the future she would leave it here on Locust Street like a seventeen-year-locust husk she found this summer still clinging with no bug inside it to the trunk of a little crabapple tree she was thinking of climbing.

. . .

The war was horrible, all those young soldiers being killed and babies being bombed and the Nazis murdering a whole village at Lidice and everything, but wonderful, too, happening so far away, in so many of what they called "theatres," and making all the movie stars go about selling bonds and putting on shows for the troops with the USO. The war gave everybody something to do. Because Lyle Dresham, the young sorting clerk at the post office, was drafted, and old Wes Freeman had retired and then died of a bad liver all by himself in his shack out by the marsh, and Mr. Horley himself was of retirement age but agreed to stay on "for the duration," Daddy worked longer hours than ever but only did one delivery a day instead of two. To the rural outskirts, including Beaver Road, he drove a khaki Jeep the Army had lent the post office so the blue-star mothers of Basingstoke would get their V-mail. In town he parked at the corners near the green collection boxes and walked a piece of his walking route and then went back for the Jeep. When he gave Essie a ride in the Jeep it was fun because it bounced at every bump and she felt what it was like to be a soldier. The bottle-cap factory was converted to making bullet casings and Momma got a job there, working through the night when she was on the dead man's shift. Coming into the house with a blurred happy face with her hair upswept according to factory regulations and wearing brown pants and a blue working shirt like a man, she would kiss Essie as the child was heading out the door to school. At the age of thirteen Essie was in the seventh grade and that meant walking the opposite way from the elementary school on East Rodney Street. It meant walking west to the combination junior-high–senior-high building built on the edge of the old poor farm in 1923, with the football field inside the cinder track and just beyond the bleachers fields of the new crop called soybeans, since there were fewer hogs now in the countryside to feed field corn to.

The high school had been built of bricks the color of throw-up, rude kids said. Separate from the big building stood a wooden shed roofed in tarpaper where the groundskeepers kept their lawn mowers and the athletic department kept the girls' hockey sticks and the square stuffed baseball bases and five-sided home plates. There were two baseball diamonds, one for softball not far from the storage shed, so that a good long foul ball pulled over third base might hit the wall or its one window covered in rat wire, and another beyond it, with a grass infield, for hardball—high-school varsity and also the town league. Beyond this second diamond the town playground offered an open pavilion with a smaller equipment shed and tables for checkers and braiding gimp, a basketball backboard on two pipes stuck in cement, two metal slides kept slippery and shiny by rubbing with the wax paper that sandwiches were wrapped in, a swing set with four big troughs worn where feet kicked, a smaller set of three for babies with chairs that had a bar across in front, and a jungle gym whose iron pipes were dewy and cold in the morning on the backs of your knees when you skinned the cat. Nobody could skin the cat like Essie at the age of ten; she liked the feeling of the world turning upside-down and the blood rushing to her head and her dress falling down over her underpants for a second. By the time she was thirteen she would never do such a thing, boys might see her hair there, at the edge of the cotton crotch. Much of the playground apparatus had become babyish but still she liked to linger, as spring lengthened the days, in the barren area between the shack near the high school and the pavilion on the edge of the old poorhouse peach orchards, a stretch that included the bleachers for the two baseball diamonds. The space held a flavor of after-school release, of a wide horizon, of not hurrying to get home. Extending her range to this space was a step, she knew, in her life's adventure. It was lazy and dirty and expectant, the atmosphere of it, the dirt full of stamped-in cigarette butts and drinking straws and used bottle caps, the back of the pavilion shed scratched with drawings and words not all of which she as yet understood.

She liked the kids who hung out here, though they were from the wrong side of town. As they lounged on the bleachers the air felt like rain clouds, hanging low and fuzzy over their heads, making them momentarily safe from possible bombers in the sky. The Du Pont plants and the Canal might be enemy targets, everybody said. Battles were raging in every direction over the horizon, in Libya and Burma, at Guadalcanal and Stalingrad, names in big black headlines and breathless radio bulletins introduced by the stutter of a telegraph key. In the movie newsreels, tanks plowed through the desert, making sandstorms, and Allied planes dropped hundreds of slowly twirling finned bombs on German cities, making firestorms. Smoke billowing, planes diving, battleships listing and sinking, parachutes multiplying in the sky over Yugoslavia like lilies in water, the Jews in the Warsaw ghetto starving and fighting guns with stones, frozen Nazi soldiers' bodies lying all over Russia: the voice of God behind the movie newsreels boomed and scolded, swollen graver and greater than ever in this feast of horror yet enclosing the audience in the ultimate security of an unfaltering American baritone. Essie did not doubt that the Germans and Japanese would be rolled back and crushed like evil bugs. Just their names, Huns and Japs, were buglike. The Italians were already surrendering, a forest of arms in the air, all of these wops looking so scruffy, unshaven, scared. Hitler was ridiculous and chewed carpets when he got mad and Hirohito was a tiny yellow man in a bulky big white uniform with a foolish big sword. Mr. Phillips said in Sunday school it was like Armageddon in Revelation in the Bible, all these beasts up from the bottomless pit, led by the one who spake like a dragon and put a mark on everybody's forehead or hand, whose name was the number 666, which worked out exactly to be code for HITLER, he said. Essie was impressed but not worried; Roosevelt and God and Churchill and Stalin were encircling and protecting her with millions of brave young men, GI Joes. She was to be confirmed into the church this

June, and Ama was busy working on the dress, with overlapping tulle skirts below and a breathtaking bodice of a fabric full of little eyelets up above.

Yet all the houses along the Delaware shore were blacked out and at night when the firehouse siren blew you were supposed to turn off all your lights and huddle on the stairs just as if that fat Goering's Luftwaffe bombers might be rumbling overhead. One night some planes did go over and Essie's heart nearly stopped, but for Ama giving her a hug and Daddy breathing the one word, "Ours." Ama sewed and knit things for the troops overseas and was always collecting canned food and old clothes for the children of Britain. To buy canned food now, along with sugar and coffee, you needed coupons, and got little round red rationing buttons in change, as well as the real change in pennies and nickels and dimes, at Hubie Drew's grocery store. Shoes were that way too, which Essie didn't mind because she loved to go barefoot from April to October; the soles of her feet got so tough and thick she could stick safety pins through them and horrify Danny, who couldn't stand to see it. Lucky Strike green had gone to war and Daddy paid her a penny a cigarette for rolling them out of tobacco and ZigZag paper in a little machine that you flipped back and forth once. The war sucked everything out of their peaceful world: butter and meat, sliced bread and Christmas cards, sneakers and gasoline. Daddy could get gasoline for his Jeep only because he was special as a mailman. Danny was the one who really loved the war, always making that "r-r-r-r-r-r" divebombing noise with his little lead P-38s and B-29s and Spitfires and collecting the insignia of all the Army divisions and jumping with a Geronimo shout on tin cans to flatten them for the scrap drives at school. He was in the fourth grade, and got sergeant's stripes for bringing in so many pounds and such a big ball of tinfoil. At night she could hear him in his room fantasizing or maybe even dreaming in his sleep making that "k-k-k-k-k" noise of a machine gun. He was always telling her ridiculous stories he picked up at school about how the Marines in the Pacific would take the little Japanese by the heels and drop them from the backs of battleships one by one into the churning propellers, and how Hitler had only one ball and was turning all the Jews in Europe into soap and smoke. She would tell him, "Cool down, little man; you're overheating your gaskets," which was an expression she had picked up from the gang she hung out with out near the playground. They were not considered "nice" but they seemed nice to Essie, nice in that they were letting her in on things she couldn't learn at home. They were a little tough but these were tough times, with everybody's parents distracted by the war.

They all lived closer to the ballfields, by a few blocks, than Essie did—Eddie Bacheller and Loretta Whaley and her twin brother Benjy and Junie Mulholland and Fats Lowe, who was a year older but had been held back, and some others from their end of town, up on the tannery side instead of east toward the old fishery wharf. They smoked cigarettes, Wings and Kools, they had stolen from their parents and complained about how all the teachers were jerks. Essie secretly didn't think that; she thought Mr. Langford, who taught beginning algebra, was rather handsome, with black eyebrows that nearly met in the middle like Tyrone Power's, and Miss Fenn was almost glamorous, if she wouldn't pull her hair back so old-maidishly but let it fall to her shoulders like Veronica Lake and straightened her spine, so she didn't seem always to be peering out at her class through some kind of keyhole. She could have taken a posture lesson from Mr. Josephs, who had left town because of the war; there were job opportunities, and his tap-dance class had gotten down to just five girls anyway. Sometimes when Miss Fenn was one of the teacher chaperones at the junior-high lunch-hour sock hops, she would step out and dance with a ninth-grade girl, and really knew the steps. That was one of Essie's personal goals: to become the best jitterbugger in her class. Others were (1) to stop being so skinny and (2) to stop blushing when she stood up to recite in class and (3) to never stutter, even for a tiny second on the words beginning with "d" or "l." Her singing teacher, Mrs. Loring up in New Castle, taught her how to breathe from the diaphragm and let the sounds come out at the top of a continuous column of air—"Breathe with your belly—your belly, Essie!"—but when she got excited or felt in the wrong she forgot about her belly. What she saw when she looked in the mirror was a face too fat and round on top of a body too skinny, with a nose a little too broad at the nostrils and a bump at the bridge like Momma had and shapeless big red hands dangling at the ends of her arms. She was one of the taller girls in the seventh grade now, and had inherited the Wilmot ranginess, though she didn't swing her arms and wisecrack like Aunt Esther. She was always studying her face, frightened but fascinated as if the mirror were a deep hollow-smelling well, tilting her head this way or that, trying to catch the best angle, the perfect angle with shadows and light like the movie stars' autographed pictures she had been collecting since she was ten. You sent away with a polite letter saying how she was your absolute favorite and enclosed a three-cent stamp, and after months went by Daddy in his mailman's uniform would bring it to the door; so as not to bend the big envelopes from Hollywood he would open the door and toss them in on the hall carpet. Marlene Dietrich was the first one ever, back before the war, to send a photo, of herself, holding a cigarette holder and top hat and one leg up on a little white box, and then Ginger Rogers, with her eyes warm and starry just like when she danced. Recently Essie had collected Linda Darnell, Dorothy Lamour, Alice Faye, Carmen Miranda, Loretta Young, Laraine Day, Osa Massen, Jane Greer, Ann Sheridan, and Rita Hayworth. The stars had big loopy signatures, full of ease and pride. Some used purple ink, and Alice Faye wrote in green, *Thanks for your lovely letter Esther.* Carmen Miranda wore her big fruit hat and frilly South American dress as you might expect but Dorothy Lamour was not in a sarong with a flower behind her ear but wearing a sensible sort of well-fitting suit, the sort she went around selling war bonds in. Rita Hayworth was wearing her

Gay Nineties *Strawberry Blonde* outfit but her signature looked like it was printed on, and so did Betty Grable's. Linda Darnell appeared a little sad the way she always did, her lower lip heavy and her eye sockets full of shadow, and her inscription was the saddest: *For a dear girl,* she had written—*May your dreams come true.* All these were pinned around the walls of Essie's room; she had over fifty now, counting a few from men stars she especially cared about—Ronald Colman, Joel McCrea, Errol Flynn, and George Sanders. George Sanders never got to be the main hero except in the Saint movies, but Essie loved him even when he had one of his nasty roles, like in *Nurse Edith Cavell* and *Rebecca;* she loved his above-it-all attitude, and the way he spoke everything so beautifully. When she practiced acting and talking smoothly to herself in her room she was most often Bette Davis or Katharine Hepburn but sometimes George Sanders, slightly drawling, and killing people in the Saint movies so calmly, with a sleepy little blink and a pursing of his elegant English lips. When Danny got really frantic with her teasing and her lording it over him he threatened to come in and rip up her movie-star collection and spatter ink all over them but she knew he would never dare commit such a sacrilege: she would never speak to him, her own brother, again.

She didn't like her own face but had to love it because it was hers. She thought it might be too broad but then Myrna Loy's and Greer Garson's faces were broad. Her skin had Momma's glow and the only acne so far was in the creases where the nostrils met the face and where the chin came out under the lower lip—there was a little not exactly crease but depression there. Her eyes were big and clear like Momma's yet instead of being a cornflower-blue like hers or a quiet milk-chocolate like Daddy's were a brown lighter than his, lighter even than Ama's, closest to Grandma Sifford's mysterious Moorish flecked honey-brown, but often changing, depending on what kind of day it was and what she was looking at; in the studio photographs Mr. Purinton took on his second-floor studio on Rodney Street last winter there was a little pinhole gleam right next to each pupil, white and black, fascinatingly, the white bouncing back from a light and the black going in and down as far as you could go. In black-and-white photographs her thick hair could look black but in the summer sun bleached almost to blond. Like Ama's hair it was very thick and began straight across the forehead, without a widow's peak. Essie wished it was the color of Rita Hayworth's in *The Strawberry Blonde,* with James Cagney and Olivia de Havilland. Olivia de Havilland was Joan Fontaine's sister and neither of them, nor Vivien Leigh either, had responded to Essie's request for a photograph; perhaps because they were over there in England under the bombs or because Essie hadn't put enough postage on to get her request across the ocean. Aunt Esther had very fine pale hair, like cornsilk to the touch. But she had almost no eyebrows whereas Essie's were long and sharp, right on the edge of the two arches of bone that ended her forehead; she loved their shape, every hair of them, and the way at the outside of the arches they went slightly up and over the edge, like Vincent Price's when he had evil thoughts. Momma said one time it made her look more mature than thirteen, she had the eyebrows of a grown woman, and Essie treasured all such remarks that helped her to see herself from the outside, as others saw her.

Aunt Esther since the war started had stopped getting her hair cut and permanent-waved but let it grow long and made of it a pigtail she wrapped around her head, as if just to get it out of the way now that she was the mother of three—all boys, all noisy and awful: Peter Junior, Jefferson, and Ira. Their father, Peter, was going bald and off in Washington all the time working for some wartime agency; he couldn't explain what for fear of giving away war secrets. The war had done Uncle Jared out in Colorado good, too. Back after the Crash that had started the Depression he had been given a piece of a mountain with a played-out copper mine in it, to keep him quiet, by his wife's father, who was a crook, Daddy and Momma told her one night when Ama wasn't listening. Now the need for copper was so great the government had paid him lots of money to get the mine working again. "That Jared," Daddy had said, and laughed a little—he never laughed a lot. "My brother will always land on his feet. It might take him years, but he'll land on his feet." Essie loved it when Daddy let slip his sense of the Wilmots' being somehow special, with a destiny that stretched above and beyond Basingstoke. Instead of being fine and shimmery like Aunt Esther's, Essie's hair was thick and unruly, so when she came in from running home from the baseball fields or working in the hot damp greenhouse it would be out from her head like a madwoman's, Momma said, sending her straight to her room to comb and brush. Essie would experiment in front of the mirror with putting her hair up like Rita Hayworth's in *My Gal Sal* or Bette Davis's in *The Little Foxes* and *Now, Voyager,* or looser like Greta Garbo's in *Two-Faced Woman* or Ingrid Bergman's in *Casablanca,* more like real hair that hadn't been shellacked or frozen in ripples like Irene Dunne's. Her face as she pondered it in the mirror was like a pie somehow in the middle: the nose a bit blobby and the lips not curving in and out as the stars' did but straight across, a slash in the dough, not cushiony and pushy-out like Betty Grable's or even Momma's when she was listening to the dance bands on the radio in the kitchen. Essie's lips were thin and careful like Daddy's and not pink and flirty like Alice Gordy's. When she experimented with Momma's lipstick and rouge it felt as if she was painting the middle of a pie. Though she began to have periods last July she had no breasts, either, though Loretta Whaley had quite nice pointy ones that pulled at her blouses and even Junie Mulholland, you could see where they were starting when she wore a sweater.

Essie sighed, leaning her weight backward on her elbows on the splintery bleacher board above the one she was sitting on. Something needed to rescue her but in the meantime the flat land that had been the poorhouse fields receded hypnotically under a soft April sky that looked like a piece of wet paper somebody had been brushing with gray in stripes. The smells of new grass and softening earth and peach blossoms from the sea of creamy pink beyond the playground were soaking into her brain, so she could hardly move, though it was getting late. Loretta and Junie had gone on home, cradling their books against their lucky breasts, and Eddie and Fats and a couple younger boys from this tannery end of town were playing basketball around the playground backboard. The ball had a slow leak and whenever anybody tried to dribble the bounce got less and less, so that everybody laughed and somebody would kick the ball away. The only other person on the bleachers with her, three boards down, was Benjy Whaley, who was reading a *Captain Marvel* comic book and yet was aware of her, she could tell. She uncrossed her ankles in their white socks and recrossed them, stretching her legs out so tight she felt the muscles squeak. At least she had nice long legs. Already she was as tall as Momma, and even though Ama was still taller a lot of it was her hair, piled up that way she had, like a big gray doughnut on top of her head. Essie sighed again, so loud she almost had to say something. "How's the comic book, Benjy? I don't hear you laugh."

He didn't turn to speak to her, a sure sign he had been really aware of her. "It's not supposed to be funny."

"Sometimes it is, though," she said. "Some of the villains. And the way he says 'Shazam.' "

Benjy said, "Shazam!" in a big voice, meaning to be funny but showing he was too nervous to think of what to say.

"You can't tell me those men who draw that strip don't think it's funny," she said. "I bet they sit there laughing at dopes like you who take it seriously."

"Without dopes like me spending their dimes," he said, "they'd be out of a living." Now he did look at her, leaning back and staring with his face upside down, a pointy chin where the top of his head should be and his eyelids blinking the wrong way, with the red on top instead of underneath. It was terrible like a creature from Mars, or a crab when you thought where its eyes and mouth were. He actually had a nice round pointy chin, like a girl's, more feminine than her own, which was a little bit too squared-off. She wished she had his chin. Benjy had always noticed her, pushing her and pulling at the ribbon in the back of her dress, but in the junior high he was milder, somehow, and more subdued, as though with the addition of the new students that had been in elementary schools over near St. Georges and that now came by bus, swelling the classes, he had discovered something about himself, maybe that he would never amount to much more than his father, who worked in Shorty Sturgis's Garage and ran a one-man gun shop on the side and in the evenings. In Delaware men loved to shoot ducks; they would get up early in the mornings and go crouch in the reeds. Benjy needed to be teased a little. She retracted her long legs in their scuffed saddle shoes and red kilt skirt and moved down to sit on the board beside him. Looking down to be careful and not fall and break a leg, which could happen on these old bleachers, she saw all the papers and bottles that had collected on the grass underneath. The grass was trying to grow, but because of the shade from the bleacher boards was coming in yellow.

"L-let's see," she said, leaning slightly against his arm. Captain Marvel was fighting some bald scientist who was within a whisker of having the secret that would permit him to rule the universe, along with the Axis powers. One panel showed him talking to Hitler over the phone, with electric zigzags leaping around the curve of the earth. "That's so dumb," she said. Benjy said nothing, just turned the page. She couldn't believe he read so slowly. "D-did you listen to Jack Benny the other night?" she asked. "I love it when he visits his money in the vault, all that creaking and slamming—even my father gets to laughing hard. We all sit listening Sunday nights right from Jack Benny through Phil Harris and Alice Faye, and he starts to snore in the middle of Charlie McCarthy."

"I forget," Benjy said, lowering the comic book and looking toward the horizon. "Sometimes we listen. My father says they're all Jewish."

"I don't think Edgar Bergen is Jewish, he's Swedish," Essie said. "Anyway, what does it matter?"

Benjy had a very interesting mouth in profile, fitted together so precisely, and a little angrily, like Vivien Leigh's in *Gone With the Wind.* That had been *such* a tremendous movie, though she didn't like it when the little girl fell off the horse and died, and preferred *The Wizard of Oz,* where nobody got hurt except the witches. Dorothy had breasts, you could see, even though she's supposed to be a little girl. "We're fighting this war," Benjy said, "because the Jews got us into it."

"Really? I thought we were fighting it because of Pearl Harbor."

"The Jews could have stopped Pearl Harbor. They wanted the war because it's good for the banks."

She was sorry she had moved down to sit next to him. She could feel from far away her mother beginning to worry. The wet brush strokes in the sky were getting thicker and darker. It always made her excited when it rained, as if God was touching her somehow. Essie thought of her little room's walls covered with stars' faces and stars' signatures and a taste came into her mouth of such coppery happiness that she wanted to punch and pinch thick-witted Benjy.

He kept staring toward the blurred horizon of low blue hills way beyond the hardball diamond. There was a round green water tank like a visiting spaceship from Mars, and the underside of the clouds trailed dark travelling wisps. Unexpectedly Benjy said, "In a couple more years I'll have to go fight in it and get killed, probably."

"Oh, Benjy," she said, sounding a bit in her own ears like Bette Davis being Southern, "of course you won't. It'll be all over by that time! Already this year the Germans are surrendering all over the place—Russia, Africa."

"Yeah, but then there's the Japanese. They fight to the death, every one. They're crazy little monkeys."

"Didn't MacArthur just k-kick them out of Guadalcanal?"

"MacArthur gives me a pain in the ass. He's a show-off."

"Why, Benjy, a person would think you weren't American!" But still she didn't move away and begin to walk the nine blocks home. He had folded up the comic book in a brutal way, doubling it like a newspaper, and his thumb against the bright paper looked sallow and strong, delicately carved and grubby in the knuckle. Car grease was in his blood. It was so funny, his being a twin with Loretta, who didn't look at all like him, and who was much more mature. Benjy's skull was narrow and his hair, so blond it was almost white, like an albino's, had been cut close in a crew cut, so she could see the interesting ridge of bone behind his ear. His ear fitted close to his head, as if the top part had been glued. One of the things she didn't like about herself was her ears—they didn't stick out, exactly, but they didn't exactly lie flat, either.

"I'm American enough," Benjy said. "I'll go if they call me. I'll do my duty."

She giggled at such a grim thought, here at the still center of a landscape so peaceful, so idle. It revealed in him a solitary brooding akin to her own private dreams. She blew lightly on his nice flat ear. "Is that what you do, Benjy—what other people tell you to do?" She saw him for all his delicate physical beauty as defeated, stuck forever in this town with its stupid prejudices and boring jobs.

He turned with a fury whitening his face, pulling back his lips from his teeth, and said, "Fuck you, Essie Wilmot."

She was not shocked. The phrase was chalked and gouged into the playground pavilion, and the shed near the school. She had once heard a bunch of soldiers on the trolley car saying it over and over, loud. "I didn't mean anything mean," she said.

"Yeah, what do *you* do," he asked, "except what you're told to do?"

The parents of the kids who hung out around the bleachers and the playground after hours weren't quite like hers; they went to bars, and bowling alleys, and had nocturnal shouting matches and brawls that sometimes leaked back into the classroom gossip. Some of the parents weren't even together—the mothers worked and the fathers had gone off to plants in Ohio or Virginia. The war was like a wind that had stirred up everything not fastened down. It made everybody a little reckless, even Momma coming in in the morning jumpy on coffee after all night in the clangor of the cartridge factory, her hair up under her bandana so she looked like Jean Arthur, if Jean Arthur were getting fat.

"Oh, I do things like this," Essie said, and edged closer with a tilted head. She pictured Ingrid Bergman in *Casablanca*, the scene where she pulls a gun on him, in the room above Rick's with the Venetian blinds, and he says in his beautiful white tuxedo jacket, *Go ahead and shoot. You'll be doing me a favor*, and she can't, and their profiles merge, her tearstained cheeks shining, her hair rimmed with light and slightly out of focus, her lips numb and thick and a little bit open, as she desperately surrenders herself in a war-torn world. Essie had kissed boys before, but in childish play, post office at parties and in school cloakrooms while wriggling in protest and whacking them on the ear afterwards. Benjy's lips were still childish, hard and pressing on hers too hard, so there was a danger of their teeth clicking together, but she liked the strange big feeling of it, this other body pushing at hers and hers pushing back through these two vulnerable moist spots, Benjy's existence impinging on hers like an invasion from one planet of another. He had a taste, of the Philip Morris he had been smoking and the licorice he had been eating, and behind that of something bland and faintly salty she supposed was simply flesh, or the taste of another soul rising up through his throat. She pictured his lips, how they fitted together, and tried to spread that fit to her own lips, to their lips mixed together. But he was quickly uncomfortable, even though the boys playing basketball weren't watching, and backed off with a frightened stare, like a white-eyed mechanic sliding out from under a car. There was nothing to say, what had happened had been so strange. But from the hangdog look in his eyes now she knew he would be back for more, and a kind of ashamed churning in her own insides

South Pacific with a case of malaria and a bellyful of parasites and was delivering on the edges of town in the Willys station wagon that had replaced the Jeep; he had a young family and was ambitious. This seemed to Essie and Danny much too cautious of their father, and rather selfish and unkind to deny them and Momma (though they couldn't exactly say this) the advantages that would come with a raise in his pay and status; but Ama took her son's side, saying to them privately, "It keeps him fit, and it's something he can handle. Your daddy has a certain temperament. They used to say in Missouri, 'Don't race a plow horse, and don't eat a laying chicken.' "

Momma had her hands full over at the greenhouse, where Grandma Sifford was having health problems. With no appetite and constant pain, she was shrivelling and looking ever darker, ever more of a Moor from North Africa. Doc Hedger's successor, handsome young Dr. Jessup, had her worked up at the Wilmington General Hospital on South Broom Street and the X-rays found a tumor, in fact several little tumors. Only Essie knew where the cancer had come from: those poisons, like nicotine tea, with which her grandmother had combatted all the bugs and spots and wilts that had thrived in the hothouse atmosphere. Poor Momma limped back and forth all the time, diagonally across Locust Street in the rainy fall weather, taking on the cooking and housekeeping for her father, mothering the elusive mother at the root of her own maimed life.

So it was relatively easy for Essie to announce that she had to go up to Philadelphia next Saturday and have some more photographs taken by Doug Germaine, and would be back by six or seven at the latest. "Be sure you are" was all Momma said. She looked weary and cross. "That boy was pushy."

"Momma, it's his job. You saw the photographs—weren't they striking?"

Momma brushed a piece of hair back from her rounded white forehead and said aloofly, "He sees you in a way a mother can't," a touch of permission and release tucked into the cold remark.

"If you get the chance," Daddy said, "be sure to look in at the Curtis Building. There's a fantastic thing in there, a big mural made all out of glass. Believe me, it's out of this world."

Doug lived on Pine Street in two rooms three floors up; the front room was his studio, with an old velvet couch he had hung a mottled sheet behind, to make a background. He had a female friend with him, which Essie had not expected, a slightly tough and hefty bleached blonde somewhere in her twenties called Gloria. Essie couldn't tell much about their relationship because as soon as they had her in the studio all their focus was on her Gloria showed Essie how to use a lip brush instead of lipstick and how to apply artificial eyelashes—it made her squeamish, the tickling at the edge of her lids, but Gloria crooned to her, "You have such photogenic eyes," and Essie relaxed. They oiled her face and shoulders to take the lights more dramatically and fussed with her hair until Essie felt as if her whole scalp was burning. Gloria, whose fingers were deft but not especially gentle, spent what seemed an hour playing with different tints of make-up, including white, to define the line of her nose and to make her cheeks look hollower. "Shadows," Doug said, much less casual and amusing than he had been in Dover. "We sculpt you with shadows." He kept moving his lights and asking Gloria to hold a silver-paper reflector as he began to photograph. His camera here was a big box with an accordion on the front and a black sheet behind. He moved it closer and closer until she had to fight blinking her eyes; it was like the false eyelashes, tickling and dangerous. There was a bulb on a white cord he could squeeze to click the lens while he talked to her. "Great. *Great*, Essie. Now let's try a single spot, to give us some slashing shadows off those cheekbones." He kept asking her to assume unnatural twisted positions, facing into the spotlight so lashlike strands of glare blinded her, while from the darkness beyond the lights Gloria's voice would reassure her, "You look heavenly, darling," or Doug's, constipated-sounding with the intensity of his focus, would say, "Don't *pose*. Keep your face very quiet.

Let us *in.* Give us your *dreams,* the girl inside. Don't think too much; it makes your mouth tense. Puff out the upper lip. Imagine something big and soft flowing through you, from behind. Good. *Good.* Now look right at the lens. Challenging—get mad. 'Who is this jerk?' Yes. Up with the shoulder. Higher. Even higher. 'Who is this idiotic jerk?' Oh, yes—nice." He had her change from that dusty-pink off-the-shoulder Jane Russell sweater into a slinky Joan Crawford kind of dress, satin and tight at the hips and knees, with a long feather boa she was invited to play with, draping it across her shoulders and down her front and for one series of plates pulling it intriguingly across her face so that only her eyes showed. Painted and oiled and every hair lacquered as firm as the fibers in a hat, Essie felt armored in pretense, formless and safe behind her face, like the rich filling of a stiff chocolate. As Doug sweatily worked away, trying to coax some kind of essence from her that she could not picture, she found he seemed most happy with those expressions where she was imagining him as Mr. Bear, a big innocent Mr. Bear with his fur scuffed off at the elbows and muzzle, his camera lens being one of the hollow round eyes with the tiddlywink pupil in it. Mr. Bear had been her first audience. She would scold him and cuddle him and tell him her thoughts on everything. She never stuttered with Mr. Bear and knew she would never stutter in this painted armor of beauty with which she faced the invisible audience gathering behind these remorseless lights.

Doug and Gloria took her out to a cheap chophouse joint at the corner of the next block. The people in Philadelphia seemed loud and forcedly jolly, and there were Negroes mixed up with them, in the booths as well as at the counter, as loud and joshing as the others, and nobody seemed to mind. You never saw brotherly love like that in Basingstoke. After lunch they went back and Doug went into the other room while Gloria asked her if she would mind posing in her underwear. Essie had put on her best panties and bra, imagining she might have to make love to Doug because he was doing her this enormous favor, but still she hesitated, while Gloria explained that more and more advertisers were switching away from illustration to photographing the models, for items like lingerie and bathing wear. Advertisers liked the real model over the stylized drawing, though of course the newspapers and family magazines were still very cautious.

Essie was cautious herself; she could imagine what Momma would say, and Daddy would silently think, if they could be there. Suddenly Gloria got earnest and spoke straight in her face with what seemed a weight of experience: "In or out, dear: choose. You can't play coy in this business. The product is you. What privacy you got, you make for yourself in here." Gloria tapped herself in the chest, between breasts grander than Essie's but starting to sag and leathery on top from too many suntans. You only had so many years, Gloria's skin said. Meekly Essie nodded and undressed, down to the nylon panties below her panty girdle, and after a few minutes felt as natural in the little pond of hot light as if she were in a bathing suit on the sunny beach at Woodland. Her lean athletic body was a gift she trusted and never worried about; it had skipped to her from hunter ancestors right through the genes of her doughy parents. When Gloria asked her to take off her bra, for "a few glamour shots, mostly from the back," she scarcely protested. That was as far as they went. Yet back in Basingstoke, exhausted and gritty from the train and trolley car, Essie felt she had more to hide than if she *had* gone to bed with Doug, as she had intended and as her mother had feared.

"Momma, there was this woman there all along, helping him with the lights and everything. It's *work*, believe me. Simple honest hard work."

Her mother was not convinced. Studying her daughter with a moment's acuteness, before rushing off into the evening dark to attend to the trouble of her parents' house, Emily said, "You're not the same. They did something to you."

"They did nothing to me but take a zillion pictures I bet nobody ever looks at. Really, Mother. Why'd you drag me to all those lessons, if all you wanted was for me to hide under a bushel here in pokey old Basingstoke?"

This Biblical allusion made Momma consider. "Maybe we both," she said, after considering, "had unreal expectations. Essie, I'm sorry, if I loved you more than was reasonable."

Momma touched her cheek, and suddenly both women hugged, to seal over the gulf opening before them. Her mother somehow knew that Essie had given up to Doug and his lights a piece of the dark treasure accumulated in the furtive and indecent smother of being loved. What her family and the boys of Basingstoke had clumsily bestowed was now to be taken to market. Not three hours removed from her session, Essie felt her stirred-up nerves craving the tickle of attention, the armoring pressure of self-display.

"Take the plunge," Aunt Esther advised. "What the hell." In the desultory scatter of her senior year—a bemused, irritable period of killing time like what Essie imagined pregnancy to be—she found herself, when she could commandeer the family Studebaker, over in Red Lion, visiting Aunt Esther and Uncle Peter. First they had had an apartment, like fugitives; then in the Depression they had flauntingly bought a big old house with formal plantings and noisy plumbing and terrible heating bills; and now they had built a modern house, on two wooded acres, with big picture windows in both the kitchen and living room, and a redwood deck off the second-floor bedroom, and a fieldstone barbecue in the backyard, and a tennis court where the three boys bopped the ball around with their parents. Essie found this house more cheerful than her own had become. Grandma Sifford's finally passing on, in December, had taken something out of Ama; she was shrivelling in the face and hunching in the shoulders, and though she tried to be as busy and cheerful in the kitchen as ever, some days dinner just didn't appear until Momma came back from the greenhouse, where Grandpa Sifford needed her more than ever. It was as if when Daddy declined the postmastership Momma took a new husband, her own father. Some days Essie would come back from school and the house would feel deserted, the front shades pulled down to save the furniture from the sun, and Ama sitting upstairs in her room on her bed in her slip and old-fashioned stockings with seams and rolled tops, gazing at the wallpapered wall as if its entwining, repeating pattern of ivy on bricks held in some shallow third dimension the answer to a riddle. Then Essie would ask her what she might put in the oven or fry up for dinner and Ama in discussing food would come back to life. Danny would be still at school. Too runty to make any team, he had become the manager of the jayvee basketball squad and also was on the debating team and ninth-grade student council—quite the little politician. It was all depressing; the shy gray house set back with its yard from Locust Street had gone stale, the furniture funky and stained and pre-war, like the crackly old fake-walnut Philco cathedral-front radio, and even the cookbooks that Ama told her to look up recipes in were tattered and falling apart and savoring of a tyrannical past where they expected a woman to stand around all day testing roasts and baking pies from scratch on a wood-stove.

Whereas over in Red Lion everything was new and sunny even in the dead of winter. Instead of dumb calendars with dressed-up Scotties and a greasy religious picture of Jesus praying in a purple robe at a conveniently flat rock while a single spotlight brought out the planes of His face, the Pulsifers had framed prints by Bonnard and Matisse in wild colors and shapes and actual oil paintings done by a friend of theirs of the marshes and the derelict old houses along the Canal. Instead of *Reader's Digest*s and *Saturday Evening Post*s limply getting out of date in a stained-maple magazine stand next to Daddy's armchair they had something brand new called *Flair* with a hole right in the cover and *Life* with all its shiny photos of people in the limelight. On the bookcase on Locust Street there were sun-bleached fat cloth spines with names like Thornton

Wilder and Edna Ferber and Sinclair Lewis from before the war, when Momma used to read novels, and an awful assortment of books in dismal dull colors dragged down from Paterson about the Bible and God along with O. Henry and Kipling, and on the lowest shelf, more depressing still, a whole row in crumbling yellow-brown leather of something called *The Popular Encyclopedia* that Essie had never opened, it smelled so of the dead past; whereas the Pulsifers had lying around still in their bright jackets new books by modern authors like Philip Wylie and Anne Frank and Ernest Hemingway and Ross Lockridge, Jr. And then that fall they had bought themselves a television set, the first Essie had ever seen in a home. It was like a little movie right there in the living room, a free movie that was running in a fishbowl. To Essie the images the tube produced looked fuzzy and dirty, worse than B pictures out of Universal, and not so much like a movie as like one of the skits at high school, some man getting into a woman's dress and falling around on high heels, and messy, everything slapdash and underrehearsed, these women knocking each other around in the roller derby and this man with all these rings on his hands playing in a kind of cellar by the light of some candles: it turned her stomach a little, like too much candy, to look at it for long. But the three Pulsifer boys flicked it on as soon as one banged into the house and kept it on as they went in and out, with their noise and sports equipment and friends. They were rich spoiled brats, compared to her friends in Basingstoke. Uncle Peter would come home from work and find the two Esthers in the kitchen or out in the screened sunporch underneath the redwood deck. "Which twin has the Toni?" he would say, stooping to kiss his thin-lipped wife but wanting, Essie could feel, to kiss *her.* Uncle Peter had come back from his wartime duty in Washington with all of his youthful bounce restored; he was baby-bottom bald on top of his head and had frizzy amber-gray hair on the rest. With his wartime contacts and new understanding of how government does things, he had established an independent practice in New Castle. Except for days when he wore dark suits to court or down to Dover, he wore tweedy sports coats and gray flannel pants and polished brown loafers. Boys and men had an attractiveness that was mixed up with power, with the ease with which they moved in the world, and on this scale Uncle Peter was about a six. "And how is my knockout niece, Basingstoke's answer to Claudette Colbert?"

It dated him, that he thought of this star, though perhaps there was a resemblance. Lauren Bacall would have been more flattering, if he ever went to the movies. He and Aunt Esther spent most of their weekends at their country club, playing golf or tennis doubles and having dinner with other people about their age. Sitting through a movie would be an insult to their intelligence and a waste of their time.

"She can't decide if she should move to New York," Esther explained. "I just told her to go for it. What the hell." Aunt Esther still wore her hair in a big coiled pigtail and when she smoked or was thinking up a wisecrack narrowed her eyes so much that they were just the tiniest slivers of blue, sagging down in the outer corners. Just being with her, Essie made an effort to keep her own eyes wide open, in case a squint ran in the family.

Uncle Peter sometimes stopped off for a drink or two on his way home, so that pink blazed in his meaty face. "You've got yourself a haircut," he said to Essie. "The New Look!" He put down his briefcase and too roughly squeezed the exposed back of Essie's neck; she hunched her shoulders to shake him off. Still, she didn't want to be rude, she liked it here in his house too much.

She explained to him, as if in apology for her fashionable hair, "This Doug I keep mentioning sent my photos to a friend of his called Wexler in a New York model agency but it took months to get a reply out of him and now all he's said is if I'm ever in New York why don't I come by for a chat?"

"I don't like the address he's given her," Aunt Esther told him. "It's in Chelsea, on West Nineteenth Street. There was nothing down there but speakeasies and dry cleaners in my day. If it's legit, how come it's not further uptown?"

"What do you know?—you're talking twenty years ago. Subway fares were a nickel then, too. If they're willing to look our Essie over, what has she got to lose?"

"Look her over with what in mind?" Aunt Esther asked. "Some of these so-called model agencies—"

"I can take care of myself," Essie said, wondering if she could. Boys and back seats in Basingstoke were one thing, high-powered agencies in New York were another.

Uncle Peter asked aloud, "Who's up for a drink?" and answered himself in a high squeaky voice: " 'I am, sir,' said Tiny Tim, casting off his crutches." He was lit, all right.

"She needs somebody to look after her," Esther said, brushing off as tedious her husband's pranks. "I was thinking, what about Patrick?" To Essie she said, "Your cousin. How well do you know him?"

"I remember him once coming to Locust Street, one time when Uncle Jared had come east. But that was before the war. I was ten or so. He seemed very grown-up and stuck-up. He thought Danny and I were little rubes, he made that plenty clear."

"He's not much more than a year older than you, actually. He was a babe in arms at our wedding. But when Lucille and Jare split she began running with this arty monied crowd, so I guess he grew up fast. He never had a man around to model himself after." There was some meaning here Essie didn't get; she could tell by the way Aunt Esther's eyes checked out her face, before resuming: "Jare was out west with his damn fool mountain. But any port in a storm. Patrick knows the ropes, or some of the ropes. Pete's right, it can't do you any harm to go talk to him before you get in any deeper with people like Doug, who's out to just milk you for his own sake, and this Wexler, who may or may not be on the up-and-up."

How strangely distrustful Aunt Esther was! Just like Daddy, though with a different way of expressing it. Essie said, "If you're afraid being a model is just a way of being a prostitute, I don't see what good that would do Doug. He wants me to succeed. He says I have great looks, though I can't see it myself. I think I'm kind of homely."

Her aunt's squinting eyes flared, for a moment, almost into circles. "Darling, no—you've got it. It doesn't show all the time, but it shows in photographs. When I see some of them, it's almost like Pop has become an angel. My dad was a beautiful man, but in you it's gone somewhere. We just don't want to put our feet wrong. I moved down here to please *your* dad and I've lost what city smarts I ever had."

Her aunt's praise felt like an X-ray bringing up in white the secret inside her ribs, the thing that told her that she was the center of the universe and that there would be no misstep. Uncle Peter, oblivious of this Wilmot transaction occurring beneath his nose, set a cloudy brown drink before his wife, with a little lurch that produced too loud a click, and said, "Essie, what can I tempt you with? I know you don't approve, but a little glass of sherry? A rum-and-Coke, very weak, Scout's honor." But he held up the fingers that mean horns, as a joke. People who drink like you to drink. Though she had stopped going to church a year or two after being confirmed, staying home with Daddy and the Sunday paper instead, she was still Presbyterian enough to fear alcohol. It ate lives, in from the edges, lurking in cupboards and becoming the secret reason for every gathering of two or three, and one day people woke up and realized that liquor had stolen their lives away. Also, drinking made you fat and puffy, and her face needed all the bony structure she could give it.

"You shouldn't offer the girl a drink when she's driving," Aunt Esther told him. She rarely said anything to her husband this contrary. She had wanted him, back there before Essie was born; she had paid the price in scandal for him; she had made herself his; this was her bed and by damn she would lie in it. These weathered marriages from the Twenties surrounded Essie like Delaware's shallow smoke-blue hills. When she thought of them at all, her aunt and uncle and her parents and the doomed marriage of Uncle Jared and Aunt Lucille, it was as beaten-down monuments to the cowardice and stolid timidity of this older generation. She was determined to have a lot of men and to be captive to none of them.

"Aaahh," Peter said in self-defense, shamed for a second, caught at corrupting a girl. "Essie could drive the road with her eyes closed. She has a good head on her shoulders." And he took the opportunity, as she sensed he would, to place a puffy strong hand on either side of her skull, with its short haircut, and squeeze, hard and soft, for what seemed a long while. Essie put up with it; it was a kind of farewell.

James Patrick Wilmot lived in the Park Avenue apartment owned by his mother and stepfather, Mr. Traphagen. Mr. Traphagen—an old Dutch name—was a frustrated artist who, after thirty years spent in his family's china-and-porcelain-importing business located on Pearl Street, had retired early to concentrate on painting. To better concentrate he spent, with his reluctant wife, more and more time in Maine, and was still up there, stoking a woodstove and watching the storm waves break on the rocks, in early December. Essie knew this much from her aunt and father. Daddy had little to say about his sister-in-law, except: "It would take a saint to be married to Jared, and Lucy was no saint. Her father avoided Sing Sing by the skin of his teeth. As to the boy, it's a wonder he's not a juvenile delinquent. She was too pregnant with him to come to your mother's and my wedding, but she showed up with him in her arms at Esther's, and stole the show. He has those black-Irish good looks, don't know where from. Old Jimmy McMullen was a homely devil—always looked like a truck-loader in his tux." All this family lore, Essie thought, was coming out of the bushes to boost her on her way.

She had been primed with instructions how to get from Penn Station to the Times Square Shuttle and then up the East

Side to Eighty-sixth and Lexington, all on a dime token. But she was an hour early and walked instead up Fifth Avenue, drinking in the caustic city air, the stony cold, the carols broadcast out onto the sidewalk, the Salvation Army dinging their nervous bells, the yellow taxis and snorting green buses, the swift-moving crowds with their averted, flitting faces. There were lavish, glittering, nodding, rotating Christmas windows from Lord & Taylor's on up to Saks and Bonwit's, of Santa Clauses and three Magi in three skin colors, of people in sleighs and fur muffs from old-time New York. She had been here only twice before—with her parents to the World's Fair and the other time to go to the Radio City Music Hall and see the Rockettes—but the city fell open before her like a chocolate apple, in crisp glossy pieces, perfectly intelligible. The numbered side streets were like rows and rows of books that some day she would read. The avenues flew straight ahead of her to a vanishing point that was Harlem. At the corner of the park with its bronze statues she turned right until she struck Park, and then walked north, inhaling exultantly though her feet had begun to hurt, to the Traphagens' address. The doorman gave her name into a little loudspeaker, which squawked in return. An elevator operator in white gloves and a maroon uniform with brass buttons took her to the right floor; a little mincing maid in a black dress trimmed in crisp white opened the door to her. So many people, to serve just you. In the parqueted apartment foyer a half-moon marquetry table held a vase of fresh flowers—mums and glads with a green backing of ferns and what she recognized from her years in the greenhouse as eucalyptus and leatherleaf.

The living room held a piano and sofa so big there seemed several of each. The space in the room, which several islands of glossy, nappy, furniture tried in vain to fill, went back and back, as if a camera were tracking forward, and velvet-curtained windows gave on brick and granite cliffs and sharp-edged deep valleys where automobiles crawled far below. She had been here before, in the movies. Patrick entered from some other room of the vast apartment and was predictably tall and handsome and gentle. She had to perch forward on her chair to hear him talk, describing his life with an amusing, drawling diffidence, like James Stewart with Cary Grant's class and Robert Taylor's moody eyebrows. Only his hair was upright, like Farley Granger's, and like her own when the hairdresser didn't flatten it. He was a student at New York University, down in Washington Square, majoring in fine arts though he didn't think he'd try to be a painter; he'd seen the effort break old Trap's heart. Trap? His stepfather. How sophisticated, Essie thought, to have a stepfather, and your real father off owning a mountain in Colorado. A piece of a mountain, actually. With the war over, there was no profit any more in the copper leavings and pillars, but Jared—he called his own father "Jared," just like that, one man speaking of another, distant man—and his partners had great hopes for developing the slopes into a ski resort. Recreational sport was becoming big business. Families getting out and doing things together, that sort of middle-class folderol. Essie was fascinated by the traces of herself in Patrick—a Wilmot way of holding his head to one side, as if listening for something; a prim fineness to the gestures of his hands and a dry cut of his lips—and felt herself, much more wholeheartedly and maturely than when sitting on the bleachers with Benjy Whaley, swooning forward into love.

All around them, as they talked, she trying to match his gentle voice with one equally soft and diffident, the apartment spread its wealth and silence and amplitude of unseen rooms. There were many antique family things and some modern boxy furniture such as Aunt Esther and Peter had but bigger and more expensive, and over all a romantic tinge of neglect, a sense of absent owners, who had brought the decor to a certain high pitch and then wandered away, bored, leaving the windows dusty and the fabrics fading. Yes, her cousin said, he would like to go with her when she had her interview with Mr. Wexler. There were other agencies, better agencies, but since Wexler had already expressed interest, had seen her portfolio, let's begin with him. A bird in hand, et cetera. He would make the call for her, he knew a chap, actually, who had worked for Wexler. No trouble, honestly. He'd like to do it, he was between terms and bored fairly silly. He talked rapidly, in his murmuring voice, as if seeking to hypnotize her. No, in answer to an earnest question of Essie's, he had no doubts, having seen her now in the flesh. She was a gem, wanting only—with some embarrassment, Patrick made vague and agitated gestures in the air—polishing. Voice and acting lessons, perhaps, once she was established here in the city. To Method, or not to Method, that was the question. An in joke, he explained. Of course there was a limit to what could be taught, they can't make a silk purse, et cetera, but these coaches have techniques, there are little tricks, ways of connecting with yourself, your inner self. . . . Everything would happen, he was confident. For years he had been hearing about her from dear Aunt Esther. In fact, his mother was always talking about driving down to Delaware for a visit, but . . . No matter, the mountain at last had come to Mohammed. Now, she *must* let him take her out for a little lunch, and then he could point her in the direction of a museum—she *must* go to the Modern, his mother was one of its founding spirits—or over to Broadway, the overrated Great White Way, rather dreary in daylight, actually, for all of its gigantic signs and pathetically palatial movie houses. Some people came to New York and then went and sat in a dark movie house, could you believe it?

But Essie had visions of a movie right here, in this lovely quiet set. He thought she knew nothing, a rube, but she did know some things. "Before any of that," she said, "I wonder if I could take a b-bath? I w-worked up a terrible sweat, walking all the way, I was so excited. This city is absolute heaven."

"No," said Patrick, with a primness she was not sure was a joke. "Heaven is quite elsewhere." She wondered how much he had been raised a Catholic. They took everything so literally, straight from the priests. Essie was grateful that her God was a Protestant one, Who gave you credit for some brains and let you work things out for yourself, at least until you died.

In her bath, she kept waiting for him to come in and see her naked, the tops of her breasts gleaming up from the bubbles. She had found some of his mother's fragrant soap in a cabinet but the tub had been so long unused there were dead spiders in it, and one living, and the water thumped out with a burst of rusty brown. Still, an abundance of mirrors gave her back in angled slices her pink-and-white perfection. Waiting to share her pleasure in herself, she thrust one taut ankle and rosy-toed foot out of the soapy water, and then the other, admiring the fine straight tendons that jumped up, and the wandering veins like rivers of delicate aquamarine. She leaned back so her nape got wet and soapy and moved her eyes from one corner of the bathroom ceiling to the other, and then oppositely, making an X. All her nerves were tensed against the click of the door opening, as it would have in any movie—amusingly in a comedy, scarily in an intrigue mystery—but eventually the bubbles all had popped and the water clammily cooled. Draped in a beige towel with a scratchy monogram, she went in search of Patrick. The little maid came down the hall, looking startled to see her, but Essie smiled vaguely through her, knowing that servants were just love's furniture. She walked on, barefoot across the textures of parquet and Oriental carpet and polar-bear rug, into the study, masculine with books and maroon leather, where Patrick was pretending to read a magazine. It was called *The New Yorker*—she had never heard of it, it wasn't on the rack at Addison's Drug Store—and the cover had a chalky drawing of white-faced shoppers walking at night along where she had just been, past a store window holding a Christmas tree and a hollow-eyed, sinister Santa Claus.

Perhaps he was truly reading it; he didn't seem to hear her and looked up only as she let the towel drop. Patrick winced, and his moody blue-black eyebrows scowled. He jumped up to retrieve the damp towel off the polar bear's massive square head, where she had dropped it, and to push it back at her, hiding her tender, radiant front. His breathing was heavy and entwined with her awareness of her own; he gave her a light cool kiss on the cheek and said in his rapid voice, as if trying to restore her hypnotized mood, "You're absolutely lovely, you know, but shouldn't you be saving yourself?"

"Who for?" she asked, correcting this to, "For whom? You'll do fine."

"Well, that's it, darling. I won't. I won't do fine. I know that much about myself at this point. *Sorry.* Oh, my. You must let me explain during lunch. Do get your clothes on—you'll scandalize poor Marie."

She had things to learn in life, Essie knew that. But her sense of herself was that she would be looked after, now, and not allowed to fail. There were too many eyes on her, ghostly and real. This particular embarrassment she deflected by picturing, as she walked away, back to the bathroom and her clothes, her naked back receding in the rectangular frame of his vision, the towel clasped casually to her chest where he had thrust it, the lithe white lengths of her legs and the unrepentant seesaw of her buttocks spelling out to him what he had with such curious gallantry renounced. Maybe, she thought, he had a fiancée. But no, he explained at lunch, the problem was that from about the age of fourteen he had found himself in the unfortunate position of being attracted only to boys. His mother had no idea; old Trap, who was somewhat queer himself, guessed, but said nothing. Boarding school—Choate, in Wallingford, Connecticut—had made it all beautifully, horrifyingly clear. Well, it was his problem. He patted her knee, there at the little round table of the restaurant, where the menu was all in French. They had an affinity: two Wilmots with a touch of outlaw. Maybe all Wilmots had a touch of outlaw.

As though nothing awkward had happened, he took her to the museum, on the far side of an Episcopal church. Such gaudy colors, such toylike shapes! And all being looked at so seriously, by men in fitted suits with double-breasted coats and women in the latest long bell-shaped skirts and wasp-waisted suits decreed by Dior. Then, as the short day drew in, making her cheeks sting with its cold, Patrick walked her down Broadway to the Times Square subway station, and told his country cousin how, in that vast underground of cement and steel and hurrying bodies, to find the IND Eighth Avenue line to Penn Station. On the train back to Wilmington she had time to reflect that sex was at the heart of show business, but was not worn, actually, on its sleeve.

She couldn't believe Patrick was really homosexual. She felt she could bring him around, if he'd just let her. The only homosexual in Basingstoke was an old man who lived in one of the rooms above Krauthammer's; the high-school boys used to play awful pranks on him, but he never got mad or went to the police, as if he had no rights. He just snuck around like a beaten dog, bent with weird longing, hoping to get lucky. Here in New York it wasn't quite so bad; there were enough of them to make a society, and not such a secret society at that. The arts, especially minor arts like window-dressing, were dominated by them. She felt it a kind of comforting accreditation, actually, at the model agency, to have a poof bring her in.

The glamour trade was run by types who didn't exist in Basingstoke. Wexler was a busy bald short man who snarled, "Show us the legs, dear," and said of the sheaf of photos Doug Germaine had sent him, "Some of these I like. Girl next door, with a little devil in her. Take off five pounds and do something about your hair; it's out of control. Also it's a little dead. Lighten it, darken it, something. O.K., young lady. You want to come try your luck in town, we'll put you in our files. No promises, no guarantees. Client satisfaction's a slippery thing. Some girls come in here you think, 'Jeez, what a knockout!' but in black-and-white, nothing happens. Something about the nose, usually. What you ask of a nose, basically, is that it stays out of the way. The eyes, the mouth—there's the action. Your nose, well, it could be tuned up but it's not a big problem right now. I hope you thank God every night for those teeth. Your mom and dad must have spent a fortune."

"Not a penny," Essie said. "Ama—my grandmother—said brush after every meal, especially when you had dessert. I've had four cavities in my whole life. She said it was all the iodine in the local spinach. My brother, Danny, has terrible teeth, but then he's a complainer about everything." She liked Wexler. She felt he liked her, in his rude Jewish way. These were her people, show people—like Jack Oakie and Jack Haley in the movie where one of them was shivering and put the stutter into the song about "K-K-K-Katie." She had been cast up on the shore of the Delaware and adopted by nice natives but in her heart knew she belonged to another race and spoke another language; the movies and radio had brought her news of her real people and now she was crossing the border to them.

"Seven fifty an hour is where our girls start; some get up to twenty-five. Minus our ten percent. Sounds like a fortune, but it's only working time. Conventions, a lot of the old bucks will ask you for a date. Handle it with dignity. Any girl takes bed money we hear of it, she's out. Runway shows, less of a problem. Right, Pat? You said you're cousins?"

Patrick nodded. "First. Non-kissing."

"You taking a cut?"

"Not a penny, to re-coin a phrase."

"Maybe she could use an agent—somebody to push her. You, Pat, you seem like a nice well-mannered guy, but I don't get much feeling of *push.* Hustle—there's no substitute. With a girl's looks, you don't have all day. Sorry, Essie, if I sound like a cynical shit."

"No, no. I know. Do you think I should leave high school and come to New York now?"

"No, Jesus. Get your diploma. You'll probably be needing it, to get an honest job. You're not even legal yet, are you?"

"Not until Valentine's Day." This was January, the Middle Atlantic region having been hit two days before by a great snowstorm. What had been a picture postcard in Basingstoke, where the hemlock boughs were bent low over the sidewalks and the chickadees hopped in the tracery of grapevines and Locust Street chimed from end to end with the scraping of snow shovels, was in New York an icy ashy slush the traffic churned with broken chains and angry claxons. Yet there was for Essie also something secretive and radiant about the storm's aftermath here, like light and cool morning air sneaking in across the windowsill. Spots of pure snow were still tucked in basement doorways and windowboxes and in fine straight lines on fire escapes. Dirty plowed snow was mountainously heaped along the curbs, burying the trash cans, and people had worn a narrow wobbling path like a forest trail, carrying their expensive parcels and wearing their expensive clothes. She loved it when it snowed in the movies—so richly, barrels of Lux flakes—and it was like that here. West Nineteenth Street seemed a brownstone village street, everybody's breath visible and lemon-yellow dog pee scribbled in the snow among the cigarette butts. She even liked the scratchy coldy feeling she had in her throat from rising so early this morning and getting snow in her galoshes and thinking, *Dear God, don't let me have such a bad cold I fall apart, let me be a grown-up who just rides a cold through,* as she rode the train north through the transformed New Jersey landscape, restored by the blizzard to a gently rolling land of villages with smoking chimneys.

"Almost there," Wexler said. "You have a nice birthday, young lady. Take care of that face. Don't go playing hardball with any wild pitchers."

But in fact he didn't wait; a couple of possibilities came in—demonstrating a floor-waxing machine at a housewares show at the Sixty-eighth Street Armory, and a Bloomingdale's ad showing a group of girls modelling the daring new Bikini-style bathing suit—for which Wexler thought Essie would be right, and by May she had become a veteran of riding the train, of getting off at Penn Station, of moving through the subway with its girder-rattling expresses and gum machines and newspaper stands and subterranean vaults, grimy expanses warmed by thousands of daily bodies. Her senior year—its basketball games where she and other cheerleaders ran out onto the floor to do the choo-choo, its weekly exams and quarterly report cards, its rasping of buzzers and slamming of metal locker doors, its herd aroma of girls' drugstore perfume and boys' Vitalis and sweat, its furtive cigarettes and furious hissed gossip of she-said and he-said and who-said, its juggling of boys and promises, its parked cars heated by a running engine and lit by a feeble dashboard glow, its class play in April (*A Change of Heart,* in which she played the mother, long-suffering Mrs. Dunlap), its May Court (she was not elected queen or even maid of honor but one of the five so-called ladies-in-waiting), its prom (she went with Jamie Ingraham, though they had broken up in April, and he kept saying how much he wanted to marry her if his parents would agree until in the back of the car she leaned back and lifted up all those scratchy petticoats and let him fuck her, which shut him up), its feeling of a sheltering world shredding and wearing thin, of her girlhood ending—all this seemed a lesser reality, like Rodney Street when she came out of the Roxie.

She moved to New York in June. Patrick had done some asking around and decided that the best place for her would be at the Barbizon Hotel for Women, at Sixty-third Street and Lexington. The rooms were pink and green and the bathrooms were at the far end of the halls. Big butch elevator operators kept the men and boys that thronged the lobby from getting into the upper floors, but there was no system for keeping the girls from spending the night out of their rooms. Essie in the next year and a half had a number of boyfriends—some her age, some older and married, and one rich besotted Iranian playboy attached to the United Nations—but it was the female friendships at the Barbizon that she thought of when she looked back on this transitional period. In Basingstoke she had missed having female friends, once Loretta Whaley and she had drifted apart in their junior year, Essie tugged one way by her lessons and ambitions and Loretta tugged another, down into virtual marriage to Eddie Bacheller, her steady since tenth grade. From the way the couple acted they had already joined their parents' generation, with its bowling alleys and Saturday-night blowouts and its way at parties of the men clustering on one side of the kitchen and the women on the other. Loretta talked of just the kind of house and car they would have, and how many children, and where they would go on vacations. She even turned dowdy, her hair all in split ends and her nails ragged, and tough, making a chewing motion with her jaw even when she didn't have gum in her mouth: a lazy coarseness of manner spread to her skin. Essie knew that, however tough she must make herself inside, the Wilmot fineness was her ticket out of Basingstoke—that, and a greenhouse freshness. Another reason that she hadn't had a lot of close high-school friends was the number of hours after school and on the weekends that she had spent in the greenhouse, moving through its sultry white light, inhaling its moist, oxygen-rich air, greeting and assisting customers, carrying trays of seedlings and sprouting cuttings from one table to another in the constant rotation the miniature climate demanded, from warmer to cooler areas, from northern to southern exposures. At the Barbizon she found another hothouse, of young women in bloom; humid confidences and gushed news about men and clothes, waitressing jobs, and *must* movies were shared from mouth to ear to mouth until it seemed the building had a single, female nervous system, vibrating each morning through the stacked floors to the same smell of coffee and the clanking of depleted shower pipes, flooding the halls with evening perfume as the girls swirled out on stiletto heels to their dates, *jeunes filles en fleur* menstruating on a single merged cycle and turning over in unison in the dead of the night as they rose through the gauze of their dreams and sank back again. It seemed to Essie that for this interval the terrible responsibility she carried, of being herself, was shared—diluted in giggles and laughter and childish pranks performed in pajamas and flimsy underwear.

She saw Patrick at least once a week and took his advice

except when it was about men. If he had had his way, she would never have gone out, except with guys he hankered for himself. At his suggestion she enrolled for acting and elocution lessons at a school—a dusty maze of bare-floored studios on Fifty-seventh Street—which had been rendered old-fashioned by the rise of the Method. Rather than focusing on inner emotional states, they still taught technique, which Patrick thought she needed. The voice instructor, an old Englishman who sipped martinis from a glass tube concealed in a silver-headed cane, winced when he heard her dragged-out, twangy Delaware vowels and had her wear a clothespin on her nose to force her voice deeper into her throat. To improve her posture, she was made to lie flat on the floor until the instructress, once a Thirties chorine, could see no air beneath her spine. There were lessons in fencing and stage duelling, in mime and in falling downstairs. When certain *grandes dames* of the stage came as guest lecturers, the girls were expected to wear hats and white gloves. The theory seemed to be that, if sufficient attention were paid to the outside, the inside would take care of itself. The shell of illusion needed behind it only a certain poise, a stillness, for the audience to feel engaged; it was better, in fact, not to reach out too boldly, but to allow the audience, like any object of seduction, the space in which to come forward and exercise its own volition. If God were too eager to please, who would worship Him?

Between lectures and lessons Essie rushed to photographers' studios. She was not gaunt enough for high-fashion assignments, but the manufacturers of floor waxers and insecticides, toothpastes and skin creams liked her solid hometown looks, her even teeth and guileless smile and dark strong Moorish eyebrows and elusive glow. Her long straight legs, those of a tomboy a few years ago, were used to illustrate the new seamless stockings, with their "nude" look. Posed with an electric fan, she appeared aristocratically cool; with an electric heater, invitingly warmed. She paid for her lessons and shelter and yet had enough left for increasingly generous presents, on birthdays and anniversaries, for her parents and Ama and Grandfather Sifford. Steuben-glass bowls, imported English gardening tools, new-fashioned electric kitchen appliances, a pair of antique hornshell curved combs for Ama's wonderful crown of hair. And she received presents—an emerald bracelet from the Iranian playboy, a silver cigarette case with a rueful inscription from one of her married friends. But she never, unlike some of her fellow aspirant actresses and part-time models, let herself be listed by any escort service, or accepted a cash present for her nights away from the Barbizon. Her lovers in this period, who in later and less reticent decades yielded up to interviewers a considerable number of candid details, agreed that Essie was striking in her energetic directness, her earthy innocence, her at times childlike gaiety, as well as in the unforgettable beauty of her naked body: the fullish breasts and slender thighs, the wrists and throat to whose pulse her fragile young life was bound, the thickly dark-fleeced *mons veneris* and the Artemislike virgin strength.

The big Hollywood movies at the end of the Forties were *Easter Parade* and *The Treasure of the Sierra Madre*, *Rope* and *Johnny Belinda*, *Red River* and *On the Town*, *Adam's Rib* and *Samson and Delilah.* Attendance was down from the peak of 1946, but only industry insiders noticed, or grasped the significance of the anti-monopolistic legal rulings which would separate the great studios from their theatre chains. In New York Essie discovered foreign films—from England, *The Red Shoes* and Olivier's *Hamlet* and *Kind Hearts and Coronets,* with Alec Guinness hilariously playing eight murdered characters. From France, *La Chartreuse de Parme* with subtitles and Gérard Philipe, and *Les Enfants Terribles* and *Le Silence de la Mer;* Essie had never seen on the screen such disillusion, such despair, such blunt black Godlessness, not even in *The Ox-Bow Incident.* The films back at the Roxie had wounded only to heal, to dismiss their consumers back into reality as even better Americans and firmer Christians. Essie was shaken and stretched above all by the Italians and *neorealismo*—the movie about the drunken soldier who picks up a whore and keeps talking to her about the pure and simple girl he once knew without realizing it was she, this very whore; and the one about the man whose bicycle is stolen and who looks for it all over Rome with a little boy: the poverty, the squalor, the vitality, the honesty so fierce that *The Miracle* and *Bitter Rice* had to be seen in a little showing room below Fourteenth Street beyond the notice or the reach of the Legion of Decency. Patrick took her to those, and to the chaste little pair of theatres in the Museum of Modern Art, where she entered for the first time the twitchy, stark, absurd, majestic world of the silents—it was like entering the silence before she had been born, when Ama had no gray hair and her grandfather Wilmot walked the earth. He had read too many books and escaped into the movies: these were two facts about him that reverberated in the family, calling out to her. Also, the museum showed the Russians—the glowering robed giants of Eisenstein, stalking one another through castle corridors like chambers of a vast crazed mind. For the first time, in a scene of charging Teutonic Knights, faceless in their tin-can helmets, she saw the Christian cross, flapping on their banners, used as a symbol of evil. These many films new to her unsealed an abyss that Essie had not looked into since she was seven and, sitting between her parents, had watched *Lost Horizon;* in that pretty young face suddenly crumbling with age had loomed an abysmal cruelty of horizonless time and space from which Hollywood and her house on Locust Street and her customarily answered prayers had sheltered her. But to remain loyal to her prayers it was necessary to face this harsh illumination and grow, though it hurt, and often the date on whose arm she walked out through the lobby did not, from his crass comments, seem to have absorbed anything, to have any idea of what a troubling revelation he had witnessed.

Patrick always knew what to say about the movie, where it went hollow and where it rang true, what bit of business suddenly fell into the rhythm of real life and made you laugh.

That was a thing about homosexuals: they were sensitive. And yet they were frustrating, not just sexually; some inner deflection kept him on the sidelines of life, studying paintings but not wanting to paint himself and even sneering at those that did try, falling in love with boys at NYU who were straight, and disdaining as "queers" and "fags" those who were like himself. He had discovered at boarding school that he could neither change nor enjoy his nature; when Essie, for whom sex had never been a problem—an entertaining smooth chute into the dark-red bliss of things—offered to prove to him that he could love girls, he said, "There you go, dropping that damn towel again."

"Didn't you feel anything when I did that? A little tiny throb? Even of c-c-curiosity, what it would be like?" She knew how to coax a man, from seeing so many movies, but none that she could remember had ever touched on this peculiar problem, of what she pictured as short-circuited wiring.

"I felt protective," he said, "and still do. You're my dear little cousin, for Chrissake." She made him feel masculine, perhaps, as he guided her education and at an uncontaminated distance oversaw her career; he made her feel effective, and reckless, and whole. He had several times mentioned a desire to get her out of the "rag trade"—increasingly the modelling agency had sent her out on assignments of modelling shortie nighties and provocative negligees and push-up bras. The ads appeared in the back pages of men's magazines like *Esquire* where it was not likely Ama or Momma or Daddy would ever see them, but in fact bratty Danny had discovered one and showed it to everybody in Basingstoke. Patrick scolded her: "Wexler is using your very charming innate exhibitionism and turning you into his house tart. Next thing you'll be posing naked for calendars."

Essie shrugged; shame was not part of her religion. "What's to hide? I mean, it's me."

"You do sell yourself short, darling, sometimes. It's one of the disadvantages of coming from the sticks; you don't know your price in real dollars. Now, try to think, what do you *really* want?"

"A house and a husband and ch-children?"

"Piffle. Oh, my, such piffle. You want a house and children and a collie dog about as much as I do. What you want is to be in the movies. Right? You want to *act*. You need a theatrical agent. I've been asking around, and I think I've found a fellow for you. He works for an outfit called the Music Corporation of America, but don't you worry, they've gone beyond music. I did a dance on the telephone and we've got an appointment for you at Radio City."

"Oh Patrick," she said, squeezing his arm through the thick black sleeve of his chesterfield. "I wish I c-could do *some*thing for *you*."

The agency was on the sixteenth floor, beyond and above the skating rink, the golden sideways-floating deity, the enormous Christmas tree and its great red balls, the revolving doors, the green-marbled lobby floor marked out with squares of concentric strips of brass, the brown murals of nudes with knotty bottoms laboring and men in Mexican hats being set free and giant obscure machines and cogwheels rolling forward in some kind of revolution, the banks of whispering elevators with pleated brassy doors and Negro operators in white gloves and braided uniforms. Essie was nervous, because as they whiningly ascended she could feel tall suave Patrick's tension beside her, but as soon as they were ushered into the agent's office she relaxed; the agent was like Uncle Peter, except shorter and Jewish. He gave her that same sense of jumpiness, of being up on the balls of his feet, and of wanting to touch her. His name was Arnold Fineman. What he had of hair was frizzy and reddish. Essie felt certain she would eventually sleep with him and went very quiet and proper, sitting in a chair with her knees pressed together and her gloved hands clasped on her black alligator pocketbook. She was so reticent that Patrick took over at first, describing her modelling and her acting and elocution lessons, and how she had been in summer stock last summer, in Bucks County.

"Yeah? Whadjou play?"

Essie spoke up: "I was the maid in that play by Thornton Wilder, *The Skin of Our Teeth.* Sabina."

"Howja do?"

"She was wonderful," Patrick loyally said. "And then she was Florence McCricket, in *The Torchbearers.*"

"The audience seemed to like me," Essie admitted. "You work so hard and feel every night you're getting better, but then in a week it's over. The director said I needed to strengthen my voice."

"In those hay barns, sure," said Arnold Fineman. "They'd muffle Ethel Merman. When else you been on the stage?"

"H-high-school plays," Essie faltered. "I was always the mother. And I was s-s-second runner-up in the Miss Delaware Peach contest in 1947, when I was seventeen."

Her stammering perked him up, roused his protective instinct a little. "How old're you now?"

"Nineteen. Twenty this coming February."

"Not getting any younger, huh?" He reached across his cluttered desk to a pack of filtered Viceroys and with a tricky snap of his wrist made a couple of the cigarettes jump out an inch, offering them across the desk before lighting his own. As he squinted through the smoke he looked like Aunt Esther, and too serious about his work to be sexy like Uncle Peter. She doubted now that she would be sleeping with him. He asked, "So you think you want to be in pictures?"

"I guess so." She amended that to, "More than anything."

He sighed. "Would you do anything to get there?"

She supposed she should say yes, but hesitated, trying to imagine what anything might be, and he rescued her with, "Move around for me. Walk around the room like you've come into a bar in Shanghai. Whoops, the Commies have Shanghai now. Make that Singapore."

Essie had put on a soft gray wool coat dress, ankle-length,

rather *chinoise,* with a high collar and black buttons and a strip of black braid down the front, and a gray felt pillbox on the back of her head. She sauntered around in the tight imaginary skin of a shady woman, Dietrich or Ida Lupino, parting the curtain of beads with a hand and knee and cruising the bar, heavy-lidded, through the pall of Oriental smoke. Peter Lorre was there, and Sydney Greenstreet, and maybe, at the bar, in a white dinner jacket, smoking a cigarette and nursing an old grief . . .

"O.K., O.*K,*" Arnie Fineman said, in this high office where the Venetian blinds turned the sun into stripes and there were signed pictures of stars on the walls just as in her bedroom. "Now pucker."

"P-pucker?"

"Make a mouth at me. What the frogs call a *moue.* Pout. Think kiss, Esther. Think melting point. You're creaming in your pants."

She put her hands on her thighs and bent her body into an S to bring her face down to Arnold Fineman's level, blushing and feeling humiliated that Patrick had to watch this. She feared that such a display would put him further off heterosexuality. But then with a little push of inspiration from behind she got into it, shuddering her eyelids at half-mast and thinking directly into Fineman's face, *You little kike shit, some day you'll pay for this.*

Fineman gingerly smiled. She saw he had a motherly, worried side. He was not only short but so stooped in the shoulders he looked hunchbacked. "O.K., Esther—good try. Great try. You could use more upper lip. Maybe you can do it with lipstick. And the hair—we gotta take it in some direction or other. Your boyfriend here says you sing. Give me a song."

"With no piano?"

"I'll hum along. Only don't make it 'Rudolph, the Red-Nosed Reindeer.' Jesus." The song saturated the air this plangent December; it was hard to chase the tune from her mind.

"Mule Train" and "Ghost Riders in the Sky"—one of the girls at the Barbizon could do a very funny Frankie Laine, with a hair-dryer as a microphone. " 'Some enchanted evening,' " Fineman began in a surprisingly rich baritone, " 'you vill see a straaanger. . . .' "

" 'You will see a stranger," she chimed in thrillingly, amazed that he hit upon an operatic song. They carried on the duet until they ran out of words, and straggled off into laughter. "O.K., O.K.," he said. "Deanna Durbin you ain't quite, but I'm sold. As far as I'm concerned we're in business. Fifteen percent off the top from you, from me lots of hustle and a screen test as soon as we can rig it. The studios are panicked right now—box office is down, bad press is up—but when haven't they been? From where I'm sitting, you're special, Esther. Satin skin on an iron frame, not-bad boobs, and eyes like they haven't seen since Pola Negri. The nose—yeah, well, they can smooth it out with make-up and lights. Only one other thing I don't like. The name. Who the hell'd ever shell out fifty cents to see Esther Wilmot? She sounds like a Sunday-school teacher. Let's think about this. Sit."

As she sat there, her satin cheeks burning with the abrasion of his rough praise, so that she felt a pressure in her face as if dangling upside down on the playground jungle gym, Fineman stared and absurdly opened his mouth like a baby bird, making the halting sound "Ah . . . ah . . ."

"Anna?" Patrick suggested.

"We call my grandmother Ama," she said.

Fineman's lips closed and he announced, "How about Alma? You look like an Alma to me. Sweet but sexy. Kind of mysterious-European, yet salt of the American earth. Alma. It's yours. It's all yours. Can you think of any other Alma who's a star?"

"A star?" she asked.

"What else?" asked Arnie. "Is it bit parts you want?"

"Does it sound a little . . . Negro?" Patrick asked.

"Let it; hell. One look, they see she's not. Alma Wilmot. No, terrible. Wilmot, will not. Wilmot will not do. No, no, Nanette. Any ideas, you two?"

"It would be nice," said Esther, "to keep something of my real name. I don't want to . . . my family . . ." Those little white faces, watching her rocket go up, getting smaller and smaller, the state of Delaware just a sliver, its round head buried in Pennsylvania's underside like a leech. She thought of the du Ponts, so grand, so distant from little Basingstoke. "De . . . de . . ." she said.

"De Mille, de Havilland," Patrick prompted, trying to be helpful.

"DeMott," she announced.

"Spell it," said Arnie, not convinced.

"Capital 'D,' no space, capital 'M.' Alma DeMott."

He was writing it out. "Mutt, demote, I don't know, kid."

"It's right," Alma insisted. "Surely I have some say in my own name."

"Let's sit on it. We'll discuss it at dinner tonight. Twenty-One, on Fifty-second, sound O.K. to you?" Arnie remembered Patrick's presence, and, standing hunched and looking toward him with a grimace of politeness, said, "Unless . . . ?"

"Oh, no, that would be lovely," Alma intervened. "He's not . . . He's my cousin." She had stopped herself from saying, *Not one of us.*

But he was, he was one of the family she was deserting, even in name.

As it happened, Alma would play opposite, within the next few years, both Gary Cooper and (in new wide-screen CinemaScope) Clark Gable. She was virtually unknown and cheap, and in those early years of the Fifties, as the great studios were slowly disintegrating, proven stars had begun to demand such large fees that corners had to be cut on the budget elsewhere. Both Coop and Gable had turned fifty in 1951, and it was not then as clear as it later became that male film stars from the classic Thirties era had no end to their careers but death. These screen gods had human worries. Cooper had a bad back, which the action scenes aggravated cruelly; he had an ulcer and arthritis. His Catholic wife was refusing to give him a divorce, and he was not finding much ease in his overpublicized affair with Patricia Neal. He seemed bone-tired. There was in his gentle, courteous treatment of Alma on the set the weary proficiency of an angelically handsome man who had handled in his days more pretty young women than he could count or remember. Accustomed to making an impression, she was offended, down deep, and became almost contemptuous. There was a quiet about Cooper, and a taciturn passivity in the hands of the director, that approached stupidity. Alma, even as a novice, established herself as a resister on the set, an actress with her own ideas and her own image to foster. As ardent on the seventh take as on the first, she felt in Cooper's arms the full edge of her much greater youth and energy and desire. Yet, seeing the first rough cut of the film (they would never let an ingenue see the rushes) and then the final product at the premiere, she was astonished at how Cooper dominated the screen—at how his leathery face, with its baleful Nordic eyes and slightly frozen mouth, so inert-seeming in the cluttered glare of the sound stage, possessed a steady inner life beside which her own apparition was flickering, nervous, discontinuous. She heard traces of her Delaware vowels and saw a shining fright in her eyes. The director's and film editor's ability to shape her performance, to whittle it after the event, by their editing of the footage, amazed and maddened her, until Coop told her, one long lunch break as he drove her out to Malibu in his famous silver Jaguar, "Don't fight it, Willie." He had found out her real name and teased her with it. "Trust the machine. Else you'll get an ulcer bad as mine. Hundreds of folks have a job that feeds into a motion picture. You've seen it—eighty men to do the sets and lighting alone. Your job is, know your lines and show up fit two hours ahead of camera call." He reached over, while the wind rushed past and the sun beat sparkling dents in the Pacific below, and cupped his hand around her skull in its fluttering bandana and gently shook it back and forth like a container. "That's all you're responsible for, what's inside you and what comes out. Let Production do the rest. Tell yourself they know what they're doing, even when it seems they don't." *They*—the inscrutable and myriad powers, the production chiefs and assistants and directors and script girls and electricians and cameramen and focus pullers and costumers and make-up artists, who processed their faces and sighs onto thousands of screens. In afterthought he said, "For a job, it don't pay half bad. Beats being a ranch hand, I can tell you that. Must beat something back in Delaware." And with the merest self-mocking twitch of those immobile lips he actually added, "Yup."

Gable was more engageable—a woman's man who had climbed up from Ohio's oil fields on a ladder of female sponsors, beginning with his stepmother. He flirted with Alma, turning on that slowly spreading smile like a ruthless squeeze of superior strength. A few times, in the thirsty, dusty weeks of the Nevada location shoot, he slept with her, like a sleepy lion obliging a female cub. But the times didn't add up to anything more; there was in Gable a loneliness too big for Alma to begin to fill. Where Cooper was a sublime accident, who had cartooned and ranched and bummed about before backing into acting as a crowd extra, Gable had never been anything but an aspiring actor. He thought in billboard terms. He had loved Lombard; in a Hollywood that had matched him with its every giantess from Jean Harlow to Ava Gardner, Lombard, all soft gay golden toughness, a foul-mouthed publicity hound and frenetic practical joker, had been his heart's match, and she had smashed herself against a mountain while trying to sell war bonds. He had been so long a star he had forgotten how to find mortal satisfactions; in his loneliness he finally found a wife on a sufficient scale of glamour, the widow of Douglas Fairbanks, Sr., with the heavenly name of Lady

Sylvia Ashley, and knew three weeks after the wedding that he had made a critical casting mistake. He was suffering the financial pains of their divorce wrangle while he and Alma co-starred. Ever since the war, his hands had a palsied tremor which had to be hidden from the cameras. Gable was unduly dependent, Alma felt, on the approval of lesser men—the technical riffraff of grips and stuntmen that accompanies a film crew into the desert—and on whiskey; in the morning, his breath, locked into his mouth by his false teeth, stank with the fumes of last night's bonding jaunt to the bars of Elko. But his breath didn't show on film; what showed was—blown up by CinemaScope to the size of Egypt's Sphinx—the peerless straight brow, the shapely fierce eyebrows, the sense of a benign force that had wedged those cheeks and lips and chin together into such a pure harmony, male beauty without a touch of the other, feminine kind. Alma liked to play with his ears, which protruded even more than her own. He called her Al, she called him Pops. Both Coop and Clark were two years older than her father, and helped her understand him, as a man of a generation tempered in hard times. Beasts of burden all but a few of them, they were unable to explain themselves and unapologetic about the lack; sons of an America where the Bible still ruled, they were justified in all their limitations by the Protestant blessing bestowed upon hardship and hardness. With Gable and Cooper, this bleakness was sexy, though her father had never struck her as so. He was the least sexy man she had ever known.

At the "21" Club, once a speakeasy and still a low crowded place, with model airplanes and other wartime souvenirs cluttering the ceiling, her future was coming close but not yet arrived. One of Arnie Fineman's first questions had been, "How do you feel about television?"

"I hate it," she said hastily, a silver gimlet having already slipped down her throat. She didn't know how to drink but had the idea, from overhearing Aunt Esther and Uncle Peter talk, that gin drinks didn't put on weight like whiskey did.

"Why is that?"

She realized she just loved the movies and hated anything that was hurting them the way television was. "It seems cheap and ugly," she said. "It's l-like r-reality, only it's in a box and has commercials."

Arnie put his plump hand, broad and uncallused like her father's but manicured, over hers. Reddish hair sprouted glinting between his knuckles. He wore a glossy black stone in a chunky ring on one finger and a broad band on another, a wedding band, she realized. He said, "Hate it, love it, it's here to stay, and it eats up bodies, babe. It's a quick way to get a girl exposure. Has Wexler had you do any commercial spots?" When she said no, he said, "I'll talk to him. Millions see these damn things. Also, there's a lot of drama on, night and day. Not bad experience, and you're in and out in a week or two. You rehearse, you do it, you walk away. Like Hollywood in the old days. Hollywood's slowing down. Even with the contacts, it takes a month of begging to get a screen test. Let's not just sit around on our pretty little asses, huh?"

She felt the second gimlet twisting agreeably within her. The level of raucous male conversation in the restaurant seemed to rise and uplift her drifting body. The little gimcrack airplanes on the ceiling banked and as if under a high sun she basked in the realization that her new agent would take more masterful care of her than Wexler ever had, or faintly pathetic Patrick, and that to all of the questions Arnie would pose this evening she would answer yes.

He had a little in-town apartment on West Sixty-sixth Street, where he stayed some nights while his wife and two teen-age sons held the fort out in Scarsdale. She was fascinated overhearing his phone call home explaining the sudden business that would keep him in town; it was like being behind the set during a play, and wondering how anybody out in the audience could believe it, it was so obviously fake.

She made television commercials demonstrating the new Electrolux, making easy strokes back and forth and showing how the alternate brushes and nozzles were compactly stored within the wheeled cylinder. Dial soap and Nestlés Quik were among the new products she dramatized for a minute or two, in live commercials. For the former, she daringly undertook a shower, produced from a perforated bucket under the hot lights, clad below in the bottom of a bathing suit and above in an abundance of lather, turning her breasts away from the camera, its tiny red eye burning as it licked her up. Those early television studios were makeshift and drab—addresses in the vicinity of the Chrysler Building or Union Square, up six flights in a freight elevator and down a linoleum-floored corridor with custard-yellow walls. Everybody seemed, like her, to be not long out of high school. Not all her assignments were in Manhattan. For a small station in Bridgeport she performed with Pillsbury cake mixes, while an off-camera announcer explained the miracle of their ease—"no more wasted kitchen hours slaving with flour and sugar, butter and eggs! Throw away that tired old eggbeater!!"—and at another, in Newark, she was the middle of a trio of models illustrating the range of Miss Clairol tints. For some weeks she was candidate for Miss Rheingold, and her face, in a fussy good-girl perm that just covered her ears, hovered like a blimp above Times Square. Minute Rice, Corningware—Arnie was afraid of her being typecast. "No more food, for Chrissakes," he decreed. "Your image will get to be a drudge. It'll get fat."

"It's my grandmother in me," Alma explained. "Oh, how I used to love being in the kitchen with her! When she'd let me stir and taste the icing, I felt so re*spons*ible!"

Arnie found her roles in the television dramas that were proliferating night and day. *Lux Video Theatre, Goodyear TV Playhouse, Robert Montgomery Presents*—she was called a few days before the show aired, to be a hat-check girl, a troubled young nun, a "daffy" roommate, a distraught wife, the cool and calculating "other" woman. Rehearsals were hectic and few; and were sometimes confined to the morning before the play went on. She learned to memorize dialogue swiftly, and to rememorize it when the director changed it all around ten minutes before air time. People held up cards spelling out your dialogue in large letters behind the cameras, but it was a mistake to focus on the prompt card and ignore the face of the actor supposedly engaging your passion. One of the few times she stuttered on air was when a man held her cue card upside down. Alma almost never stuttered, except when she remembered she was Essie. There was an urgent forward flow of television action and passion that didn't allow for self-doubt. Drinks spilled, lines were garbled, phones failed to ring on cue, paintings fell off the wall when a door was slammed; it didn't greatly matter. The drama was being flung into living rooms where drinks were being spilled, people were getting up to go to the bathroom, children were noisily fighting, dogs were at the door begging to be let out. Television was people; an insidious mutually forgiving dishevelment permeated the studio, with its flimsy pseudo-rooms and its tangle of snaking cables just off camera. It was a far cry from the luxurious polish and perfection of Hollywood films as Essie had viewed them back at the Roxie.

Arnie at last did secure her a screen test with Columbia. He had an in with a man who had an in with Harry Cohn. "Even so, kid, these things take time. The bigger they are, the less they like being rushed. And Cohn, let me warn you, in an industry loaded with crude and ruthless pricks, is absolute tops. Every year he would get the Oscar for biggest bastard."

Alma had never flown in an airplane before, and not only was she terrified but she didn't understand how to let the tray down when the stewardess came clinking along the aisle. Arnie had come with her, and his friendly red-haired paw reached across to undo the latch, and he murmured to her explanations of why the plane's propellors kept changing pitch and why the whole thing, a long can with them in it, kept tilting and dropping. Her stomach cried out that God had left her, He didn't exist, she was going to fall to the earth below as from a hideously tall tree and never be any more than the nameless girl in the Pillsbury ad. She should never have aspired to this height. Her bra felt soaked; she was lactating acrophobic sweat. Arnie gruffly murmured, "It's like waves in the ocean, babe. You can't see them, but they're there. Air is like water, always moving. But this aluminum boat we're in—hey, these DC-9s are *solid.*" He rapped on the curved wall beside his little chilly oval window and it gave off a dull, padded sound.

But Los Angeles itself—the palm trees, the pink low houses, the Spanishness, the endlessness, the air like the air of a late-spring day in Basingstoke only purged of the chill that would gust in off the Delaware—enchanted her. The city as its sections flowed one into another was as full of people and stores and cars as any city in the East but strained clean of the grit back there, the history and industry. There was nothing old except the Spanish names and the La Brea Tar Pits, which did exist, on Wilshire Boulevard just as they said on the Jack Benny program, where mentioning them had always gotten a laugh; all the names and places on Jack Benny were here, including the towns called out by the railroad announcer's voice: Anaheim, Azusa, and Kukamunga. And the Brown Derby and the big letters posed raggedly on the hillside to say HOLLYWOOD. Hollywood was almost a little town like Basingstoke. She was not prepared, though, for the width of the streets and sidewalks and the winding palm-lined streets of Beverly Hills, where there was no live person in sight but Japanese and Mexican gardeners wheeling dead palm fronds out from behind hedges of oleander and fuchsia. The big half-hidden tile-roofed houses looked owned but not lived-in, like movie sets. The wealth here was gentle wealth, humorous wealth even; these fortunes derived from art and illusion and personal beauty and not, as back home, from cruel old riverside mills manufacturing some ugly and stupid necessity like Trojans or bottle caps.

Arnie explained to her why she would be a lucky girl to sign up with Columbia. "Listen," he said, "this is 1951, not 1937. Fox, Metro, Paramount, Warner—they're all fucked up still from being forced to cough up their theatre chains. Columbia never had any theatres; until the war it was purely B movies and Frank Capra. More important, it's the only major studio with a practical attitude toward television. If you can't beat 'em, join 'em: Cohn may be an ape but he's not the dumb ape people take him for. He's created a subsidiary to make TV movies—Columbia Screen Gems. They finance production with sales of their old movies to television. Clever? Clever. The dinosaurs are giving way to the mammals, sweetheart, and Columbia's the only studio growing fur."

For her black-and-white screen test Alma did Sabina's two concluding speeches from *The Skin of Our Teeth* (beginning "Mr. Antrobus, don't mind what I say. I'm just an ordinary girl . . ." and "Oh, oh, oh. Six o'clock and the master not home yet") and then sang "Can't Help Lovin' Dat Man of Mine." For her color test, without sound, she chatted with the cameraman as he came in close, manipulating his focus. He showed her how movie cameras work, the two wheels for up and down and sideways, and how when you get to be really good you can write your name with a pen attached to the lens. He asked her out to dinner but she and Arnie had to fly back to New York. After two weeks he brought word that Columbia had pretty much liked what they had seen but the guy who had an in with Cohn reported that Harry had been troubled by her lips—her upper lip, specifically. It was too thin. There was an easy operation, Arnie told her. They inject collagen.

But it didn't feel easy; she woke in her hospital room with its expensive gray view of the East River and Roosevelt Island feeling she had been punched in the face, hard, by a telescoping succession of men. While they were at it they had taken two little tucks in her nostril-wings as well, paring them down, and straightened the little bump at the bridge of her nose, just like Momma's. Wounds heal fast, however, when you're only twenty-one; on her next flying trip west, all the men's heads turned when she coolly walked down the airplane aisle to the little blue lavatory, with its whispering toilet. When he saw her, the head of new talent, on orders from above, proposed a seven-year optional contract, beginning at two hundred fifty a week for the first six months and going up to thirty-five hundred a week for the seventh year. She said it sounded nice but she could not sign without her agent's approval. Arnie had been overworked and under the weather—he kept talking about giving up smoking and had been impotent with her a few times in his place on West Sixty-sixth Street. Alma had flown out alone. The talent head, a man called Max, was impressed by her resistance and after several phone calls told her that Mr. Cohn would like to see her.

Compared to the great acreages that Paramount and M-G-M occupied, the Columbia lot was a modest fourteen-acre hodgepodge bought bit by bit on old Poverty Row, on Sunset Boulevard, between Gower Street and Beachwood Drive down to Fountain Avenue. But Harry Cohn's own office was huge, and where people pushed the outer door open the paint had been eaten off by the sweaty palms. The room smelled of cigars the way Addison's Drug Store used to, and this soothed Alma's nervousness. Cohn, the last of the monster moguls, had turned sixty, and Columbia was riding high for the moment. He was more businesslike and polite than she had expected. He wore a pale-gray suit, his white necktie with its silver scribble no doubt a Countess Mara; a red-bordered handkerchief was artfully fluffed out of his breast pocket. His nearly bald brow was fabulously broad, like that of a bison or rhino, whose lowered head is its fiercest weapon. He stayed standing behind his desk until she took the dove-gray chair an underling held for her. The pugnacious set of his face reminded her of Mr. Horley at the post office—he had been crusty and mean on the outside but had always liked Essie, she could tell, ever since the time he put her in a mail sack and pulled shut the drawstring and told her he was sending her to Cincinnati.

"A lot of young ladies would jump at that contract," Cohn told her, unsmiling.

"I *am* jumping, Mr. Cohn," she said. "But what's that expression—look before you leap? Your friend Arnie Fineman has been wonderful to me; I depend on him."

"My friend who?" he asked, and added, "In this business yesterday's friend is today's pain in the ass." His eyes kept flicking, to her new, plumper lip—or was it that she was still self-conscious about it? It felt stiff when she smiled. Harry Cohn tried to smile back. He had a wide wry mouth that related uneasily to the dark flat stare of his beetle-browed eyes. He had had his way so often, he had pushed so many people around, that his expression had become as blank as the end of a battering ram. "Saw your test," he said. "You can't act for shit yet, but you've got a glimmer of what Rita had—has." He had still not given up on the disintegrating star who had carried his studio through the Forties. But he was looking for another. He reminded her, as he talked, less of Jeb Horley than of the high-school principal, Mr. Pritchard, with his carefully groomed dwindling gray hair and froglike mouth and crafty way, behind his bossy front, of trying to pick up the secrets the young always have. Mr. Pritchard would turn severe when a boy or girl did something really bad, but then talked about it afterwards with a kind of twinkle. "Flesh is funny stuff," Harry Cohn announced. "A lot of it, even on a girl you think is a great looker, photographs as pasty dead meat. What you want is flesh with candlepower. Harlow had it. Clara Bow had it. Am I losing you?"

"No. This is interesting, Mr. Cohn. I loved the movies since I was a little girl."

"I bet you did. You and everybody else. L.A. is drowning in twat, and don't forget it. Lift your head. Yeah. Good job. Now you got a mouth that goes with your body. And a refined nose. I don't see you as any Hepburn, I'll tell you right out. You got an ass; Hepburn never did. One bony broad—who needs more? You've got a dirty side, can you go along with that? You're no God-damn Alice Adams. You got those old-fashioned vamp's eyes. Your hair—has Arnie or Artie or whoever talked to you about it? It's that Christ-awful wishy-washy brown."

"It's my natural color."

"Not for me it's not natural. I see you as an inky brunette, to go with those vamp's eyes. But let's not get ahead of ourselves. We got no contract. Did I tell you, a lot of girls would kill for this contract?"

"I'll sign the contract, I'm sure. Once Arnie passes on it. But I was wondering, now that fewer films are being made—suppose another studio ever wanted to use me in a picture?"

He relit the big dead cigar in his hand and squinted at her through the smoke. "Then we'd make a deal with our opposites," he said. "That's called a loan-out. But you haven't been in any picture yet. You haven't posed for a single publicity still yet. You haven't begun, Miss DeMott, to pay your dues."

"I know that, Mr. Cohn. I'm very anxious to get started."

"I mean, O.K., you've done some acting on TV. But what's TV? It's for kids and paraplegics, that can't get out of the house to go to the movies." Alma loved having herself described and discussed, even when the approach was harsh; but she could see the man's eyes sinking in, weary of her as a subject. "You know what I was doing in 1912?" he asked.

"No, Mr. Cohn."

"Playing vaudeville with Harry Ruby. Harry Rubenstein. I sang, Harry played ragtime. Before that, I hustled pool and sold hot furs. I was even a trolley-car conductor, till they fired me for raking too much off the fares. They expected a little rake-off, but nothing that ambitious. The joke in my family was they thanked me for bringing back the trolley at night. I'd dropped out of school after my Bar Mitzvah. I had a beautiful voice—tenor. Can you believe that?"

"Yes, I can, Mr. Cohn."

"First job I had was a singing part in a play, *The Fatal Wedding*, as a choir boy. Anyway. There I was, hustling, and the movie bug bit me. It bit my brother Jack first. He worked for Carl Laemmle—ever hear of him?"

"No, I don't think so. I'm sorry."

"A great old Hun. I was a song plugger, and I got the idea of plugging songs with movie shorts. *I'm on My Way to Dublin Bay* was the first—don't laugh. Theatre owners liked them. Jack and me got Laemmle interested, and one thing led to another. Carl hired me to be secretary, over at Universal City. That's what brought me out here. I never looked back. The movie bug had bit me, but good. I paid my dues, is the point. We all got dues to pay. Want to sing for me?"

"Sing?"

"Yeah. You know, sing. Belt it out. That phony darky crooning on the test, that wasn't you."

Alma stood up and swallowed, trying to breathe from the diaphragm, and gave him the first sixteen bars of "Oh, del mio dolce amor." Harry Cohn liked it better, she could tell, than the audience in Dover, though he tersely nodded and puffed on his relit cigar, blowing smoke, perhaps accidentally, all over her. "Alma, I got a yacht," he told her. "You like to come for a cruise sometime?"

"I'd love that," Alma said. "I've never been on a yacht before. Not on any kind of a boat in the Pacific. Would Mrs. Cohn be on board?"

He lowered his head and was like a rhino going to charge. But he then, by some shift in his unfathomable rhino brain, laughed, one dry beat. "Joan," he told her. "You'd love Joan. She'd like you. She's always saying she knows there are nice people in Hollywood but she never meets them. My first wife, Rose, was a Christian Scientist. You a Christian Scientist?"

"Oh no," Alma said, for the first time shocked. Christian Scientists were thought to be quite crazy in Basingstoke—people who refused to call Dr. Jessup even when their leg was broken or they were dying of pneumonia. "I'm a Presbyterian."

"I bet you are. Well, whatever helps you through the night," he said, and sighed in dismissal.

Columbia placed her, once under contract, in small non-speaking parts—as a gangster's black-haired nightclub date in Hayworth's soggy *Affair in Trinidad,* as one of the dance-hall "hostesses" in *From Here to Eternity,* as a motorcycle moll in *The Wild One.* But it was her two minutes jitterbugging on-screen with a groggy-looking, overweight, over-the-hill Jack Carson (caught on the dance floor while escaping two thuggish hitmen) in a quickie comedy called *Sweet and Low* that made an impression on audiences. That was followed by her first speaking roles, the haughty salesgirl in the José Ferrer vehicle *False Dawn,* and Ernest Borgnine's treacherous, touching Mexican mistress in her first period film, *The Gadsden Purchase.* This led to her first starring role, opposite Cooper in the less successful *High Noon*–follow-up, *Red Rock Afternoon.* As the only woman in the cast—a schoolteacher trying to bring the rudiments of education to Indian children—she was courted and wooed by the film crew to the point that the director complained about circles under her eyes in the morning, and she had a to-do with the fat bitch in charge of make-up. On location there was an away-from-home vacation feeling that could get in the way of the work. Being a star, Alma discovered, was drudgery, tied to the union hours of all the technicians and the teamsters. She had to rise for her seven o'clock make-up call at six, and leave her apartment in West Hollywood just as some of the hookers who lived in the building were returning from Sunset Boulevard. And there were diction lessons, and dance lessons, and posing for publicity stills, and interviews set up with *Modern Screen* and *Screenland,* and gruelling hours spent standing in Wardrobe while they poked and prodded for the perfect fit, and more hours under the ungentle hands of the hairdressers—many workdays didn't end until eight and nine at night. In those days, the film crews still worked Saturdays. She would fall asleep over the script of

Monday's lines, and spend Sunday doing a publicity appearance before a crowd of soldiers about to be shipped off to Korea.

After the Nevada movie with Gable, she insisted to Columbia on no more Westerns. She was sick of hiding her legs in calico skirts. She had grown up on glamour and knew she could project it. Cohn issued his usual blast of threats and profanity, but in 1953 they arranged a loan-out to Paramount for a musical, with a typically long title of the era, *The Last Time We Saw Topeka.* It was filmed in Paramount's brilliant answer to Fox's CinemaScope—VistaVision, whose film fed horizontally and could be projected at variable widths, depending on the theatre's screen capabilities. It seemed to Alma she and the rest of the cast (Dan Dailey, Vera-Ellen, Oscar Levant, Kathryn Grant, Georges Guetary) were always lining up for wide shots, with those on the ends worrying that they would be cut out of projection on the standard screens that still occupied most of the movie theatres. But no one who ever saw the film (the box office was disappointing) would ever forget Alma's crooning of "Melancholy Baby" while stretched out at full length on heliotrope sheets in a dress of scarlet satin slit, it seemed, all the way up her immense white thigh, like a white Caddy fender without the fin. Her strongest impression, however, was made not as a glamour queen but as a fiery waif, a woman wronged and wronging, flawed by more desire and impatience and restlessness than society could accommodate, in those gritty *noir* melodramas whereby smoldering Fifties discontent sought expression—*The Delinquents, Safe at Your Peril, Howl from the Streets, Trouble in Memphis,* and, most daringly, *Colored Entrance.* In this last, she became the first actress to bestow a screen kiss upon a black man, though on his forehead; in *Safe at Your Peril* she risked a brief but breakthrough nude scene, from the back and in an indistinct middle distance, a misty-woods skinny-dip viewed by an escaped lunatic (Richard Widmark) with a bowie knife. In all these roles her hair was left dark, though sometimes short and curly in a poodle-cut, and sometimes with bangs and to the shoulders, with a page-boy roll and a moody Stanwyckish swing and toss.

She had been there, the audiences felt—in the musty back seats of Plymouths, at the lunch-hour sock hops, in the alleyway behind the drug store and the ice-cream parlor, at the edge of town with its stupefying view of rural emptiness. Alma had paid her dues, out in the desolate America of earning and spending and eating and breeding and listening for the music, in a way the princesses Grace and Audrey had not. Kim and Marilyn had paid or were paying theirs, but somehow numbly, with anesthetized blonde wits; it was Alma's heartbreaking gift to suggest that she was fully aware, knowing more than she could say, more than the script could say, even as the plot demanded that she be cast out—murdered, exiled, imprisoned—for failing to conform. Each movie, under the Production Code dating back to 1934, was a moral mechanism that had to function toward the elimination of all defective parts. As the Alma-character was borne off by the inevitable censorious rectitude of the script, audiences felt that something precious in themselves was being carried away, in this land of promise where yearning never stops short at a particular satisfaction but keeps moving on, into the territory beyond.

She was surprised at how easily she located in herself a tragic vein, she who had been raised in such a sweet small town, by such loving parents and grandparents. But, when the script demanded she shriek or weep—and not once, but for take after take, until her eyes were red with the salt of tears and her lips sore with being contorted—she was able to worm through her memories and find something terrible and irrevocable enough to feed grief: Momma's poor stunted foot; Daddy going around and around the town like a stupid wind-up toy because everything else scared him; Ama widowed so young and stirring all those heavy unhealthy sweet things on the stove and stirring by telephone the sickly messes of unhappiness cooked up in her church circles. Grandma Sifford dead of cancer, shrivelling up in her bed like a poisoned aphid, leaving the old farmer to bumble around in his greenhouse alone, the wilts and spots thriving and the putty slowly crumbling from the overlapped panes, everything that needed tending slipping away from him. So much loneliness in living, so much waste. So much unredeemable loss. And the grandfather she had never known fallen into a shining white hole of damnation forever. And pretty-lipped slender-headed Benjy Whaley condemned to life as a grease monkey and knowing just enough to hate his fate, like a zoo animal whose instincts keep telling him there is something beyond his cage; and Patrick trapped too, though he got better every year at being supercilious and idle, to hide his romantic dreams of being carried off somehow like a bride in a *Redbook* story; and Arnie with his Scarsdale wife and kids and crumbling health, coughing and hardly able to climb a single flight of stairs or get it up for the fanciest call-girl in Manhattan; and poor Mr. Bear with his tiddlywink eyes, always so faithful, always listening to her childish chatter and letting her hug him, hug and snuggle so she could fall asleep, and now up in the Locust Street attic gathering dust and staring at nothing and wondering why that little girl never comes to play with him, never comes to say hello . . .

"Cut. Print. *Wunderwerk,* Alma. We came in even closer then; your eyes were stupendous."

She was modest, efficient. "Fred, please—if you decide you need yet another take, I'll need at least half an hour to cool down my poor eyeballs. Where's my Murine?"

"It's back in your camper, Miss DeMott. Shall I run get it?" She had her own attendants now—her own hairdresser, Leonore, and her personal secretary, Paulette.

Zinnemann was still enthusiastic; his violinist's hands fluttered, and his Viennese accent peeked through. "Vat a goot shport you are. But you nailed it, guaranteed. It's in the can. Sound says it may have heard a crackle in the boom mike; if we need you to loop, keep your voice down like it was, *husky. Piano,* but not *pianissimo.* Like you are shpeaking for your own brain to hear."

Alma loved the craft of it, using her body with a detached precision, walking to a spot marked with tape without looking at it and saying just the same thing she had said ten times before, and putting the identical passion and verve into it, where she could see her co-stars flagging, getting tired and impatient, losing tempo and relatedness. She felt, coiffed and in costume and make-up, encased in a fine and flexible but impermeable armor; the bright island of make-believe, surrounded by scaffolding and wiring and the silhouettes of those many technicians who operated the equipment, was a larger container, a well-lit spaceship carrying her and the other actors into an immortal safety, beyond change and harm. A cosmic attention beat on her skin as when she was a child God had watched her every move, recorded her every prayer and yearning, nothing unnoticed, the very hairs on her head numbered, Essie and the sparrows sold two for a farthing all over Delaware, brown sparrows rustling in the sparrow-colored underbrush. She had been lifted up from the underbrush to this heaven and she blazed with the miracle of it.

The camera missed no tremor, no blink, no nuance of facial tightening. Nothing was unobserved; even her unconscious thoughts poured out through her skin, her eyes. Though she delved within herself for emotion, she was by training anti-Method; at the school on West Fifty-seventh Street the emphasis had been on outward gesture, the body as a succession of clear signals. "Move dis*tinct*ly," one of her instructors, the strictest, Professor Berthoff, would repeatedly say. "Move in*tell*igibly. The audience must know im*med*iately ex*act*ly what you are doing. There is no room on the stage for the uncertain, ambiguous movements that in real life we make all the time." Essie had wondered why anything in real life should be excluded from the stage, but then, when she became Alma, she saw that this clarity makes a refuge for the actors and audience both, lifting them up from fumbling reality into a reality keener and more efficient but not less true. Even the face: acting for the camera, in close-up, was facial athletics, with eyelids and irises and all those little muscles that form a cat's-cradle around the mouth. From older, wiser stars she had learned how minimal the athletics can be: it is a star's privilege to be the still center which the supporting actors swirl about, generating the action. Sometimes, when she couldn't locate through a tedious succession of takes what the director wanted, she would shut down her memories and think of nothing, and something from God would flow into her face from behind, and Zinnemann or Wilder or Walter Lang would cry out from the darkness around her, "That's it! You've knocked it, Alma. Print!"

With the cry "Print!" she would know that once again her poor precious perishable self as of that exact moment had been—unless the director or editor or producer or some studio higher-up fucked with the footage—transported to a realm beyond time and space, into "the can" and thence into a thousand projectors, into a million hearts as impressionable and innocently magnanimous as hers once had been. Since 1950, by one more of her strokes of good fortune, the industry had switched from film based on cellulose nitrate, intensely flammable and prone to turn into chemical mush in storage, to cellulose acetate, which does not burn and will last theoretically forever. Most of Mary Pickford was lost utterly, but the world would never lose Alma DeMott. She would always be there, in some archive or rerun, in eternal return perennially called back to life.

"How many times did you actually kiss him?" Loretta Whaley breathlessly asked her, on one of her rare visits back to Basingstoke. She was talking of William Holden, in a movie in which Alma had played a war wife who is unfaithful to her husband under the illusion that he has been shot down over Guadalcanal; even though it was an honest mistake, she suffers for it. It was 1957 and Loretta had married Eddie Bacheller six years ago and was the mother of two darling little boys, born so close together she could push them up and down Rodney Street in the same stroller.

"Oh—a hundred."

"A hundred? How could you stand it?"

"It's not easy, they keep making you do it over and over again. Sometimes a door slams off the set or the actor hiccups or the dolly pusher misses his cue and it's not your fault, but you have to go back at it as if kissing this strange man's face is something worth dying for, 'cause you know that's what the script calls for, you're going to die in the last reel."

"Oh, Essie!—Alma. How does it feel?"

"After a while, like nothing much," she told her, a bit spitefully. "The older stars are very strict, they never open their mouths, it's like kissing a zipper; but the younger ones, like Holden, they can French, though the camera isn't supposed to see too much of it. Like there never should be any spit show." In some corner of herself she was jealous of Loretta; these two toddlers, round-faced and shiny-eyed, gazed up at their idiotic mother in her cheap polka-dot sundress as though she was half the world. They had Eddie's cheerful trusting temperament, and that fine apricot-colored hair the Bachellers had. Essie had always rather liked Eddie, not only because his older brother worked as usher in the Roxie. That day on the bleachers she would rather it had been Eddie than Benjy, who had had a mean streak and now was drinking so much, Loretta told her, he had been fired from Sturgis's Garage; their parents were real upset but couldn't do a thing with him. Junie Mulholland had married a boy from St. Georges, and Fats Lowe, who had seemed the most stick-at-home meatball possible, living with his drunken mother in a one-story house almost out in Niggertown, had "hit the road," as he told people, and was out in Oregon somewhere, bumming around and taking drugs, people said. He was going to hell in a handbasket, just like his ma, but over an improved highway.

"I mean," Loretta insisted, "doesn't it get you all hot and bothered? I know when Eddie and I—"

Alma didn't want to hear it; she turned her back, there on the sunstruck sidewalk squares near where Addison's Drug Store had displayed its two old-fashioned vials of iodine-pink and watery ink-blue. Old Seth's widow had sold the store to the Rexall chain when he finally died, and the plate-glass window held a curved pyramid of cartons of L & M cigarettes and a cardboard woman in only a towel smilingly holding a Schick electric razor against her bare shin. Alma's abrupt half-turn of her body felt to her like an invisible scythe extending out into the hazed late-summer sky above Basingstoke. Even naked of her make-up and costumes, she had more definition, more visible edge, than these shapeless shuffling others who had frightened her that day she first went to the movie alone and then, when she came out, looked like a herd of bumbling blind cows. Halfway down Rodney Street, the Roxie had *Funny Face* on the marquee, and this added to her irritation. Alma had felt snubbed by Audrey Hepburn at one of Joe Mankiewicz's parties—all that fey European dimply charm, so darling and pure, here in Hollywood for just the lark and the dollars of it. The highly refined Mrs. Ferrer had stiffened when Alma was introduced, and held out, with a flare of her eyes, a slender tentative hand as if a bit fearful of being contaminated by the bushy-haired heroine of gritty movies from King Kong Cohn's asphalt jungle. From the other side of the industry's tracks. As if that were all Alma had done and could do. She took it out on Arnie: "If all Cohn can think of for me is one more stripper in one more pathetic *Bus Stop*–type tearjerker, if all he can think of me is to out–*Baby Doll Baby Doll*— Why wasn't *I* considered for the Natalie Wood part in *The Searchers?*—I'd look a damn sight less phony in a squaw outfit than she did. Why can't I do another musical? I can sing rings around that Hepburn. Get me something *fluffy.*" The complaints and battles rattled on in her head, even here in remote Basingstoke.

"I know when Eddie and I," Loretta was going on, "are watching television, the boys asleep finally, and we start foolin' around—"

"Loretta," Alma said decisively. "Filming a romantic scene isn't fooling around. It's *work,* hard work. Sometimes it takes several days of shooting to get footage from all the angles, to do all they'll need for the montage. Your main emotion gets to be a feeling of protectiveness toward the guy stuck there with you under all those lights, especially if he's old enough to be your father. It's supposed to simulate fucking but you don't fuck around." In Hollywood "fuck" didn't hide in the shadows of the language but named a fundamental process, a common coin of the realm.

Loretta couldn't be derailed, any more than she could be dissuaded twenty years ago from telling Essie the entire story of *One Hundred Men and a Girl.* "I mean, what happens if, while you're stimulating, the guy—?"

"You work around it," Alma said, grateful to see in the corner of her vision an autograph-seeker approach, with that characteristic hesitant yet inexorable gait.

"Miss DeMott, I don't mean to intrude into your privacy—"

"Oh, shit, come right ahead," Alma said, irritated to the point of screaming by thoughts of Audrey Hepburn and Natalie Wood.

"—but I know your folks so well, your father's been our mailman as long as I can—"

"He's everybody's mailman," Alma told the young man. "He even used to be my mailman." The interloper held out an old fountain pen. She scrawled her signature, which got bigger every day, over a grubby newspaper clipping from the Wilmington *News-Journal* he had brought up to her, a ridiculously exaggerated account of the local furor caused by those few seconds of exposure in *Safe at Your Peril,* something he had saved as a dog saves a grubby slobbered-upon bone; yet she took care to cross the two "t"s. She believed in not letting standards slip—you saw it again and again in Hollywood, a little drinking habit leading to a weight problem and memory gaps, one little pop at lunch leading to a couple and a wasted afternoon on the set for a crew of fifty, an occasional sleeping pill turning into a continual daze, one hack job taken purely for the money starting a director on the skids, one less-than-professional performance tainting an actress's name throughout the industry. She kept herself professional, trim, sober, taut. Not for nothing was Alma a Calvinist minister's granddaughter. She looked at her index finger; as she had suspected would happen, the creep's fountain pen had leaked.

"Jesus, I just *loved* you in *Colored Entrance,* but *Safe at Your Peril,* wow, I think I must have seen it a dozen times—" This was so excessive, even for an enamored fan, that she at last tried to focus on him—he was tall and pale and wet-lipped and made to look even more cretinous by the green plastic sun visor and the plaid Bermuda shorts. You never used to see a grown-up wearing shorts on Rodney Street. The man was young but old enough to know better. His shoulders and arms were sunburned pink, his eyes were pale and apologetic, and she recognized something in him, some fallen distinction: he had a sheepish stale scent of downscaled expectations, of genetic washout. Yes: he looked, only taller and duller and less self-disciplined, like whey-faced Mr. Phillips, who used to own the Basingstoke Savings Bank and was the superintendent of the Sunday school. This must be his son, Wayne Junior, whom Essie had last noticed when he was a lumpish thirteen or so and she was in her senior year, going back and forth to New York. The bank had been absorbed by First Delaware and the son had become an Alma DeMott fan.

"A dozen times?" she said. "Didn't you get bored?"

"No, Jesus, Alma, never—every time through, I see something new. The way, for instance, in the scene with the gun, with just that little flicker of your eyes, hardly even a flicker, more like a blip in your pupils, I can see you thinking, *Well, death wouldn't be so bad.* And then he plugs you, right in the gut." She had a lot of queers and misfits in her fan club—the same types as were morbidly fascinated by Garland—and at times they irritated her.

"It was very nice to meet you," she said, in the level tone

that sent all but the most deranged stalker packing, and turned her shoulder on him, and again had that sensation of invisible rays from her body sweeping like a scythe across the sky.

Wayne Junior retreated down Elm Street, clutching his carefully scribbled-upon piece of newspaper, but Loretta was still there, demanding her prerogative as one who knew her when —as, indeed, her best friend, insofar as fanatically dreaming Essie had had friends. Standing ignored in the hot sun on the corner across from Pursey's Notions and Variety Store, her boys in their stroller beginning to whine and quarrel, Loretta had felt snubbed and become spiteful in turn. "And you know, of course," she told Alma, "about Jamie Ingraham—how he's married this lovely blonde girl from Brandywine, her father's very high up in one of the Du Pont divisions. They have a little baby girl already."

And yes, shrewd stringy-haired overweight Loretta was right, this did hurt, the image of Jamie impregnating a lovely well-born blonde, not in the back seat of his father's blue Chrysler but in a wide bed blessed by all the powers of church and corporation.

At home, when Alma described, with omissions, her encounters downtown, Momma said, "Yes, poor Wayne is a little impaired. I remember his mother carrying him, Danny was already toddling so you must have been five or so, and there was a scare that Basingstoke Savings would go under to the Depression, and I wonder if that didn't pinch off the fetus."

"Mother! What a ridiculous theory!"

"Well," Momma said, swinging with her infuriating hopping gait around the kitchen table (her limp was getting worse with age) to check on the turkey roasting in the oven, "you haven't had the experience yet of carrying a child, and believe me there *is* communication, from about the fifth month. The little thing is listening to your thoughts, and letting you know about it."

Ama, sitting idle at the table, said in a shaky voice, "Clarence used to say, if the baby cried while being baptized, it meant the parents had a good love life." Ama had turned ninety in May. Alma had wanted to come to the birthday party, but she was on location in England, doing a tearjerker, *But Now Is Forever*, set in the American Midwest. Shooting in foreign studios, with smaller foreign crews working at less than Hollywood union scale, had become the latest maneuver in an industry desperate over its dwindling audiences and blockbuster flops. But the outdoor scenes in *But Now Is Forever* had been plagued by rain, and in any weather the sky was wrong, loaded with hurrying British clouds, and the highways were miscast as American roads, even when all traffic had been blocked off so the rented American automobiles could drive on the right; after the cost of constructing an American-style roadside café and a piece of a spacious Midwestern Main Street had been calculated in, it would have been cheaper to stay on a Burbank sound stage, with a week's worth of location work in Kansas. Like a gambler growing desperate, the industry was making silly mistakes. Aside from the dismal English weather, Alma had found Frank Capra, aged twenty years since the glory days of Mr. Deeds and *Lost Horizon*, capricious and corny-minded; the kind of moral ambiguity and wary, wounded pessimism that Alma DeMott represented had no place in his sentimental concept of America. He directed her to lighten up. "Let the audience know you love the bastard, down deep. When sparks fly, that's love." Old-hat folk psychology. Alma was tired, in any case, of playing "gutsy," suffering women; she knew she could do a musical sexier than any that poor dazed Judy or one-dimensional Doris could whip up. Feeling guilty, Alma had run into Harrod's and sent off to her ancient grandmother for her birthday present a sumptuous black cashmere greatcoat with wide sleeves, stand-up collar, and slashed pockets. Seeing Ama now, she realized the coat had been not only too stylish but too big; her, remembered as enormous, ancestor had shrunk, and even her head of hair, gray with a few pallid streaks of chestnut, had become skimpier, so the old lady's scalp showed through in the harsh overhead kitchen light.

Yet she still made Alma laugh. "Why, Ama, what a racy thing for Grandfather Wilmot to say!"

"Oh, yes," Ama said, in a voice that if Alma closed her eyes sounded through its quavers like the voice in which Ama used to read little Essie and Mr. Bear their bedtime stories, "he was a normal man. At those church socials back in Jackson Bluffs he had to fight the ladies off, and not all of them unmarried either. He wouldn't have been one of those who preached against my own sweet granddaughter for showing the whole world what it knew she had anyway, a cute little backside."

Was this going to be what Alma was remembered for, that fleeting nude scene in *Safe at Your Peril*? It had roused protests and cost bookings throughout the Bible Belt, though not as many as the interracial kiss in *Colored Entrance.* It made the star impatient and weary to hear her films mentioned in this her old home; they had been made so far away, in another climate and time zone, and their challenges and triumphs were so hard to grasp without the technical background, and without understanding how embattled and ingeniously self-regarding the art of the cinema was, that she would rather her family would pretend they didn't exist. It was bad enough for Daddy and Momma to show up dutifully at the Roxie, where they said the heads of the audience these days were sometimes few enough to count, but it carried family piety to an obscene length for them to drag dear shrunken Ama down there, subjecting the ancient lady to two hours of simulated love-frenzy and of the increasingly graphic male violence that was another aspect of Hollywood's attempt to update its product, to shave away at the Production Code, to offer the public something, besides distorting width and flashy color and blaring stereophonic sound, that they couldn't get on the cozy little screen at home. Internationally public as it was, Alma's film career embarrassed her here in Basingstoke—her instinct was to hide it, as something private and shameful and impossible to explain, just as her daydreams in childhood, and her masturbation and then her experiments with the opposite sex, had been. Mentioning her movies at this kitchen table was, she irrationally felt, poor taste on her family's part.

Aunt Esther, clutching a Kent in one hand and in the other an orange-juice glass full of neat whiskey, volunteered, "Disgusting hypocrites. They should have been around in the Twenties—some of those dives in Harlem and the East Village Jare used to take us to had shows after midnight that would make your hair curl. Prohibition took the lid off. Breaking one law, you might as well break 'em all. People got so upset at Josephine Baker over in Paris, but at least she wore a bunch of bananas." Her voice was slurred; she slid her slivery blue eyes across their faces, uncertain of who her audience was.

Uncle Peter said, to back her up, "Not to mention some of the tent shows in country fairs right around Basingstoke—Basingstoke that's supposed to be so innocent." That social shunning, the loss of clients, back then still rankled. Holding his own tumbler of whiskey, he rested the other hand on his wife's shoulder. He had made her, his gesture said; they had made each other.

Alma didn't like being grouped with the performers in tent shows and Harlem dives, but when she inhaled to protest she knew she would stutter if she tried it; her father, always alert to others' pain, saw her famously voluptuous mouth open and close in this pathetic way, and said, "Essie, we're all just dumbfounded at what you've accomplished. I don't think any of us can actually comprehend it. Isn't that right, Mother?"

"It is," Momma said simply, and produced the familiar shadow of her dimple. "But I was never surprised. She was perfection from Day One."

Danny, as if hearing himself slighted, came into the kitchen from the living room, where he had been watching the six o'clock news on television. "Well, the Soviets have successfully tested their intercontinental ballistic missile," he announced aggressively. "So they have one, and we don't. First Rudolf Abel, now this. A master spy sitting right there in Brooklyn for nine years, with a radio transmitter!" He sounded the way he did when Essie had been allowed to do something that he wasn't. Though, being a boy, he eventually got to do a lot of things she hadn't. Since she had been in Hollywood, Danny had grown awkwardly tall, with the round Sifford head on the skinny Wilmot frame, and had graduated from Rutgers and, rather than go on to business school or one of the professions (though Alma had offered to finance him), had accepted some kind of job with the State Department, who were sending him to school to learn Slavic languages, eight hours a day. He wore thick glasses, with flesh-tinted plastic rims. "And oh yeah, Sis—this would interest you. The Southerners in the Senate are giving up the filibuster so it looks like the voting-rights bill will get to Ike's desk."

"Well, good," she said, taken aback. "I don't know why you think that would especially interest me. I would think it would please any American. It's about a hundred years late." *You nigger-kissing cunt,* one of her fan letters had begun, and went on, getting worse. But she didn't like being seen as a wild Hollywood liberal here in Basingstoke. She felt besieged; family holidays had always been like this, everybody crowding into the kitchen and getting in the cook's way, with the smells of the meal getting warmer and riper and a little sickening. Now her infrequent homecomings had become a kind of holiday, with townspeople walking slowly by the house and peering in, and every jerk who ever went to Basingstoke High claiming to be a classmate of hers, and her own parents acting a little uncertain and shy and deferential. Only Ama, and Alma's other surviving grandparent, Daniel Sifford, made her feel like a child again—safe and casually cherished. They were both absent-minded enough to forget who she had become. Arthritis and dropsy had so slowed the old farmer, with just Momma and few increasingly insolent Negro boys to help him, that there was talk of Daddy giving up being a mailman so he and Momma could take over the greenhouse. "If I retire at fifty-five," he had explained to his daughter, "I'll get two-thirds of the pension, and now that you were good enough to pay off our mortgage there isn't the need for steady income there was. But Mother and I want to run it by you before we do anything."

"Goodness, Daddy, it's your life. If you want to quit, do. Money shouldn't be a problem any more." She was conscious, as she said this, of the light from the front parlor defining the good side of her face, so she looked, her chin demurely down and her eyes lifted with a composed filial ardor—like Olivia de Havilland as an heiress.

"Oh now," he said, and looked sad and wise, though his pale-brown hair was hardly touched by gray and his daily buffeting by the weather had kept his face young and full and undefined, "money's never not a problem," and that was true. The more she made, the bigger Arnie's slice became, the more the government took to pay people like Danny to fight their Cold War, and the more people in general expected her to spend. To house her first marriage four years ago—to a director's assistant who yearned to become a director but lacked the balls as well as the touch, that brash and clever European touch the Jews had brought to it when the industry was young and pliant—Alma had bought a house in Beverly Hills, north of Sunset Boulevard in Coldwater Canyon, on a high winding road called Montevideo Drive. The house was old for California and, in a neighborhood of mock-Tudor timbering and sprawling wings roofed in Spanish tile, unusual in looking Victorian, with a slated mansard roof and spindly wrought-iron pinnacles ornamenting an off-center six-sided cupola; it was a heightened version, she slowly realized, of the big old house on Willow Street where her great-aunt Esther had lived, and where her father had come to live and then brought his bride, until Uncle Horace like a movie villain had moved back and ousted them. Little Essie had never ventured inside, though from the sidewalk she had often admired the place, her childish eyes drawn to the white-painted backyard gazebo. The first marriage had lasted little more than a year, but she still owned the house, with its taxes and falling slates and leaking old-style concrete swimming pool.

Irritated by thoughts of money, she turned on her brother. "What are you going to *do* with all those Slavic languages?" she asked him. His presence in her life had always seemed a kind of babyish squawking. If she was as perfect as Momma said, why had he been called into the family, too?

But he had grown suave, in a gray-suited anonymous Washington way, and smiled like a man who keeps many secrets. "Do? I'll speak with the Slavs, Sis, and make friends for America. I'll help the U.S. keep a presence, even in countries presently disposed to be unsympathetic. You think this is silly, your tone of voice implies. Sillier than making movies?"

"Well, Danny darling, the movies have never pretended to be anything except entertainment. But what you're doing pretends to be a good deal more."

"It pretends to be history," he said quickly. "It *is* history. Cast of billions. The future of the globe at stake. I kid you not." He looked around at the others of the family gathered here in the kitchen. No one budged a tongue to interfere; was Alma paranoid, or were they watching to see how much this kid brother could chop her down to size?

"Oh," Alma replied, with a languid and ladylike gesture, "I'm sure you're right, dear Danny, but it seems so much like boys' games. Two big bald boys, now that Khrushchev has foiled his little coup."

"It wasn't so little, actually," Danny said, with an insider's authority. "It was back to Stalinism, is what it was. I guess even you Hollywood reds don't want that." He leaned toward her earnestly, his glasses flashing: "Sis, how can you be so blithe, after what those bastards did last year in Hungary? They're bar*bar*ians."

Alma said, wishing to wave this awkward political heat away, "This country wouldn't be so high and mighty if it weren't for Stalin and Stalingrad."

Now Jefferson and Ira Pulsifer, who had been watching television with Danny in the front parlor and had ransacked the channels in his absence, followed him into the stiflingly hot kitchen. Their older brother, Peter Junior, was bumming around Europe this summer, the way young people did now, as if the Atlantic were no wider than the Delaware. The boys had Peter's preppy bounce but something of their mother's papery white skin and wised-up way of talking. "Aunt Alma," fifteen-year-old Ira called, "when are you going to come on television?"

"I was on television when it was young," she told him. "It was a rat race, my dears." Interview mode came naturally to her by now.

"Television's where it's at," Jefferson, called Jeff, chimed in. "Lucille Ball is making out like a bandit."

"Dinah Shore's on television," Ira added, his voice rising and cracking as he picked up on the curious atmosphere in the room, the celebrity electricity. "Jack Benny, Alfred Hitchcock."

"Some people sell out, Jeffie," she said, tapping the ash of her cigarette—a charcoal-filtered Herbert Tareyton—into a saucer, with a pattern imitating sampler stitches, that had been a Tuesday-night giveaway at the Roxie twenty years ago, "and others try to make enduring art."

The boys decided this was meant to be funny and laughed. Their adolescent hunger had injected a fresh heat into the kitchen. Daddy had got up to help Momma lift the turkey out of the oven and ease it onto its platter, and to take the pot of mashed sweet potatoes off the stove. Though they had bought one of the new tinted refrigerators, an enamelled lime-green, and an electric stove to match, and the plywood counter had been covered with Con-Tact paper patterned in hollow boomerangs, it remained an old-fashioned kitchen, with geraniums on the windowsill above the sink and a wainscoting of stained tongue-and-groove boards and a host of agitated flies. They still tacked up flypaper here in Delaware—amber helixes some of whose captives showed a spark of buzzing, slow-dying life. Alma had forgotten how muggy and buggy Delaware was in August. This humid heat used to be her element, in which her skinny brown limbs waded to the playground and back, to the greenhouse and beyond, to where the marsh, with its furtive citizenry of turtles and minnows and egrets, stretched miles toward the broadening river. She found she was homesick for the dry desert heat of southern California—the nights so cool a light sweater comforts your shoulders and arms, the gaudy stars close overhead, the giant lit grid stretching south from the Santa Monica foothills. When you climb up from the pool a rainbow like an oil-glimmer is caught in your lashes, and as you arrange yourself on the chaise of plastic ribbons you shiver with the speed of evaporation and hear the sound of Spanish being spoken by the gardeners and the maids, the murmur of traffic from Doheny Road and Coldwater Canyon Drive; you hear the accent of action, of deals among beautiful people being transparently done, in the air, the bare blue desert air getting ready for its winter role, as indigo background, soft as velour, for the grassy hills' winter dress of flammable gold.

She had allotted three days before Labor Day for Basingstoke, between an appointment in New York—Arnie found less and less strength for the flight to L.A., though the new jets cut the flying time in half—and a party in Bel Air where her escort would be a young curly-haired scriptwriter who, like Ama, knew how to make her laugh. But even three days seemed long. Her parents were a bit frightened of her, she realized, and not entirely approving. Her name had been bandied about by the gossip industry (ridiculous supposed liaisons—Rock Hudson, for God's sake!), and too many journalists, piqued by a mailman's being a movie star's father, had intruded on the truce Daddy had arranged with the world. When the reporters came, Momma would hop upstairs and hide, just like her own reclusive mother.

Ama had her lucid and energetic intervals and then spells of what Dr. Jessup called "sundowning." On the third day, she felt too tired to come downstairs and had asked Essie to sit by her bed a little. She rested a dry claw, still warm, in her granddaughter's moist, shapely, long-nailed hand and gazed at her with a pleasure that pierced the rheumy veil across her plum-black eyes. Her eyes had been so strained by a lifetime of fine sewing that their black skiddingly flooded the thick lenses of her glasses; without her glasses, her eyes seemed pathetically small. "You are a miracle," she pronounced at last, having gazed her fill. "Though I don't know why they had to make your hair darker than it was. And change your perfectly good American name. I always knew it would happen. Oh, I always knew. When Clarence—when he—fell," she brought out, "it was so sudden and uncalled-for, there had to be something to—you know, I *do* believe it was the Devil himself, there's no other explanation, it was pure temptation, though you may take me for a fool when I say it—"

"No, no. But you were saying, 'There had to be something to'—"

"To make it come right in the end."

"Like in the movies," Alma smiled.

"Like a movie, dearest. Oh, exactly. Give us a kiss from those gorgeous lips."

Alma aimed for the dry old cheek but Ama turned her face to be kissed on the lips. When Alma backed away, a dulling veil had returned to the old woman's eyes. "I'll try to be here when you come again," she said, fumbling like a blind woman for the other's hand, "but I can't make any promises. You know," she added, in quite another, rather aggrieved tone, "—this is something I can say to you now that you're no longer a Wilmot—the Wilmots, well, they have a trait, if I can bring myself to name it—"

"Yes, Ama? What? A trait?"

The old lady had turned a bit pink. "They're, well, *self*ish. It comes out in different ways, but that's what they are. Your grandfather could have gone on in the ministry—a lot of us have doubts, but we just brush them under the table and get on with the job. My goodness, yes."

Papa Sifford, pottering around in the great glass prism that a visitor stepped down into and that was floored with mossy dirt, less directly extended his blessing. His mode was silence, and letting Nature take her course. The fat had leaked from his creased jowls and they fell like hound flaps. "It gave me a start," he admitted, "when you came in, you have such a likeness to Tabitha the first time I saw her. They were picking squash, over toward Cheswold, and here this smallest of the field girls was carrying the biggest load in her bushel basket. Now, Essie, since you're around, I could use a strong back. The cyclamen have been getting too much heat at night, and I thought to put them under the tables over on the north side. The boy who waters for me won't take the trouble to keep the water off the leaves, he just turns the hose on spray and daydreams. They don't follow orders any more, they do everything their way. Now he's off, would you believe, at practice for the high-school football team. This is the first year the squad's to be—what's the word?"

"Integrated?" For more than an hour Alma performed with her grandfather the old ritual, which to little Essie had seemed to take endless patience, of moving the flats holding six potted plants from one table with its rusty grid and white-painted wood over to another in another portion of the greenhouse, where the sun's rays fell with a slightly different intensity and the circulating air caressed the mute green leaves somehow more encouragingly. A few customers came in and out of the greenhouse, but with her hair up in a bandana and her lips and face innocent of make-up, they did not recognize her. Perhaps they were strangers brought to live in Basingstoke by the new refinery and holding tanks built along the river, in the saltwater marshes, just north of where the Avon used to find the sea through a maze of tidal channels and a set of rocks that boys could fish from. There was no fishing now; just an eight-foot electrified fence, and several new tracts of ranch houses between here and there. Or perhaps they were townspeople who, inching through their own lives in that molelike small-town way, assumed that Essie Wilmot had never left.

She carried plants back and forth—potted yellow and orange mums into the direct sun on the south side, checking under the leaves for spider mites; red and pink rosebud impatiens grown in hanging pots; some garish flats of *Kalanchoe blossfeldiana,* which the old man called Flaming Katie, pinching back the flowers to give better fall blooms—and imagined herself one of them, lifted up and set down in a place where she would be happier and could better grow. Her arms ached when she was done. He took her down into the bulb cellar, beyond the giant disused old coal-burner, converted after the war to oil with an automatic feed, though there was still a broad wooden bench beside it, and a grimy mattress. "That bench would get mighty hard after a solid week of tending," he allowed. In the dim cool light of the dirt-floored cellar, freesia and hyacinth, daffodil and lily bulbs were laid out in plastic trays of potting soil like so many tidy gravesites certain of resurrection. When they got an inch or so high, with a good root system, they would be suspended in the dark at forty degrees until it was time to take them up into the greenhouse heat and light and force them for the Christmas trade. Participating in the old man's numb, silent pride as he surveyed this buried wealth, Alma was aware of, for a second or two, forgetting herself.

"What a lovely time we had together, Grandpa," she said in parting. Tears, since she had learned to cry on cue, rarely came to her eyes spontaneously.

"It kept us out of mischief," he allowed, with a twitch of one of his dewlaps, hinting his private opinion that mischief was what her life now mostly consisted of.

In Essie's experience, her prayers were generally answered, if not always as promptly as she wished. She did get her wish to make a musical comedy—a Warner remake of *The Straw-*

berry Blonde, resplendent in Vistarama, co-starring Bing Crosby, with Dick Van Dyke in the Jack Carson role and Janet Leigh as Olivia de Havilland. Crosby did not let the nearly thirty years' difference between himself and his leading lady show onscreen; he had recently married the even younger actress Kathryn Grant, who had been with Essie in the making of *The Last Time We Saw Topeka,* and who now visited the Warner lot in a majestic state of pregnancy. The child, Harry Lillis Crosby, Jr., was born a month after the film wrapped. The film couple—Alma in a henna-rinsed pompadour, and the senior Harry Lillis Crosby in a toupee that had its own red tinge—weightlessly waltzed from one side of the curved screen to the other, and entwined voices for a gentle duet that amazed the musical insiders by going platinum. "And they wanted me dubbed," said Alma at the 1959 Grammy awards, as the audience roared with laughter. The Hollywood crowd had softened toward her, as she had grown from a challenging, willful ingenue to a seasoned, adaptable screen veteran.

She had become a comedienne by letting herself be infected with Crosby's marvellous lazy lightness, in banter that felt ad-libbed even when carefully rehearsed. Unlike her other leading men, Crosby owed little of his success to physical handsomeness. He had conquered the worlds of radio, recording, and film with sheer performance; as a boy in Spokane, he excelled at any sport he took up, and was so clever at school the Jesuits had hoped to make a trial lawyer of him. The aging crooner's occasional flashes of impatience and coldness did not alienate her. A certain inhuman efficiency had to lie at the heart of such achievements. She observed in him what she already sensed in herself, the danger of becoming a performer purely, of coming alive in proportion to the size of the audience, and being absent-minded and remote when the audience was small. She knew enough Irishmen—Patrick, for one, and the bachelor algebra teacher back in Basingstoke, Mr. O'Brien, and Spencer Tracy and Donald O'Connor, and indeed until the emergence of the Jews hadn't the Irish been the soul of American entertainment?—to understand how an unflappable charm and wit could enwrap a pinched, rigid private morality, a spoiled priesthood. She, too, had her religion. She had trouble understanding how people could doubt God's existence: He was so clearly there, next to her, interwoven with her, a palpable pressure, as vital as the sensations in her skin, as dependable as her reflection in the mirror. When, in the wake of her dawn risings, she submitted under the merciless make-up lights to the probing, licking, stabbing ministrations of greasepaint sponge, eyebrow pencil, and eyelash brush, and let her hair be tightly drawn around the horrible dead-looking rats—those hairy net sausages she had once found in Ama's bureau drawer—to form her Gibson-girl pompadour, and her waist was cinched into the boned corset and every pleat and velvet ribbon of her lace bertha and shirred and flounced hobble skirt was smoothed and pinned into perfection, and her dog collar of brilliants and pearls was hooked snug around her throat and her high hairdo precariously topped with a large black velvet "Gainsborough" hat trimmed with ostrich plumes, then Alma held herself in the back of the Lincoln limousine that carried her from the make-up rooms to the sound stage like a sacred statue, her weight balanced on one buttock on the seat's edge, her gloved fingertips braced against the back of the seat to minimize the pressure that might wrinkle or disarrange a single fold of cloth, her eyes held wide open under the load of cream and kohl and belladonna, her painted lips ajar and unspeaking, and eased herself out of the limousine to offer up with a static priestly reverence her image to the cameras.

Yet sixteen months were to pass before she made another film. The critics applauded the new, light, "good" Alma DeMott, but the public was not so sure. *Casey and His Strawberry Blonde,* as the remake was lengthily retitled, was not the box-office smash it needed to be in this era of soaring costs and budget overruns. A sprightly, singing, Technicolor innocence was not enough to bring the public in from the steady drizzle of television. Musicals, except for M-G-M's cut-rate series of

Presley vehicles, were a thing of the past. So, in a strange way, were film goddesses; women, however gorgeously shadowed and intricately vexed, had lost their sway over the box office, perhaps because housewives were staying home, tending the electronic fires. Phenomena like Garbo and Crawford and Greer Garson required the complicity of discontented, dreaming women. Despite the growing stir of Fifties feminism, American women of the Depression and the war had had more practical equality, more of the stature that earning power brings. The scripts Columbia offered Alma held ever smaller and more disagreeable female parts, in a poisoned male world where Tony Curtis licked Burt Lancaster's boots or Ben Gazzara invited homosexual bullying at a military school. She complained to Arnie, "Bring back the Communists—at least they could write parts for women. The scripts now are all by kids, writing for kids." Including, she did not add, the curly-haired kid she was living with.

Arnie and Alma were lying naked together in his suite at the Beverly Hills Hotel, since the young scriptwriter, Matt Lazlo, had moved into her house on Montevideo Drive and hung around "working" all day. Her beloved agent puffed a semi-medicinal Salem to hide his embarrassment over his impotence, which they had spent a sweaty hour proving to themselves. He would have it, and then his mind would begin to wander, back to Scarsdale or the MCA offices in Rockefeller Center. Or was it her mind that began to wander, at the very moment when his prick was growing slightly harder in her mouth? It was one of those surprisingly dark-skinned pricks Mediterranean men have, as if grafted from an African race. Though ritually circumcised, it tasted rancid. Its spark had become very delicate, and needed a concentrated passion to flare up. Like a camera, it sensed any faking. With her young lover, Alma's mind could be a million miles away and he would come off in three minutes and think she was the greatest lay since Cleopatra. "Babe, the industry's all shook up," Arnie explained, relieved to be performing with words. "There's no such thing as a sure thing any more. Even Esther Williams bombed for M-G-M, and then that big proxy fight. When you got mutiny on the flagship, the whole fleet's in trouble. Pickford and Chaplin have sold out of U.A. Hughes made a mess at RKO and sold out. Warner's sold off its library. TV's the buzzard, we're the carcass. CinemaScope's pooped. People get bored with gadgets; they even got bored with sound, at first. The old hardball guys, the guys with a nose for the public, are dying. Mayer, and now your guy Cohn." He snorted, and hot cigarette ash toppled into his gray chest hair, sending up a scent of singe. She was thinking she'd love to get into the bathroom for some mouthwash. "That was a funny gag," Arnie said, "about Cohn giving people what they want. But so many showed up at his funeral because they knew it was *their* funeral."

"I liked Harry."

"I know you did. He liked you. Nice Gentile girls that wouldn't fuck him, he had a great respect for."

"Who says I didn't fuck him?" Perhaps jealousy would rouse him. Her sexual failure rankled. It was like a flop at the box office; your whole self was on the line. Men might think they were crazy for virgins, but in her Hollywood experience what turned men on was a woman they knew had been used by other, bigger men. A way of getting in touch: channels.

"My friend of a friend says." He sucked smoke down twice and let a thin yellow-blue vapor bounce out with his words. "Don't tell me I was misinformed." She squeezed Arnie's muscleless bare arm, in amused salute to the Bogart echo. He mistook perhaps the message behind the squeeze, and announced, staring at the ceiling, "Speaking of dying, Alma, count me in. My doc says my cardio-vascular system is that of an eighty-year-old man. And my grandfathers on both sides lived to their nineties, back in Poland."

"There's a price I guess for leaving Poland."

"Helluva price for staying, too." To bring them back from these abysses he sighed and said, "You've done great, kid. I'm a hundred percent proud of you. A scruffy kid from Delaware without even a straight nose at first."

She toyed with the frizzy gray hair above his ear, a translucent ear with its own silky coating of colorless fuzz. "Then how come I'm not working?"

"That's the reason. You're a star. Your price has gone too high."

Thirty-five hundred a week had years ago become too little; there had been two renegotiations, and two idle threats of suspension, and at last Columbia had released her from the final year of her contract. She was on her own, in a game whose rules were changing fast, with an agent who couldn't even focus on getting his prick up.

"Then couldn't you lower my price?"

"Honey, it's not that simple. It wouldn't be fair to our other talent. We come down on you, it throws off the whole scale. The town's lousy with bargain hunters as it is."

"Arnie, I've got to keep working. They'll forget me."

"It takes a little time to forget. You're only twenty-eight. Listen, Alma. Here's what's happened. The studios turned out a lot of crap, but they hired, and those they hired they kept at work—grips, stunt guys, continuity girls, carpenters, everybody right up to the top. They brought a star along, and once you were up there they experimented a little, to see how far you could stretch and keep your audience. The audience showed up, week after week, Westerns, thrillers, A, B, they didn't much care. You know what the banks used to figure?—that *any* film, no matter how lousy, would make back sixty percent of its cost. So any picture you always had sixty-percent backing, no questions asked. All that's gone. Product's down from five hundred films a year to two hundred. The studios are relics. What's going to be left is deals—independents and agents. MCA had a third of Hollywood signed up already, and Stein and Wasserman have bought up contracts as the studios began cutting people loose. We got more talent than we can sell. We're supposed to do what the studios used to do. But those are big shoes. We don't have their plants. They don't have their chains. Actually, don't be surprised if MCA doesn't wind up buying a studio. We just formed Revue Productions, to make series for TV. Hey—how'd you like to be on TV again, till we find a package big enough for you? That *Strawberry Blonde*—you were overwhelming. You made Der Bingle look dead on his feet."

The image made Alma feel slightly guilty and sick. "I don't want to go back to TV. TV is for midgets who never quite made it here in Hollywood; I'd as soon go back to playing summer stock. Am I that washed-up? When did it happen? How, Arnie? I'm only twenty-eight!"

He sighed one last lung-deep plume toward the ceiling and put out his king-sized cigarette in an ashtray on the glass table at his side of the king-sized bed. "I gotta give up these things. O.K. Listen. Alma. We're working for you day and night. Be a little patient. Take a vacation, take some guitar lessons. Go to a dude ranch. You could lose an inch or two off your waist, I was noticing."

His words added to the irritation of her stirred-up, unsatisfied sexual desire. At least Matt always finished her off, with his tongue or hand if he had to. He was a European gentleman in that, even if his scripts did seem adolescent—espionage, science fiction, all-male technology wars. Arnie had closed his eyes. Staring up at the white, sparkle-plastered ceiling, Alma drew imaginary diagonals with her eyes from one corner to the one opposite, and then made an X, though the far corner was cut into by the walls of the luxurious bathroom, whose whirlpool tub was mauve and sunken and whose glass shelves Arnie had already loaded with a standing army of pill bottles. This lack of a fourth corner struck her as bad luck and gave her a shiver of dread. "I think it was a mistake to make a musical," she said. "It's made me harder to typecast."

"Well," Arnie said, his eyes unopening, "you couldn't keep playing rebellious kids forever. Be patient, babe." He sighed and got out of bed and wearily stood, looking more hunch-backed than ever. His useless liver-colored prick hung heavily below his white puff of pubic hair. Beyond his silken ear, turned abruptly blood-red by a stray sharp beam of afternoon sun, some flaw in the calm California day, as tightly sealed on the other side of the hotel window as a diorama, permitted a frond of a palm in the foreground feebly to lift, like the dying hand of an overacting extra in a scene of battlefield carnage.

It was no time to be patient. Already in the mirror the line of Alma's jaw was unclean and flesh was closing in on her eyes. In her anger with Arnie she got herself pregnant, by the script-writer boyfriend, Matt Lazlo, the Matt short for not Matthew but Matthias. His parents were Hungarians who had come to California in 1921, escaping from the anti-liberal, anti-Semitic excesses of the first years of the Horthy regency. His father, György Lazlo, a professor of music back in Szombathely, found work as a piano tuner and teacher in Pasadena. Matt had grown up as a California golden boy, drifting into the arts and scriptwriting. Alma's marriage to him did not last long—none of her early marriages did. Her husbands were envious and abusive, one trait leading to the other. Matt melted away more amiably, less graspingly, than the first, or the third, a rock instrumentalist for a group that never quite jelled. Alma had little patience with husbands and lovers—after such a child-hood dose of adoration, she was quick to decide that she wasn't being loved enough.

Her only child, a son, was born in April of 1959, the same year her career entered its second, triumphant, platinum-blonde phase with the (considering that this was still the Eisen-hower era) daring and somewhat feminist sex-comedy *Cream Cheese and Caviar*, opposite Paul Newman. Calling her solemn-faced infant Clark was not, in view of Gable's sudden death in the following year, auspicious. As Gable had lived by acting, so he died by it: it was said that doing his own stunts and putting up with the drug-addled Marilyn Monroe while shoot-ing *The Misfits* in desert heat killed him. But the Sixties were to be a good decade for death. Arnie Fineman died the same year, in his sleep at home in his Scarsdale mock-Tudor, and Ama the next, with Daniel Sifford and John Kennedy following in 1963.

Among the many roles that Alma undertook, motherhood proved one of the few for which she was clearly miscast. The boy grew from being a winning, timid, rosy-cheeked toddler to a rather sullen, bland loser, with little of the Wilmot sense of election or the Lazlos' continental flair. He had the small wary features and stocky build of his grandfather Teddy, whom he loved. He was never able, in the scrambling, structureless Hollywood scene, to find his niche. He had a noncoöperative streak. His mother's fame enabled him to get jobs in agencies and on independent production teams but some quarrel or missed appointment invariably balked his progress. There was more than the usual number of problems with girls, drugs, and wrecked cars. Alma was relieved, really, when in 1987 Clark, while working as a ski-lift operator for his great-uncle Jared in central Colorado, fell under the spell of a very religious mountain-man called Jesse Smith and joined his supposedly utopian commune, called the Temple of True and Actual Faith. A move so odd, she reasoned, must gratify the need to distinguish himself that any son of hers of course would have. Off her hands, and into God's. So be it. Good riddance.

iv. *Clark / Esau / Slick*

"There isn't an awful lot to say about me," Clark would say, making an acquaintance, to fend off the oppressive, overshadowing fact, which came out sooner or later, that he was Alma DeMott's son. Son and only child. "Oh, she did the best she could," would be his answer to the inevitable question. "I didn't see her much except on weekends. She was out of the house before I'd get up for school and a lot of times didn't get back till I was in bed. People don't realize how hard these poor stars work; the poor saps are *slaves.* Even weekends, there were things she had to do—special appearances, charity crap, interviews, trips to New York to be on some talk show. After her original agent died—he was a pretty laid-back guy from what I gather—she got this purely West Coast woman agent, Shirley Frugosi, who was *ruthless.* She had Mom hopping all the time—London, New York, Rome, wherever she could get up a little publicity hustle. And then, when she *was* home, Mom I mean, she had to keep going to these parties and stuff where it would be helpful to be seen, with a lot of these L.A. drunks and deadheads. Mom went, but you could never say she was a drinker. That was really the main thing that soured the marriage with Rex—Rex Brudnoy, the rock singer, you've probably never heard of him—that, more than the groupies and the fact that her career hit some kind of a wall in about 1969 and his never *did* get off the ground. In Hollywood you can maybe have one flop in a marriage but you can't have two."

Rex would have been out of bed for a couple of hours by the time the driver had dropped Clark off after school at Beverly Vista Elementary and they would have a game of Wiffle Ball with a plastic orange bat out on the flat part of the lawn, beside the concrete pool. Rex had played on his high-school team back in Texas before dropping out and becoming a musician and he could tell Clark just the kind of fungo he was going to hit to him: *This'll be a high one. Here comes a line drive. Start stretching, Superguy, I'm going for the fucking fences.* Rex called him Superguy as a joke based on Clark Kent's being Superman. Looking back, Clark supposed that Rex was the closest thing to a father he had had. He was wiry and athletic in his motions but not tall—no taller than Mom, really, when she had on heels. His beard was black and patchy and smelled of beer and an incenselike sweetness. He was generally stoned, Clark supposed now, but it never seemed to affect his Wiffle Ball skills. When, after he had let Clark make his five catches, his turn came to take the field, he could make the most amazing grabs, of screamers whistling at his feet or twisting pop-ups which more than once Rex snagged on the edge of the pool or beyond, falling in with a splash that lifted a great scatter of small green balls of water into the dry California air. He would come up out of the water displaying the perforated white ball daintily in his hand and his drenched beard all in little wet points around the neat white teeth of his casually triumphant grin and the hair on top of his head showing in his soaked strands that it was thinning; Rex was going bald and still his group, Brudnoy and His Boys, couldn't get onto the charts, couldn't get out of the rut of dates in dives in Santa Monica and Redondo Beach where after midnight the kids kept screaming and dancing themselves blind no matter what you did as long as the drummer kept up a beat. Though Mom's name had gotten them sessions at Decca and Columbia the records didn't take off, people said they sounded like the Beatles without Paul's wistful appeal or John's sardonic edge or the Stones without Mick's fury or the Monkees without the cuteness or Led Zeppelin without the balls. It was no life, Rex confided to Clark. Straining every night to pull out of himself the personal electricity to connect with a mob of kids stupid with pot was wasting him away, making him thin as a long-distance runner. When the group came around to the house in the afternoon sunlight you could see how small they were, how slight, however long their hair was and woolly their beards; in their purple tank tops and leather vests they were boys, kids looking for a break, kidding each other for Clark's benefit though he was just ten, their eyes sideways on him to check out his reactions, and talking to Mom politely as if she were an older woman, which she was, actually. She had been thirty-one when she married Rex and he twenty-five. Once, when about sixteen, Clark had asked his mother why she had married Rex and then stuck with him until 1970, by which time he had become a very pathetic drunk. She had given him a look, like *And who the hell are you?*, with those famous long eyebrows arched under her cap of carefully tousled platinum hair, and told him calmly, "Rex was all cock." Clark didn't think then or now that this was a suitable thing to say to a son, even a son growing up and accumulating some experience of his own. It shocked him, it stuck in his mind: he could still see her, her flat defiant calm way of saying it, implying, *Get off my case, kid*, the long red nails of her hand aligned around a Virginia Slim uncoiling blue smoke into the air next to her ear. The white edge of her ear protruded a bit through the bleached feathers of her hair. Cartoons of her always emphasized the cup ears but when you were with her they just seemed to fit her face, which could look homely or tired but never lacked life, a kind of hungriness he could never blame her for, it was so simple and innocent.

Clark had used LSD and PCP a certain amount before he began to scare himself and the trips had left him with some windows in his head open a crack, so these bright little movies sometimes ran without his asking. One was Mom saying Rex was all cock—a kind of slap in the face when he had just been trying to be friendly, on some basis or other, since for once they were in the house together. He must have been back, at that age, on school vacation from St. Andrew's, where Uncle Danny had gone for two years before Rutgers and the State Department and Mom for some sentimental snob get-even reason of her own insisted on sending her son, once Beverly Vista ended in the eighth grade. Clark had missed California like crazy and hated the raw Delaware winters and the general boggy climate, like your feet were always wet and your nose was always runny and stuffed-up. People said Delaware was beautiful but to Clark it looked like a crummy little cramped piece of the past, a historical set out in the weather too long, everything brick and tacky and weedy and industrial, there by the dreariest most oil-polluted river he ever saw. The East was full of these greasy black rivers not worth one sparkling gallon of the Hollywood Reservoir. He could see why Mom got out as soon as she could.

Another inner movie was Rex flopping into the pool in that dead-serious silent-comedy way, all to amuse a ten-year-old kid, while Clark cringed in shame at hitting so many twisting pop-ups; he was anxious and kept swinging too quick and just ticking a piece of the Wiffle Ball at the bottom. "Easy, *easy,*" the Texas athlete might say, "think *contact,* Superguy." But Rex never blamed him, just climbed out on the pool ladder, saying something like "He emerges triumphant" in a sonorous third-person voice-over, and took a tug on the Coors can on the glass table and went back to a crouching position on the carpetlike lawn in his sopping jeans and T-shirt, shivering slightly like an underfed dog, water streaming from the points of his beard and the long hair on his head, unaware of how his skull was starting to show through on top. Clark could even see in the little movie what was silk-screened onto Rex's T-shirt; the front said VIVA LA V.C. and the back had a picture of that spaceman in a polar-bear suit saluting beside that funny stiff flag they had planted on the moon only it was the North Vietnamese flag with its single yellow star on red and Ho Chi Minh's face was smiling out of the astronaut's helmet. Mom, too, wanted North Vietnam to win, which seemed strange to Clark, since America had been pretty good to her.

"Rex wasn't a bad guy, though onstage he went for this wild-man image. It wore him out, actually. We'd play Wiffle Ball or Frisbee in the yard and then come in and watch old movies on Channel Nine until my mother got back or he had to go off on a gig. They broke up when I was eleven. He got to be such a drunk he'd piss on the living-room sofa in his sleep. Mom told me the real problem was he couldn't take any more of being Mr. DeMott. Of course, there *was* no Mr. DeMott."

"Of course."

"DeMott was a made-up name," Clark needlessly explained, sensing that he was slightly lost and that this ski-bunny was several steps ahead of him. She was a plain little item looking like Sissy Spacek used to—fine straight strawberry-blonde hair falling around a slightly tense freckled face, with a nose taut like an animal's, so the nostrils showed—in a booth in the main café at the base of the mountain, called Golddigger's. The various après-ski groups had shuffled and reshuffled themselves around the long mahogany bar, and some had gone off to eat Mexican down the road and others had piled into a van to go try the new Thai place one valley over, and he had been left here with this girl, as if by plan. He couldn't figure it out but was letting it happen. She had the washed-out, rabbity, starry-eyed look of a pioneer woman, except for the vivid white band the goggles had left across her face, like the bathing-suit ghosts you see on actresses in a porn video. Clark supposed he would be sleeping with her tonight but wasn't excited about it yet. Women were a trap—like drugs, like booze, like fame—he had decided a while ago, about the time he left L.A. for these beautiful mountains. God's country, people called Colorado.

You had to nibble the bait, it was human nature, but you

tried to get out before the steel door fell. The lower half of her face held about a three-days' depth of freckles and tan, he estimated: out from the Coast or Denver or the East for a week of higher altitude. These bitches expected to get screwed. If they couldn't screw a ski instructor a chair-loader would have to do.

Great-Uncle Jared had promised him chair-loading would just be a transitional job, until a spot higher on the staff opened up. His mother used to take him and Rex to Squaw Valley over Christmas when this was still a fashionable thing film people did. Clark had loved the blank dazzle of the slopes, the sliding leaping motion of the sport, the ultra-violet blueness of the mountain sky. Mom would stick him in a kiddie class all day, but at best they went twice a year—again during the Washington Birthday week—and then, when he was around twelve, they stopped going altogether, maybe because Rex wasn't with them any more; he skied like a pro, until his morning nips and the beers at lunch made him lazy and reckless. So Clark's skiing never got good enough. Three times he had failed the test for instructor, with all these baby-faced twenty-year-old rube locals brought up on skis smirking. "If you dun't haff zuh reflexes by aitch sebenteen, the botty has too much to remember": this was the consolation offered by Bighorn's head ski instructor, Rolf Koenig, from Austria's Wild West, a crew-cut dimple-chinned Nazi type who even pushing fifty wedeled down the lift-line like a feather twirling to the floor.

Clark met resistance everywhere in the hierarchy of Bighorn, as Jared and his Denver partners had named the resort back in the Forties, when rope tows and single chairs and bear-claw bindings were the state of the art. The founder's great-nephew didn't like taking orders and wasn't much good at giving them. He thought the lodge cafeteria should deëmphasize artery-pluggers like cheeseburgers, French fries, and glazed doughnuts; he thought that somebody would be killed one of these bright sunny days if Art Marling, the head of Patrol, continued to open expert trails when the spring melt was exposing rocks and stumps. "Experts don't hit rocks," Art told Clark.

"Yeah, but a lot of non-experts go down anywhere where the chain isn't across. You see these teenage girls that can hardly snowplow. Their boyfriends talk them into it."

"That's their problem, then. The trails are clearly posted," Art told him, giving him that dead-eye, do-it-my-way stare that always made Clark see red, though he usually cringed and backed off. His worst fight at Bighorn had been with Johnny Ponyfoot, the middle-aged full-blooded Ute who was operating, that particular Sunday, the new triple chair up to Silver Saddle, the halfway point. The trails down were broad and gentle but to keep the weekend crowds moving the lift had been so speeded up the chairs were slinging around the pulley wheel and chopping into the backs of the skiers like machetes. The skier in the middle, with no sidebar to grab on to, was especially threatened; three times that morning some little kid failed to get his ass in his slick Gore-Tex jumpsuit up on the seat in time and went sprawling in the slush here at the base, headfirst in the thousand bucks' worth of flashy equipment his parents had poured all over him like Technicolor paint. At the speed the chairs were moving, a snagged skipole could break an arm, crossed skis a leg. It was aggravating work in any case, the trios of skiers nosing up to the mark half-hidden in the slush waiting for you to catch the chair and ease it under their butts like a bedpan—it got to your back, and your nerves, the way the chairs kept coming, *blang, blang, whoosh, blang, blang, whoosh.* The third time he had to pick up a sprawled little guy and settle him, red-faced and teary, on a stopped chair, he signalled *ease off* to Johnny, and was rewarded with an acceleration that had him grunting and the skiers giggling as they hurried up to the mark a second ahead of the chair. Clark saw red and put a hand up to halt the line and planted himself in front of the next chair, daring it to knock him down. The cable was braked, bouncing and swinging chairs halfway up the mountain. Clark stepped to the shed and opened the door and told Johnny, "Hey, ease it down a notch, for Chrissake. You're going to kill somebody."

"Haven't yet. Not in twenty years. Manufacturer made the lift for this speed. Get your ass back loading those chairs."

"Ease it down, or I'm reporting you."

"I'm reporting *you,* DeMott."

"That's not my name, Tonto. I'm walking."

The line was building up, and everybody, all these rosy-faced kids in their goggles and headbands, was listening. Clark in his stomach felt like backing down but his body kept stomping away, sloshing his wet-toed cowboy boots through the mashed potatoes here around the ski racks, toward the lodge. As he walked away he could hear Johnny Ponyfoot's phone ringing—the operator at the top asking what the problem was—and he knew that by the time he got into the lodge management would have heard the Indian's side of the story. It made him weary. His back ached, his toes felt cold and wet. Let these rube locals have their fucking mountain. Except where else did he have to go? The California he knew and loved had been for boys, a theme park for young people.

He asked Sissy Spacek, "Want something to eat, you? I'm getting squashed."

"My name's Hannah. Maybe you didn't hear it the first time."

"Hey, you, don't start scolding. How'd I know you and me were going to wind up on a desert island? Suddenly everybody else is elsewhere. You can get a steak and fries here, or there's Mexican down the road. New Age Vegetarian closes at nine, we've missed it."

"Or we could get a bite back at my place."

"Your place? Just like that?" They usually didn't come this easy any more, not since AIDS.

"It's a little more than half an hour from here, over in Lower Branch."

"Lower Branch. That's a place?"

"It was a fair-sized town, once."

"One of those. Mined out."

"It's just over the line, in Burr County."

"Jesus," he said, not knowing why.

She told him, "All Colorado was called Jefferson once, you know that? The Territory of Jefferson. The miners got together and named it. But Congress said it was illegal, somehow. This was just before the Sand Creek Massacre." She was a little schoolteacher, was what she was. Clark had been sitting here getting zoned out on margaritas and she'd been sipping away at a brandy glass full of soda water with a splash of cranberry. She'd be sober in bed and up for a great time and he'd be a flop. Ten years ago he wouldn't have known that he could flop at this, too. He thought every time you scored was a success. But now it had become just one more of the things he was mediocre at.

"Always seemed funny to me," he admitted, "this whole big territory he purchased and not a state in it named after him. Andrew Jefferson. No. Wait. Thomas. Right?"

Uncle Jared had been puzzled and philosophical over Clark's latest scrap, up there in his corner office high in the lodge like a captain's bridge, gazing out through plate glass at the white slope served by the triple chair, a profitable glaring expanse dotted by little swaying figures. They trickled down and like silver dollars out of a slot machine got fed right back in. This slope had been the beginning, back in the Forties—a simple T-bar, and then a single chair, before the big double chairs were run up on giant tubular stanchions to within spitting distance of Bighorn's needlelike summit. The runs down had such daredevil names as Smoking Gun, Shootout, Aces 'n' Eights. Jared's useless withered arm was safety-pinned in its flannel sleeve to the body of his fancy shirt, the white suede yoke set off by a waxy black string tie with a miniature ivory steer's-skull pull. His old eyes, their color filmed over, picked up an icy green glint when he looked out at the snowfield—his sun-withered profile had an emerald chip in it. He turned and said, not unamiably, "Clark, you remind me of my little brother. Always fearful. Fearful of this, fearful of that. Feeling sorry for everybody, himself foremost. Why the fuck bother, was my way of looking at it. Worst case in any set of circumstances is that you die, and there's some good to be said for that, when you get to be my age. So what went wrong this time?"

"Sir, Johnny Ponytail was operating that lift at an unsafe speed. I had three small children, one of them a girl, knocked down trying to mount a chair."

"Your job was to see that didn't happen. Johnny's job was to move 'em along. Johnny does his job because he knows not everybody in these parts likes to hire a Ute, though the government says we should. They're not considered dependable. I said, 'Let's see about that.' Johnny's been with me a good while. You have any problem with his being Native American?"

"Absolutely none."

"They were here first. Don't forget it. They sure as shit don't."

"No, sir. But—"

The shrivelled old man eased his weight off the desk, where he had perched on one buttock to gaze out at his mountain, like a cook easing a heavy pot off a hot stove. "Do you still hear from Teddy much? How in hell *is* your granddaddy?"

"He doesn't write me as often as he used to, but I would have heard from Mom of any change. He and Grandmom keep busy driving each other to the doctor and puttering in the greenhouse. One of Esther's boys, Ira, really runs it now."

"I tried to get Ted to come join me in New York—make him a junior partner in McMullen. Old Jimmy had us where we were cleaning up, the suckers were forcing money down our throats. My fool kid brother couldn't take the pace and ran himself home to Emily."

"I guess we can't all be ambitious," Clark said. Was this to be his punishment, hearing these old facts, worn smooth with the telling, told once again?

"I always liked Emily. Good-looking woman, never mind the leg. Your mother's the one with the spunk, though."

"She's amazing," Clark lamely contributed, while Jared, careful of the useless arm, eased the stiff weight of his skinny body into his old-fashioned wooden-armed swivel chair. "Even now," Clark thought to add. "I talked to her on the phone a couple weeks ago and she's all excited about marrying her new boyfriend, this Boston banker brought in to help run Columbia, now that Coca-Cola owns it. He's married to somebody else, but that wouldn't worry Mom."

Jared mused, "Never could quite figure out where she got it. My dad didn't have it, I know that. Born licked. Left us all in the lurch." The old man's eyes were looking at something Clark would never see, a vanished scene—a table, a room, frame windows giving on an uphill cobbled street holding trolley tracks—that took away the glint. He became impatient. "Son, you're here on her say-so," he told Clark. "Don't think you're better than our other hands."

"I don't, sir, it's just—"

"If your damn granddaddy hadn't been such a sissy he'd of gotten a piece of Bighorn, most likely. It was all Jim McMullen had to keep me quiet, when '29 called all the margin players in, those we'd let get way over their heads. He thought it was worthless. He'd been stuck with it himself, as security. Eight thousand acres of emptiness, Lucille—that was my bride back then—"

"I know. My grandparents have shown me photographs."

"Eight thousand acres of emptiness, she called it, and gave me a horselaugh. It didn't help our marriage."

"No, I guess it wouldn't."

"But I took it. The East was played out for me. There was silver and gold traces, still, in the old tunnels. The Utes who worked the old girl before were still around, or their kids were. Two dollars a day for crawling on your belly with a candle on your head didn't look so bad then. Then the war made the copper worthwhile again. Best damn thing ever happened to this country, that war. God bless war, that's what I've learned to think. Stirs it up, the whole kaboodle. The first one took something out of me, but the second put it back. We even reworked the old tailings, with the improved methods. Henderson still had the big smelting plant down on Cinder Creek, so the transport was economical; the rails had been laid. You have to smelt the copper-pyrite ores; copper oxide needs the leaching. Molybdenum was the coming thing, after the war. It used to be just a by-product; they dumped it out with the gengue. But a couple smart chums of mine from Denver saw there was going to be a market for recreation, and we gave the old girl's guts a rest. There's more good in her, though, for them that would have the desire and the new equipment. It was a slow start, with the skiing. To the ranchers and apple farmers around here, snow had never been anything but a nuisance. Before the jets, you couldn't expect to see Easterners. Some winters the snow wouldn't show up, and others too much did. Before Sno-Cats came along in the Sixties there wasn't any what you'd call grooming. We'd take a big two-man cross-cut saw out and saw off the tops of the moguls. Honest to God, saw 'em off like tree stumps! You could say it's been one helluva ride. Ninety-three last January, and I can still remember my own name. Can even get it up on occasion, when I'm having a naughty dream." He swivelled challengingly, with a brutal squeak of the rusty spring. "So you're asking yourself why is he running off at the mouth? You're kin, Clark. Kin's strange stuff. Sticks to you for no good reason. I haven't seen my brother since our mother's funeral but if he walked through that door I'd do a jig standing on my head, that's how pleased I'd be to see him. We were Paterson boys together, for a while. Needed to do things his own way, and that was just like me. That was the Wilmot style." Gingerly Jared moved his butt forward to the edge of his chair, to give Clark the benefit of a filmed-over, colorless stare. His good hand on his knee was like tobacco leaves wrapped around chicken bones. It had a tremor the bad hand didn't. "But, young fella, you got no right to disrupt an old man's show. Learn to take orders, or it's back to your momma, or whatever other broad'll give you a bunk."

During this monologue Clark had been fascinated by the old man's boots: they were cream-colored with a swirling wealth of stitching and leafy tooled relief, and heels higher than an inch, and inflexibly pointy toes: a young buck's boots, with red-plaid polyester pants tucked into their raked, scallop-cut tops.

"Now, in case I croak tomorrow, to nobody's great surprise," Jared had said, "here's a piece of wisdom I'm passing on: money gives, and pussy takes. You need to get your act together, son. You need a trade." That had been the word from Great-Uncle Jared.

He and the girl—Hannah, Sissy, he struggled to remember—stepped out into the parking lot. The packed and rutted snow underfoot squeaked. The mounds plowed up around the lot were fifteen feet high, though spring was in the air and there had been considerable melt on the south slopes. She led him to her pickup, a Ford Ranger a couple of years old, with those square double headlights and plenty of slanted mud streaks on the underside. His own little '84 Nissan Maxima V6 waited a few steps away, calling him back to his two rooms in the lodge near the lifts, back to his bed, his Michael Crichton paperback, his sleep. Up at six-thirty tomorrow. "Maybe we should put this off to another time," he suggested. "You drive home, and I'll get a burger down at the Wendy's."

"Don't be so chicken," she said, smiling and flaring her eyes wide, so the whites gleamed, there at the side of her muddy Ranger. "I won't bite."

Pussy takes. Clark actually nodded off for ten minutes when the heater warmed up the cramped little cab. The side of his skull bounced on the window frame; he folded his ski cap to make a pillow. There was a chill deep through him that was hard to shake but why would he be scared of this little freckled schoolteacher type? She drove mostly downhill from Bighorn, south from the lights, neon and otherwise, of the shops and restaurants and ski boutiques and sharp-gabled condos that had accumulated at the foot of the mountain, along the two-lane highway. The lights dwindled to a scattering of windows back from the road, tucked up in the forest like faint Christmas lights. There was a sudden lonely brightness around a shacky café advertising in fading letters TOPLESS ENTERTAINMENT NITELY. They passed on the left the huge cement-colored ghost of the Henderson copper-smelting plant, its steel-roofed sheds and diagonal feeder chutes and bucket belts crouched in an encirclement of slag heaps like some great crusty engine of war disabled during battle. The ruin was still owned by a company somewhere; the mineral war could be resumed. The cab radio murmured the news of early March 1987: bodies of those drowned and trapped were still being pulled from the British ferry *Herald of Free Enterprise,* which capsized on its way from Zeebrugge, Belgium. In Bergenfield, New Jersey, four teenagers were found dead in an exhaust-filled garage, apparent suicides; three were high-school dropouts and the fourth had been recently suspended from classes. In Rome, the Vatican condemned test-tube babies and artificial insemination, while in Washington, the reaction to President Reagan's claim of "full responsibility" in the Iran-contra affair has remained mild. Japanese investors, it has been calculated, last year bought up to six billion dollars' worth of American real estate.

After some miles this mysterious girl left the highway for a narrower road that went uphill for a while, through close masses of pines and firs, and then turned down again. Clark felt these motions in his leaden, dozing body. He was travelling miles, way out on a limb. Once, when his eyes fluttered open, he saw far below, as if he were in an airplane, a nameless vast lake, flat as a mirror, giving back to the moon its own cold light. The moon picked out the slender pale trunks of the aspens and birches at the edge of the sloping dark forests of featureless evergreens. Clark seldom came in this southwesterly direction; his trips when he took them were north to

Route 70, which went to Denver one way and back to California, through Utah and Nevada, the other.

Hannah woke him by braking to a stop and taking a turn at a cluster of weathered signs one of which said LOWER BRANCH. The forest—a national park, perhaps—had fallen away; they were in high ranch country now, miles of rolling open grassland interspersed with wooded clumps, and not a light anywhere but the diffused, sickly moonlight. His stomach ached; he could taste all the salt from the margaritas and his septum stung from the two lines of coke he had done on a toilet seat in the Golddigger's men's room. The Ranger turned left onto a dirt road and bumped and rattled for a half-mile, at just the speed that made the most of the corrugations. This bitch had misled him: he thought from sizing her up that she had a rental, probably with a girlfriend or two, not far from Bighorn. Well, by the time they got to the sex he wouldn't owe her much consideration. Except he needed to get back and she was his ride. They came to what looked like a fence of new barbed wire, its points glittering in the headlight beams. There was a gate she had to get out to unlatch, giving him time to study a sign that said in smallish grouted silver-filled letters, LOWER BRANCH—TEMPLE ENTRANCE.

"Temple?" he said, clearing the sleep from his throat. "What kind of place is this?"

"We call it a temple. It's where I live," Hannah said. Like Sissy Spacek, she did not have much of a profile, at least in the dark of the cab. Her voice had changed, dropping into a sort of purr that went with the flat cat's nose.

"You own a ranch?"

"I share a ranch."

"Who with?"

"Spiritual brothers and sisters," she said. "We all contribute, work and money if we have it. You could say it's a commune."

Trapped. This was beginning to sound freaky. He didn't like the hypnotized sound of her voice or the institutional look of this place. Onto an old-fashioned clapboarded two-story farmhouse, with a front veranda and gingerbread trim along the eaves and porch pillars, had been added wings of utilitarian wooden boxes, some shingled and some finished in vertical boards and two-inch battens, like chicken sheds. As the Ranger parked and its headlights wheeled, more additions and outbuildings than Clark could mentally organize were pulled from the darkness. His first thought was that this would go up like bales of hay if it ever started to burn. Perhaps the thought was suggested by the live glow at the windows, the secretive orange illumination of kerosene lamps rather than electricity.

The air outside the heated pickup cab had a different scent from Bighorn, whose aroma to him was of engine grease and stale beer and the boot-battered redwood decks baking in the lunchtime sun. Here there was, layered into the night, woodsmoke, and animal dung, and hay. Somewhere in the wilderness of buildings a sheep bleated, and several others blindly answered with their stammering *maa-aa.* The wide porch was stacked with split wood. An unpainted storm shelter boxed in the front door, which seemed unusually narrow; its faded blue paint was webbed with crackle and its two gaunt windows were frosted in one of those swirling leafy patterns, like uncoiling ferns, that were tooled onto Western boots. An old-fashioned bell on a rusty spiral spring jangled as they pushed the door open. A narrow country staircase faced them across a small entrance hall; beside the blunt-tipped newell post a small cherrywood sewing table held a pewter vase holding a dozen or so stalks of last summer's wheat beneath a cross of two sticks tied together with whippings of coarse brown string. The cross gave Clark the creeps but at least the symbol suggested that no outright harm would come to him. In a long parlor to the right, a fieldstone fireplace threw out heat and a dancing ruddy light into a ring of chairs and shadows. Some of the shadows rose up and came toward them. More or less his and Hannah's age, with names like Tom and Jim and Polly and Mercy and Luke, they shamblingly stood and said "Welcome" or "Howdy" or "Peace, brother." Depending on where they stood, they had pinpricks of flame in their eyes. They had hard hands and by and large gave a country person's rather lame handshake. Some seemed weathered and stringy ranchers, and others as professionally amorphous as Clark himself. "And this is Jesse," Hannah said, in that same smug betranced voice in which she had mentioned spiritual brothers and sisters.

"Well now isn't this a treat," Jesse said, giving Clark a firm handshake with one hand and gripping his elbow with the other as if to steer him somewhere. He had been talking to the little circle around the fireplace; these others went so quiet at the sound of Jesse's voice that it sounded louder than it was. He was a few inches taller than Clark and maybe ten years older, with a wide mountain-man's chest and a level, challenging gaze. His hair on the top of his head had gone the way Rex Brudnoy's was going nearly twenty years ago. What hair Jesse did have fell in a dirty-looking grayish fringe to the back of his collar. He wore a camel-colored flannel shirt over a black turtleneck, tucked into stovepipe blue jeans baggy at the knees but tight as spandex at the hips. He had forgotten to shave about three days ago; his eyes looked rubbed red and pink, perhaps from staring at the fire. He spoke carefully, as if reading a blurred text, in a voice husky from overuse but deep and confident and gently onrolling. "Sister Hannah always brings us congenial visitors. She has a fine eye for those to whom our company might prove a blessing."

"He's starving," Hannah said at Clark's side. Her ordinary female voice sounded light and nimble, after the echo-chamber intonations of the other. "He wanted to go to a restaurant but I promised him food here."

"Food and fellowship are among the Lord's weapons. 'Thou preparest a table before me, in the presence of mine enemies.' Dear wife, you go see what meal you can scrounge up in the kitchen, while I sit here a moment with our new friend."

If Clark had had a car of his own he would have bolted for the door. He got very restive when people appeared to be taking him over. Still, this seemed a setup he could outsmart, if necessary. The others had resumed their seats by the fire, those who were not saying good night and leaving the room. There were children among them, two or three little ones fast asleep and carried on a parent's shoulder, their faces flushed and heads helplessly lolling. The frame farmhouse, with its porcelain doorknobs and cracking plaster walls, dated from somewhere around the turn of the century. The furniture in its long low-ceilinged parlor was either homemade or bought cheap; plastic bucket chairs as if from an airport waiting room were mixed with the bentwood and cane lightweight stuff fashionable in the Seventies. The old velvet sofa in front of the fire looked as if a family of dogs had used it for years as a bed; striped Indian blankets covered the most worn spots. To Clark it all suggested some neighborhood drop-in center or halfway house, held together by charity and grudging civic grants. Bright crude acrylics of a staring Jesus and his crowd of stick-stiff disciples and torturers on the plaster walls repelled his glance. With that gentle steering touch on his elbow, his host tugged him toward a corner where two old green-painted kitchen chairs stood near a half-empty bookcase holding a few rows of black-backed books—Bibles, hymnals—and several stacks of photocopied pamphlets, the covers busy with hand-drawn insignia: flames, eyes, rays, pyramids, stairs, stars. His host took the chair in sounder condition, leaving Clark with one whose broken spindles did not permit him to lean his weight back. "Wife?" Clark said.

"In a manner of speaking. We are all spouses in Christ here at the Temple. Tell me about you, son."

"There isn't an awful lot to say about me."

"Now, if that were really true, and not just a way to fend me off, you'd be the first, the first soul in the history of the universe without a powerful story to tell, the first soul that God left totally empty of eternal possibilities." His rubbed-looking eyes in the flickering half-light had yellow glints; he had a way of staring for a frozen second, as if what he was seeing had to be translated out of a foreign language. For all the unearthly confidence of his husky, practiced voice, Jesse had the air of a man who had suffered, with more to come.

Clark told him, "My mother was—*is,* she would want me to say—a movie star. I'm sure you've heard of her—Alma DeMott." As he said it he realized the name didn't have the ring it used to, as it had sounded all through his childhood, deafening him in a certain way.

Jesse smiled, but smiling didn't come naturally to him. A reluctant slant slit revealed gray glimmers of rather ragged teeth, one of them capped in gold. "My friend, I fear I come up empty on that particular name. I was never much of one for movies. My mother and my stepdad were old-fashioned pious people, Seventh-Day Adventists, and they regarded such entertainments as issuing straight from the pit of Hell. We moved around from one ranch to another, back up there"—his thumb jerked over his shoulder, toward what Clark took to be the mountains—"hiring out to whoever would have us. My stepdad was right handy. He could mend most anything with his hands, and wasn't slow to use his fists, either. Before you knew what you'd done wrong you'd see sparks and be lying stretched out on the dirt. At the age of sixteen, however, I strayed from the rigor of parental discipline, and lived apart, like a young wild dog, until King Gog, as I call our United States government, drafted me into military service, which was still obligatory at that time, since we were fighting the Communist foe overseas in Vietnam. Now, the point of my story is that King Gog, no doubt to distract us poor boy-sinners from the dreadful deeds we were being asked to perpetrate, made motion pictures mightily available to us, right there on the base as well as in the pleasure-district of the city nearby. One of those motion pictures, if I recall exactly, portrayed the seduction of an innocent college graduate by a whorish friend of his mother's, in a variety of luxurious hotel rooms. Another, I do believe, bodied forth the violent crime rampage of a pair of young lovers, the young man of whom was impotent except when he had just committed murder. Did your blessed mother perform in either of these?"

"No. They sound like *The Graduate* and *Bonnie and Clyde.* Terrific pictures, actually."

"These patterns of damnation, I was astounded to behold, were set forth with every sign of endorsement by the film-makers. The color was overwhelmingly glorious, and such a wealth of attention was paid to every detail that you thought you were looking upon reality itself. The Devil's work is lovingly done—give Satan his due. The harlots paraded in shining raiment, purple and scarlet decked with gold and pearls, and it all went down as smooth as ice cream, right down to almighty death itself. That couple up there on the screen died in a hail of bullets but you could get up and leave your seat a whole man. The ways of damnation are glamorous. Lucifer was the fairest of the angels. But God scraped him off the edge of Heaven like a little piece of goat shit."

Clark said, to keep the talk impersonal, "Sixty-seven was a real turnaround year for movies, actually. They got back greatness. Did you happen to see *Blow-Up?* Or *In the Heat of the Night?* I was eight or so, but Mom took me all the time; it was the one thing we did together. The picture that wowed me most, I guess, was *You Only Live Twice*—the best James Bond picture ever made, in my opinion."

"See now, Clark, there *is* something to say about you—you have gorged yourself on ephemeral trash. As far as garbage goes, you remember every empty can, every orange peel."

"Please, don't call it trash. We lived and breathed movies around the house. If she was between projects we'd go out to a matinee and pig out on popcorn and Raisinets. Some afternoons we saw two in a row. You would have thought, it being her business, she would have been critical, but she wasn't—she liked most anything."

"Your mother was a good mother?"

"Like I tell people, she tried. She had a lot of natural fun in hèr. But she was usually working, or else worrying about why she wasn't working, poring over these crappy scripts Shirley kept bringing her. Shirley—that's her agent, Shirley Frugosi—would have had her doing guest spots on *Laugh-In,* or a dumb television series like Doris Day got talked into, *any*thing to generate Shirley's twenty percent. Yeah, I guess you could say her career took the best part of her energy. Being a star makes you very narcissistic."

He looked at the high-ranch messiah, to see if he understood. Jesse nodded. In 1987 everybody knew about narcissism.

Yet something urged Clark to make himself very clear to this man. He became, in part, his mother. "You know, like, 'Should I get another facelift?' The more you get, you know, the faster they wear out. The skin stops moving like real skin does." He pushed his own skin back toward the points of his jaw, to dramatize. "Or 'Should I get another husband? Would a young stud juice me up enough to keep me in romantic leads for a couple more years?' She used to complain, without the studios the way they used to be, nobody took *care* of you, and always there were these kids coming on, out of college film studies and all the film-acting schools. There didn't use to be such things. To these movie brats, you were already history." He wondered if it was the two lines of coke making him talk so much.

"Clark, I can hear in how you tell this that you loved your mother very much. You suffered along with her, though you were helpless."

"Did I? I didn't think I did. She was so famous my only way out from under her was to poke fun of her, really. She had these Fifties mannerisms—arching her eyebrows, pushing her mouth at the lens—that were easy to poke fun of. I used to do an imitation of her at school. People thought it was hilarious, coming from me. Hey—could I get a beer, do you think? My mouth's drying out."

"Friend, we keep no alcohol here at the Temple. We consider each body a temple in miniature."

"Not even a beer? I was reading the other day how some scientific studies prove that it's actually good for you—"

Jesse had touched Clark on the upper arm; now he touched him on the knee. "Scientific studies show, brother, that alcohol and tobacco impair sexual potency, and this impairs a man's bounden duty to disseminate his seed, as enjoined in Genesis, Leviticus, and the Song of Songs. In the Song of Solomon, six eight, we read, 'There are threescore queens, and fourscore concubines, and virgins without number.' " The gold tooth winked; the tawny eyes flared; the hand lightly resting on Clark's knee squeezed. There was a humidity in Jesse's close presence, and a restriction in Clark's throat, a kind of tight internal collar, though he prided himself on not, whatever his failings, having inherited his mother's ridiculous tendency to stutter. "Keep that temple pure," Jesse told him, "and it will *func*tion."

"Yeah, well. What was I going to say? Something. I don't want to bore you."

"You will never find Jesse bored. Never by a recital of the truth. Weary, yes, and sore-laden with the sorrows of mankind, but never bored."

Clark had these irritating memory blanks, more and more of them lately; but then the break in the film was mended and the inner movie resumed. Loving his mother. Basingstoke, and Locust Street, and the greenhouse. "Yes. I don't know what all I felt about my mother, but I loved her parents. I was sent to prep school near this town in Delaware where they lived and got to know them. They'd tell me all these stories about Mom when she was a little girl, and I would feel jealous, I guess. She had been a celebrity to them right from the start. They had given her all this *attention.*"

"Attention is a good thing. Awareness of the Lord's love is a better. 'I love them that love me; and those that seek me early shall find me.' Proverbs, eight seventeen."

"Yeah. You know, Mom never mentioned God to me. One of the few times my grandparents came out to the West Coast, she had me baptized at the Presbyterian church over on North Gower in Hollywood, but that was as far as religion went. Her father was kind of notorious in the family for never going to church."

"False witness is more to be deplored than no witness." Jesse shifted weight in his chair, making the rungs squawk. He had long arms and a wide bald skull. Clark could see him as a hunter, narrowing one lion-yellow eye behind a gunsight. Jesse's voice softened, explaining. "Your mother perhaps was *jealous* of her God and did not wish to share Him with the world, even with her son."

"Well, that seems a bit—"

"God has a relation with us all, friend or foe, atheist or otherwise. God had brought your mother a long way, it must have seemed to her, by allowing her a role in these whorish entertainments, and she did not wish to imperil their pact by breathing a word of it. What she called God was Satan, and I tell you she did not wish to share her indecent joy in Satan, her copulations and blasphemy."

Clark had to laugh at that. Maybe Satan was all cock. He found himself strengthened by this conversation. It was shaking up his head and settling the pieces in a new order. This guy's head did even crazier riffs than his did. "Hey, if I may ask, who are you, you know, to tell me about my own mother? You've never even seen one of her movies. You sure about that, by the way? *Cream Cheese and Caviar,* with Paul Newman? Or the one after that, that I thought was even sexier, *A Stitch in Time,* about the model business, with Steve McQueen as this blocked, pansyish couturier—it's the one time they let McQueen show what he could do being *funny.*"

"I am the only person you will meet," said Jesse Smith, "who is not interested in your mother. I am interested in *you.*"

"You mentioned those '67 movies; maybe in '68 you saw *Baby Breaks the Bank,* in which she played a mother for the first time? It *killed* her, to be bumped up a generation. 'Next thing,' she told me, 'I'll be doing Bette Davis's sister!' When I saw her on the screen I was fascinated, she was such a better mother up there than she was with me—so warm and perky and really on top of the kid and his needs. She was *great.*"

"In 1968," Jesse told him, shutting those pained red-rimmed eyes, "I was not viewing motion pictures. Courtesy of King Gog, I was in Vietnam, as a PFC, humping the paddies."

"Oh, 'Nam! You were *there?* That's cool. Was it as wild as they had it in *Apocalypse Now,* all that rock music blaring and explosions all over the place?"

"There was music," the mountain-man said heavily. "There was drugs. There was fear, and there were wounds. We prayed to be wounded, and thus sent Stateside. We had the phrase, 'a million-dollar wound.' I cannot say that God pulled me to His bosom in Vietnam. I cannot say, Clark, that I took consolation in prayer. I was not there to draw close to the Lord. That was not the Lord's purpose at that point in time. I was there to witness evil. I was there to descend into Hell."

"My uncle's in the CIA, but of course he never admits it. It's part of their code."

Hannah reappeared, still in her scarlet bell-bottom jumpsuit and après-ski boots in a purplish fake fur. Her eyes went wide as she approached Jesse; she was in awe of him, and hesitated to approach closer. "I don't mean to interrupt—"

Jesse grunted and pushed his weight up from the chair onto his spindly legs in their tight jeans. On his feet he wore not cowboy boots but wool socks and those sandals that have little curved sides and a German name. What was it? Jesse put a heavy hand on Clark's shoulder and told him, "My brother, you have unholy antecedents. And yet, 'The stone which the builders refused is become the head stone of the corner.' Psalm one eighteen, also found in Matthew twenty-one. I sincerely love you. You have qualities yet to be tapped. I think you will learn to love me. Now here is Hannah, announcing her meal; go, eat."

In the primitive whitewashed kitchen, with its black woodstove and dangling iron and copper pots, she fed him a bowl of thick lentil soup, and a chunk of dense home-baked bread, and a dish of sliced pears in a peppery syrup; she said the pears came from an old orchard on the property and had been put up as preserves by the women of the Temple.

"How the hell many of you are there?" Clark asked. The talk with Jesse, so hypnotic and lulling while it had been going on, had left him irritable. All he wanted was to get back to Bighorn and grab some sleep. He had to be manning the double chair to the top when it opened at seven-fifteen for the hotshots who liked to ski the night's fresh powder. He remembered a few sparklike flakes of snow fluttering in the truck headlights. Above their heads on a high kitchen shelf an old hand-wound wooden-cased clock with a ruddy moon on its face dropped—*plock, plock*—hollow drops of time into his echoing skull.

"Close to forty, counting the children. People come and go, there are no rules. Jesse doesn't believe in controlling people that way."

"In what way *does* he believe in controlling them?"

"With love and instruction," she answered, her catechetical promptness amusing her, too, denting the corners of her dry, Sissy Spacek lips.

"That works?"

"Yes, it does, usually."

"How much of this skiing do you do? Isn't that sort of extra-curricular?"

The synthetic fabric of her jumpsuit faintly crackled and hissed as she moved about, serving him. "We move in the world," she said, "until the Reckoning. A number of the men hold jobs outside. One is an accountant, another a carpenter who hires out. The Temple runs a sheep ranch, and two of the women make pottery we sell. There are expenses: we have farm vehicles, and central heating in the main building, and a generator that runs on diesel fuel. We try to live as the lilies, but we must eat, we must wear clothes. We're not angels, Clark; we're human beings waiting to be saved."

"At the Reckoning."

"Yes. Then."

"When is it coming?"

"Sooner than we think. Jesse is always studying Revelation, to find the exact date."

There was a buzzing expectancy in his head like the static that speckles a television screen before the video clicks in. "You don't think your pal Jesse might be pretty thoroughly crazy?"

Perhaps the look she gave him was only mock-reproachful. "How can you say that, after talking with him for all that time? Some of our guests he hardly says a word to—he takes quite a dislike to them. He didn't to you."

"I did most of the talking."

"Yes, darling. He draws a person out. You want to tell him everything. I told him I missed skiing, and he said, 'Go, do it.' Jesse believes," she said, keeping her face very straight, "in doing it."

"I was filling him in on old movies. Why are you calling me 'darling'?"

She moved back and forth, clearing the long plank table at whose end he had eaten, wiping his place clean with a blue sponge. "May one not call a husband 'darling'?" she asked. "Would you like a cup of herbal tea?"

"I'm not your husband. Jesus. Let's skip the herbal tea. All I want is to get back to Bighorn."

"I'll drive you back to Bighorn if that's what you really want." The sponge stopped describing its quick circles, and she swept breadcrumbs into her palm, cupped at the edge of the table. The sink was a long steel trough; above it, shelves held stacks of thick plates and square-bottomed cups. The same crude artist who had done the bright Crucifixion scenes in the living room had done a Last Supper in here, with the thirteen pairs of bare feet lined up underneath the tablecloth like a row of pink buns in a pastry shop. Dry snow ticked at the black windows.

"You can't do that. It would take you two hours."

"An hour and a half if the snow doesn't get worse."

"Isn't there any place here I could sack out?"

"Of course. My room."

"How would your local spaceman feel about that?"

"Spaceman?"

"Your guru. Jesse."

"He would approve. We try not to be selfish here. Sleeping with you is a way of sleeping with him."

"Oh, great."

"Of being his perfect bride."

"You're his bride."

"All the women at the Temple are his brides."

"The old skunk. He's fucked all of you? Whose children were those I saw?"

Hannah's face, still bent close above his, reddened in color as she said, "Not mine. None of them. Yet." Then, solemnly, she did a thing he really liked, a dash of mischief from the normal world: she dumped the breadcrumbs her cupped hand held onto his head, into his hair. Clark laughed, jumped up, scrubbed his head so the crumbs flew from it. Standing, he felt her tense body, slight and muscular, as a challenge, a physical unit equal to his.

"Your skiing," he said. "Is it skiing, or fishing?"

"I do love to ski. I was a junior champion, back in Minnesota. The fishing, sometimes you get lucky. It has to be the right fish."

"What's right about me?"

"You acted lost. Talking to you, I got the feeling you weren't going anywhere but weren't content with that. You got drunk but didn't like it in yourself. You're ambitious, just like your wonderful mom. Let's go to bed. You don't have to make love to me."

"Thanks a bunch. That was the one thing that was still making sense."

Taking up a four-battery flashlight resting with others on a shelf, Hannah led him through a panelled white-painted door beyond the sink, through a storeroom stocked with cans and boxes of food that did not need refrigeration, down makeshift chilly corridors floored in bare plywood or industrial carpet, past closed doors and unlit branchings-off. The further they moved from the central farmhouse, the colder it got. Her flashlight's watery bull's-eye of a beam flitted across surfaces of bare pine and untaped sheetrock. From behind some of the doors that they passed he heard voices muttering, coughing, settling for the night. A child's voice piped some unanswered question. A male and a female voice were entwined in a recitation that Clark recognized, from the single word "trespasses," as the Lord's Prayer. From a smell of wet clay and heated brick he gathered they were passing close to the pottery. At St. Andrew's School in Delaware he had gone to many chapel sessions and this Spartan setting reminded him of a verse that had struck him as sadly human—Jesus complaining that the foxes have holes and the birds of the air have nests but the Son of Man has nowhere to lay his head. Birkenstocks—that was the name of that funky kind of sandal. Hannah came to an unpainted flush door she pushed open; it lacked a lock.

Her cubicle held a single, headboardless bed and a plain bureau and table and kerosene lamp and a few pegs from which to hang clothes; the room had been storing cold air all day and their breaths were visible in the skidding flashlight beam. It was March but not yet spring. She found matches with which to light the bedside lamp and then a cylindrical space-heater standing on the bare floor. Ornate perforations on the heater's top projected a wide wavery image, an abstract rose, on the seamed ceiling of plasterboard, so roughly slapped-up some of the joint tape drooped down. The bathroom with its icy white fixtures and sloppy caulking was down the hall; she went first, and when he came back—having dipped his finger in baking soda and rubbed it across his teeth in place of a brush—she was already within the narrow bed, looking like a child, her hair fanned on the pillow, her eyes two dabs of shadow and her nostrils two more.

"Turn off the lamp, my darling husband," she said, in a

return of her betranced voice. Though the heater flame softly roared and its rosy projection wavered and swung on the ceiling as if warmly alive, every surface in the room was still cold, including his own skin and the brass knob of the kerosene lamp. The orange flame leaped up in a last flickering as the wick withdrew into its circular sheath. Hannah's staring face went dark and then returned in the rosy tint of the heater glow, which permeated the room as if its plywood walls might sympathetically spring into flame.

"What are you wearing?" he asked.

"My flannel nightie. It was too cold to be naked. The nightie lifts up."

"What do you think about a condom?"

"Jesse says—"

"Let's think for ourselves on this one little issue. They're clammy, but they save many an itch. Not to mention—"

"I know. Don't mention it. I hate even the word. Do you have one?"

"As it happens, with my debonair bachelor lifestyle, I do. Right next to my driver's license."

"You're dear, really. You're a dear fish, Clark."

"We don't have to fuck at all, you know."

"Don't you like me even that much?"

"Please—I do, I do. It's just I'm so beat." Nowhere to lay his head. "I'm freezing out here. My teeth are chattering. Can you hear them?"

She listened, they both listened. The wind was picking up, the window sash shivered in its frame, a ceiling joist creaked, a coyote howled far away, a sheep nearby baaed in fright. Back in Beverly Hills he would occasionally hear a coyote, out in Coldwater Canyon or beyond. Maybe the same coyote, cruising the West. Clark took off his boots but left on his thick socks; he took off his Norwegian sweater but left on his turtleneck; he took off his work pants and silk long johns and his underpants. He held his Trojan in its oily foil packet like a ticket of admission and slid into the bed. The margin of sheet beside her bit into his bare thighs so sharply he convulsively embraced her for warmth. Her flannel hug was tentative, fumbly; they were strangers. They attempted to kiss but had trouble making their lips meet. Hers tasted medicinal, of zinc oxide and lip balm. Their fuck indeed felt marital—sleepy and dutiful, a poke and a submission. She made no pretense of coming, and he was too chilled and freaked, in their narrow space of warmed bed, to exercise much sexual courtesy. This was her idea, after all. Still, there had been a splendor, an onward momentum as of music, in the slithering up of her nightie and its baring to his touch her curving surfaces, both furry and smooth, and in her opening her thighs to him and her breathing "*Ooh*" with soft surprise into his ear.

He hardly had energy to strip off the Trojan (the damn pubic hairs always caught) and to drop it on the floor before turning his back and falling asleep. The bed was so narrow Hannah had no choice but to curl her arm around him and to fit her body against his. Between fits of cloud the moon, that debunked deity, poured its borrowed light through the invisible wind; the sash vibrated and coyotes sang mournfully to one another. Even the foxes have holes.

Fuzzy dawn light met his eyes when she awoke him. The frosted shade of the kerosene lamp had the shape of an old-fashioned big-hipped woman. The heater had purred all night and the cubicle was so hot his neck was sweaty. Hannah was bent above him, whispering insistently, "Clark. It's six o'clock, darling. Shall I drive you back to Bighorn?"

"Bighorn," he said, as his consciousness escaped from his dreams, which had been as entangled and shallow as the pattern on Uncle Jared's boastful boots. "They think I'm a jerk," he told her. "Let me sleep, honey. I'll give them a call later." It was as when a boy he travelled to Europe with his mother, and after that first sleepless day of dazed excitement—the crooked damp streets, the shops with iron shutters, the strange rapid language, the buildings that looked different, solid and rhythmic and gray like monuments—a profound need opened within him, a need to fall and fall into the gauzy substance of oblivion, the bottomless world beneath the waking world—a need his mother would explain with the breezy phrase "a change of air."

Uncle Danny had travelled a lot between Washington and the Far East in the years when Nixon was winding down Vietnam and visiting China, and he would stay a night or two en route with his famous sister. Clark didn't go off to St. Andrew's until 1973, when he was fourteen, so he was around, and he and his uncle would drive the freeways in Mom's white Jaguar convertible while she was off working. His uncle seemed to own only gray suits, so the most casual he could get was to leave his jacket and necktie off and turn up the cuffs of his white shirt. He seemed to Clark tremendously tall, though his grandfather told him Daniel was no taller than his great-grandfather Clarence had been, and not as handsome. Uncle Danny had the dull pale-brown family hair, cut in a businessman style that seemed bizarrely short in those shaggy years, a sort of military statement, and thick glasses behind which his eyes wore a constant, slightly bewildered and evasive but not especially troubled squint. Behind the wheel of the Jag he looked boyish, the wind mussing his hair and then flattening it in colorless patches, and he steered, Clark thought admiringly, with a very light, two-fingered touch on the steering wheel. Uncle Danny was sensitive; he scanned the dial for classical radio stations, tucked in among the loud rock and angry talk stations, and once took Clark to the Los Angeles County Museum of Art, right next to the La Brea Tar Pits. Rex Brudnoy was gone from the household by then, and when Clark was eleven and twelve he and Uncle Danny would head down to Disneyland or Knott's Berry Farm for a day of rides. But by the time he was thirteen he was too old for that, and it seemed more adult just to drive, south to San Clemente or north to Santa Barbara or east into the desert, enjoying the meditative sensation of eating up the miles, the miles of pink and powder-blue and adobe-colored houses, to views of the Pacific so vast you could see the earth curve or else out into the desert, where the L.A. megalopolis crumbled into little sun-flattened towns left over from the days when California was a part of Mexico. "Any time you want to turn around," Clark would say. "Don't do this just for me."

"It's pure pleasure for me, Clark. I don't get to drive much on the job. I'm driven, but that's not the same. Listen to that—pure milk and honey. And fire. That's Mozart. You should learn to listen to these guys."

"What is your job—is that O.K. to ask?"

"Absolutely it's O.K. to ask. I am a State Department political officer stationed at present in our Embassy in Phnom Penh, Cambodia. A very pretty country with a lot of problems. A beautiful people, Clark, and some amazing temples. Angkor Wat: the largest religious structure in the world, so they say. Make yourself a vow to see it before you die. It's one of those countries, like Poland, that happen to be in the wrong place. They've had some shaky times, under their two-faced little king, but we have a good man in there now, I think: Lon Nol. Heard of him?"

"Sure, I guess." He knew Uncle Danny could tell he was lying. That was his job, to know when people were lying. "So what do you do all day?" he asked.

"Oh, hard to say. Push paper, meet people. Gather information, and pass it on. I guess I'm a communicator—people like me are the means whereby other countries communicate with ours, and we can present ourselves to them. Communication's the difference between 1972 and 1914; it's what's kept the Cold War fundamentally cold. Know what the other fellow won't stand, and go to the edge but not over. If you look at World War One, those people had no idea what they were getting into. Franz Josef didn't even come down from his vacation house while his ministers were declaring war on Serbia."

Beyond his uncle's pale, amiable, squinting profile, bleached mountains crinkled up out of the desert. Nearer to the highway Clark could see a golf course—garish strips of green that had no business being there—and a foreground of gas stations and truck stops and cement-block stores advertising PEPSI and HOAGYS and TIENDA DE COMESTIBLES. Clark tried to picture hydrogen bombs wiping all this out, but it seemed too vast, too vast and too delicate, a semi-transparent vision spun out within a serene, basking, blue-tinted emptiness. "What do you think of Vietnam?" he asked.

"It's over. All but the shouting. Henry's in charge."

"How could the U.S. make such an awful mistake?"

Uncle Danny pushed out his lips, thinking, so from the side he looked a little like Mom trying to be sexy. "Was it a mistake?"

"Well, it got us fifty thousand dead soldiers, and South Vietnam is worse off than when it started."

"It got us into China," Uncle Danny told him. "It got us the two SALT agreements. We've got Mao and Brezhnev each trying to kiss our ass. Nobody's supposed to say this, but Vietnam impressed the right people. The superpowers all agree, the North Vietnamese are pricks. They've got Laos. They won't get Thailand. They won't get Cambodia, if I can help it." He turned to face his nephew, the two fingers keeping their light contact with the wheel, as the speedometer needle quivered around eighty. "Vietnam was a hard call," he said, "I'm glad you won't have to fight in it. But somebody always has to fight. You and I walk down the street safe, if we do, because a cop around the corner has a gun. The kids today say the state is organized violence and they're right. But it matters who's doing the organizing. King George the Third, or George Washington. Joe Stalin and his disciples, or our bumbling American pols. I'll take the pols, every time. What the kids don't seem to see is that their freedom to grow long hair and smoke pot and shit on poor Tricky Dick is based on the willingness of somebody else to do their fighting for them. What you can't protect gets taken away. The class or tribe or country that can't fight gets swallowed up. I try to be cool about it—I mean, look at you, for Chrissake: your *hair*, that little Mary Jane leaf on your polo shirt—but frankly it pisses me off, Clark, this whole decadence thing, this whole spoiled stoned slogan-mouthing generation of rotten know-nothing ingrates, so I'm glad I'm not in this country for long at a time. I might turn conservative." A new Mercedes with opaque windows whipped by as if they were standing still. "The U.S. doesn't want trouble," Uncle Danny said. "We don't need more territory, more client states. What good has South Vietnam ever done us? It's just cost us a bundle, and no thanks either. But we can't hide here between our oceans and let the bully boys have the rest of the planet. Their so-called system stinks—I've been there. Name me a Communist country where fair elections wouldn't throw the thugs out. There's real grievances and these thugs come in and steal the issues and screw up the solutions. If your mother weren't my sister, it would really get my goat the way she and these other pinko Hollywood fatcats and bleeding hearts talk as if the late great Ho would suit them just fine. Let them try it on for a week. They'd all wind up in reëducation camp at best. Don't get me started, I don't want to get emotional. I try to be dispassionate about it, but I love this crazy, wasteful, self-hating country in spite of itself."

"I don't think Mom's political really." Clark, who had never had a brother or sister, was fascinated by his mother and uncle, who a minute after a quarrel over Mitchell or McGovern or whoever would fall to kidding and smiling as if it had all been a kind of rough-and-tumble play. She treated him like a little boy who loved his collection of cap pistols and lead soldiers and who was innocent of the real wars, the wars of Hollywood she had fought by putting her whole self on the line, her looks and muscle-tone and emotions and sex all out there on offer, for the bankers and the veteran flesh-merchants and the kids fresh out of film school to mock or ignore. She would flare up at Danny and say that he was a fascist, and he in his gray or seersucker suit from the height of his six feet two would give the Hitler salute and put two fingers on his upper lip for a Hitler mustache the way they must have when they were kids in that war. Her face unclenched and broke into her big smile. She loved him, Clark sensed, because he knew her, knew her as she had been before she was Alma DeMott, and thus was one of the few who had witnessed the full, miraculous performance.

"You don't know her," Uncle Danny said. "She shot off her mouth about how we shouldn't hunt down domestic subversion and cost herself being Miss Delaware Peach." They were coming back into L.A. along the Pomona Freeway, the San Jose Hills off to their right, the Puente Hills Shopping Mall on their left, its acres of parked cars twinkling in the sun, which hung like a red moon in a silver band of smog. "Maybe just as well: if she'd won it, she might have gotten conceited and married some dumb local nob like this Ingraham she was dating. She wouldn't have had her *drive.*" He squinted into the sun and looked like a professor, with his thick-lensed glasses. "To do the drill in life, you've got to have something to prove. You should meet my Uncle Jared some day soon, before he kicks off."

"You've got a lot planned for me to do. See Uncle Jared, see Angkor Wat."

"I don't want you just to sit around here and be a beach bum. I want to have a famous nephew. I love my dad, but don't play it safe like he did. Now listen to that. That's *Sturm.* That's Beethoven. The Mozart gloves are off. Beethoven goes for broke, every time."

To Clark Uncle Danny seemed a treasure, a man from space who was somehow his own, a little like that robot who with his deep echoing voice and flashing lights waited on Will in *Lost in Space,* which Clark had faithfully watched as a child. He still thought *Lost in Space* was better than *Star Trek.* He asked his uncle, "What language do you communicate in, in Cambodia? I thought you had learned languages like Russian."

"I'm picking up bit of Khmer, but French does pretty well.

For some reason I've never had much trouble with languages. The secret is, don't be easily embarrassed. I love trying it out, and seeing what the hell I get back. Your mother isn't the only ham in our family."

The sun was making longer shadows between the freeway and the mountains, and a thin transparent half-moon showed in the cloudless sky, to the right. Clark could never figure out the relations between the way the moon looked and where the sun was, though Mr. Sourian the eighth-grade teacher at Beverly Vista tried to show them on the blackboard. The cooling air, the radio thundering Beethoven close to Clark's knees, the return into the smog-domed heart of Los Angeles against the pressure of commuters' headlights, his youthful uncle companionable and protective in his white shirt beside him—this was one of the movies his head would sometimes run, though perhaps it actually happened only a handful of times, three or four. In the ninth grade he went off to St. Andrew's. Uncle Danny was stationed next in Czechoslovakia, after Pol Pot had replaced Lon Nol in Cambodia and anti-Communism had been routed throughout old Indochina, so he didn't fly through Los Angeles any more. He had actually gone and married a Cambodian woman, and having a family of his own further took him out of his nephew's orbit.

Clark had been living at the Temple some months before Jesse took him on a summer's morning into the sheep barn and showed him, in a loft behind a concealing wall built of bales of hay, the guns: shotguns, rifles, machine guns, pistols. Barrels and bolts and triggers of dark machined metal in wooden crates or wrapped in plastic, scented with oil, possessed of a smooth inarguable beauty, haughty in their power to administer death. Clark sensed flagrant illegality but did not cringe, for Jesse was standing near in the semi-dark, watching closely for his reaction. Clark asked, "What are these for?"

"Brother, those are for the Day of Reckoning."

"Do you have permits for them? There's enough here for an army."

"Why, yes, Zeb has a ton of permits, somewhere in his files. And those otherwise have their permits in the accounting of the Lord of Righteousness, stamped and dated right there where He sits on His Almighty Throne," Jesse said in his husky, onrolling voice, which made the motes of hay dust swirl in the narrow beams of light the barn shingles admitted. "Some were bought legal, at a shop in Leadville doesn't ask too many bothersome questions. Others, there are ways—you can order parts separate and make yourselves a dandy package. Brother Luke is right clever at that, from his days at a lathe in a machine shop." He pulled a rifle from a crate and held it erect before his face. "You take an old AR-15 like this, and add an AR-15–M-16 upper receiver part, and you got yourself an M-16, fully automatic. You just pull the trigger and it's *k-k-k-k-k*—good-bye, gook. The M-16's what they issued us in Vietnam. She's a sweetie, when she don't jam. There were a lot of complaints from deceased users about it jamming, so they renamed it from the M-16A1 to the M-16A2 and it worked much better. Here, son. You hold her."

The gun was surprising: provocative like a woman, both lighter and heavier than he would have thought. The seven or eight pounds of severely interlocked and fitted metal was somehow buoyant, ready to become a magic wand. The stock was plastic instead of wood, and the sight a little intricate house of dull black.

"Ever held a gun before, Esau?"

That name had been bestowed upon Clark when he had finally broken all his connections at Bighorn, telling both Johnny Ponyfoot and Art Marling what he thought of them at Golddigger's one last hard-drinking evening, and he had come here to stay. The name did not feel like him yet; he was still Clark to himself, in the credits in his head. He felt a mockery in the name, after he had read about Esau in Genesis: Isaac and Rebekah's firstborn, born red and hairy, a rough hunter who was his father's favorite but was cheated of his birthright by his twin brother, Jacob, who had been born clinging to his heel and became their mother's favorite. With her connivance Jacob had cheated Esau of their father's blessing, deceiving the blind old man with the hides of kids laid across the backs of his hands. Esau had been a rube.

But Hannah told him that the secret of the story was that Esau later forgave his treacherous twin; he, Clark, had a good heart. He was not allowed to live with Hannah, as he had thought he might; he was instead assigned to a men's dormitory at the other end of the compound, and compelled each night to dive for sleep amid the coarse barnyard snoring of the other men. Rubes, he had come to dwell among strange rough rubes. Just as Esau founded the nation of Edom, alien to that of the Israelites, so he had come from a world alien to that of most of the Temple-dwellers, who were men and women of rural background, haunted by the apocalyptic expectations of Adventism. Adventism should have died near its beginning, when the predictions of its founder, William Miller, met, in 1843, the First Disappointment, and then, revised to October 22, 1844, the Great Disappointment. For all the chances they gave Him, Christ declined to come. But rubes are accustomed to disappointment, and the Millerite sect trickled on without Miller, twisting and splitting and arriving in one of its rivulets at the sensation in Jesse Smith's balding head that God was about to act through him.

"Not that I remember," Clark answered.

"You'd remember," Jesse said, and leered. "It's like sex—you don't forget that, now do you?"

In truth, Clark did. Healthy airheaded girls you met at the beach or a club and were next day a dim part of an acid trip or coke binge you wanted to forget. It made him uncomfortable when Jesse talked about sex: sex ran like a widening crack through the image he projected as their lord and savior. He had become obsessed by impregnating as many of the Temple women as he could, so his seed would be richly represented in the hundred forty-four thousand of the saved after the Reckoning. Hannah was pregnant. Clark thought he could not be the father, because he and she, in their infrequent, sneaked times together, always used condoms.

Jesse sensed his unease, his virginity in regard to guns, and pulled a bigger weapon from the concealed array. "Now, this is what we were up against, the daddy automatic rifle of them all, the AK-47. The good old Kalashnikov. Developed in Russia, now mostly manufactured by the Chinese. The gun of choice for all those who wage war upon Gog. See this banana clip? That's the identifying mark. Thirty rounds; you ram it in her slot. There must be fifty million of these old girls out there in the world, making things hot for the Devil and his crew." He elevated the gun so its barrel exactly bisected his face, there in the shadows of the loft; he focused on the barrel and slowly went cross-eyed.

What did they mean, Jesse's bursts of clownishness? That he kept for himself not only the privilege of sex but that of joking? Who was the joke on?

Clark could not remember when he had decided to believe in Jesse; the big man had just stepped into him like a drifter taking over an empty shack. In Jesse's presence he felt possessed of a value he possessed nowhere else—not in the presence of his mother, to whom motherhood had been an interruption of her real life, nor of any of those to whom he was, foremost, his mother's son. Jesse in his canny craziness saw around the corners of Clark's soul to what had been overlooked. Clark was the least of Jesse's cubs but was licked and cuffed with the others. He could not project for himself the moment of his conversion; in one frame he was on the outside, wondering how Hannah had tricked him into this rat-trap, and in the next he was inside, unable to leave, tied by gravity to this savior's unpredictable orbit.

" 'And I will call for a sword against him throughout all my mountains, saith the Lord God; every man's sword shall be against his brother.' Know where that's from, brother Esau?"

"Ezekiel, somewhere." Jesse's interminable sessions of Bible study often put Clark to sleep, weary as he was with his work at the Temple, helping Luke and Jonas and Mephibosheth build more barracks for the expanding tribe of children, wielding a hammer and saw all day as the hot summer winds swept up across the grasslands, whitening in waves the slopes the voracious sheep had not yet nibbled bare.

"Ezekiel, thirty-eight twenty-one. 'And I will plead against him with pestilence and with blood; and I will rain upon him, and upon his bands, and upon the many people that are with him, an overflowing rain, and great hailstones, fire, and brimstone.' That frighten you, son?"

"Not if you are my friend, Jesse." This was a rote answer, chanted in Bible study.

"You know who he's talking about, don't you?"

"His enemies. The Lord's enemies."

"Not just any old enemies. He's talking here about Gog, of the land of Magog, chief prince of Meshech and Tubal. You remember my telling you all who Gog really is, don't you? Think about it—G, O, G."

Clark let the letters revolve in his head, but all that came to him was how close they were to spelling GOD. These fervent believers seemed to him always skirting the edge of blasphemy. Blasphemy was everywhere, like sex in the movies before the Production Code was abandoned and scenes became explicit, and boring. He was staring down at a skeletal little stubby gun, still in its plastic wrap and form-fitting packing of Styrofoam. He guessed, from Arnold Schwarzenegger movies, that this was an Uzi. "Made in the Holy Land," Jesse said softly near his ear. "By the same Israeli craftsmen who have brought you the Galil rifle. The genius stroke of the Uzi was to fire a dandy little pistol bullet, nine millimeter, full metal jacket. A fold-out butt for compactness. G, O, G. What have you come up with?"

All this hay scratched Clark's sinuses and the image flashed through his mind of how quickly the building would blaze if a single match were set to it. Sheep screaming below, ammunition exploding up here.

"Government of the Godless," Jesse pronounced, with satisfaction, lowering the Kalashnikov. "That's what Gog means, and that's what we've got. This fake cowboy Reagan says he believes in God but he never goes to church, you'll notice. Scared to step out of doors since that other movie actor plugged him."

"Not an actor," Clark said; though Jesse didn't like to be corrected, Clark felt, after being lectured about guns, entitled to make a point. "A young psycho who was in love with an actress, Jodie Foster." He passed over the M-16, glad to be rid of it. It wanted to come alive in his hands.

Jesse went on unheeding, "And he let the Pope into the country, to go around spreading his infernal poison. Come the Day of Reckoning, those two will be Number One and Number Two Antichrist, begging these mountains to fall on them and hide them from the Wrath of the Lamb. Sure as manure."

Clark had been too young for the President's films, but *Knute Rockne—All American* used to show up on Channel Nine and what enchanted Clark was the giant soaring kick, from the bystander in street clothes, and the dodging, dancing run the length of the field that had signalled Pat O'Brien that a miracle was at hand. You knew all along that somebody as good as George Gipp was bound to die. The world can't have perfect people in it; it throws off all the tolerances. A strange thing was that, until he got to be President, Reagan's greatest scenes were in bed: dying and asking they win one for the Gipper, in *King's Row* asking where the rest of him was, and in bed with Bonzo.

The movies in Clark's head were flickering too fast; he was beginning to panic up here in the dark triangular loft, with these mummified bundles of guns smelling of the oil that kept them eternally young. Jesse with his preternatural alertness sensed Clark's discomfort and held the two rifles aloft in a priestly gesture, one in each hand, prolonging his disciple's torment, confident that torment is what holds a disciple to the master. Torment is interesting.

"'Thus will I magnify myself, and sanctify myself,'" Jesse said. "Swordpower, they called it back then. *Gun*power's what it is now. 'She brought forth a man child, who was to rule all nations with a rod of iron.' Revelation, twelve five. I bet you thought Jesse's rod meant my prick, didn't you, brother Esau?"

"I hadn't thought about it," Clark said, moving around the bales toward the built-in ladder that would take him down from this claustrophobic, scratchy, oily-smelling loft.

Jesse followed him down. Clark watched the older man's Birkenstocks grope, slippery and cautious, on each worn ladder rung. Jesse arrived on the barn floor, with its litter of stray straw and sheep pellets, slightly pink in the face, and panting. He wore a buckskin vest over a red flannel shirt and Clark could see his pounding heart moving the leather just slightly, like the featherless bald wings of a bird still in the nest. In a skip of his brain, a slip of the sprockets, Clark perceived Jesse as himself trapped, trapped by his mission, by something like live worms in his head. Jesse had the two-edged gift of inspiring pity as well as obedience. He said, as if apologizing for having alarmed Clark in the loft, "We need to defend ourselves, Esau. The unrighteous are relentless. Gog keeps saying we owe them taxes. County, state, Lower Branch Collector's Office, we keep getting these envelopes with little windows in 'em every day. I ask Zebulun, what's this and what's that?—he doesn't know. He's a strong believer, and a mighty man of means, Zebulun, but he's not a man for figures. Me neither, brother Esau. The ways of the world are not mine."

Zebulun was a young rotund Hawaiian of complicated bloodlines who had been recruited by Matthew in a Pacific fishing expedition among Seventh-Day Adventists impatient for the Second Coming. This sect of Millerites, the most successful of a number, had explained the Great Disappointment by saying that on October 22, 1844, an investigation had been launched in Heaven to lay the proper foundation for the Judgment Day still in the future. Like other heroic believers—like Mormons or Moonies or, for that matter, adherents of the Athanasian Creed—they had grown over their fantastic elaborations a skin or scar of worldliness, of conventional dress, business success, and pleasant manners; yet underneath burned a pus of frustration, an inflammation of hope deferred. Matthew, like his namesake, could promise that "it is near, even at the doors." Matthew told Zebulun that the Prophet had come, and was living a few miles north of Lower Branch, Colorado, in Burr County. Zebulun's father owned Honolulu real estate and pineapple fields on the Big Island, and his access to wealth had given Zebulun the position as treasurer to the Temple, though he was in Clark's view a butternut-colored mental defective tranquillized by Jesse's good news. It must be he who was paying for the guns.

Jesse continued his lament: "Gog has more snoops in his employ than there are devils in downright Hell. Some Board of Sanitation inspectors has heard our plumbing isn't up to code and wants to come sniffing at the septic tanks. Some damn social worker got as far as the inner gate, saying there'd been reports of child abuse—child abuse, when we're giving our little ones the only true religion that will keep their hides from frying in the everlasting flames! Luke was on guard duty that day—he put a bullet next to her front tire and said he wouldn't miss next time."

"If I may say so—" Clark hesitated, testing.

"Speak, Esau."

"You need better PR. There's ways of avoiding such incidents. In Hollywood I used to work for the Nova Talent Agency—one of our jobs was to keep these young stars out of scrapes."

"I never should have come down," Jesse confided to him, taking off the little round wire-rim spectacles he had worn to admire the guns and rubbing his eyes with pinched fingers as if milking them of sadness. "I never should have come down this low." From the wide square mouth of the barn they gazed east to the mountains above them, the grassy slopes turning into rocky heights and then to a distant ragged and unapproachable profile tinged even in August with snow. "Up there where I was, you don't owe anybody and they don't owe you. You eat what you shoot and burn what you cut."

"So what happened?"

"I got the call. Faith filled me like a fire, hot and cold. I had to share the news."

A half-moon was emerging from the blue sky, like a stone from an ebbing tide. "That must have been a wonderful feeling," Clark said, politely.

"No, it was terrible. The responsibility was plumb terrible; it was pure terror. That's what I do for you folks—I carry off the terror. To carry off the terror for all mankind—believe me, I begged for the cup to pass, but it didn't. Back from 'Nam a couple years, and just finding my feet under me, looking for an old played-out ranch to make my own, and the Lord hit me with this."

Among the things Jesse believed in was not washing too often; his aura was at times, with a shift in the air, unbearably strong. Clark felt a desire to get away and meditate upon his vision of the guns. They inarticulately held a deep meaning for him, he believed.

"It hit me like a grizzly bear's hug," Jesse was telling him, caught up now in a movie of his past. "It put a weight on my mind that near drove me off my head. It's damn lonely, being the bridegroom the universe has been waiting for." Jesse looked at Clark intently, testing him, seeing if Esau would betray him. "Don't tell the others everything I tell you. They're simple folk, by and large, and can't take too many mysteries at once."

Clark said crisply, by way of concluding, "You better tell Zebulun you want me to help him. He wouldn't believe it, if it came from me."

. . .

Those four years he went to St. Andrew's, in the middle of the Seventies, he visited his grandparents once a month on the average. He liked his grandmother fine, though he wondered why her leg had never been fixed by one of these simple operations that the doctor shows on television are always performing, and why she kept feeding him this rich sweet country food that had made her so fat she could hardly hobble between the stove and the kitchen table. But it was his grandfather he loved—the way people called him "Teddy" though he was over seventy, and the old man's patient way of moving, of listening, of suffering in silence. If there was one thing Mom did not know how to do, it was suffer in silence. Though she had had fits of trying to be a mother, as he achieved the shape of a man she was generally distracted if not thousands of miles away, on location in Mexico or Louisiana. After 1970, when she hit forty, she weakened and began to accept TV work—older-woman roles in four- or six-part adaptations of last year's popular novels, in costume dramas with an enlightened slant on ethnic issues. Her platinum-blonde phase was over; her hair went dark again. She played the obstructive but eventually enlightened and forgiving mother of an aristocratic Mexican girl involved in a romance with a peon turned revolutionary, and in another the Creole madame of a New Orleans bawdy house burned down for accepting clients of mixed blood. Older sisters, female executives, women with tortured pasts that had come back to haunt them—television, relatively cheesy though its production values were, embraced a world where middle-aged women could still play a role. The big screen, bewildered by its liberation from censorship, clung to the ideal of youthful beauty, and there was no shortage of fresh examples: Ali McGraw, Katharine Ross, Karen Black, Maria Schneider. They wouldn't last the way she had, Mom said, but then she hadn't lasted the way Crawford had.

Teddy had more time on his hands now that his nephew Ira had energetically taken over the greenhouse, and he welcomed his teen-age grandson's inarticulate companionship. The two were physically akin—stocky, squarish, with mild brown eyes and straight dull hair. Teddy walked with the boy around the town, pointing out vacant lots where there used to be houses, and new houses where there had been fields, or houses that had once been neighborhood grocery stores, or a dilapidated mansion where the man who founded the bottle-cap factory had lived, or a big run-down house gone into apartments which had belonged to his father's sister and where he and Em had lived when newlywed, or shacks where black people had lived in deplorable conditions, when you think about it now. From his days as a mailman he knew the name of the family that had occupied every house years ago. Many of them were still there, some had passed on. Oh, he could tell a story or two, if regulations didn't forbid it. A letter carrier, coming to the door every day, gets a sense of a house, and sees things—women in bathrobes asking if he'd like to come in for a coffee, cars parked out front that belonged on the other side of town, children left unattended squalling themselves blind upstairs, signs of the heart going out of a house by the peeling paint and broken screen doors. "You can tell," he told Clark, "by the kind of mail people get—if they have the interest to subscribe to a magazine or two, if there are any picture postcards and hand-addressed letters from acquaintances who are keeping up in the world, or if they get too many bills stamped ATTENTION, if there are registered return receipt requesteds from some legal outfit. It's a terrible thing, Clark, when a house starts to sink—when the man of the house is being dragged down."

The boy heard a note of personal grief, of grievance. He asked, "Is that what happened to your father?"

"Yes. Yes, it did. I don't like to remember it, if you don't mind."

"But then your daughter became rich and famous."

"That helped. But she paid a price. There are no free rides.

Look at the television bilge they have her in now. No better than soap operas, I don't see how Em watches 'em day after day. She ought to retire on her money, your mother, but she can't. That's the penalty of success. Nobody knows when to stop. Everybody always wants more."

He and Clark would get into the family Chrysler—a stately sober gray-blue, it was one of the few luxuries they had allowed Alma to buy them—and drive around Delaware, up to Wilmington, where he would point out the buildings that held the old movie theatres and O'Connell's School of Practical Business, before the downtown was pretty much given over to the blacks. "Not their fault everything runs down," he explained. "They don't have the money for upkeep. They don't have the money because they don't have educations. They don't have educations because nobody had any use for 'em, once they stopped being slaves. You know this was a slave state, right through the Civil War? They wouldn't ratify the Thirteenth Amendment until 1901. Any black tried to vote, he was in big trouble. We had it all—lynchings, whippings. People are meaner than mules." Clark's grandfather laughed, as the Chrysler purred through blocks of tumbledown, boarded-up Wilmington. "Well, here's the result. American cities are the black man's revenge. They've taken them over. A white man's scared to go into town, after dark. There used to be shops all through here, and pretty gals riding open trolley cars in their bonnets. Don't think back then we didn't look at the girls, and they didn't know it, even though they didn't show us everything they had on the first go."

Nothing made his grandfather indignant. He was a man at peace, still curious about the world but with never any hope of changing it. Even the monstrous white-painted holding tanks, acres of them behind an eight-foot silver playground fence, down along the river where he and Jared used to fish, and where there used to be marshes full of heron and muskrat and terrapin, he found admirable in their way, as a triumph of expenditure and engineering, of Man's ability to impose himself on Nature. They parked on the roadside and he rolled down the window, so they could smell the tanks, the rich and intricate chemistry of their processed petroleum. A sunlit shoal of cirrus clouds arching in the direction of New Jersey seemed to carry flakes of the tanks' white paint up into the sky. Freon gases released in aerosol spray cans are destroying the ozone layer, scientists had announced that fall. Clark was fifteen, and at St. Andrew's had been exposed to small doses of Machiavelli and Plato, Byron and Camus, even some Nietzsche—enough to know that there was less to the sky than he had once vaguely assumed. Every trip to the moon took something away from God. He was jealous of his mother; she had had a God, here under the cozy close sky of Basingstoke, and in her Hollywood egotism hadn't bothered to pass Him on to him. He didn't know what to believe; he only knew that he was going to die some day, and that was unthinkable—everything going out like a light bulb, and people and planets going on and on without him, even beyond the time when the sun exploded and became a cinder. He lay down at night into this charred and leaden eventuality; it belonged to the adult smells of his body as the sheets warmed, and masturbation's headlong relief eclipsed the knowledge with a kind of inner light only to have it sourly wash back, even as he blindly dabbled at the sheet with his handkerchief, hoping the school laundry would mistake his ejaculation for snot. Lynette and Bobbi Anne and (most down and dirty) Alicia, eighth-grade girls he knew in his last year at Beverly Vista Elementary School, starred in the little movies he projected in his head, but when they were over the bottomless black truth remained. In Hollywood there were these well-groomed churches and synagogues along the palm-lined boulevards but his mother had never led him into them, except for a crowded funeral or two, the death of a star, photographers snapping and excluded fans crowding the sidewalk and the tone inside that of a publicity handout or a roast with fewer than usual jokes. Who was this God everybody talked of but no one ever met? The Episcopal chapel services at St. Andrew's seemed perfunctory and weightless, the same words every time, like a mumbled foreign language he had never learned, the homilies by faculty members chatty and down-to-earth if not, in tone, downright mocking. Where was the hidden miracle? Who could he talk to but his grandfather, who had mild, unblaming opinions on everything? He asked, one November day when they had gone to the beach in the car, and were happy to be back out of the wind in the Chrysler's warmth, "What was Mom's religion like when she was a girl?"

It could have been put better, but his grandfather grasped the gist. "She went to the Presbyterians over on North Elm, with her mother and mine. The Siffords had been Methodists, but it seemed easiest once the baby had come for Emily to switch, my mother was so keen for her own church. The family always said she should have been the parson, not Dad."

"Was Mom, you know, real sincere?"

Teddy reflected back. "She never said one way or another, that I can remember. Went to church school every Sunday, and was confirmed at thirteen. Pretty as an angel, in a white dress my mother made with her poor old eyes. I didn't go generally, but I went to that service all right. This was my *girl.*" He studied his grandson, his face looking worried, wondering what the boy wanted. "Then, about your age I guess, the age when she began to do with boys, her attendance began to slump off, and she'd stay home with me, doing her homework or going off and seeing some friends. It was normal, even Mother agreed. She'd say you expect to lose them at that age, they'll return when they have children of their own. Mother had been head of Sunday school out in Missouri; that's how Dad met her."

"How come you never went?" Clark asked.

The retired mailman turned his profile into the tinted glare of the windshield and his thin lips gathered into a pugnacious pursed hardness—a Wilmot kind of mouth. "Never seemed to need it," he allowed. "Stopped dead after Dad died." He reflected a bit more, thinking back. "I must have had a grudge."

A patch of whiskers his razor had skimmed over showed white stubble in the glare. Just by the silver fence a strip of marsh lay undisturbed and out of it flew two great blue herons, the S of their necks straightening as their shadowy wings labored to beat their arrowing bodies into the air and away.

"Grudge?"

His grandfather slowly scratched his jaw at the very spot where the razor had skipped. "This'll sound strange, coming out of the way people used to think, but it seemed to me God could have given Dad a sign. To help him out. Just a little sign would have done it, and cost God nothing much. Damned if I'd go to church to sing His praises after that. Mother never pushed me on it, either, much as church meant to her. Actually I think I scared her. Emily came along, and went in my place. I would never take the comfort away from those it comforts, and I don't mean to bother your head with this, Clark—you asked, and I answered the best I can remember. It's all a long while ago. Now we have a President resigned, and nothing's sacred."

He waited for Clark to say something, to argue with his position possibly. But Clark could think of nothing to say; the thought of God, right there by the glossy white gas tanks that could explode in a fiery ball as big as an atom bomb might make, frightened him, so his tongue felt enormous and numb.

His grandfather put the key in the ignition and said kindly, "Sometime when you're here for a weekend we ought to drive up to Paterson and see how much is left that I remember. It seemed the center of the universe then; the silk strike made headlines all over the country." He put the heavy Chrysler in gear. "Now let's go home and see what good thing Mother has cooked up for us." In this sentence "Mother" meant his wife.

After he had graduated from St. Andrew's, and come back to college at U.C.L.A. in Westwood, and dropped out when it seemed a really good opportunity in an independent production unit of mostly young people had started up to make a picture that would cash in on the Superman craze (only he wouldn't be called Superman or after any superhero in copyright, and all of his superhuman effects like bending a crowbar or lifting a steam engine wouldn't come off, hilariously, which also meant a big saving on special effects), and drifted back to take some classes when he couldn't take any more crap from the snotty head of production, who seemed to get his kicks putting a star's son down, just with little nasty subtle things, and Clark had told him what he thought of him—after all this, while waiting for the right combination to click, sleeping to noon and watching MTV or the old movies on cable and wondering why the people in these black-and-white screwball comedies talked so fast and loud—audiences then must have understood them but he couldn't—and phoning around and showing up at Ma Maison or Jimmy's or Spago or the Colony with the right-looking chick, who for all her leather mini and see-through blouse and pierced nostril and stiletto-heeled purple vinyl boots and the butterfly tattoo on her left shoulder blade was a nice-enough good-hearted girl who like him had improved her mood with a few too many chemicals and hoped that just showing up at these places redolent of success would catch her up in the gears, the magic mechanism that maneuvered the trip to the stars, and then going to the parties in somebody or other's absent parents' house with everybody a different flavor of stoned it seemed and the water in the swimming pool lit from underneath like a piece of sky upside down by wobbly golden bulbs and the pet Russian wolfhound lying out on the terrace watching with a worried look and wanting to play with the chewed yellow tennis ball between his long white paws but nobody playful, everyone too wasted and self-absorbed and carefully moussed and pinned together to go entertain a dog, all this arduously attained and Mex-trimmed multi-million-dollar home being turned into the shit of boring chatter going nowhere, not even to bed, people too strung-out and scared of or tired of the idea of love, the moviemakers had *done* love, the songwriters had done it, what was left were jagged images, one after another, mocking, slicing in MTV like shark's mouths in a feeding frenzy in that documentary about the Great Barrier Reef—during all this his grandfather would send him patient letters from Basingstoke, in stamped envelopes and the address very tidy in its numbers, the high Los Angeles numbers that amused the former small-town mailman. The letters were in acknowledgment of the affection the boy had shown him and attempted to respond to the need he had sensed in his grandson, for a faith. But Teddy had no faith to offer; he had only the facts of daily existence. Weather, family news, local change.

February 19, 1983

Dear Clark:

It's been a mild winter so far but it's only February so anything can still happen. I have seen it snow a foot in March.

Emily has been having a time with her leg and her breathing; an infirmity like that certainly adds to the bothers of old age, but she has never been a person to complain. It gives me pleasure to wait on her, after all the years she's waited on me.

The drug store, you will remember, where she and I met down at the corner of Rodney and Elm has changed hands again. It's been empty for some months, even the Liggett's up the street couldn't match the prices at the cut-rate at the mall over toward Red Lion.

It is sad to see the old big windows empty and the door at the corner boarded across. When I was your age I would have thought if anything was going to last forever it was Seth Addison's drug store and Wayne Phillips' bank down the street but both were just here for a time it turns out.

The whole block has changed—a pit full of bricks where the Roxie was and the Oddfellows' Hall locked up for lack of new members. A video store where the pool tables used to be. People blame the malls but it's not all the malls it's that people don't have the loyal sense of community they used to. Also the young people are too busy making ends meet.

Your grandmother and I were both sorry to hear from your mother that your latest job hasn't been working out. It sounds like they don't really want anybody to be creative. They just want to imitate what has proven to be a success before. That's the mall mentality all over.

Don't be discouraged, Clark. We all know you have ability to spare to do the necessary and make your future. There were plenty around here ready to laugh at your mother but she held fast to her dreams. Now those same people come to me expecting some touch of magic to rub off. I tell them, Essie did it herself, we just loved her. We had never expected something so pretty to come out of us.

Your Uncle Danny has been posted to East Germany and that's all he's allowed to say about it. We enjoyed seeing him and his family several times when he was back in Washington on leave. His little ones are cute as buttons and he's putting on some weight. These Asian women know how to take care of a man.

Even the post office has been moved out of town to a new facility located on what used to be beet fields, meant to serve three communities. But you're supposed to buy your stamps from a machine and the men and women at the window are mostly colored and don't know you and don't care. In my day we gave everybody personal service and often delivered letters without an address, just a name.

Well that's enough grousing from this old party. We still have some of the books and little tapes you used to bring down from St. Andrew's on weekends and then forgot. Whenever we talk about wrapping them up and sending them it gives us the blues so we've been lazy about it. Next time you're here you can take them away.

It was the same way when my sister Esther died and Pete was keen to get their place ready for sale but I couldn't make myself go over and sort out the old things she had in the attic from the Paterson days. She hadn't wanted to move down here from that area but came because I begged her. She was always a good sport, thinking of others, never of herself.

Now Mother is calling me to dinner. The six o'clock news says a storm may be heading up from the Carolinas this weekend but I doubt it will amount to more than rain or a few inches.

With the big ones there's a taste of iron in the air and the hair on your arms stands up in the electricity.

Mother says a hug from her to you and to get your rest. Sufficient sleep is the *sine qua non,* my father used to say.

Fondly,
Grandfather Wilmot

Clark sometimes thought being better-looking would have solved his problems. Hollywood was a town based on looks and those who didn't meet the minimal standard were non-persons; people looked right through you. Not that he was ugly: like his grandfather, he was harmless-looking, bland. But he had not inherited either his mother's fine-whittled bones and glowing skin and taut, sultry features or his father's lithe charm and head of curly hair. Matthias Lazlo was in and out of his son's life like a rumor of grace. His failures as a script-writer, his unwavering commitment to last year's formulas and the ageless power of pure triteness, did not destroy his career; people liked having him around. He was a native golden boy with a seasoning of Hungarian charm. He blended in. Hollywood, its sunshine and sexual plenty and cheerful rapacity, its comically desperate dependence on the whims of a global public, made him happy. He was incorruptible in his happiness, and that made the people around him feel better. Clark's mother saw the industry as fraught with peril, a wheel turning faster and faster beneath her slowing feet; Matthias Lazlo, with maybe one screen credit a year, saw it as swarms of talented, hard-working specialists in beauty and excitement whose epic task had shifted from easing a nation's pain with entertainment to easing the pain of the entire free and third worlds, not excluding parts of Eastern Europe. His idea of fatherhood had been a night game against the Mets at Dodger Stadium, a birthday dinner at Chasen's, a game of tennis at the Hillcrest Country Club, a couple of lo-fat mushroom-burgers at Carneys on the Strip, or, a few years later, an attempt at a double pickup at the Hard Rock Café, over on La Brea. It was his father, depressingly, who always got the play, from, say, the magenta-haired girl with silver sprinkles around her eyes and a bleach-spattered denim vest over a flesh-colored bra and bare belly.

So he liked it that at the Temple of True and Actual Faith he was the suave one, the slick outside operator, the one who gave the TV interview when Jesse refused to come out of his bedroom. Zebulun was a well of money but his brains had been baked somewhere back in the pineapple fields. Matthew—the broad-faced, near-sighted, fast-talking son of an Adventist preacher back in Indiana—had his relentless, humorless powers of persuasion but could only talk to other Adventists; when he got among people reared on other premises, with no expectation of a Prophet and of the world's soon ending, he was lost, dumbfounded by the vastness of such skepticism. With his mother's milk Matthew had taken in heated, fine distinctions in scriptural interpretation; that the Bible was not divine in every phrase and comma had never seriously occurred to him. Luke and Jonas had been with Jesse a long time, from near the start, and had his cowboy hardness without the playful streak, the mystical bemusement. Their clothes, but for the big polished silver belt buckles, looked as if they had rolled in the corral in them. Their wiry bodies and withered, unforgiving faces made Clark feel soft and smooth; he sensed their dislike. He was an outsider, a non-rube. In their minds the wagons were circled and anything that moved outside the circle presented a target. Mephibosheth was far milder, an intensely practical man—a skilled carpenter and amateur electrician and plumber who with his wife, Mercy, had been converted after reading a hostile, sardonic account of the Temple in the Grand Junction newspaper. Belief, unaccountably, had dawned on them both; they had talked through that night all about it, discovering this miracle in each other, and, the next day, began to sell their home. They had brought three half-grown children and devoted themselves to the orderly running of this commune on the lines of their former household. Tom and Jim, like Clark, were a few years one side or the other of thirty, and like him had found the outside world unrewarding. They were educated; Tom had been a trained physical therapist in rehab clinics, and Jim (Tom's first cousin) and Jim's wife, Polly, had both been high-school teachers, of business math and Spanish respectively. Though Clark should have felt most at home with them, and did not dislike them, their commitment had a casual, half-hearted quality—a kind of "Well, why not?"—that disturbed him, quickening what was left of his own incredulity. They were too much like the California people he had come here to escape. He preferred the quaint, stolid company of Mephibosheth, who spoke of himself and Mercy as "sunk in the pit of Hell so deep we didn't know we was burning," and of Zebulun, whose alarming gaps of sense were smoothed over by a Polynesian benignity as deep as the Pacific. Each day took Zebulun slightly by surprise, giving him a small perpetual smile and a giggle quick to spring forth and quick to shut down. He lived to please Jesse, and brought back guns from trips to Texas and Nevada, those free-wheeling super-American states, as a lover would bring bouquets of roses. A company of believers is like a prisonful of criminals: their intimacy and solidarity are based on what about themselves they can least justify.

August 28, 1988

Dear Clark:

Now with Mother taken from me I rattle around and the day seems so long there's no getting from one end of it to the other. I wake up feeling like I've been dumped at the foot of a mountain and can't possibly climb it. Just to shave my kisser seems more than a body can do.

Those years when we had your mother and Danny and my mother all here with us I would never have thought the day would arrive when this little house is too big. But it feels like the governor's mansion.

A girl comes in once a week, one of Loretta Bacheller's girls, and gives it a going-over with the vacuum, but I make it easy for her by hardly setting foot in more than two rooms, my bedroom and the kitchen and back. When Em was slowing down we put a TV in both rooms, to spare her the steps.

They keep thrashing this Iran-contra thing but they'll never get Reagan the way they got Nixon. The American people like him too much and we're tired of agitation. This Roseanne character on TV tickles me. Vulgar some would say, but she tells it like it is.

I confess it raised my eyebrows when you first joined up with this Temple but if it settles you down and gives you comfort there's no complaint from me. I never minded other people believing, and maybe being surrounded by two good believing women as I was freed me up to coast along with the Lord's forbearance. Looking back I wonder if Dad didn't believe more than he knew, and that's what made him so serene at the end. I hope when my turn comes shortly I make no more fuss than my old man.

I'm not expecting to omit dying from my schedule entirely the way my brother Jared seems to be. I must say it is a strange development to have two Wilmots out on those Colorado peaks. Back in Paterson we couldn't imagine anything bigger than Garrett Mountain. On a Sunday half the town's laboring class went up there and it was a glorious sight to see, the pretty Irish girls and the young Italian dyers.

Speaking of Paterson, I finally did get back there. Ira had some business with a nursery in Clifton and asked me if I'd like to ride up, now that I'm on my own. He and Benjy Whaley try to keep me entertained now and then. Benjy has done real well in electronic repair and I'm not just any old local geezer, I'm your mother's dad.

It knocked the wind out of me, seeing the old town. The Falls is still there, bigger than when I was a boy because the mills aren't drawing water off, and the grand buildings, the City Hall and Courthouse and the old Post Office, the prettiest of them all I always thought, standing on the edge of acres of rubble.

Pretty near everybody is black. Those that aren't are spic. Market Street looked like something out of Haiti, it felt to me like carnival time, all these boom boxes and the girls in bright rags and not much of them, the men standing around laughing as though every day was a legal holiday. It makes you real proud of welfare.

There are parking lots the size of tobacco farms all over town. The mills are gone from one side of the river and some of the others have been turned into a museum. The highway dumped us off into all these streets that have become one-way.

Dad's church up near the Library had become an African Baptist and didn't look like it was thriving. The brick parsonage with all the lovely old walnut woodwork inside had been torn down for a housing project along Straight Street.

Ira had his appointment in Clifton so I didn't press him to drive up Twenty-seventh Street to where we lived after the parsonage. I couldn't remember exactly the number anyway, which surprised me.

Don't think I was put off. The memories weren't so happy. There was a lot of ugliness to the mills, and the noise they made you could hear all over town, grinding up human lives. The noise and the streets filthy with horse manure. Today we have problems but we did then too. I'd rather see people jigging down the middle of Market Street than huddled in those slave shacks over on Beaver Road.

This Jesse Smith seems a sincere and interesting man from the material you sent me. I can't follow a lot of interpretations, bringing these old stories up to modern times. What I never liked was the way the voices of ministers sounded when they got up there in the pulpit—like they were simultaneously begging and bossing. My dad lost his voice, literally, under the strain.

I don't expect anything of dying but then I never expected too much of life. That way, you can't be disappointed. I got more than I expected, as it turned out. Em and the Postal Department were mighty good to me.

I'm trying these days to make myself stop listening for her step. One thing about her, her step was like nobody else's. You always knew where she was. It impressed me when I first got to know her how fast she could skip along regardless.

It's been a sultry summer, the worst I can remember. Late every afternoon, thunderstorms over in the west, but they don't come to anything. The lawns have been brown since late July. So I guess they're right about the hole in the ozone. Darlene Bacheller tells me the frogs are dying out, their skins are too thin for the cosmic rays.

Steer by your stars, young Clark, and know that I'm pulling for you in your new commitment.

Fondly as always,
Grandfather Wilmot

There were other adherents, who came and went, camping out in the unheated outbuildings and melting away as the weather turned cold; but over the course of two years after Clark's arrival, and especially in the third year, coming and going in the band of disciples became increasingly difficult, as the scope of Jesse's mission widened in his vision and afflicted ever more sorely the world outside.

Without outside pressure, nothing might have changed. But what era or empire has ever failed to exert outside pressure? Even the Mormons by their remote and bitter lake had to be subdued to Gog's domination, and accept a President's appointed governor. The children of the Temple were the flashpoint. Why weren't they in school? Were they being abused? The social worker whose front tire Luke had threatened to puncture returned with a state trooper and a sheriff's deputy from Burr County. These three delegates from the land of Magog moved through the rooms and corridors, looking askance at the bleak ramshackle barracks, the obliquely branching halls, the arcane religious symbols carefully painted on doors and walls by Mephibosheth's Mercy, an artist who also did, from Polaroid photographs, fanatically detailed watercolors of the Temple's sweeping views and sold them through a gallery in Aspen. In the men's barracks, Jonas was spitting out vows to kill these invaders, while Luke looked on as if snakebit into paralysis and Jim placidly, with amused side-glances at Clark, argued the fatal folly of making any resistance at this moment. "This is not the time," Jim said. "Injure or alarm these three, and three hundred armed devils will follow with tanks and helicopters. They want an excuse to destroy us." But for all this cool advice the simpler men felt as a fever the presence of aliens and disbelievers in their secret, sacred space, hammered and gouged together by their own hands.

It had come to Jesse to bury an entire old school bus beneath the complex of wooden buildings, with a single trapdoor under a colorful carpet the women had made from rags: in this long hushed space, the folding doors sealed and the windows black with dirt, their guns were stored, not just the M-16s and AK-47s but handguns—Beretta 92s and Smith & Wesson .357 Magnums—and a .50-calibre anti-tank rifle and pounds of gunpowder and crates of grenade casings and more than one M-79 grenade launcher. Upon this treasure the Temple reposed; Jesse preached from Exodus 15:6: *Thy right hand, O Lord, is become glorious in power.* He cited Ezekiel 9:1: *Cause them that have charge over the city to draw near, even every man with his destroying weapon in his hand.* And he preached from the twenty-first chapter of Revelation, which describes the new Heaven and earth that will replace the old Heaven and earth—the walls of jasper twelve thousand furlongs square, and the city within, of pure gold like unto clear glass, with foundations adorned with sapphire, and chalcedony, and emerald. He read, "And the city had no need of the sun, neither of the moon, to shine in it; for the glory of God did lighten it, and the Lamb is the light thereof." Jesse was the Lamb: they took him to mean that even if the Temple were all buried like the old school bus his light would continue to shine in it. His light would never leave them, in that eternal temple of gold and emerald which lay beyond the horizon of mortal existence and human understanding.

He met the three visitors in the little auditorium, with a graceful high clerestory designed and built by Mephibosheth, which served the adults for their Bible-study sessions as well as the smaller children for their classroom. There were seventeen children at the moment, some fetched here with their parents but most conceived in the years of the Temple; as many as eleven were thought to be Jesse's own, by the testimony of the mothers. "We love our little ones," Jesse told the three interlopers. "We show our love by teaching them righteousness, so that on the Day of Reckoning they may be transported without delay to the Lord's abode."

"We'll need a census, to see what school-agers you have here," said the sheriff's deputy.

"The public schools of this country," Jesse said, "are cesspits of thievery, bullying, cigarette-smoking, glue-sniffing, pill-taking, instruction contrary to fact, and free condoms. Sex without procreation and science without God are the watchwords. The children learn to adore the devil-gods of rock music and licentious television commercials; they worship images on a screen until nothing else means squat. All of God's creation—the beasts of the field, the birds of the air—less than squat. I beg you, gentlemen and ma'am, don't destroy these young souls by dragging them off to be schooled in atheism and electronic black magic!"

The social worker, a plain plump woman with buck teeth and low-slung big breasts, said, "I was raised a Mormon, I can't disagree with a lot of what you say. But the law's the law for everybody; otherwise there won't be a country. Our evidence is these children are being brought up as ignorant little fanatics. Further, there's word of irregular sexual morality and physical abuse."

Jesse's eyes darkened, so their yellow glints sparked. "Our creed is love. Love is what we feel for one another. We do not always spare the rod," he admitted, "but any punishment is administered in love, for right reason. The children know in their hearts. Ask them yourselves."

"We love Jesse," one little boy quavered, and then, the ice broken, a nervous shrill chorus of professions followed. Standing behind the children, freckle-faced Hannah, pregnant for the second time in the ten seasons since she had brought Esau here early one night as winter was yielding to spring, bent and whispered, "Shall we sing our song?" Her sweet slight voice, shaky on the first notes, led theirs:

"Jesse is our Master,
 Jesse is our Lord:
Jesse makes us safe within
 His blessed, blessed horde."

The second stanza was less well memorized and harder to understand; its last word was "sword." Uneasily the state trooper, in his columbine-blue shirt and black-striped brown pants, wandered to the wall where a bulletin board displayed tacked-up childish drawings of a bald smiling man with a fringe of hair hanging to his shoulders, his hands together in prayer, radiating shaky hasty crayon lines of divine power. In some of the drawings, Jesse's eyes were prayerfully closed; in others, open and oval and unevadably staring. The trooper, a muscular humorless youth with a chin so deeply cleft it seemed a scar, asked Jesse, when the word "sword" had died away, "Mister, what are you claiming to be here? God Himself?"

Jesse in his huskiest voice, with a little smile, told him, " 'Thou sayest it.' Luke, twenty-three three."

But the trooper did not answer, as Pilate did, *I find no fault in this man.* He grunted and said, "There's laws against false claims and allegations. There has to be some limits, even in this day and age, where people say anything, right on the radio and TV."

The deputy, an older, smaller fellow in a gray suit and tarnished badge, interposed, "We understand a lot of your residents here have signed over all their life savings. This could be fraud, depending on the circumstances and the judge."

The children sensed a serious challenge and looked to Jesse to resolve it, to banish these doubters. "We of the Temple do not break laws," Jesse told the delegation sonorously. "On the contrary, the laws that are true we recast in everlasting steel, rolled from a fire hotter than the hottest forge. 'As therefore the tares are gathered and burned in the fire; so shall it be in the end of this world.' Think, my friend," he told the young trooper, "of what a second would be in the furnace of that pure fire, let alone ten seconds, let alone a minute, let alone eternity. You would burn, every cell and hair of your body would burn, the cells of your eyeballs and your most tender parts would burn, and each second would be reconstituted to burn again. You would beg for extinction, for merciful annihilation, for the one gift that does not lie within God's almighty power to give. 'Behold, I am alive for evermore, Amen; and have the keys of Hell and of death.' "

The beefy trooper's gaze broke and he glanced away, out the window, at the sere bright day gleaming in rapidly moving waves on the long autumnal grasses, buffalo grass and wild rye, of the front meadows. Jesse sighed and in a more conversational voice said to the social worker and the sheriff's deputy, "Talk to my brother Esau here. He'll give you a list of the children if you must have it. Those of school age, we'll have at the end of the road when the bus goes by. The time we got left before the Reckoning ain't long enough to fuss over. Our little ones know God's truth."

Clark had become Esau gradually. He had grown a beard, which though straggly and colorless at first had thickened and declared a surprising reddish tinge, and some wiriness to bulk it out into a spade shape. It abraded the skin of his neck and upper chest and reminded him of his new self; when he looked into a mirror—there were few, here at the Temple, but a wavery one hung in the men's washroom, to shave by—his eyes looked mild and younger than they had before and his lips in their nest of springy cedar-colored hair plumper and more sensual, though his last sex with Hannah had been months ago. It had to be stolen sex, since all the younger women now, all five of them, were brides of Jesse. She had granted him entry from behind, lying on her side as unexcited and docile as a sheep, since she was queasy with the beginnings of her second pregnancy. How strange that had felt to Esau, his prick reaching up into her as if to push away Jesse's burgeoning seed; the thought was blasphemous, and exciting. Having wiped herself with toilet paper and tugged her pants and skirt back into place, Hannah told him she couldn't let him do that any more. If he got too hard up he could go after one of the others, such as Deborah or Jael, whom Jesse had been neglecting. But—her mouth stiffened like a schoolteacher's—if he loved Jesse enough he wouldn't need this; the other men didn't, except sometimes Tom, and then Polly would oblige her husband's cousin. So there was a traffic of sexual information among the women: with this knowledge, Esau's appetite had lessened. He needed his privacy.

He led the three visitors to the upstairs room where he was allowed to have his computer terminal and telephone. The room had been a bunkroom when this was a ranching family's home; now it was the untidy interface between the Temple and the world. Zebulun worked at an old black-lacquered kneehole desk whose cubbyholes were overflowing with receipts, permits, bills, bank statements, ultimatums, summonses. Esau had persuaded him to invest in a computer, a Formica-topped work-station table, some filing cabinets, and a laser printer; it meant stringing an electric line along the half-mile of dirt road up from the asphalt road that led to Lower Branch. With the kerosene lamps and log fires and the generator, they had been self-reliant, Jesse and Jonas pointed out. But Esau argued that, unless they could control their publicity, they would get only bad publicity. Jesus Himself instructed the disciples, *Go ye into all the world.* If they were alive in today's world, Peter and Paul would be using computers. Jesse's pamphlets and analyses of Scripture could be beautifully worked up on the home-printing program with its variety of types and sizes and easy pictographics, and mailed and faxed out. "Hate to get it down on paper," Jesse admitted. "Once a thought's down, it's dead; it can't grow." Passed from mouth to ear to mouth, testimony grew and enlarged and became infused with every man's wishes and thoughts. "That wire," he said, of the electric wire, "is the Devil's tightrope; he'll walk it in, sure as birdshit falls from trees." Esau promised that his equipment, as morally neutral as an automobile, would spread the word, keep the Temple's accounts, and hold the authorities at bay.

The largest desk in this room—a bunkroom, once, for the seasonal ranch hands, its floors scarred with spur-marks and its walls spiky with clothes-pegs—was reserved for Jesse, but his desk stayed clean-topped and unused. He spent his time in the other big upstairs room, his bedroom, with a wife or wives, or haranguing his faithful in the auditorium, at whatever hour of the day or night inspiration struck him, or walking the perimeters of the yard, within the barbed wire the Temple had strung, gazing up at the mountains where he had once lived. As the summer waned, giant clouds with scum-brown centers poured out of the western desert onto the peaks, hiding their snow-streaked tips. "It won't be long," he would say to Esau, his tawny eyes glinting in amused foreknowledge. "We're wired for disaster." Yet thanks to his equipment Esau was now able to call up and print out in swift triplicate a list of the Temple's children, with their ages, thus establishing a gingerly credibility with the social worker and her two protectors.

The deputy wore a shiny gray business suit with a star-shaped badge pulling one lapel awry and a spine that made him carry his skinny body with a twist in it; of the invaders he was the least hostile, the most conversational. He handed Esau back a smaller piece of paper—several pieces attached together, with carbon-paper interleaves. "You owe Burr County three thousand seven hundred and twenty-one dollars in back property taxes," he said.

"We know that, we're working on it," Esau said, and with several taps of the keyboard called up for display a glowing screen of mostly negative numbers. "Our leader, Mr. Smith, resists the idea that we owe the government anything. We live independent here, and ask no services."

The deputy said, "You ask for roads to drive down to Lower Branch on, for supplies and employment, those of you that got jobs. You ask to be protected from the Russians. There's a lot you people ask, without knowing it. If it was this simple to hide from taxes, everybody would be doing it. Everybody would go for some squirrelly religion if that's all it took."

"O.K., I guess I see your point," Esau said, stalling. "How about you, Zeb?"

Zebulun had come in, big and waxy and foolishly, nervously smiling and blinking. He wanted the apparition of these intruders to go away and was counting on Esau to perform the magic—like pressing DELETE on the computer. "No problem for me," he agreed, but asked suspiciously, "What does Big Daddy say?" Big Daddy was the name some of the younger wives and older children had given Jesse, and it had impishly spread through the Temple. Jesse didn't seem to mind it.

"Big Daddy wants to stay out of it," Esau said. "He wants me to handle it." To the reasonable-looking, twisted, and half-obliging deputy he said, "In principle, we pay our taxes. We render unto Caesar."

"There are some other problems." The big cleft-chin state trooper, moving closer with rather menacing baby steps, said, "Neighbors on both sides been complaining they hear gunshots from dawn on, some of them, from the sound, from automatic repeaters. You know those aren't legal."

"We got a right to target practice," Zebulun said, giggling without meaning to. "It's set up in the canyon, where there's only rocks around." He loved his guns with a truly feeble-minded love. He and Luke and Jonas had fierce target-practice competitions; Esau had surprised himself, taking a ten-pound Kalashnikov into his grip one day, by being not a bad shot himself. You keep steady and squint and squeeze. Two hundred yards away, a can jumps, a piece of old crockery explodes. Magic. Quick and neat as a computer key.

Blushing behind his beard at the sweep of the attempted deception (but the tingling of his skin signalling that at least he was alive; he was playing the game of life), Esau punched some more keys and swirled his mouse around and clicked it and produced a screen listing their guns, the number of the permit for each neatly aligned beside. "There's our armaments," he lied. "Less than a gun per man, and all standard single-shot hunting and sport weapons. Look," he told the state cop, and smoothly turned to widen his plea to the other two agents of Gog. "You don't want a legal hornet's nest. There are constitutional issues here—freedom of religion, right to bear arms—that really resonate in this part of the U.S. Is this still a free country or not? Sure, our theology isn't your standard Sunday-school disposable generic brand. We try to take the Bible at its word. True and Actual Faith—we try to live by the literal Word of the Lord. This is un-American? What are you telling me? We want to be left alone. Is this un-American? I say it's *real* American. You heard the Big Man. He said, O.K., you're bigger than we are. When the Day of Reckoning comes, we'll see who's bigger, but for now, O.K., sure, you win. We'll give you our school-age children. We'll catch up on our taxes. But don't push. I'm reasonable, Zeb's reasonable, but our Big Man here is very sincere. You've seen him, you've heard him talk. Human life to him is just a phase we're in. A preliminary phase. If he tells us, *Die,* we gladly will. That's our advantage over you guys. We see life in proportion, in relation to the last things, the ultimate things, whereas to most people—I don't say *you,* necessarily—it's something to cling to no matter what the price. Most people are afraid to die, and that acts as a stumbling block. They're not *free.* We're not afraid. We're *free.* We know that no matter what happens we're going to be saved. Isn't that right, Zeb?"

"That's right. Jesse's going to save us."

"He *has* saved us, brother," Esau gently corrected. "We're beyond harm. We're living already in the light of the Temple above. 'Whosoever will save his life shall lose it'—you folks know the verse?"

The deputy and social worker nodded; the beefy state

trooper took one of his aggressive baby steps and said, "Hey, give us a break. We've all heard preaching in our lives. This is a Tuesday morning."

"You see," Esau concluded patiently, "you of the world are still trying to save your lives, that's why you're losing them. Look. I'm not naïve. I've lived in the world. I've tasted its pleasures right down to the bitter, bitter dregs. I've done dope. I've done women. They leave you worse off than you were before. I have nothing left to lose. Neither does Zeb. This is a delicate situation, is all I'm saying. You come in here with your six-shooters and your summonses and legal crap, you might get more back than you bargained for. I'm not talking for myself, I'm talking for our Big Man. The Lord's righteousness is like unto dynamite—don't play with it."

"You threatening us?" the state cop asked. "Let's not forget, buddy, the government's got some dynamite of its own."

Esau shrugged. It was as when, back in Hollywood, trying to put together a package, he did his best to sell a tableful of bankers on a project, and without their saying a word he could feel resistance rising, the atmosphere congealing. He backed off a bit. "Tact," he said. "I'm asking that you folks show some tact. What laws are we breaking?"

"There's been a lot of talk in town about polygamy," the social worker said.

Esau said, "Mr. Jesse Smith is married to nobody. He is a legal bachelor, as am I. The married couples here are married only once at a time. More than that, we have a Constitutional right to privacy."

"Maybe less than you think," the state cop said. "There's laws protecting minors. There's laws against perversions."

Esau looked at the half-tolerant deputy and winked. "Yes, and there's laws against ripping the tag off a pillow," he said.

He sometimes remembered a night back in 1984, when one more package of which he had been a minor but salaried part had not been bought by the banks and collapsed, and he had given himself the satisfaction in parting of telling the faggy would-be director what a phony pretentious prima donna he was, and he had gone on with some geek who wanted to become his dope dealer over to some newly opened club in the Valley with a lot of these identical fascist surfer types with great tans and studded leather vests and close-cropped blond hair standing around staring like bit parts from *Blade Runner*, zombies invading from the super-queer cool future. Clark had had four vodka-and-oranges and done some lines in the men's room and not only was his stomach upset and empty but his septum itched and burned hellishly and whenever he blew his nose he got blood. The Olympics were all over television that summer and a woman was running for Vice-President; cases of AIDS were adding up and so were the bodies of starved children in Ethiopia; the first black Miss America resigned because of some old nude photographs in *Penthouse* and Jim Fixx dropped dead while jogging; a fired security guard armed with three guns walked into a McDonald's in San Ysidro and killed twenty, including a number of children. That was the ten o'clock news, which Clark watched in his room. Downstairs Mom was entertaining a portly shadowy man with his temples grayed as if air-brushed. Coming into the house, Clark was invited to sit with them, and was too stoned and spooked to resist; any company was better than facing himself alone in his room. He could tell from the smell in the air, an extra dab of perfume, a musky whiff of excitement, that Mom was putting out her heat for this guy, who looked to Clark not much younger than his grandfather.

"Dear, do say hello to Mr. Wentworth. Mr. Wentworth comes from Boston and is part of the new management team Coca-Cola is installing at Columbia." They had got back from dinner somewhere; Mom was wearing a clingy loose crackly pajama outfit of lime-green silk, with red-strapped stiletto heels that clung to her narrow tan feet like bright little traps; she kept crossing her legs and swinging her ankles, to show how thin they were. Clark had often heard her say that, having seen her mother balloon up, she would never tolerate an extra ounce on her own body, and she had stuck to it, with diets and a treadmill and weights to keep the arm flab off; she weighed no more than she had at eighteen but the weight was brittle, and her face after her most recent lift and lid job looked pulled, as if by wires hidden under her hair, which was dyed rust-color and cut in a sleek short Isabella Rossellini–style tousle. She was telling the man in his smoke-gray suit about the old days at Columbia: "Harry was a *dear* to me, though I know a lot of people hated him. He could be crude and inconsiderate, it was true, but I think a lot of the dislike was simple jealousy; he was so much more clever than the studio mafia in general. They were ragpickers, most of them, or the sons of ragpickers, whereas Harry's father had at least been a tailor. He had brought the company up from absolute Poverty Row, doing these pathetic Hall Room Boys two-reelers—one time on his yacht he re*galed* me with how they would save money by using short-ends of film bought from Paramount and Universal and painting *both* sides of the scenery and even, you won't believe this, making up only one side of the actress's face if she was going to be shot in profile during that scene—up from being this kind of penny-pinching sweatshop—the original name was Cohn-Brandt-Cohn or CBC and people called them Corned Beef and Cabbage and so Harry, who was a snob really and like most snobs terribly easily hurt, grandly called it Columbia—up to all those Academy awards for Capra and then of course Hayworth and *Eternity* and *River Kwai* and so on. The year after he died was the very first year the studio went into the red. This at a time when all the majors were *deep* in the red. After that, of course, it was the British productions, *Lawrence* and so on, and to give her her due Streisand that carried it, kept it alive, all through the Seventies. Oh, yes, you're going to say *Easy Rider* and *Bob and Carol and Ted* and whoever the other one was, but these weren't exactly the bread-and-butter kind of pictures, were they? They lost a fortune, I know, on a ridiculous musical remake of *Lost Horizon*, one of my *very* favorite pictures when I was a girl. I watched the original again on video the other week and really it *was* absurd, I had to admit, these tatty sets and the backdrops so obviously painted. A girl doesn't see any of that. But Clark. You must tell us about yourself. What fun did you have this evening? How did the pitch for your little romantic comedy go?"

"It didn't. It's *fini*. I quit. I told Don what a shit he was."

"I'm sure he was *so* glad to hear it. From such an expert on shits as you."

Mr. Wentworth fussily cleared his throat and said, "Young fellow, would you like a drink?" His face was round and clean and closed, with red flecks of actinic damage on the cheekbones; he knew a thing or two, his small eyes told you, in a not especially friendly fashion. They were an intense deep blue, like the glass in certain old-fashioned medicine bottles. He had a dry, squeezed-nose way of talking; Clark supposed that was a New England accent. To Clark his suit was sending out vibrations: the gray wasn't exactly one shade or another, and a kind of ultra-violet shimmer came off it, in waves. Maybe all these qualities were in Clark's head, like Vaseline on the lens when the picture goes misty.

"Thanks, sir, but honestly I'm afraid I might throw up."

His mother stared at him, to see if he needed to have his stomach pumped. She hadn't worked for a year, and he knew it drove her crazy. Her last role had been as an astronaut's mother; they had given her big also-featuring billing but couldn't write enough new lines to make it more than a cameo. She had been offered Eleanor Roosevelt, with fake teeth of course, in a four-part TV docudrama about the lead-up to Pearl Harbor, and she had gone into a rage at being offered a part so old. When he did the math in his head it wasn't so far off. Among movie people Clark's age she was a joke, a relic still walking and talking like something at Disneyland. They confused her generation with that of Myrna Loy, when in fact she was a well-preserved fifty-four, still capable of vamping as he could see. "Then perhaps you'd like to go up to your room, darling," she said. "There are all sorts of messages Conchita and I have been writing down for you. You must be lending your friends money again, though I *beg* you not to. As Mr. Wentworth was very amusingly telling me, all Hollywood is going on lean-mean rations. So your friends must suffer along with the rest of us."

As he made his way up the stairs, he heard her continuing, in that breathless accentless onrushing voice she had been taught, "Now they have these terribly high hopes for this thing called *Ghostbusters* but from all that *I* hear it's just another brawl with those *Saturday Night Live* juveniles, who become utterly *charmless* on the big screen."

In his room Clark looked out the window at the lights of Los Angeles receding in their checkerboard from West Hollywood south to Inglewood and the clump of lit skyscrapers downtown and beyond to a thin dissolve of oceanic blackness under a sky that didn't look like a sky, it was so full of reflected light the stars were drowned, rubbed out, but for the multicolor winking planes slanting in to the airport. He remembered how in Delaware in the fall the stars got bigger after first frost, big as blue plums above the defoliating trees, but those days were rubbed out, too. School days, Golden Rule days. He felt hungry but couldn't think of any food that wouldn't make him sicker. He looked over the messages but Mom was right, it was all people who wanted something, nobody who had anything to give him. The eleven o'clock news disgusted and saddened him, especially the hungry healthy way the two talking heads gobbled it off the TelePrompTers and spat it out, their mouths moving like busy little parasites attached to their faces. The world as entertainer fell flat some days. He used his room as a place to come in the morning to change clothes. He hadn't slept here for two nights. One night he had spent in a girl's bedroom with her mother and her boyfriend grinding away right on the other side of the wall, and the next he had crashed over in Simi somewhere with some guys he had picked up at The Ginger Man.

In the drawer of his bedside table he found a half-smoked joint and a porno video he had been watching and got bored with. He put the roach in his mouth and lit it and put the video in the VCR and clicked it to play. He turned off all the lights so there was just the red glow moving back and forth to his lips and the rectangular jiggling glow of the TV screen and the lights of Los Angeles at his side like those of a giant runway receding on a screaming takeoff. The pot began to mollify his sense of recent injury and the action on the video switched from the mistress of the mansion doing it with two African-American burglars who had bound and blindfolded her to belowstairs, where the maid and the young long-haired butler were getting it on. The brunette maid in her black-and-white mini maid's uniform, which came off to reveal red garters, was lithe and nimble-tongued and seemed to be getting into it, her ass perched up on the hard kitchen counter, having her brunette pussy eaten out. She kept on her little lace cap and lace choker. She reminded him of someone, the quick avid elastic way she moved and flared her nostrils in supposed ecstasy.and rolled her eyes back into her skull so mostly white showed. His mother. His mother when young, before he was born, when her hair was dark. This supposed French maid even had an upper lip like Mom, puffed up and like a bent pillow, so when the camera came in close on her tipped-back face while her pussy was being eaten its flesh formed two sides with the lower lip of a black triangle so full of saliva a momentary bubble formed that you could see the camera lights reflected in. Of course it wasn't his mother but it could have been twenty-five years ago. When she was pregnant with him: the thought made him queasy.

There was an innocence flickering through the supposed French maid's act, a down-home girl from somewhere's simple wish to please; the sound track under its disco throb caught little words she said softly, "Nice" and "Mmm" and "Oh, yes," less for the camera than for the other performer, encouraging him to keep up his end. When her turn came in the unvarying scenario of these films to blow the butler, she really put herself into it, her whole head thrusting down the shaft with a little extra effort, deep-throating, teasing the veined skin with her slightly buck teeth, her lips pushing all the way to his pubic hair while her hand with its long red curved whore's nails played scratchingly with his balls. The guy's hard-on got big enough to choke on; some of these girls can never produce the excitement, the spaces of sly tenderness that bring a man up amid the harsh lights and tight schedule and silently scoffing cameramen. Clark had been involved over in the Valley with a couple of hard-core productions and he knew the technical problems. The "wood" problems. Women on women was much more dependable. He had slipped his pants and underpants down on the bed and with his left hand matched the brunette's mouth stroke for stroke, as she kept glancing hopefully upward to the male face, which was off the screen—his mother's look of bright expectancy at its purest, a look he seldom saw any more, as she expected less and less of him. He'd show her, the bitch. His own eyes rolled back into his skull and his airplane lifted off with a shiver of propulsion and a set of diminishing throbs. When he looked again the butler was jerking off on the maid's face, white gobs like Elmer's glue which she was licking off her fingertips, still girlishly, shrewdly eager to please, and Clark had come all over himself, his hand and pubic hair and the band of his underpants. God, people are disgusting. The roach still burned in his other hand. He took one last toke deep into his lungs and resolved to get out of Los Angeles, out of reach of the fucking movies.

The Temple didn't grow, but it didn't shrink much either. Zebulun's parents came to visit all the way from Maui, and though the shy old couple—like a pair of carved dolls that couldn't stop nodding—didn't stay, when they left there was more money available for defense weapons and stockpiled canned goods and frozen food in the giant humming freezers installed in the buried school bus, now that they had electricity. Jesse's sense of foreboding and his readings of Revelation grew more dire. He asked that white robes be made for his disciples, to be worn at Bible study, in accordance with Revelation 7:9, wherein multitudes stand before the Lamb "clothed with white robes," and with 6:11: *And white robes were given unto every one of them; and it was said unto them, that they should rest yet for a little season, until their fellowservants also and their brethren, that should be killed as they were, should be fulfilled.* Putting on one of the gowns the Temple women had made from bed-sheets, Esau felt the slither of death's touch. Yet he continued to drive the Ranger pickup into Lower Branch, its scattering of steep-peaked houses and its Total gas station and 7-Eleven and, below where the branching road made a triangle, Mildred's Breakfast and Diner and J.C.'s Café and Tru-Value hardware store and a struggling unpainted non-denominational church and the two-story cement-block civic building combining town hall and police headquarters and a one-cell lockup: there he would deal with the minions of Gog—paying the tax collector, placating the social worker, striving with the sheriff's deputy to keep the Temple within the letter of state and county law, arranging with the occasional newspaper or TV reporter an interview with Jesse and a carefully supervised tour of Temple premises. Returning then, besmirched by contact with the corrupt world, to put on his disciple's gown and sit and listen to Jesse rant upon the most ghastly passages of Ezekiel and Jeremiah and Revelation, pounding this desert lode of old grief into a present furious sword until his hoarse voice croaked shut, was no more strange, Esau told himself, than shifting from one to another of any of the layers that make up human existence—from wakefulness to sleep, from social dress and conversation to the mute nakedness of lovemaking, from eating blessed cereal at a ceremonial table to shitting in hunched solitude on a cold bowl. Man is a mixed bag, a landscape of swamps and caves as well as sunlit slopes. Reality is a kind of movie the self projects, and the director of special effects just needs a decent budget to turn the sun as black as a sackcloth of hair, and roll back the scroll of the sky, and cast the stars down from the sky as a fig tree casteth her untimely figs when she is shaken in a mighty wind.

The fall of 1989 turned bare and brisk. Karen, the oldest of the three children that Mercy and Mephibosheth had brought to the Temple, brought back from the regional high school, where she had been placed in the tenth grade, word that her biology teacher, a smart-aleck young son of Ham from the Five Points section of Denver, had told them that though so-called creationism was a theory still entertained by many backward people, including state legislators, the evidence overwhelmingly rules out a Creator in favor of random cosmic events producing amid many hellishly hot or frigid planets one suitable for life, life which arose when accidental permutations of complex molecules present in the warm primeval soup or sludge fell into combinations that replicated themselves; from there on it was all the carnage of big critters eating small ones and survival of the fittest as described by the self-employed English naturalist Charles Darwin, one of the nineteenth century's great men. When Karen had shakily asked her African-American instructor about Jesus Christ, he had said, in front of the whole class, that, while Jesus and the rumors that attached to him have been a fixation of white-dominated European culture since about the year 300, the vastly greater majority of the world's population have through recorded time believed in other gods or no distinct god at all. And their lives, he added, were probably no less happy and unhappy than ours. Religion is a curious appetite, the instructor mused, and as with the appetite for food a great variety of substances will satisfy it, including some pretty bizarre dishes if the hunger is strong enough. The girl, though she knew there was evil out there, had never heard it expressed so bluntly, by a teacher and not a rudely taunting other child.

The next morning, in the heavy dew, Luke told the children to stay in the Temple and went out, into a swale in the lower right-hand meadow where a thicket of little gambel oaks grew, with an M-16 he had fitted with a telescopic sight. When, at seven-thirty, the orange-yellow school bus came along the macadamized road, and stopped and tooted at the end of the Temple's dirt road, Luke from about a hundred fifty yards away shot out the two tires on his side. It was a crisp November morning, with the foretaste of winter in the wind and the sky overhead as blue as a lupine and the leaves of the little oaks turning a papery khaki color. In his telescopic sight, with the rifle steadied on a low branch, he could see beautifully. He could see the bus driver, a plump bleached blonde in an ochre suede jacket, roll down her window to look at her front tire; he could see the glint on the chrome edge of her side mirror. He could see, as he swept the rifle in a gentle arc, the little faces cramming up against the cloudy windows in curiosity. The windows made their faces look dirty. Their mouths were open making a shrill noise he couldn't hear. When he took out the back tire and swept the sight back, the faces had all disappeared—ducked down, he guessed—so he took out a few of the windows for good measure. It made him cackle to see that safety glass vanish into a thousand crumbs. The bus driver was so foolish or non-comprehending as to lever open her door and stand there, looking first up the road and then in his direction. That woman should lose some weight. Luke rested his cross-hairs on her round blond head, that painted hair pinned tight against her head, but you could bet she let it down at night, this pig-fat hussy hauling off righteous children to drink from the foul wells of Godlessness. It would be a righteous deed to put her out of her misery, but he contented himself with the elongated mirror glinting a foot above her ear. When it shattered, she ducked as fast as if the spinning lead had grazed the shining yellow hair of her harlot's skull. There was a silent peace, an utterly still intimacy in the gunsight that he hated to leave, like a peephole drilled straight through to Paradise, but he figured he better hightail it back to the Temple walls, having made his point.

He came in the back way and the men of the Temple, having heard the shots and seeing the stalled school bus from the upper windows, greeted him in the kitchen with a gabble of agitated voices. "I can't believe you did that," Esau said. Luke sneered at the soft recruit's face, which had gone pale above the ruddy crescent of its pseudo-Biblical beard.

"You've been flirting with the Devil's troop too long, Slick. Go on out to them, now's your chance."

But Clark doubted that he would get very far down the road without a bullet in his back. His groin went watery at the thought; he pictured his body as terribly apt to puncture and tear in the jagged company of these hard men, hard by nature and hard by creed.

Jesse came down from his bedroom, looking like an old woman in a loose nightshirt of striped flannel. Of late he had been sleeping the mornings away, sometimes to noon, his duties with the women and his study of the Bible keeping him long awake. The women reported in whispers how visions churned in him at night, making him shout out and break into a sweat. The skin of his face was unshaven and slack, and his bare feet below the hem of his nightshirt touchingly lumpy, chafed pink in spots and callused yellow in others, as if they had never been made to be walked on. He listened to Luke's account and tension returned to his face, and light to his tawny eyes, naked of their circular glasses. Jesse lifted his sleeved arms now, there at the end of the long harvest table where they ate, and announced, " 'The days are at hand, and the effect of every vision. For there shall be no more any vain vision nor flattering divination within the house of Israel.' Ezekiel twelve. The meaning of that, my brethren, is, the fat's in the fire. 'These shall make war with the Lamb, and the Lamb shall overcome them, and they that are with him are called, and chosen, and faithful.' "

The other mountain-men, Luke and Jonas, sent up a jubilant whoop, and Zebulun and Mephibosheth shut their faces against any course other than following their master. Esau looked toward Tom and Jim and saw there shades of his own trepidation, but then Jim, the married one, caught Esau's eye and winked and shrugged; so Esau felt complicit. He was conscripted. He had been too young for a military draft and the most danger he had known had been from hard drugs and cars driven fast along the curves of Mulholland Drive in a fog. He was in some underdeveloped sector of himself gratified. The time had come to convert his faith into deeds. He imagined that Jesse's sore-looking eyes had turned toward him when the prophet had spoken of vain vision and flattering divination—as if Esau's traffic with the civic forces surrounding them had been a betrayal instead of a service, the propagandizing of the Lamb's good news. He'd show them.

The ruckus had drawn the women and the children downstairs and in from their rooms along the wooden corridors. "Fear not, my gentle ones," Jesse announced to them. "The day of our glory approaches." The women were told to prepare for a siege, and to gather warm clothes and bedding and all that was needful and to repair with the children to the underground bunker. Zebulun and Mephibosheth were instructed to fetch guns from the places where they had been hidden. Jonas and Jim were commanded to mount watch from the roof, which Mephibosheth had made accessible through building a trapdoor and a small platform behind the chimney. Within minutes these sentries shouted down that the bus driver had opened the emergency exit on the far side and was ushering her charges in double file along the road, in the direction of the neighbor a mile distant. "Shall we give 'em some lead?" Jonas asked in a yell.

"Those are *chil*dren!" Esau told Jesse.

Jesse had dressed himself in jeans and sneakers and several

sweaters and over them a bulky green vest, his Army combat vest with its many square pockets. He was moving faster, with more energy and grace, than Esau had seen for months. "*Negative!*" he yelled back. "Hold your fire!"

"The man's crazy," Esau told him.

"Some would say inspired," Jesse said huskily, his eyes darting about the living room, checking the windows, the other men coming in and out, the crystalline out-of-doors. Yet he found time to minister to this one of his flock. "Brother Esau, it was bound to come. It's all in the Book. There has to be a day of wrath to pare it down to the hundred forty-four thousand of the saved. That's the math of it, and the truth of it. There has to be a winnowing. Scared?"

"I don't know. I've never been in a fight like this."

"Some take to it, some don't. You might surprise yourself."

Jesse and Luke calculated that the bus driver would need half an hour to shepherd her children to the neighboring ranch. If she met a hired hand out in a vehicle or on a horse, the time could be less. Then allow the authorities a half-hour to get organized and drive out from the center of Lower Branch.

Sure enough, within half an hour the phone began to ring, piercingly, upstairs in the Temple office. Esau raced to answer it, but somewhat to his relief Luke, with an olive-green cloth bandolier of ammunition magazines slung across his shoulder, was explaining in a patient twang, "Well, see, that was a kind of lawful protest against your hauling off our children and filling their innocent heads full of a lot of atheistic propyganda. Wasn't nobody hurt, that's the way we intended, but any armed men come around I can't make that same promise. We got a God-given, Constitutional right to defend ourselves."

Esau picked up the extension on Jesse's unused desk and said, "Eddie, that you? We'll pay for the tires and the windows—send us a bill. Just don't send anybody around. Things are touchy right now. The mood here is explosive."

"Clark," Eddie, the sheriff's deputy, rather languidly said, "you don't go shooting up county school buses. That's just not done. I'm afraid we got to bring somebody in for it. Already, we've got reporters on the line, wanting a story."

Luke broke in, "Mister, don't pay no mind to what Slick here says—you're not getting no tire money out of me nor Big Daddy neither."

Esau was not surprised that the mountain men called him Slick behind his back. At times, after an afternoon spent in Lower Branch sharing a brew with Eddie at J.C.'s or jollying up Charlie Rowe, the Burr County tax commissioner, he had felt slick to himself. But Jesse appreciated him, he knew. *From each according to his talents.*

Luke was going on into the phone, "We been paying taxes like royal suckers and what've you morons been doing with the money? Feeding a ton of welfare freeloaders and pouring Hell's own slop into our children's heads." Then he hung up.

Within twenty seconds it rang again. Esau reached for the extension but Luke yanked the main phone so the wires pulled up the box at the baseboard, and the receiver at Esau's ear went dead. There was a purity to the silence, and a bliss in the fact that he could do no more; he had gone the extra mile, it was out of his hands. He reported Luke's crazy action to Jesse and Jesse smiled, a little the way Jim had winked. The prophet searched his mind for a quote and came up with, " 'Every branch in me that beareth not fruit he taketh away.' "

Jesse seemed a foot taller, taking charge, assigning men their posts, stroking the heads of the gathered children and looking for a second into the faces of each. Before they descended into the bunker, with their blankets and stuffed toys and food supplies, Jesse asked them all, the women and children and men still in the living room, to huddle in front of the cold fireplace for a Bible reading. He read to them from Revelation 21: " 'And God shall wipe away all tears from their eyes; and there shall be no more death, neither sorrow, nor crying, neither shall there be any more pain: for the former things are passed away.

" 'And he that sat upon the throne said, Behold, I make all

things new. And he said unto me, Write: for these words are true and faithful.

" 'And he said unto me, It is done. I am Alpha and Omega, the beginning and the end. I will give unto him that is athirst of the fountain of the water of life freely.

" 'He that overcometh shall inherit all things; and I will be his God, and he shall be my son.

" 'But the fearful, and unbelieving, and the abominable, and murderers, and whoremongers, and sorcerers, and idolaters, and all liars, shall have their part in the lake which burneth with fire and brimstone: which is the second death.' "

Jesse looked up and told his frightened flock, "Those murderers and idolators, those whoremongers and liars will soon be at our gates. But, little loved ones, I am Alpha and Omega. My enemies shall be thrown into the lake of fire and brimstone, and I will give the faithful freely of the water of life. There will be for us no more death, or sorrow, or crying. Children, what did God promise He would do? Who can remember what I just read?"

He looked hopefully into the little faces, and all were silent until a scared boy of about five said tremulously, "Wipe, wipe away—"

"God shall with His own beautiful hand wipe away all the tears from our eyes," Jesse paraphrased. "Now, is there any more beautiful passage in Holy Scripture than this solemn promise in Revelation? Better believe it, my little ones, and allow the fear to ease from your systems. Jesse is watching over you. Big Daddy promises to take you with him wherever he goes. Amen. Now hustle your butts down below with your mommas and don't come out till a voice you know for sure calls you out."

Some of the older children laughed at the sudden "hustle your butts"; the smaller ones were in a transfixed state, beyond laughing or any expressed emotion. An animal freeze reflex had rendered them numb, clustering close to their mothers; a number of their noses were running, and one little girl had a bright nosebleed from one nostril, which no one was attending to, as they all shuffled in a hush off to the bunker.

Luke and Zebulun both had their tactical ideas but the more urbanized, younger men only trusted Jesse. The mists that had lately been befogging his spirit—from excessive simmering in Revelation and female sexual juices—had burned away; he was calm and faintly aloof and lazily leonine, the way Clark remembered him the first time they met. He sent Luke up to the roof with his telescoped M-16 and the lightweight M-79 grenade launcher; Tom and Mephibosheth were to guard the back with AK-47s, Jonas and Jim were brought down from the roof to join Matthew on the second floor, and Zebulun and Esau and himself were stationed on the first floor, the first line of defense. Jesse kept an M-16 for himself, tucked some spare rifles—converted AR-15s, mostly—and a stack of ammunition magazines over against the fieldstone fireplace, and put Zebulun in charge of the .50-calibre Browning machine gun. They mounted its tripod on the overturned bookcase, which they lifted some inches up on Bibles, behind a shield improvised from a rusty old tractor seat jammed into the half-open window. The plump Hawaiian dimpled and giggled in delight at this sign of trust from his leader; in his apprehensive happiness he kept testing different chairs in which to seat himself behind the gun, like a pianist finicking over the bench height.

Jesse said, "Slick, here's a special gal I know you're going to love," and placed in Esau's hands a graceful old-style hunting rifle; the long blued barrel floated outward like a flexible, sensitive wand when he embraced the polished stock, of silky checkered walnut. "Ruger M-77," Jesse said. "Three hundred Winchester Magnum. Pop the pimple on your girlfriend's nose at five hundred yards." It was Jesse's teasing way to speak to his men as if they had roguishly active sex lives, when he had taken all their women from them. But one of his cryptic salutes or recognitions lay in giving Esau not a coarsely murderous military automatic but this delicate bolt-action scalpel of a weapon; he was finer, he felt Jesse was saying, than these hammer-handed rubes around them.

The Ruger's rear sight was an intricate leaf shape, the front sight a beaded ramp that seemed to Esau, waving the barrel through the window, to swing into its target like a ball of mercury popping into the bottom of a cup. Jesse had shown him his window, there in the living room; Esau took the creaky green-painted kitchen chair Jesse had sat on when they had first talked. He propped open the loose worn window with a stick of kindling and nestled his face into the cool smooth concavity of the stock's cheek piece and let his gunsight follow the drifting flight of a hawk cruising the valley below. The November wind was sharp on his face and his eyes watered as he took in the beauty of the morning: the mountainside falling away in blowing grassy terraces interrupted by clumps of cottonwood and pine, the sun hidden behind an approaching slant sheet of cloud whose edges were white eddies of fish-scales sculptured like curved ribs of sand left by a receded tide, the receding valley miles beyond and below struck by yellow sunlight beyond the giant cloud so that its ragged lake gleamed a blind blue and the tilled and fenced fields in these lowlands seemed a checkerboard of nappy, nicely sewn fabrics. He did not want to give up this world but must believe that its glory was the pale shadow, the weak foretaste, of a better. *If God so clothe the grass of the field, which today is, and tomorrow is cast into the oven, shall he not much more clothe you, O ye of little faith?* He clung to his gun lightly, as if this slender machined construction of steel and wood were indeed a woman, a slim resilient mother who would bring him through this fever, this fear, this burning water above his organs of excretion. His strained nerves seemed to be lifting him off the floor, so his feet in their scuffed orange Frye boots belonged to somebody else and were as remote as the hawk he had lost sight of. He kept swallowing something thicker than saliva. He had a sudden vision of something he enormously wanted—one of those peanut-butter sandwiches he used to make as a child, of two Keebler saltines, square in shape but breakable into two, at the counter of the kitchen overlooking the swimming pool, when Rex wasn't there and he had hours to kill before Mom showed up full of her day and dying for a Spritzer.

Above him the men on the second floor were tramping loudly, in circles it seemed, to work off their nervousness. Each minute of waiting was so long a thousand small noises filled it. "Gog's having a slow day," Jesse drawled. "Must be a bake sale over in Magog City." It occurred to Esau that Jesse had taken the two least dependable men, himself and Zebulun, under his wing here. *Upon this rock.*

The footsteps upstairs went still; Clark heard the murmur of the approaching cars, a murmur so subtle it might be imaginary, like a breeze in tree branches, or the rustle of blood in your skull. Then the breach in the morning's peace rapidly enlarged, though still out of sight, since the road was at a lower level than the pastures where sheep nosed after green leftovers in the frostbitten brown grass. Two tiny vehicles appeared far down the dirt road—a white police car with its blue rooflight whirling and a pale-blue van behind it. "Murderers and whoremongers and sorcerers," Jesse quoted aloud in a light voice, to amuse himself or to hearten Esau and Zebulun. "The beast and the kings of earth have sent their disbelieving weasels."

The four-rail gate to the Temple yard, fenced off from the sheep by barbed wire, had been closed and chained with a plastic-sheathed padlocked chain. It took the three men from the state-police car—two in state troopers' wide flat-rimmed green hats and black winter jackets, the third in a gray suit, with a bent way of holding himself—some minutes while they puzzled at the chain and the situation. One cop produced a bullhorn but Esau's blood was pounding in his head so hard he couldn't hear what was said. It was an urgent, barking mumble. Then came the sound of a gunshot, rather puny in this vast out-of-doors beneath that huge leaning leaden sheet of cloud crumbling above at its edges into the light of a hidden sun. The shot might have come from above, from Luke on the roof, or been one of the policemen shooting out the padlock. Very quickly, and like a film in no synchronization with the rattle of gunfire and indignant yells of men, the police car rammed through the gate, shedding its shattered long boards as it moved forward fifty yards or so and then stopped, when its windshield shattered and holes began jumping up in its hood. The two cops got out with drawn pistols and one of them immediately did a hippety-hop and fell in the dust by his back tire; the other crouched behind the car but it wasn't giving him enough shelter. From the angle of Esau's window, the farthest to the left, a silhouetted slice of the crouching figure showed through two upright slats of the porch rail. The blue-barrelled Ruger's sight moved to place its bead on that target almost of its own snaky will. Not only was Clark's head suddenly as clear as an adjusted TV screen but his eyesight too; he could see the buckle on the cop's belt and the shine on his boots and the duller black gloss of his empty holster. Esau held the bead steady just above that holster and squeezed off a round; the recoil pushed his shoulder like a girl's playful tap of flirtation and the abstract target flipped away like a tin cutout in a shooting gallery. Then it became a man, a dark shape trying to writhe to safety underneath the car, a now-hatless trooper with the round white face of a boy, not even a boy, a white-faced mammal, a frightened hurt creature staring from its burrow. The trooper was trying to lie still but something, pain, kept stirring his body around underneath the car. The car, a new white Camaro with the black letters STATE PATROL on its hood, was swaying on its springs as bullets slammed lavishly into its thin metal. Zebulun was going into raptures with his machine gun, filling the room with smoke and the tinkle of brass cartridge shells hitting the floor, and the men on the second floor were pouring a racket out of their automatic rifles and whooping, ugly ecstatic noises out of their throats, and stamping on the floor with such a drumming of footsteps that Esau tried to picture the dance they were doing. There was a fat wet thump on the veranda roof; then a split-second's shadow such as a buzzard or an airplane passing in front of the sun casts flicked at the corner of Esau's vision. Whatever it had been was out of sight now beyond the porch boards, where he couldn't see. He could only see the porch rail with its upright slats, their dry paint raggedly scabbed off, and framed between them the little figures of the scene beyond.

The blue van hadn't come into the courtyard; two of the men in it had produced rifles and were firing from around its corners while the third man, crouching, raced up to the riddled police car with its shot-out windshield. Now the man in the gray suit who had come in the police car emerged from the back of it and began waving his arms in some kind of surrender. Clark recognized his friend Eddie, the sheriff's deputy. The bead of his gunsight just nicely covered the man's head at that distance but when he squeezed he evidently missed, because the deputy kept waving and holding his arms out in a wide frantic gesture as of benediction. Jesse, leaning against the frame of the window next to Esau's, snorted softly and said, "Looks like they've had enough of the power of the Lamb. Now they beg the mountains to cover them. What's your pleasure, Zeb? What do you say, Slick?"

Esau asked, "You can't shoot men not firing back, can you?"

"They've tres*passed*, brother. They'd never sin again, and would thank us from Heaven."

Zebulun asked, "Shall I do it? Shall I let 'em have it?"

Esau slipped the bolt back to reload and the naked oily metal in such close-up struck him as obscene, like an aroused dog's red bared penis.

" 'And death and hell delivered up the dead which were in them,' " Jesse quoted. "Revelation twenty. Those devils are already dead and damned forever, Slick, in the eyes of the righteous God. We got to brush you up some day on the fine points of true and actual faith."

The two men by the van had thrown their guns into the grass and were moving forward with a stiff caution, one step at a time, arms out from their bodies, to help with the two bodies. The one first hit had never moved after doing its hippety-hop and the one under the car, whom Esau had shot—though he couldn't be sure, there had been so many bullets flying around—had rested his head on the earth so the white disc of his face no longer showed. He had lost his fancy hat. A quick round from upstairs, making the dirt leap up in a rope of dust pellets, froze all motion, out there on the bare front yard. Jesse, holding his M-16 with its muzzle down, pushed off from leaning against the window frame and sauntered out to the porch, the creaky porch stacked with firewood, and stood at the top of the steps. Esau had never heard Jesse's voice lifted so loud—lifted to the hills. "Take 'em away!" he yelled. "Take your carcasses into town and don't come back! This is the house of the Lord!"

The men upstairs shouted approval, and a line of lifting dust spatters raced toward the men frozen at the gate, and looped back, and made a galvanized bucket by the old pump dance.

Esau tried to remember Jesse firing a single shot, and could not. He was in a daze, like a trembling dog after copulation. His arms were still cradled around the slender gun. The day was darkening; the great slant cloud had lowered so close above them that its outriggers of white fish-scale could no longer be seen. The grazing sheep had moved lower down in their pasture, away from the bullets, but the hawk was still hung high over the valley, hunting in an effortless circular glide. A few specks of snow, dry as ash, skidded through the air beyond the porch rail. At first Esau thought the flakes might be spots in his vision, but no, they were real, tracing agitated paths in the air. In the distance—in long shot—the three tiny men hastened to carry the two limp bodies back into the van, a van, Esau realized, driven here to haul some of the Temple members off into custody. Now all of them were as guilty as hot-headed Luke. *And whosoever was not found written in the book of life was cast into the lake of fire.* Esau looked within himself at this turning point of his life and found only the sensation that Ezekiel calls "a voice of a great rushing," a deafening brook of pure being hurling through him in whirlpools and glittering frothy spines, the world's spacious life accelerated by being funnelled through his narrow self.

Jesse had come back inside and was calling up the stairs, "Looks like they nailed Luke. He's out there on the tulip bed—fell from the roof."

Jonas's voice twanged angrily, "He shouldn't've been put up there, for anybody to take a pot shot at."

"It was where he wanted to be," Jesse said. It was not within his divine powers to admit a mistake. If it *had* been a mistake. Luke had got them into this. There was justice in it, if he was dead.

In its screaming reverse gear, the van was backing back down the dirt road. The riddled patrol car sat there in black and white like a nightmare piece of a junkyard. Jesse went out the door and down the veranda steps and placed his fingers on Luke's scrawny throat, below the jaw the man had not bothered to shave this morning. Esau and perhaps the others clustering around wondered if the broken body would rise at the touch, but Jesse didn't say the words that might have done it. Maybe he was afraid they wouldn't work. Maybe he wanted Luke to stay dead. Luke had been trouble. Esau glanced about and assumed only he had thought these things. He caught Jim's eye and Jim gave a light little grimace and shrug. He and Jim knew something together, but what was it?

The men and women of the Temple buried Luke behind the barn, in a corner of the upper pasture, where tenacious farmers years ago had grown wheat. That night, four inches of snow accumulated, and it seemed Nature wanted to swaddle the Temple in silence and safety, for snow kept falling, as November became December, and the dirt road drifted shut, and there was rarely the sound of an engine, except that of a news helicopter, a Bell 206, taking photographs and television footage of the snowbound compound of religious criminals, or that of a reconnoitering Huey borrowed from the Colorado National

Guard by the FBI or the ATF. The description of the firefight, in which one state trooper was killed and another paralyzed in the legs for life, had convinced the Bureau of Alcohol, Tobacco, and Firearms that illegal combat weapons or illegally adapted sports guns were stockpiled in the Temple. To the faithful, the approaching and retreating rotors sounded like the beating of the wings of mechanical angels of doom; children would run outside and wave, though Jesse forbade it, promising them they would be machine-gunned.

The helicopters dropped pamphlets, imploring surrender. The guilty would be given a fair trial, the pamphlets said; the rest would be granted safety and freedom and the forgiveness of the state. The authorities had cut off their electricity, within hours. The Temple members lit their kerosene lamps and burned wood in their fireplaces and iron stoves. They hitched up the generator to the freezers to keep the frozen food from spoiling; they had laid in enough food to last months, feeding thirty people—eight men, with Luke gone, and five women and seventeen children, nearly a dozen of them Jesse's. Then there were sheep to slaughter. And laying hens. Years ago an iron hand-pump in the kitchen had been tied into the well, so that even when the generator ran out of diesel fuel pure water would flow for the faithful.

The main lack, Esau felt, was communication. The helicopters dropped their unctuous ultimatums, and loudspeakers set up on the edge of the neighboring ranch's property—the Triple H, belonging to Hank and Hortense Harden—poured out, on advice of a siege psychologist, a curious hellish nonsense of acid-rock music and screeching sounds and official pronouncements that drifted their way, when the wind was right. But the Temple had no way to respond; not only had Luke ripped out the office telephone but he or some other zealot had, in the wake of the first assault, cut the phone wires where they entered the house at the corner of the second story. Esau explained to Jesse that, with no communication facilities, there was no way the Temple could get its message out. He said, "Gog's is the only voice being heard. But there's millions now who want to hear your side of it." So he and Jim and Tom got up on the sheep-shed roof, which had a shallow pitch, and stamped out the letters PHONE. But the helicopters, though one came and hovered over them like a giant rattling dragonfly, couldn't read the white on white, it seemed. They tried giving the letters contrast with straw but the wind kept blowing them away and fresh snow kept falling. Then it occurred to Esau that the Temple was being watched, through telescopes and telescopic gunsights, from the government-operations center over on the Hardens' property to the northeast, as well as from the press encampment that the Temple's other neighbors, the Menéndez brothers, had allowed to spring up on a fallow rise of their land beyond the road, a half-mile to the southwest. Satellite City, it was jokingly called.

Esau climbed out from his office onto the roof of the porch and slowly waved his disconnected telephone back and forth like a semaphore. His beard had grown longer and the AP telephoto shots of him looked eerily messianic, his beard and uncut hair blown sideways by the winter wind. A number of newspaper captions mistakenly identified him as Smith himself. The next day a news helicopter dropped a radiophone in a box full of Styrofoam peanuts, with several spare batteries, and communications began to flow. "Our leader wants to tell his side of the story," Esau explained to the press. "We were attacked. We have been consistently persecuted. Our rights have been repeatedly violated. The Temple member who fired at the school bus was himself killed in the shootout. He is a martyr. We are the victims, not the aggressors." He didn't believe all of what he was saying, but he loved the sensation of saying it into the little coffee-colored Panasonic phone and feeling the words being drunk up by a thirsty world. It wasn't like the old days in Hollywood, when he'd do the breakfast meetings at the Polo Lounge and the lunches at Du-Par's or the Bistro Garden and still nothing would happen—the package had no buyer, the backers backed away, the coke-addled anorectic bitch of a star changed her mind. Esau asked that electricity be restored, so that a computer hookup could be arranged. Their bargaining chip, he knew, was themselves as hostages, especially the women and children. The government could not afford the bad publicity of any more bloodshed. He broadcast into the phone, "We are not afraid to die. We know the Day of Reckoning is at hand, tomorrow or the day after doesn't matter that much to us, believe me. We welcome the day when it comes. To us, it's just a trip to the heavenly Jerusalem. In the meantime, let's talk. The Lamb of God wants to get out his side of the story."

At first, Jesse was mistrustful. Isolation had bred an intense solidarity with his little flock; his expositions of the Good Book had become, after the first hour or two, a kind of rapture. Men as well as women at moments rose up and gabbled liquidly in tongues and fainted. Esau tried to let the voices in him speak, but something watchful in his head, that little motionless sardonic spectator, though shrunk to the size of a computer chip, prevented it. The mountain-man in Jesse enjoyed the lack of electricity, the cold nights wherein all but those on watch in the four directions of the compass slept in close rows on the floor of the living room with the roaring, sparking, flue-licking fire in the fieldstone fireplace, or else in the kitchen with its woodstove in full blaze. They were all growing thinner on the diet of rationed oatmeal, canned peas and beets, roast chicken and mutton; in the shadow of death, beneath the throbbing clatter of the guardian helicopter, under the erratic barrage of the barking, shrieking loudspeakers aimed at their sanity and resolve, the Temple's spiritual body became leaner and more supple. Jesse's first interviews over the radio hookup were stilted and full of sullen, defiant silences, when the questions struck him as impudent or off the point. The point was eternal salvation, preceded by imminent destruction. " 'Thou fool,' " he quoted, " 'except a seed dieth, it is not quickened into life.' First Corinthians, fifteen thirty-six. That's the whole Christian religion in a nutshell. Most of you millions out there call yourselves Christians don't believe it; you're scared of death. Scared of losing your imported Japanese rattletrap, your mortgaged heap of plywood and Fiberglas, your deck of credit cards. You're scared of losing out on the abominations of the earth, scared of waking up inside your seven-thousand-dollar coffin with your nose two inches from the wood. You've wasted your lives staying in the middle of the stream and now you hear the waterfall roaring; you're scared of roasting in eternal Hell. 'So then, because thou art lukewarm, and neither cold nor hot, I will spew thee out of my mouth.' That's Revelation, three sixteen. That's the voice of the Lord, no wonder you're all scared. Those two state-employed vermin tried to storm our sanctuary with their Smokey the Bear hats on, they were lukewarm, I spewed them out. They lacked that good hot faith. If they'd of had it, they'd've been here on the inside looking out. Right, Slick? Right, Zeb?" Jesse would forget he wasn't just talking in this upstairs farmhouse room with a few of his disciples but, through the miracles of electronics, to the nation and the world. His unsophistication was very effective. Millions were fascinated, for a time.

Alma had been on location in Turkey, on one of those isolated eastern islands where classic temple ruins have been scarcely disturbed but for earthquake and erosion; she was playing, for a two-hour cable-television drama, a Greek peasant woman who kills a man, an evil snickering German tourist, for seducing her feeble-minded daughter, and then must kill the pregnant daughter. It was based on a true story that had been in the news. Alma's face, with a few days of Mediterranean sun and some stylized pencilled wrinkles added to the taut corners of her eyes, suited the stark drama very well; the something implacable and Moorish in her spirit had worn through her dulcet youthful skin, the glow of her girlish flesh. Jennifer Sprague, the young female director of *The Sharpened*

Knife, who had done her apprentice work on television commercials—their dizzying quick-cut style and eighteen-year-old epidermal paragons—marvelled, as she peered through the viewing lens, that this bronze crone was the same woman who thirty years ago had so sweetly and demurely sung with Bing Crosby and done *Uh-Oh, My Show Is Slipping* with Jack Lemmon and Jerry Lewis, including that breathtakingly choreographed section where the trio, fleeing indignant investors, mistakenly get into a bowling alley on roller skates, dodge balls, and hop the gutters. How many takes did it need, that shot where Alma not only slides headfirst into the pins but comes out of the automatic pin-setter actually riding the ball, in her roller skates, up the return trough? Jennifer had clicked the video back and forth and couldn't find the spot where the stuntwoman was spliced in. Alma must have been blue with bruises. Her natural gaiety and bounce had bridged the utter lack of chemistry between Lemmon and Lewis, and now her flinty, weathered face looked as if she had never smiled, as she leaned in her black headscarf and widow's weeds against a whitewashed wall, squinting into that black sun of death, her destiny. She would kill, who could doubt it? These old troupers still give you your money's worth, Jennifer thought to herself, and, what's weird, still want to. Why would this woman, on the verge of sixty and married to a rich husband and rich on her residuals from her platinum-haired Sixties comedies in any case, want to subject herself to this baking sun, to the Turkish food, to the lonely nights in a fleabag hotel, to the direction of a woman young enough to be her daughter? They shared the evening meals, the two of them plus the head cameraman and the male star, a former East German who was gay to his eyeballs and in a kind of heaven of boys here on this Turkish island. He often vanished in the evening, and the head cameraman joined the gaffers and grips and their local assistants, leaving the two women alone. Jennifer was learning something about devotion to this glorious, much-prostituted art of the cinema, and Alma was realizing how much she had missed by not having a daughter.

Alma's husband, Caleb Wentworth, didn't realize for six days, as he busied himself with a bachelor's rounds in Boston—his State Street office, his Chestnut Hill home, Monday night at the Tavern Club, Wednesday lunch at the Country Club, Thursday dinner at the Somerset—that this religious maniac whose murderous clan figured in the front section of the *Globe* and claimed a few seconds of the Channel Five news every evening was the same one that his stepson, whom he hardly knew, was involved with. At about the same time, the reporters realized it also. SON OF FIFTIES MOVIE STAR AMONG THOSE UNDER SIEGE. *From "Safe at Your Peril" to Real-Life Drama.* When her husband reached her by phone, they could hardly hear each other. "I *can't* come back," she screamed. "There's three weeks left of shooting, all of it of *me*! Anyway, what can I *do*? You know how hysterical the media are; I'm surprised, dearest, you've fallen for it." Ahead of her was the filming of the murder of the tourist, the exoneration by the court, and the final *coup de grâce* of fate, worthy of bloody Euripides.

But once she was back in Hollywood, ten days before Christmas, Shirley Frugosi urged her to fly to Colorado and show the world a mother's heart. Alma's name hadn't been in the news so much for years. Not just interview requests but real offers were coming in, including the part of a zany mother in a biracial sitcom that had Cosby money in it and was sure to run five years at least.

Her maternal phone call, placed a few days after her return from Greece, had not been very satisfactory. All calls to the Temple went through an FBI switchboard, and it was a four-hour wait before she was cleared through and Clark came to the phone. "How was Greece?" he asked. His voice seemed deeper, brisker.

"Hot, darling. My skin dried and cracked so much I looked like a Gila monster but this twit of a girl director thought it was all wonderful. The more wrinkles the better, from her point of view. I'm just a *monster* to these younger people coming up. They assume I'm dead; it's like being poor Rita, only without the Alzheimer's. But how are *you,* sweetheart, is more to the point."

"I'm good. Things are good, Mom. We've settled into a routine and Jesse seems happy. When he's happy, we're all happy."

"Oh, *Clark,*" she burst out. "You sound so *brain*washed!"

As was his way with her, he stayed polite. He was a real Wilmot in that. Where had his father's Hungarian flair gone to in this boy? "That's the sort of thing people say," he mildly conceded, "but my head's never been clearer, actually. When I think back to Hollywood I was always in a daze. Not your fault—we had to live there, for your work. You did your work, I'm doing Jesse's work. He's sort of like what Harry Cohn was for you—crude, but inspired. The real thing."

"But, b-but, baby, wh-what's going to *hap*pen?"

"Don't stutter, Mom; nobody's asking you to feel guilty."

"You-you're surrounded by a virtual army and they're surely going to put you all in jail, for that one p-p-policeman being killed, though of course you had n-nothing to do with it."

"I said, calm down. It's just a life. Mine, I mean. A time to be born, a time to die—you've heard that. We have wonderful feeling here right now. It's like we're one mystical body. I've lost a lot of flab, but there's enough basic provender to last to spring at least. We'll just have to wait to see what the Lord ordains. Read Revelation, especially the last chapters, if you want to know more. Everything's in there, once you know how to look."

"I'm c-coming out there. This is ree-ree-ridiculous, to hear you t-talk like such a simpleton."

"Mom, I can't advise it. You can't get a motel room within fifty miles. You'll get pestered to death by reporters. They're all out here, hundreds of 'em, and are starving for something to happen. You know those people in New York that get out on ledges and everybody yells 'Jump'? It's like that. Well, fuck 'em—we're not jumping, at least till we get a sign."

She laughed, she was so relieved to hear him sound halfway like himself. "Don't jump, Clark. I love you."

He gave no sign of hearing. "Till Jesse gets the sign, I should have said." But perhaps he had heard, for his tone became more confidential: "It's a media circus, and I'm the coördinator at our end of it. I just wish those dickheads at Nova who said I was too abrasive to handle sensitive talent could see me now."

"I'm sure they're reading about it, darling." She was over a hump, the blockage of self-doubt, and spoke fluently. "You'd be interested in a story Shirley was telling me. Apparently, when they approached Spielberg and told him they thought it would sex up the new Indiana Jones if they brought in Sean Connery, he's supposed to have said—"

"Mom, incoming calls are limited to three minutes."

"Oh. You mean the FBI—"

"No, they don't care, they'd love it if we'd gab all day and give 'em some ideas. It's Jesse's rule; he says the outer world distracts us from God."

"From him, he means. Clark, I know his type. This town is full of megalomaniacs; it's the environment. Any man who can sleep with a new girl every night of the week naturally gets to think he's God. Then they get in so deep embezzling and lying they can't back out. I've been studying this man's photographs in the paper and he's one of those bluffers."

"*Mom.*"

"When it catches up with them they don't honestly think they've done anything wrong. At Columbia, even after they had all this evidence against Begelman—"

"Mom. Goodbye."

"Clark? G-g-g-" She couldn't say it, couldn't get past the "g." This simple word. He hung up while she was still trying. His own mother, and all those FBI eavesdroppers listening to her humiliation. "Goodbye," she said in her bedroom to herself, looking into one of her mirrors, tilting her head this way and that. "Goodbye, goodbye, goodbye, you idiot," furious with herself.

He had scared her about the motel rooms. She had had experience of motel rooms, back in Basingstoke—little musty shacks huddled between the road and a strip of woods, next to a roadhouse, with the sheets on the bed smelling of mildew at best. She telephoned Bighorn Mountain, Uncle Jared's private number. She blamed him for Clark's involvement with this grotesque sect anyway. An unexpected voice—a New York voice, overripe and elderly and almost ironically smooth, like a butler in Thirties comedy—answered. "I'm sorry, miss, but my father died this October. To whom am I speaking, please?"

"Patrick? Is it you? Don't you know my voice? When did he die?"

"Essie. My Lord. Didn't you get the announcement? It made the Denver papers, but I guess not L.A. The whole funeral was agog at the thought that you'd show, but you didn't. Your father didn't make it either. My mother was quite hurt, and said the Wilmots had never liked Jared marrying a Catholic."

"How ridiculous. We loved it. Ama loved underdogs. I was away for two months making a movie in which I kill somebody. My first onscreen victim. *Very* satisfying. My secretary is supposed to sift through the mail for what's important. Darling, I'm so sorry. How old was he? Incredibly old, I suppose. And you—you're incredibly rich now, I suppose."

"Always hopeful—God, I love you. The perpetual ingenue. No, it turns out that by the time Dad was done wheeling and dealing he only owned a sliver of the mountain, something under an eighth. And the ski resort loses money all the time. The smart people go to Aspen or Vail, or like to be helicoptered into the Bugaboos. I'm just out here to tidy up the wreckage. Your son, by the way, has been making quite a name for himself, if you favor the Christian right. I must say, Pope John

Paul Two looks almost reasonable, compared to what you heretics come up with."

"Clark is compensating—you mustn't mock. But it's about that, yes. I need to come out and where could I stay?"

"Where else but with me, who made you what you are? Essie, it would be bliss. Only no towel-dropping this time."

"I d-don't know what you're talking about. I have a perfectly lovely husband, a proper Bostonian."

"God, if you could have seen yourself that day. I should have had a camera. So young, so lovely. Your hips had points, you were so skinny. You probably had Band-aids on your knees, and scraped elbows. The waif from below Wilmington. You thought it was part of the drill, you poor dear thing."

"Well, it often was," she said, and sniffed. "You're making a motel sound not so bad."

"Don't be huffy, cousin. We're *fam*ily."

He met her at the Burr County airport; he had filled out, so in his black chesterfield and white muffler he bulked like Jimmy McMullen in the newspaper photographs Ama had kept in a scrapbook back on Locust Street, when the financier was being hauled into court for fraud. Patrick's black hair, long as a musician's, had grayed becomingly, in white sweeps above his ears, but age had emphasized a pugnacious Irish coarseness to his nose and upper lip. In Uncle Jared's topaz Cadillac Brougham, with a silver bighorn ram for a hood ornament, they drove east and north. "An awful lot of nothing," Alma said, gazing out the window at the darkness as they climbed.

"Wait till you see Lower Branch. It's Times Square before they cleaned it up."

They drove through the crossroads hamlet on the way to the mountain. Snow had been plowed into heaps that went halfway up the telephone poles. Feebly blinking Christmas lights were strung on a cement-block building that must be the town hall, and on a steepleless wooden church across the street. Between the heaps of snow dirtied by the flickering polychrome tints, dark crowds of people—media people, she supposed—clustered like bees in agitated, buzzing swarms outside the entrances to the one bar and the one hash joint, called Mildred's. Even the 7-Eleven was being overrun, in the cold fluorescent light of the Total station. So many cars and television vans were parked at improvised angles that the main street became one-way traffic in spots. A silhouette in a parka and headphones waved them forward; it was not a policeman but a drunken newscaster, who had nearly arranged a head-on collision, amid encouraging chaotic shouts, with a car coming the other way. It was a dismal carnival such as might be held on a frozen shelf of Hell.

In another forty-five minutes, along a winding road with an endless pine forest to the right and on the left a deep long valley holding a ragged receding lake white under the moon, and then an abandoned mass of gray buildings saying HENDERSON tucked into a mountainside, Alma was brought to the family condominium at Bighorn. Among the framed photographs on Uncle Jared's dresser, she found herself as a little knock-kneed girl, with a bathing-suited little brother and two young parents pale as lard in the summer sun of a Delaware day before the war. Patrick would have sat up for hours serving weak Scotch-and-sodas and trying to relive old New York days, days when flesh merchants like Wexler and Arnie Fineman had the power of gods over a young model, and a girl could ride the subways at any hour without fear, and the art world still produced something you could call art, instead of this trash that was worse than performance trash because it stayed there, on the wall, with its glued-on broken crockery and absolutely hopeless drawing copied from old *Life* magazines which supposedly makes it very *iron*ic. "Nobody is *buy*ing it, thank God; the Eighties are over and money is *ter*rified of everything except Treasury Bonds." She couldn't rise to his prattle; the altitude or some deep black fatigue Alma was still carrying from Greece or this melodramatic business with Clark got to her; she could scarcely keep her eyes open. It depressed her to realize, from the way Patrick was trying too hard to bring back their common past, that knowing her for those few years back then—he who had seemed so suave and superior and in command when she first met him—had become a high point of his life, a justification of his inconsequential, sterile, mannered existence, an acquaintance he must peddle to others; the story of the towel had no doubt been told and retold, in cheerful, gleeful betrayal. That innocent wanton girl and that closeted, pained, elegant young man had deserved at least privacy. Patrick showed her her room and practically put her into bed, for all she could remember. She was too limp to even do her night cream. In her dreams something very big was pressing, pressing at an elastic door, growling and spitting; but in the morning, as the ski lifts started up, she deduced that it had been the sounds of the Sno-Cats grooming the slopes through the night.

"Tell me about your new marriage," Patrick said at breakfast. In morning light he looked puffy from drink, his jowls still glossy from being shaved, and touching, his old handsomeness come down to a mere dignified bulk, too dignified now for the scramble of the art world, with its violent young bodies and wills. ("Everybody's *mu*tilating and *punc*turing themselves, these girls come in with the faces like absolute *sieves,* God knows what they've done to the rest of their bodies, it's *ter*rifying," he had complained last night.) His close-shaved face was a blue-pink old querulous queen's.

"It's heaven," she answered. "A stable older man. Why did I keep marrying those ridiculous boys before?"

"Because you were a ridiculous girl, my dear. Where do you and Number—is it?—Four live?"

"Well, that's complicated right now," Alma said. "When Coca-Cola sold Columbia to Sony for that insane mark-up in the billions—the *poor* Japanese, really—it left Caleb without a job, after all he had done to get TriStar started, so he went back to Boston of course, which his heart had never left. But I hate to give up the Coldwater Canyon house after all these years, and even the cottage in Malibu, the capital-gains taxes would *kill* me if I sold, so that's how it stands." Patrick's lips mockingly quivered, and she said with all her actressy dignity, "Caleb and I are apart a good deal, yes, but what we give each other we don't need to be physically present to receive. He loves my fame, and I love his dear old money."

From his face, pursed in distaste like Charles Laughton's when mutiny loomed, this was more than Patrick had wanted to know. Marriage between men and women was an area where he was invincibly ignorant; even his parents' he had not been privileged to witness, and then his mother and Mr. Traphagen had given themselves to art. Alma went on, in revenge because Patrick had been rather boring last night, "Oh, I know you think I've made a lot of my own, and I have, but Hollywood money is like snow, didn't somebody once say? It melts. Caleb's is *Bos*ton money. It hides, and grows. These New Englanders have really never discovered the pleasure principle. They all love Maine because it's so uncomfortable. Caleb has a house in Brookline and a shingled place on Martha's Vineyard. I love it on the Vineyard. Cagney went there for years. Everybody on it thinks they're some kind of star, so I get no attention. I go barefoot. I even go shopping barefoot."

"You sound happy," he said, subdued as she had wished.

"Oh, who can tell? When the ambition bug bites, happiness stops being the point. I should be happy, God knows—I think I would be, if Clark and these crazies of his weren't such a desperate worry. Could you *pos*sibly, poor dear Patrick, drive me back to Lower Branch, or is there a Rocky Mountain taxi I could call?"

They arrived in time for the press conference that the FBI spokesman, Mr. Fred Dix, gave every eleven in the cement-block town hall, upstairs in the meeting room. He reminded her of Wayne Phillips, Sr., in front of the assembled Sunday school, looking uncomfortable and evasive and whey-faced from leading such an indoors life. Alma had not seen folding chairs like these—double, dark brown, with close-set slats on the curved seat—since Sunday school. The big room, with its industrial steel windows and an American flag drooping in the corner, was full of these chairs, but, even so, some reporters had to stand along the walls. The monotone briefing stated that the situation was basically unchanged. As per Mr. Smith's request, two of his thirty-minute tapes on the real meaning of the whore of Babylon and related texts had been broadcast on radio stations in Gunnison, Salida, Leadville, and Glenwood Springs. Mr. Smith was still prayerfully meditating on the matter of releasing women and children. Physical access to the Temple and its grounds continued to be denied to television crews on the grounds of personal danger; on three separate occasions last week cameramen who had ventured inside the thousand-yard perimeter established by the coördinated law-enforcement team drew rifle fire from inside the main house. An exasperated reporter shouted, "Sir, is your so-called team going to do anything at all or just hang outside the perimeter forever?"

The spokesman's jaw lifted, a bit like the President's when he spoke of Manuel Noriega, and he said, "This is a highly delicate and volatile situation. Jesse Smith is a pathological liar and a known killer who is holding seventeen minors and five women in there. If he wants to prove me wrong, all he has to do is come out of that compound and submit to American justice." This was a dare, meant to reach Jesse Smith as a sound bite, and the television cameras duly rolled. To make another bite, Fred Dix went on, "The winter is our friend, not his. Every day they hold out, they have less fuel, less food, less patience. More anxiety, more friction between them. We can wait all year. We can certainly wait till the snowdrifts aren't there to impede operations."

"What about cutting off their electricity again?" another reporter asked.

Dix's patience was not as endless as he suggested. "We're trying for a peaceful resolution and full communications is the way to bring that about. The FBI, the ATF, the Colorado and county forces of law enforcement are running this operation, not the news media. Our aim is to save lives, not provide a sensational story for the public. We're not going to let the tail wag the dog here."

One of the bored reporters noticed that Alma had come into the room. Like a beast with a hundred eyes and mouths and a single will, the forces of news-gathering rushed to consume her. She answered their questions one by one, taking care not to stammer and not to blink as the flashbulbs went off in their blue cascades: "I am here because I couldn't bear to stay away—any mother would do the same. . . . No, I have never met Mr. Smith or read his pamphlets. This decision was Clark's, and I have never pried. We all have a right to a private religious life, surely. . . . He was baptized as a Presbyterian on North Gower Street in Hollywood. . . . I have talked to him just once over the phone, for three minutes, and I must say he sounded more focused and alert than I have ever heard him. . . . No—I would be, of course, and you would be, but he did not sound frightened. . . . A quiet boy, basically, interested in much the same things as other boys are. He took after my dear father, I used to think. . . . Theodore R. Wilmot, W, I, L, M, O, T, Basingstoke, Delaware . . . That's right, the mailman, though actually he retired many years ago. . . . Same-sex marriages? They do now? I didn't know this. But any denomination has to keep up with the times, I suppose, including the Presbyterians. . . . Yes, with the wonderfully talented Jennifer Sprague, who is going to be I am sure one of the truly creative forces in American film of the Nineteen-nineties. . . . *The Sharpened Knife,* based on a true story in the news . . . Quite grim, yes, but cathartic . . . Two and a half months in Greece . . . Not really—how could I, considering when I was born? I think one of the good effects of television has been to promote more roles for mature women; the old Hollywood gave us a very artificially heightened sense of life and beauty, and it placed a terrible burden upon everyone, actresses and audience alike. . . . No, there is no truth in that rumor. We are very happy, though because of our work we are not as much together as we'd like. . . . Goodness, no, I wouldn't think so, though I'm not sure I know quite what you mean by 'all-out assault.' . . . Perfect confidence. I've had some reservations about J. Edgar Hoover but never about the FBI as a whole. . . . Yes, I thought the blacklisting was disgusting, and still think so. . . . Well, I haven't seen everything, being as I say on location in Europe, but I loved Andie McDowell in *Sex, Lies and Videotape.* For the best actor—"

Patrick stepped in front of her and said, "All right, you vultures, enough. This is a frantic mother you're dealing with." To Alma, in private, he said, "My God, Essie. You don't have to answer every crappy question. Your problem is and always was you're too damn anxious to *please.*"

She had felt sorry for these media people; they looked so exasperated and weary, so underfed and overdrunk, stuck here at this standoff and supposed to send back a story a day, a little revelation or miracle every day, to feed everybody. Why should she mind being their tidbit for the moment? She might make the network news, unless Bush invaded Panama.

Rather roughly Patrick steered her through the news personnel, who were still shouting and murmuring questions and requests for a private interview at her convenience, up front to where Fred Dix was coping with his own beseechers. Dix reached above a reporter's shoulder to shake her hand. He said, "These are terrible circumstances, Miss DeMott, but it's a privilege to make your acquaintance. I've been adoring your films since I was a kid. Just about my favorite, if I can say so, was that *Strawberry Blonde* you did with Cagney."

She thought of telling him it had been Crosby, the one with Cagney had been Rita Hayworth, but what did it matter? She had been mulched in—what had once seemed to her absolute immortality turned out to be a slow dissolution within a confused mass of perishing images like a colorful mountain of compressed and rotting garbage. "Thank you," she said, and since Dix was momentarily too starstruck to continue, she added, "That was one of the most fun. Nobody makes musicals like that any more."

"And a damn shame it is," Dix said. "The world'd be a less violent place if they did. Tell me, Alma—if I may—what you hope to accomplish by being here?"

She didn't know. Her agent had insisted she come. "Well, I thought m-maybe if I could see Clark face to f-face."

"Face to face," Dix said, something of a performer himself, of the dry macho variety. "Half the world wants to see those fools in there face to face, the investigation team foremost. Do you know"—and now he was including Patrick in his discourse, having sized him up as her protector or agent, and as a man more understanding of a man's problems—"these various media keep telling us they'll take us to court if we don't let a crew approach the house at their own risk? First Amendment rights, they say. First Amendment, Second Amendment, it's all I hear these days. And would you believe we got dozens of wackos showing up wanting to be let into the Temple so they can join up? We got food parcels pouring in from all over the country and Canada we're supposed to take over on our choppers and drop. We got about ten different psychotics telling us Jesse Smith should be put in jail because *they're* the real Jesus Christ, not him. Including some women—that's a new one. The amount of human sickness a thing like this stirs up is enough to make you puke. I had to smile at that question about the same-sex marriages—I'm hardshell Baptist myself, and we'd never hold with that."

Alma had been retaining her next line in her head throughout this long expository speech. "Mr. Dix, what can I do? I want my son to know I'm here for him."

"He'll see it. On the box. They've been dropped a couple Zeniths. Our Jesse over there's become quite an addict, I understand. Their electric bill comes to us, and it keeps going up. Don't mean to be flip about life-and-death issues, but you got to see the comedy of it now and then or you'd go crazy yourself."

"Is it true that this man has said anybody who wants to can leave?"

"He says that, but keep in mind he's got those people in there hypnotized. They have no wills of their own. They're no more likely to run away than a whipped dog from his master. Also, they'll have to face some outstanding charges."

Something—the image of the whipped dog—pushed tears suddenly over her lower lids. "He's trapped!" she blurted out.

Patrick put an arm around her and said to Fred Dix, "Suppose the boy wants to reach her, how will we know?"

"Esau—that's what he calls himself—checks in with us three, four times a day. He's having the time of his life. Handles it all like a real pro, I must say. Where shall we tell him she's staying?"

"Bighorn Mountain, forty-five minutes from here. Let me give you the private number."

Dix took it but felt the need of some ceremonial remark, some acknowledgment that a goddess had descended to be among them. Essie was afraid he would try to kiss her hand. He said, "A true honor, ma'am. I guess a thing like this shows the movies weren't exaggerating, they were telling the simple truth."

Dear God, forgive me for my mistakes, my selfishness. Always I was seeking to do Your will, that my talent not be hidden, that my light would shine forth. Forgive me if I could have done more for Clark. Save him from this sadness, this farce. Give him back to me as he was, helpless and so eager at my breast. Forgive me if I should have nursed him longer, as You know I had committed to Cream Cheese and Caviar *and Newman wasn't available later. Dear Lord, make me again the young mother I was; let me pour into him all the love his little being needed. Heal our lives and take us back and make us all perfect. Do the impossible, Lord, for him, as You have done for me. Rescue him from that terrible house. Reach down, so that none but I can see. I will not tell. Let me love You again. Amen.*

It had been so long since Alma had prayed that she fell into the vocabulary and near-nonsense of the little girl praying with Mr. Bear clutched against her face. God had been her secret then and was still. She felt Him still on her skin, though His pressure had become less passionate. She stayed in her uncle's condo a week, surrounded by blazing-bright snow, the rumble of the lifts, and the strange red-cheeked armies of young skiers, alien and mesmerized, but her son never called—just her husband, her agent, and her father, sounding amiably addled and maddeningly passive. He even said, "It's in the Lord's hands," he who hadn't spent a minute in a church except the time she was confirmed. A great number of respectful but inexorable news reporters somehow got her number and called, and a young British producer—passed on from Shirley's office—wondering if she might be able to tackle a British accent for a television adaption of a novel called *Memento Mori,* all about these dreadful old artistic people, very clever and amusing. "We're hoping for Maggie Smith for the lead. You'd just mainly have to roll your eyes and look vampish." At night, Alma tried not to keep pace with Patrick's drinking, to save on calories, but it was hard. He had a whole life's grievances to recite. He had known her when she was nobody, and such people were fewer and fewer: blessed islands in this acid sea of celebrity. He deserved some attention for this, but not as much as he wanted. He had become a pathetic fame-fucker, and wanted to fuck hers, her poor old tattered fame. One night as she went into her room, from the wet kiss he gave her you would have thought he was making a pass.

The year 1990 brought an inch or two of fresh powder every night. The routines within the Temple rarely varied. The main event of January, which they all prayed over and discussed for days, was Matthew's defection. The big, puppylike, near-sighted Hoosier had loved his mission work—the trips to Hawaii and Australia and even Israel and Thailand, where against all the odds he had created nuclei of converts back in the Eighties—and perhaps, so outward-turned, had been simply too lonely. He crept out in the night; the sound of the police car with its escort of news vans taking him away had woken some of those within the Temple. By morning a fresh fall had erased even his tracks in the snow. He was charged, television told them, with murder, conspiracy, attempted murder, and interfering with the duties of a police officer. In his jail cell he became, for a week or so, a great favorite of the press, and, his fervor for Jesse's Word unabated, did continue to spread the gospel. But the media have a brief attention span, and soon he sat unattended in his cell, waiting out the yawning intervals in the legal process. Jesse took a mild view of the betrayal: "Well, I guess Matt was one of those seeds that without looking it had gone and fallen on stony ground."

Toward the end of January and through February there was the lambing. Day and night, the bleating of new arrivals on this earth, and men and women coming and going into the barn with heat lamps and blankets, wearing bloody aprons and green Platex gloves, to assist in the muddle of birth—the little black hooves outthrust through the woolly vagina, the slippery purple-yellow placental mess, the new lamb staggering to its feet with the umbilical cord still dragging in the straw. Coyotes smelled the afterbirth and, winter-starved, came close in skulking, howling numbers, so that the men armed against the armies of Gog turned their guns against a natural foe. Clark explained to the siege headquarters in Lower Branch that this shooting was not directed against the personnel manning the perimeter, and relayed Jesse's refusal to let a team of veterinarians ski into the Temple. "Slick, that's how they do with them airplane hijackers," Jesse explained. "Send in a crew to take away the rest-room shit that turns out to be Israeli commandos. 'The treacherous dealer dealeth treacherously.' That's Isaiah, twenty-one two."

The February snows were the heaviest of the winter and yet the sun strengthened each day, dazzlingly, burning bare margins of mud at the base of southern-exposed walls and outcroppings, with the first shoots, by the end of the month, of spring grass, and of snowdrops with their blue-green leaves and pearl-white hanging heads, and the probing pale tips of the avalanche lilies. Even on clear cold days a softening was felt in the air: the woodsmoke from the chimneys smelled stronger and sweeter; puffy broken cumulus replaced the leaden nimbus layers or bald steely blue of January; and the birds, the chickadees and juncos and finches, came out from the shelter of the spruces and hemlocks and peppered the air with excited twittering, sharing some news that electrified their densely programmed little brains. The tracks of small animals, squirrels and marmots and wood rats come to steal the sheep's feed grain, multiplied in the barnyard, and in March, on an early morning when fog was lifting from the softening snow, two elk had moved past the house, migrating up from the valley into the mountains. The male was shedding his antlers, and by furiously rubbing them against the rough dry boards of the house he brought men scrambling from bed to the windows with their guns, thinking that the long-anticipated assault had begun. Ghostly in the fog, the elk couple hightailed it upward, into the shrouded vast realm of the mountain lion and grizzly bear, the horned lark and the white-tailed ptarmigan and bald eagle. With the stirring of spring, traffic along the road at the end of the snowbound dirt road had picked up, too, while Clark found the cops and agents down in Lower Branch and even his old friend Eddie, of the gray suit and bent spine, less and less communicative.

In mid-March, Tom and Jim's wife, Polly, deserted, with Polly and Jim's three-year-old girl, named Fidelity. It was not as adulterous as it seemed; they had begged Jim to come, and he had seemed to agree, but at the last minute had told them to go without him. From his bunk in the men's barracks he explained it to Clark: "It's simple math, in a way. You know about Pascal's bet? The odds are long, but the rewards are infinite, so the bet is infinitely worth making. I'm betting Jesse's the real thing. Some might say it's mighty strange for the Lord to come again in the form of a limited, gun-crazy guy like Jesse, but that's the Lord's style, to work in mysterious ways." Jim added, with a sly shrug and his cool slant smile, "If I'm wrong, Polly and Fidelity are safe, and my cousin will take good care of them. Tom's a straight guy. Dumb but straight." Clark knew he should like Jim, but something held him back, something fishy and too easy, as if life for Jim was like watching television. Clark felt he had come a long way from home and yet here was this man who kept slyly trying to engage him in the accent, the language, of the old country.

Not a week passed before—another miracle—their number was replenished; a party of four, who had come to Lower Branch months ago, shortly after the siege had become news, finally made it into the Temple, by snowshoeing at night through the weakest spot in the authorities' ring, the steep rocky bowl to the northeast, having bribed the Hardens two hundred dollars to let them through on the Triple H land. "Jesse, we are yours," they told him. "We are saved." He bestowed upon them the names Benjamin, Medad, Mehetabel, and Elisabeth. They brought with them hundreds in cash and the certificates and passbooks to their life savings, but until the day when connections with the banks and merchants were reëstablished, they had brought mainly the burden of their bodies to the Temple, where the supplies were running low. The miracle solved nothing.

Jesse appeared disheartened and distracted. His spirit had fattened on the publicity of the winter, but the convergence of thousands of converts and untold numbers of angels, ushering in the new Heaven and Earth that Revelation promised, had not come about. Now he felt an approaching famine in things, an unease of coming change. Satellite City was almost a ghost town. The foreign networks and major papers had pulled their correspondents, and then the national newsmagazines had shifted to local stringers, and the smaller-budget and remoter radio and television stations had faded away. A reporter population once numbered in the hundreds—so vast that the Salvation Army had set up a meal truck on the Menéndez brothers' tent-covered rise of land—had shrunk to representatives of the major networks, the Denver *Post*, and a few local papers and stations within commuting distance. Jesse's tapes had been played to audiences of millions, his onrolling voice had huskily twanged through any number of recorded interviews, his pamphlets of exegesis and prophecy had been publicly quoted, ridiculed, and psychoanalyzed; and yet nothing, in any cosmic sense, had happened. The world remained insufficiently perturbed. It rolled on, untransformed. Heaven expected yet more of him, and under this demand his spirit writhed, sleepless. The fringe of hair falling to his collar had whitened; his wire glasses were worn awry, or absent, so his golden eyes stared without a focus. He spent days at a time among his women, but—claimed a rumor that crept out through his bedroom walls—impotently. Meeting Esau in a corridor or before Bible study, he would ask, "How goes the battle, Slick?" and not wait for any answer. Once, as Clark was hurrying to bed after dinner so he could rise for the sentry watch before dawn, Jesse, who had not been at the table, materialized on the tilted loose boards leading up to the men's dormitory. He looked through his disciple and in a tranced voice recited, " 'And then if any man shall say to you, Lo, here is Christ; or lo, he is there; believe him not.' Mark, thirteen twenty-one. Ha! Believe him not! Those old Gospeleers told it like they saw it, didn't they, Slick? Here's another puzzler: 'Neither shall they say, Lo here! or, lo there! for, behold, the kingdom of God is within you.' Tell me what *that* means."

"Well, I think—"

"No thinking now, Slick. None of your clever PR bullshit. Too late. Too late, boy. He's got us by the balls. Gog. Ever crush a big black ant under your thumb? That's us right now—feel it? *Feel* it?" He squeezed Esau's arm like a drowning man dragging down his rescuer. Esau gasped and squirmed away, obscurely, illicitly pleased to see Jesse brought low, tasting what Clark himself had tasted those empty early L.A. mornings when he had returned from one of the clubs with a burned-out buzzing brain and gazed down the grid of lights receding over this total velvety blackness until it seemed an angelic cage door was rising up to lock him in.

Jesse's Bible-study sessions had moved from Revelation and the Old Testament prophets, with their rageful violence, to the Gospels, as if he were looking for his own story there. " 'O my Father,' " he read, " 'if it be possible, let this cup pass from me.' " His audience sat in their white robes of used sheets, holding dry stalks of high-country wheat instead of the Biblical palms prescribed by Revelation 7:9. "Now, dear friends, what's this all about? This is a man in agony talking. 'If it be possible.' 'With God all things are possible,' Jesus has said earlier in the Gospel of Matthew. So He knows God could remove the cup if He wished. But God does not wish. Jesus looks up there from praying at His rocky cold table in the Garden of Gethsemane and says again, 'O my father, if this cup may not pass away from me, except I drink it, thy will be done.' God wants Him to drink it, that's how it will pass away. It will pass down His throat and out the other end. What else does Jesus have to drink in this gospel, a little further on in His horrible ordeal? Vinegar mixed with gall. 'They gave him vinegar to drink mingled with gall: and when He had tasted thereof, He would not drink.' He was thirsty but He was not going to choke down that cruel mockery of wine, that unpalatable rotgut, no, not after giving His disciples His own sacred sweet blood to drink—the blood of His body, given for them! And no sooner had He taken that one repugnant sip and shook His head in simple manly revulsion than, the next verse says, 'And they crucified Him.'

" 'And they crucified Him'! The Roman officials of Judaea and the high priests and elders of Judaism and the social workers and the FBI agents and the murderous agents of the Bureau of Alcohol, Tobacco, and Firearms, they crucified Him, for bringing perfection down from Heaven to earth. They crucified the perfect Lamb. And what did His disciples do? Believe it or not, my dearest friends, they slept, they pretended they didn't know Him until the cock crowed, they ran this way and that like sheep when the coyotes carry off one of the little lambs. And Jesus up there on the cross cries out 'My God, my God, why hast thou forsaken me?' And the people on the ground taunt Him, saying, 'Save Thyself. If Thou be the Son of God, come down from the cross.' And the thieves crucified next to Him join right in, razzing Him in the midst of their own agony, you can see why, for if He hopped down from that cross He just might bring them with Him, His new buddies and sidekicks. And the folks hanging around poke a sponge full of vinegar in His face, and have themselves a laugh, and He cries out with a loud voice, a *loud* voice"—and Jesse made his own voice here so loud that it cracked painfully, over all their heads, including those of the children, the youngest of whom whimpered at the noise, while those older stared, trying to see through this man's shouting into what the world had in store for them—"and yielded up the ghost. No 'Father, forgive them; for they know not what they do' in this version—that's in soft-hearted Luke. No friendly aside to the thief on the cross beside Him that 'Today shalt thou be with me in Paradise'—that's in Luke, too. In Matthew, He takes the cup neat, like a bolt of bitter, bitter whiskey, that makes you cough, and makes the tears come to your eyes, so you swear you'll never take another drink as long as you live.

"Now, what was in that cup? I'll tell you what was in that cup. The wrath of God was in that cup. In Revelation, fourteen ten, what do we read? We read that, if any man worship the beast and his image, 'The same shall drink of the wine of the wrath of God, which is poured out without mixture into the cup of His indignation; and he shall be tormented with fire and brimstone in the presence of the holy angels, and in the presence of the Lamb.' We don't want that, now do we, boys and girls? You know who the Lamb is, don't you? You know who the beast is, don't you? His number is 666, and if you sit down with the figures and break them down and add them up that comes out to be U.S.A., I've seen it calculated by experts. In chapter sixteen, now, I was reading the other night while you all were sleeping like ignorant possums, the angel has poured out the seventh vial, and a voice from the temple of heaven makes a terrible earthquake, 'And every island fled away, and the mountains were not found,' and there's a 'great hail out of Heaven, every stone about the weight of a talent,' and men blasphemed God, which is what you all do when you sleep while the Lamb of God is awake studying to save your poor sinful hides, and Babylon, that great unholy city greater even than Denver and Washington, D.C., Babylon that unholy city where the great mother of harlots sits holding her golden cup 'full of abominations and filthiness of her fornication,' that city of Babylon came in remembrance before God so He could 'give unto her the cup of the wine of the fierceness of his wrath.' Hear that, children? *'The cup of the wine of the fierceness of His wrath.'* Her cup runneth over, you could say, with the Psalmist. Yea, we are walking 'through the valley of the shadow of death' here—that's what this here sacred verse indicates."

Jesse looked lost amid his texts, his many cups, sweating and pale, his skin shining like a lampshade, his body contorted as if wrestling with an invisible antagonist. "Why," he asked, in a suddenly conversational voice, as one small child, who had been sobbing, was shushed by his mother, in mid-sob, "why does God set before us and Jesus this cup brimming with the wine of His wrath, with fire and brimstone and hailstones the size of a talent? Why not just give us a nice Coca-Cola or cold cider? Jesus wanted it to pass. He was a young man, with a great future in preaching and healing. But He had to drink that cup, He had to be whipped and humiliated in His naked body and nailed to that cross by big ugly spikes right through the palms of His hands and hung there so He could hardly get breath into His lungs in order to take away old Adam's sin, the sin of the world. That was the only way God His father could do what He wanted to do; He couldn't think of any other feasible way. Sure, Jesus would have liked the cup to pass from Him. I'd like it to myself. I'm not so old, though this winter has been a long one, hasn't it now? You—you'd like it to pass. But it won't pass. The cup is on the way. It's sailing through the air, friends. The cup is here." He held out his broad hands shaped as if they held a chalice. "Drink it. We must drink it together. We must drink it because this beverage, God's wrath bottled by Him personally, sealed so tight you can hear it fizz when you open the cap, is the liquor of eternal life. It's the drink of Paradise. It makes champagne look like vinegar and gall. It makes milk, little ones, taste like castor oil. None of you remember castor oil but some of you older-timers like friend Mephibosheth and his missus probably do. It was nasty stuff. It was rough stuff. But it did you good. The cup of the wrath of God will do you good. We'll drink it together, when the time comes. We'll make a little party of it. 'Drink ye all of it; for this is My blood of the new testament.' What does our Lamb Jesus Christ say in Gethsemane? He says, 'My soul is exceeding sorrowful, even unto death: tarry ye here, and watch with Me.' "

There were gleaming places below the preacher's eyes. His voice had become so husky and dry and twisted it must soon stop. "Watch with me a little longer, dear friends in this Temple of True and Actual Faith. Around the world millions say they believe the verities in the Bible but almost none of them do. Almost none of them do. They think it's a myth, they think it's an idle story told by tired old shepherds who didn't know any better tall tales to pass those long cold desert nights. But this is the Temple of True and Actual Faith, my dear friends. Faith, faith is the jewel, the pearl of great price, for which the merchant 'went and sold all that he had, and bought it.' He bought it, as we used to say in Vietnam. That was our way of saying a fellow soldier had bought the farm, had entered the land of death. 'The kingdom of Heaven is like unto treasure hid in a field,' and when a man finds it, for joy thereof he goeth and selleth all that he hath and *buys* that field. We are here on that field. We are soldiers in the field, the *e*lite corps of the one hundred forty-four thousand who will reside forever in that heavenly temple with walls of jasper and foundations of sapphire and emerald. Our human eyes would not withstand the glory of it; the glory of it will wash away our tears, our hungry stomachs, our fear and our cold here this long hard winter, our memories of the easy pleasures of the land of Magog that we left behind; a thousand-thousand-fold we will be repaid, everlastingly. Christ said it: faith as small as a grain of mustard seed will see you through, but only faith. Oh my faithful friends, when that cup comes, drink ye all of it. Though it be hot as molten lead, you wash it right down. 'I am Alpha and Omega, the beginning and the end. I will give unto him that is athirst of the fountain of the water of life freely. He that overcometh shall inherit all things; and I will be his God, and he shall be My son.' Amen. Now, good folks, let's hear some discussion."

The spring light in Colorado had become as sharp as a searchlight. The authorities, goaded by the criticisms of their inaction in the press, reasoned that, if any more frost went out of the ground, their vehicles might encounter problems of traction. The vehicles were tanklike M60A1 armored vehicles, bought cheap from the post-Vietnam Army by the National Guard and mounted with 105mm. ordnance and for this mission specially fitted with retractable booms and twelve-inch loudspeakers. The plan, approved by the Attorney General's office in Washington, called for the vehicles to approach the Temple close enough for grenade launchers to fire, through windows and holes broken in the walls, packets of the chemical agent CS—a non-pyrotechnic form of tear gas that would not, Fred Dix assured a press conference given while the assault was taking place, harm the infant lungs of even the youngest children. The FBI and ATF operatives, and the helicopter pilots and artillerymen of the Colorado National Guard, were under instructions to exercise extreme restraint in the return of gunfire. This rescue mission was to begin at dawn, but complications, including a caravan of press and media traffic alerted by a news leak the night before, delayed the schedule, so that the first armored vehicle did not make its breach, with its strangely antediluvian, proboscislike boom, in the wall of the main building until after nine o'clock. Silhouettes of Temple members flitted past the windows of the old farmhouse. Exploding packets of CS crashed through the panes and hurtled through the splintering clapboards with a muffled popping noise. A lively spring wind, smelling of rising pine sap and thawing sheep dung, had come up beneath the sharp white sun. Reporters speculated into the radio mikes and television cameras rimming the thousand-yard razor-wired periphery that on such a breezy day the tear gas might be blown in one side and out the other. Further, the extensive Temple armory was known to include gas masks. "With all winter to prepare for this, Peter," the ABC correspondent broadcast to New York, "it seems unlikely that those inside have not developed a battle plan."

Government choppers—big ones, Bell 214s, beloved in Vietnam, with the sliding doors that provide a wide field of fire for the mounted machine guns—swayed and clattered overhead, drowning out the loudspeakers assuring those inside the Temple that no harm was intended and that they should come out and surrender. "This is not an assault. Do not fire. We are introducing non-lethal tear gas. You are responsible for your own actions. Come out and you will receive medical attention. No one will be injured. Submit to proper authorities. Do not subject yourself to further discomfort." These words in doom's barking voice were chopped up by the Huey rotors and carried off on the wind. The armored vehicles, their breastplates of iron shielding frightened young National Guardsmen, roared louder as the booms nudged and chewed at the walls. There were abrupt cracklings of exterior boards, and the higher-pitched glassy crunch of a window being shattered, and then the dull popping of the launcher, the flat whack of the packets exploding, and the ghostly rush of the gas, gas that though non-toxic would sting like clouds of enraged bees.

Yet for minutes within the compound there was an apparent peace, an uncanny meek silence. The telephone no longer answered, though the FBI kept ringing it. A government sniper saw through his scope, through the windows of the battened family quarters, the shape of a man making a scattering motion, as if sowing seed. At the other end, from the men's dormitory, two men were firing what appeared to be .50-calibre armor-piercing rifles with such effect at an M60 that the co-driver felt obliged to reply with a long burst from his turret-mounted 105mm. repeater, blasting a wall to splinters and blowing Jonas and Medad into the next, merciful world. A number of television trucks, making a break in the wire-fenced official periphery, had moved in close enough to be drawing fire from the Temple as well, a turn of events the exhilarated reporters breathlessly described. After so long a news fast, this feast.

Now a lull was ordered, and the clumsy machines backed off fifty or so yards, on the churned-up mixture of mud and ice and snow and straw, and the fleet of helicopters, which included a Bell AH-1 Huey Cobra with heat-sensor cameras, lifted up so high that the sound of their wings was like that of many distant horses running. In the momentary quiet could be heard the bleating and baaing of the unfed sheep and their lambs. It was after ten o'clock. The sun was a white sore spot in a thin high haze. The air was invisibly, inaudibly full of urgent electronic communications and consultations and bulletins. The combat engineering vehicles, uneasily shifting on their treads and moving their howitzers like nervous antennae, waited in a loose circle for those within the Temple to come out and surrender. But for answer instead there rose, from the family end of the ramshackle set of linked buildings, a curl of smoke that was not tear gas. The smoke went from white to yellow, thickening. A second plume, from an upstairs window above the porch roof, joined it. The wind whipped the smoke nearly sideways, then let it straighten like a spinning top for a second, its color deepening to an oily, boiling black. Only the watching cameras, implacably whirring, knew what to do. Several explosions, ammunition or propane tanks, sent jets of orange flame shooting out the old sash windows and through the curdling asphalt-shingled roof. "Dan," CBS's correspondent panted, "this has to have been set, it's spreading so fast."

Within the Temple, the sounds and shouts, the splinterings distant and near, the unintelligible blaring voices from outside, the thuds and gusts of tear gas and wind-whipped flame had been merged in a great rushing, a dragon on the other side of the wall. Smoke billowed past the upstairs windows and sped in black curls along the ceiling. It struck Esau in the face and flooded his eyes and throat with a peppery, unbreathable heat. It felt personal, a deliberately insolent gust of Satan's poisonous breath. He had a gas mask dangling from his belt but couldn't decide to put it on. He was upstairs in the office; he had wanted to answer the phone, its incessant ringing yet another voice of this many-headed assault. But Jesse had told him, "Let the bastards ring—no more truck with the Devil, Slick." Jesse had looked glassy-eyed and sweating and paper-pale but smiling moments ago, limp with a kind of relief, when Esau had last seen him, standing at the office windows staring at the arc of momentarily stilled vehicles in the flat front area where four months ago the state-police car had been halted and the invaders pinned down by bullets. "The rod has blossomed," he said. "The Lord is at hand."

Sheets of smoke and invisible gas hurried through the room and it seemed a shutter kept dropping in Esau's head. His eyes watered and stung to the point of blindness and suddenly Jesse was gone from the window. Fat Zebulun, waddling, giggling in his excitement, had come splashing pungent kerosene through the room—over the desktops, the floors, the cardboard files, the vanilla-colored computer and laser printer with its stacked supply of glossy paper. Esau wondered. According to the plan that had been drawn up, Mephibosheth and Jim were to ignite the barn and the family wing, with the pottery workshop and the auditorium Mephibosheth had built. When had the plan been put into action? Esau hadn't heard Jesse order it, but he must have. Jesse had been now here in the office with the men, now there in his bedroom with the women and children, and again no place at all that Esau knew of. The whoosh of lit kerosene added itself to the rushing, the hellish transformation of the air. A tangled knot of women and children burst, coughing, eyes streaming, out of Jesse's bedroom. Esau, crouching to see and to find air for his voice, shouted for them to follow him down the stairs. He could not get it out of his head that the insulting, billowing, insinuant, ubiquitous smoke was a person, a malevolent soul with a mind.

He would be in Heaven within minutes, he realized. The ordeal, the cup of wrath, and then an eternity of Jesse's company. The thought seemed no stranger than the fact that he had once been a boy playing Wiffle Ball fungo with Rex Brudnoy by his mother's concrete swimming pool. *Start stretching, Superguy.* How had he acquired this clattering scorpion's tail of women and children? They clambered after him down the narrow stairway to the little entrance hall with the pine newel post and the pewter vase still holding some dried stalks of wheat. The front door was locked, locked and barred against the minions of Gog with their guns and telescopic lenses aimed like horns of the beast. He pulled at the knob, and the bell on its rusty spiral spring softly rang. The wailing people behind him kept grabbing at him. They were trying to ride out to birth by clutching his heel. There was no avoiding the birth blossoming around them but their bodies still sought escape and comfort. The blubbering and shrieks of the children were especially aggravating. He called for them to get low and hold their breaths. The long living room, a shambles of sleeping bags and broken glass and bales of straw fortification around the windows, was packed with smoke, a series of thin acrid walls, but, taking a gasp and crouching, he shouldered his way through, with this terrible thick tail of scrabbling sobbing innocents behind him. In a few minutes they would be all out of this into the icy-cool clarity of Heaven, gold and blue and jasper, with marble stairs and still lakes and the women drifting about in tiaras and silken gowns falling in parallel folds like Elizabeth Taylor in a movie whose name he had forgotten. Angkor Wat. *See it before you die.* Life is such a quick little mess. The rubes had kept boasting of burning the Temple down but there hadn't been enough thought given to where people should arrange themselves to die. Hands fought to hold on to him from behind. Scuttling, eyes clenched, Esau touched the fireplace's round blackened stones, the plaster walls, a table, a sofa; the old iron latch of the door to the kitchen materialized under his fingers.

The air was relatively clean in the kitchen. There was only a haze stirring between the blackened ceiling of tamarack beams. He took a breath. Here more people were gathered, multitudes. The others must have come up from the buried school bus. An event was in progress; Esau saw through the mullions of the upper window sash and the bunches of drying onions and herbs hanging from ceiling hooks a man running up the stony barnyard slope toward one of the armored vehicles. He recognized Benjamin, one of the newcomers who had fought through the snow to get here. The vehicle had opened its plated door and almost swallowed him when something made Benjamin pitch forward like a scarecrow thrown off his stick; he had been shot, by a bullet from the Temple. Jim lowered the rifle whose barrel he had jammed through a pane, smashing it, there under the hanging bunches of drying herbs.

The back kitchen door, like the front door, had a winter storm shed built around it, so getting out would be a clumsy operation. But Jesse was blocking the inner door in any case. In a haze like the mist on a river's edge they had gathered around Jesse and he was smilingly distributing something. What he had in his hand was a box of Triscuits. " 'This is my body,' " he was saying, " 'given for thee.' You'll feel no pain with this, honey, absolutely Scout's honor; take, eat." Weak white hands were reaching out and taking greedily. The women and taller children, some of them wearing white robes, had faces distended by a kind of rapture. In the same uplifted minister's voice, Jesse called, "Start launchin' 'em, boys! Set 'em free!"

Jim came closer with the Ruger hunting rifle and gave Esau that flip little sideways look of his, suggesting that both of them should have known better, but why not? Zebulun held a snub-nosed Colt .38 and, all in a sweat that stained his colorful short-sleeved Hawaiian shirt, he jerkily raised the revolver and pointed its four-inch barrel and a woman, Jael, fell to the floor of the kitchen, the side of her head spouting blood, blood all over her shiny young dark-brown hair with its plastic butterfly barrette, there by the foot of the iron cookstove, the hole spurting like a water bubbler, pulse after pulse until it quickly dribbled down to an ebbing red nub, pumping less and less into her matted hair. Jael had been plain, overweight, with acne, but her voice had been surprisingly melodious and precise; when her turn came to read the Bible, she had visibly preened, singing every syllable. "She's there already!" Jesse yelled out, through the thickening mist. "Our sister has reached those pearly gates!" His face was glazed with happiness; he had arrived at the fountain of faith.

The little throng sent up a wail Esau could not tell was terror or jubilation. The fire had gotten louder on the other side of the white kitchen door which led through a food storeroom into the crooked patchy corridor Hannah had led him down his first night here. There was heat under their feet, where the generator was, with all its stockpiled diesel fuel. Smoke was leaking up through the cracks. Jael had had a small daughter with Jesse's fine reddish hair and wide brow and now that little girl stepped or was nudged forward away from the others and a rifle loudly, flatly spit and Jim lowered its muzzle with that bunched-up expression on his mouth people use when they make a small mistake or eat something distasteful. "She's among the saints!" Jesse yelled. "She's a dove on the mountains!"

The boys among the children had got the picture and were fighting their mothers, scratching and screaming; but the women, grimacing with eyes closed to avoid injury, were embracing these frenzied children with the fury of those who know what is best, who know the way to be saved eternally. The heat on the other side of the door was breathing, roaring, a beast chewing wood. The plaster overhead was dribbling sheets of dust and crumbs; the air was becoming dizzyingly strange, its oxygen going. One of the women still standing, scrawny long-nosed Mehetabel, who was another of the newcomers, insufficiently seasoned in faith, fainted on the floor.

A flock of sparkling dark immaterial bubbles descended into Esau, and he knew what to do. He felt his physical body existing within that electric hyperclarity that for years had come and gone in his head. "Zeb, give me that a second," he said, holding out his hand, knowing that the other man in his rich-kid childishness would oblige.

Jesse saw the revolver in Esau's hand now and jubilantly cried, "Take 'em to Heaven, Slick! Big Daddy needs his girls!" The woman foremost in the pack was Hannah. She held her infant in one arm and rested the other hand on the head of her toddler, to steady him. This two-year-old boy looked up at Clark with a thin-lipped wised-up smile that seemed familiar. Hannah waited to be killed, struggling not to cough in the thickening smoke. Her eyes were shut. Her freckles were like pinpricks of dried blood and her nostril-holes were taut.

Clark had always had a non-coöperative streak. "Slick," he said to Jesse, "you fucker, I'll give you Slick," and shot the false prophet twice, once in the chest and the second time in the top of the head, where it was all bald, as the man doubled over. He had never liked looking at the supposed holy man's bald pate, the way the shiny skin clung to the fitted plates of bone underneath like a turtle's shell. He hadn't liked his gold tooth either.

Clark had time to wheel and plug Zebulun in his fat butterball gut and might have taken out Jim with the next shot but a surge of smoke got in the way. His blinded eyes burned; in all the rushing and screaming he seemed to hear Jim snicker apologetically. The rifle bullet struck him in the left shoulder, knocking him backward like an uncalled-for fist. The sensation was broader than he would have expected, and painless, in the first seconds, before it began to burn, all the way through the roots of all the nerves gathered with veins and gristle there, where arm intricately meets shoulder. He still had his gun arm and lifted it to get a bead on Jim with the Colt but the target ducked behind the other heads and melted backward in the intensifying smoke. The stunned women and children stared stupidly. Mehetabel was rousing. Jesse's body had flung an arm around Clark's feet so he had to kick it away. His pain was growing every second, taking over his body—his neck, his side—like a burning heart, and with it grew his towering anger; he had become a vessel of wrath. He yelled at the women, "For God's sake, you idiotic bitches, get *out!* It's *over!* Git! Git!" He cried with his inspired certainty, "Can't you see, there's nothing *here* any more! Those people outside are your *friends!*" He waved his gun in their faces and they scrambled toward the door, the children leading the mothers.

He stepped over Jesse's arm in its red flannel sleeve and then across the fallen little girl with the back of her beribboned head blown off, the long stain flowing out of her flaxen hair surprisingly brilliant, like Day-Glo paint. The nailheads in the floor glinted, hot to the eyes. He kneeled on one knee, tucked his pistol under the armpit of the ruined arm, and with the other fit the gas mask to his face. It stank of rubber and the camphorish chemical filter, and had a greenhouse quiet inside, with murky plastic lenses for the eyes. It reminded him of a virtual-reality helmet, with reality's imperfections computer-corrected. The brief torment, and then green cool Paradise, did Jim really believe that? A level head, a high-school teacher, he should know. Back beyond where Jim had disappeared in the smoke, the panelled white door into the storeroom was surrounded by a scarlet line of fire, neat as a mechanical drawing, and at each step Clark took toward it the heat on his face went up a notch. But it was the way he had to move, deeper. There was nothing for him on the outside now, just hassle, and embarrassment for Mother. Whoremongers, sorcerers, the whole pack of supercilious shits. He wasn't worried; the living God had laid hold of him, the present-tense God beyond betting on. His shoulder was screaming, outraged and paralyzed. Esau's beard, below the mask, was burning, each exposed hair curling up with a tiny crisping sensation. His breath was coming back to him suffocatingly. Even through the chemical filter, the smoke was palpable, like a fine rich coke being stuffed very fast up his nostrils, down his throat, into his eyes. His head was losing its ability to make pictures. *The second death,* when had the first been? *The Lamb shall overcome,* how could a Lamb overcome, by letting Its throat be slit? That vast indignant beast with seven heads was *whuff*ing and beating on the panelled white door as if entitled to admission. Esau was a cunning hunter. He had a twin, somewhere in the smoke. He heard a noise, soft but pointed, over where the cups and plates used to be: a cup settling on a saucer or a twig snapping in the fire or the bolt of a rifle being stealthily slipped back. *Go ahead and shoot. You'll be doing me a favor.*

Then there was no more pain, but for the briefest burning edge, like the crinkly orange margin that consumes the paper of a cigarette in advance of the growing tobacco ash.

Lower Branch was the lead story that night on all three networks and on Fox and CNN. Alma heard about it on her Jaguar radio as she was driving from her English-accent lesson over on Fountain Avenue near Flores to her facial on Hollywood Boulevard beyond Cahuenga. She believed in facials as the way to keep natural flexibility after several lifts. She was very anxious after *The Sharpened Knife* not to be typecast as a crone but to be eligible for senior romantic roles, of which there were going to be more and more: look at *Cocoon* and *On Golden Pond.* Her heart came into her throat as she heard this bleat of news but she wondered if her reaction was sincere; she checked her face in the rear-view mirror to see how actressy she looked. No, her sudden shocked haggard look was genuine. The color had bleached out of her face, an effect you could never fake. She turned right on La Brea and sped home on Santa Monica Boulevard; she brushed past Conchita, who was flirting with one of the wetback lawn men in the front yard. "Call Annette and cancel my facial," she told her in passing. She turned on CNN, where the news was continuous. When she had watched enough to know how real her problems were she closed her eyes and tried to sort them out.

There was no way to avoid going, when she had just been there. There would be charred bones or teeth to identify, legal forms to sign, reporters to fend off but not offend. Caleb must come and meet her in Colorado; she just couldn't face Patrick again, he had become an oppressive bore, laying claim to her the way no actual lover would, somehow making her whole life feel seedy and shameful. Caleb would be staunch and understated and wonderfully Bostonian with rude intrusive types. But she hadn't been enjoying their conversations lately; there was always his reproach, stated or implied, that she wasn't living with him there in Brookline, in that stifling big house, among those stuffy people. It would mean giving up, ceasing to act, when she knew she still had a career here—oh, not like it was in the old days, those days of the studios just pouring them out will never come back, but films are being made, these video stores have created a whole new market, and the overseas audiences love to see the American old-timers, there is an imperial nostalgia at work. Not that she was an *old* old-timer, having just turned sixty last Valentine's Day. Yes, she must call him, she needed him now, and she could count on the gravity of it all to keep him from being too reproachful and clingy. Poor little Clark. He tried so hard as a baby to be good, working on how to nurse, to crawl, to walk, to talk, to *be a person.* Perhaps she had been just too much mother for him. She saw his solemn square infant face peering up at her out of the crib, freshly awakened and trying to focus away from his dream; how puzzling dreams must be to their little brains, trying to grasp the real world. Tears achingly welled from beneath her closed lids. While her eyelids were still shut she prayed in the blood-tinged darkness they made, *Thank you, Lord, for letting my son become a hero at the end.*

In Bethesda, Maryland, Daniel Wilmot had tuned in the news to go with a bourbon before dinner. He and Bophana and their four children—Sotra John, Emily Bopha, Esther Sisopha, and Norodom Clarence—had been called back to Washington, now that the Cold War was won, and he was given a desk job in the Middle Eastern section, trying to figure out how to keep Saddam Hussein as a burr under Iran's saddle. Bophana had caught the same news on the television set in the kitchen and came into the study and touched Danny on the shoulder, and then on the little scar on his forehead, a trace of the childhood forever out of her reach. He rubbed his cheek against the back of her thin golden-brown hand, without taking his eyes off the images of leaping flames, of maneuvering M60A1s, of FBI spokesmen grimly explaining that their plan had been sound and their intentions the best. "This boy the same you said was loser?" Bophana asked in her lovely chiming English, so much gentler than her guttural, voluble Khmer.

The commercial came on, and Danny straightened his head and stretched his long legs and took another sip of his bourbon. "Well, I've been wondering lately if losing and winning are as different as we like to think. I liked Clark, the little I saw of him, passing through L.A. in the Seventies. He liked me, was the funny thing. Not everybody does. He struck me as a needy little guy, not quite knowing what was up. I told him what I thought was up, but I guess he needed more. That sounds pompous—of course he needed more. There's never an end to needing. We beat the Communist pricks and now the world is full of other pricks." He lit a Merit.

"Shall I feed kids while you call sister?"

"I guess I should call her, you're right. But no rush, let's all eat together. If I know Essie, she'll make a big production of it."

Teddy hadn't heard his daughter sob that way since the time she messed up the Miss Delaware Peach contest, and maybe before one of her divorces, the first or the second. Em and Mother had been alive then and they had handled it. He hoped this time he said the right things—he didn't always know what was going to hop out of his mouth these days. People he'd known all his life, and face to face with them downtown he can't think of their names to save him, just sees in his mind what their front porches looked like, and their old-style wooden storm doors, and their cocoa or stippled-rubber welcome mats. It shook him up, too, a Wilmot shot to death and charred to cinders out in some Godforsaken nowhere out west. They could save some transportation and bury him next to Jared and that brother of Em's nobody ever heard from once he took off. Or maybe the Siffords had and never told. They were a strange pair, those two, acting like they had something to hide whether they did or not. How they ever came up with that angel he married Teddy could never figure out. Families are mysterious things.

He usually got enough national news on the six o'clock out of Wilmington on Channel Twelve; what they don't tell you wasn't generally worth knowing. How grieved Dad used to be by the paper, all the terrible items in it, and the world then wasn't anything like as bad as it is now. People still held themselves to standards. All the men, even factory hands, wore bowlers or, in summers, straw hats. Even here in Basingstoke, you could walk every street in town and never come to a locked door—just toss the magazines and parcel post inside, though it was against strict regulations. In a place small enough so the people have to meet each other face to face you don't need all the regulations. Simple human decency and self-respect should do it. That's pretty much gone now, with the world so full of handy excuses. Kill a man one day and plead insanity the next.

But tonight on account of Clark—poor boy, he used to come down on the bus from St. Andrew's starved for a little home cooking and plain talk, he never tired of hearing about his mother as a girl—Teddy turned on the six-thirty national news as well, on Channel Three, the NBC affiliate good old KYW, that he had been listening to on radio since those old crystal sets with the headphones. Seth Addison had had one. Of the three network anchors Teddy preferred Brokaw; he was the youngest, and though he swallowed a lot of his words he seemed to suffer with the news most sincerely, and there seemed to be fewer commercials about denture fixatives and hemorrhoid medicine and these feminine-incontinence pads, as though anybody who took an interest in the world's news had to be on their last legs, not able to keep their own juices in.

Farrah sat down with him, though he told her she could do up the dishes and run home. Farrah was Loretta Whaley's granddaughter, from the older of her two firstborn boys, born close enough to be twins; those Whaleys and Bachellers make quick generations. The boy married one of the Ingraham girls. Farrah was thirteen, old enough to come cook an old man's supper, everybody agreed, most of them just popped into a microwave anyway, now that her mother was taking night classes in computer science.

They sat down together, Teddy in the blue easy chair he had just about worn the color out of in the seat and the arms, and little Farrah with her tidy Whaley mouth and apricot Bacheller hair in the velvet wing chair with the curved legs and matching velvet stool Em used to rest her poor leg on. Some nights he gets to watching the comedies, one after another; they run together as he bobs in and out of sleep, and it's as if Em is sitting right there, if he doesn't make a mistake and turn his head and look.

Many of the clips had been shown on the local news, so it was like watching a movie twice, a silent movie even, because Farrah had tuned it to suit herself and he was hard enough of hearing to miss a lot of the commentary. There were the military vehicles, the same green as in Vietnam and before that. Photos of this Smith madman as a round-faced young farmer boy and then talking and waving his arms in some interview they flattered his craziness with. He looked a little like Harlan Dearholt that used to be big in Dad's parish—favored the same kind of little eyeglasses. Quick still photos of Clark and Essie from ten, twenty years ago, posing as mother and son out there in Hollywood, and then some group photos of the other poor deluded souls. Pictures of the old farmhouse with its wings, and then pictures of it burning like a stack of kindling soaked in gasoline; it made your stomach hurt to think of people in there. A commercial about a cruise ship that looks like a New Year's Eve party, with this big-mouthed woman singing how you should see her now. Then Brokaw earnestly mumbling and close-ups of the skinny guilty-looking man who was shot trying to get out but would live, and then one of the women, with a freckled face, describing the shooting that had taken place inside and how Clark had done it to save them all. Then a concluding zoom of the four or so women with smoky faces coming out of this storm hutch like they're scared they're going to be shot, then stepping into the open, squinting, blinking as if just waking up, carrying or holding on to the hands of their children, too many to count. The children.

Afterword

FOR INVALUABLE HELP with the particulars of this novel, I thank Herb Yellin, Emily and Gregory Harvey, Carole Sherr, Elaine Burnett, Theodore Vrettos, Stephanie Egnotovich and Davis Perkins of the Westminster John Knox Press, Clifford S. Wunderlich of the Andover-Harvard Theological Library, Yvonne Lavelle and Paula E. Rabkin of the United States Postal Service, Jeffrey W. Gmys and Kwaku Amoabeng of the Paterson Free Library, Dennis Santillo, Norma Harrison, Robert Atwan, Steve Golin, Rodney Dennis, Ray and Joyce Smith, Peter and David and Cindy Gordon, Ray Maguire, Hugo Weisgall, Arthur Griffin, Donald Burt, Frederic R. Bernhard, Cyril Wismar, Barbara Platt-Hendrin, Mary Yuhasz, Paul L. Singer, Diana Waggoner, Kathy Zuckerman, William Koshland, Judith Jones, and the ever-obliging staff of the Beverly, Massachusetts, Public Library.

The following books were especially useful: *The Fragile Bridge: Paterson Silk Strike, 1913,* by Steve Golin; *Delaware: A Bicentennial History,* by Carol E. Hofecker; *Greenhouse Gardener's Companion,* by Shane Smith; *Cinema: The First Hundred Years,* by David Shipman; *The Story of Cinema,* by David Shipman; *A Biographical Dictionary of Film,* by David Thomson; *The Film Encyclopedia,* by Ephraim Katz; *One Hundred Years of Filmmaking,* by Jeanine Basinger; *American Cinema: Hollywood at Sunset,* by Charles Higham; *The Hollywood Story,* by Roy Pickard; *The Columbia Story,* by Clive Hirschhorn; *A Million and One Nights,* by Terry Ramsaye; *Grace,* by Robert Lacey; *Legend: The Life and Death of Marilyn Monroe,* by Fred Lawrence Guiles; *Doris Day: Her Own Story,* with A. E. Hotchner; *King Cohn,* by Bob Thomas; *Acting in the Cinema,* by James Naremore; *Making Movies,* by Sidney Lumet; *Mad Man in Waco,* by Brad Bailey and Bob Darden; *Inside the Cult,* by Marc Breault and Martin King; *Religious Cults in America,* edited by Robert Emmet Long; *Less Than Zero,* by Bret Easton Ellis.

READ MORE IN PENGUIN

In every corner of the world, on every subject under the sun, Penguin represents quality and variety – the very best in publishing today.

For complete information about books available from Penguin – including Puffins, Penguin Classics and Arkana – and how to order them, write to us at the appropriate address below. Please note that for copyright reasons the selection of books varies from country to country.

In the United Kingdom: Please write to *Dept. EP, Penguin Books Ltd, Bath Road, Harmondsworth, West Drayton, Middlesex UB7 ODA*

In the United States: Please write to *Consumer Sales, Penguin USA, P.O. Box 999, Dept. 17109, Bergenfield, New Jersey 07621-0120.* VISA and MasterCard holders call 1-800-253-6476 to order Penguin titles

In Canada: Please write to *Penguin Books Canada Ltd, 10 Alcorn Avenue, Suite 300, Toronto, Ontario M4V 3B2*

In Australia: Please write to *Penguin Books Australia Ltd, P.O. Box 257, Ringwood, Victoria 3134*

In New Zealand: Please write to *Penguin Books (NZ) Ltd, Private Bag 102902, North Shore Mail Centre, Auckland 10*

In India: Please write to *Penguin Books India Pvt Ltd, 706 Eros Apartments, 56 Nehru Place, New Delhi 110 019*

In the Netherlands: Please write to *Penguin Books Netherlands bv, Postbus 3507, NL-1001 AH Amsterdam*

In Germany: Please write to *Penguin Books Deutschland GmbH, Metzlerstrasse 26, 60594 Frankfurt am Main*

In Spain: Please write to *Penguin Books S. A., Bravo Murillo 19, 1º B, 28015 Madrid*

In Italy: Please write to *Penguin Italia s.r.l., Via Felice Casati 20, I–20124 Milano*

In France: Please write to *Penguin France S. A., 17 rue Lejeune, F–31000 Toulouse*

In Japan: Please write to *Penguin Books Japan, Ishikiribashi Building, 2–5–4, Suido, Bunkyo-ku, Tokyo 112*

In South Africa: Please write to *Longman Penguin Southern Africa (Pty) Ltd, Private Bag X08, Bertsham 2013*

BY THE SAME AUTHOR

Rabbit, Run

Rabbit, Run introduces 'Rabbit' Angstrom – on the move, on the make and on the run. 'Rabbit' has never outgrown his adolescent triumphs as a school-games hero. Bouncing between an alcoholic wife, a demanding mistress and a futile job in a banal town, his powers of indecision are unlimited, and anyone except 'Rabbit' – can see where it will end. 'A small-town tragedy . . . convincing, vivid, and awful' – *The Times Literary Supplement*

Rabbit Redux

Ten years on from *Rabbit, Run*, Rabbit Angstrom has changed – as America itself has changed – somewhat for the worse. His marriage is collapsing; his job is becoming redundant; and the urgency of racial tension and the conflict between generations present a challenge that neither his conscience nor his sexuality can resist. In the end, after confrontation and despair, betrayal and tragedy, Rabbit achieves a kind of peace. The peace of exhaustion, perhaps.

Rabbit is Rich
Winner of the 1982 Pulitzer Prize

Now Chief Sales Representative of Springer Motors in Brewer, Pennsylvania, Rabbit is enjoying the fruits of middle-aged affluence. With a secure niche in the wonderland of Middle America, he's got it all wrapped up – except for the slow, creeping onset of decay.

Rabbit at Rest

'Among prose works which address the American century, Rabbit has few obvious betters . . . this novel is enduringly eloquent about weariness, age and disgust, in a prose that is always fresh, nubile and unwitherable' – Martin Amis in the *Independent on Sunday*. 'Dark, glittering and abrasive . . . The carnal rubs shoulders with the cosmic, and it works' – *The Times*

Rabbit, Run, *Rabbit Redux* and *Rabbit is Rich* are also published in one volume, **A Rabbit Omnibus**

BY THE SAME AUTHOR

Couples

Prosperous, thirty-five-ish, the ten couples living in Tarbox, New England, form an exclusive, competitive group. They are sociable, articulate and unhappy. They enjoy sailing and skiing in season, word-games in the evenings – and adultery all year round. In this brilliant treatment of their involvements and aberrations, the sexual revolution of the Sixties is laid bare – giving us, in every sense, the anatomy of a generation. 'Rich, intoxicating, incantory ... sexual experience is described with a rare and eloquent insight' – *The Times*

Forty Stories

'Delightful to read ... full of the unexpected ... Updike's world is a kind of sanitary junkyard of cars and cats, oranges and onions, wives and unheard whines; he wanders through it, gently looking for precious metal. When he finds it ... he is a master and collects the essence with devastating effect' – *London Magazine*. 'The acute dialogue, perfectly accurate, but never quite expected, the capture of the strange surrealistic quality in American life' – *Spectator*

Marry Me

Sally Mathias is big and blonde, expensively dressed and married to Richard. He is a generous husband, making the kind of benignly drunken compromise a man has to make when he's married to an exceptionally desirable woman. Jerry Conant met his wife, Ruth, at art school. He's a talented cartoonist; she has a good eye for colour. Three children later, their marriage could be seen as a question less of mutual possession than of mutual aesthetic admiration. 'Updike has never written better of the woe that is marriage' – Paul Theroux in the *Guardian*

BY THE SAME AUTHOR

Memories of the Ford Administration

History professor Alf Clayton, narrator of Updike's blackly entertaining new novel, receives a questionnaire asking for his memories and impressions of Gerald Ford's presidential administration. But Alf perplexingly finds himself straying away from politics in the Seventies towards sex, adultery, guilt, and to his unfinished biography of James Buchanan, prelapsarian President in the run-up to America's Civil War. 'Updike's luminous prose gives the story a dimension of beauty that no other novelist could bring to it' – *Daily Telegraph*. 'Quintessential Updike, an exploration of a modern American terrain of desire, guilt and moral ambiguity that he has made distinctly his own' – *The New York Times Book Review*

The Centaur

The centaur Chiron has problems – his difficult pupils, an arrow in his ankle, and a bad report from Zeus . . .

Psychological chronicle and tragic comedy fuse in this story of three days in the life of George Caldwell, a small-town high-school teacher, and his fifteen-year-old son, Peter, an aspiring artist. Caught up in their imagined existences, the middle-aged man and the teenager struggle to make sense of the real world, which is also the world of Olympus, with its gods and nymphs and commonplace marvels.

Trust Me

'Updike's story collection is marvellously good . . . he manages somehow to combine the display of being the best at the sport with quite different human qualities – warmth, eagerness, tentativeness, an air of complete approachability . . . Inconspicuously, these are very precise social chronicles of how the Sixties turned into the Seventies and Eighties' – John Bayley in the *London Review of Books*

BY THE SAME AUTHOR

The Afterlife and Other Stories

'Updike has never written with more poignancy and power, more passion and compassion ... Fiction of this distinction ensures his own afterlife as a writer who will surely be lastingly acclaimed as a consummate portrayer of the intimacies of American life and death in the closing decades of this century ... magnificent' – Peter Kemp in the *Sunday Times*. 'Here we have an Updike afterlife of revisitings, uneasy remarryings, leave-takings, and stocktakings ... when he gets his hands on the short story the master can do no wrong' – *The New York Review of Books*

Collected Poems 1953–1993

'Whether writing in formal verse or prose, John Updike has always been a poet. Everything turns to metaphor beneath his swiftly moving pen ... His poems reveal a fine intellect, as one might expect; they are genial and sophisticated, and they possess a wonderfully tactile quality that becomes, finally, the subject as well as the texture of his best poems' – Jay Parini in the *Independent on Sunday*

Brazil

Tristão Raposo, a nineteen-year-old black child of the Rio slums, spies Isabel Leme, an upper-class white girl, across the hot sands of Copacabana Beach, and presents her with a ring. Their flight into marriage takes them from urban banality to the farthest reaches of Brazil's wild west, always holding on to the faith that each is the other's fate for life, as they pass – in Shakespeare's phrase – 'through nature to eternity'. 'A brilliant performance' – Michael Dibdin in the *Independent on Sunday*

also published:

The Poorhouse Fair
Of the Farm
A Month of Sundays
The Coup
Your Lover Just Called
The Witches of Eastwick
Roger's Version
S.
The Complete Henry Bech
Self-Consciousness
Hugging the Shore

B. Sundary Books.
Pam.
Tom.
Jonathan.